Funky Shrooms and Other Exquisite Delights

Charles Clemons

Portal Press

Soddy Daisy
Tennessee

Funky Shrooms and Other Exquisite Delights

Special thanks to Dr. Louie Edmundson for editorial work.

Published in the United States of America by
Portal Press
Soddy Daisy, TN 37379

ISBN 978-0-6151-7467-9

First Printing
November 2007

To my son Alex, my number one fan, I love you.

"The oldest and strongest emotion of mankind is fear."

-H.P. Lovecraft, author (1890-1937)

Table Of Contents

Introduction

Funky Shrooms

And Other Exquisite Delights

Pictures and Artwork

Introduction:
Strange Has A New Name

Strange fiction will never become part of the mainstream literary market for to do so would be a conundrum within itself, making it the usual, instead of the unusual. To better understand strange fiction, one must understand the relation to its nucleus from which all fictional genre branch, fiction. A generally accepted definition of fiction is; prose literature describing imaginary events and people, meaning by description, that all fiction is merely a creation from the mind of its author. While some fiction claims to be "inspired" by true events, to be classified as fiction it must be fabricated or it would become another primary form of literature, nonfiction. While this is not in any way an enigma, it is not uncommon for people to claim they do not read strange fiction because they find it hard to believe.

While fiction is rarely categorized as simply fiction, since it is broken down into dozens of genres to appeal to readers of particular taste, strange fiction is the branch that has moved further from its mother than any of its sister genres. It is this distance from normal fiction that both allures and isolates many readers. In standard fiction the protagonist and antagonist normally have clear cut allegiances representing good versus evil, making the plot straightforward and easy to read as well as to understand. This anodyne format allows readers to follow the protagonist with a relatively safe sentiment throughout the narrative even through the climax of the story to come to a customarily happy ending. Strange fiction stands apart from other fiction having ambiguous protagonists and antagonists with narrative climaxes that are as likely to end in tragedy as in comedy.

Strange fiction finds its origin before most other forms of fiction in having roots in the early fantasy, the Epic of Gilgamesh, believed to be written somewhere around 2000 BC. This tradition continued through ancient literature contributing to strange tales like The Odyssey, Beowulf and The Divine Comedy. Strange fiction began its development into modern fiction in the novel Phantastes written by George MacDonald in 1858. As literature grew in complexity dividing into different categories, strange fiction incorporated aspects from other fictional genres as they developed, collecting aspects of horror, science fiction, mystery and suspense while staying quietly behind the scenes being published in small pulp magazines and by specialty presses as other genres became best sellers.

The golden age of strange fiction came into its own with the turn of the twentieth century brought on by a barrage of high quality strange fantasy, horror and science fiction from authors such as Lord Dunsany, H.P. Lovecraft, Clark Ashton Smith, E.R. Eddison, Robert E. Howard and H.G. Wells. These and other authors stretched the limits of the paper upon which they wrote creating alternate worlds and questioning reality through the usage of the supernatural and the unknown altering the reader's preconception of truth.

During this period, strange fiction expanded creating a staple of venues for its authors and readers supporting publications such as Weird Tales, Arkham House, Amazing Stories, Astounding Science Fiction, Famous Fantastic Mysteries and limitless others, but although the material being produced during this period flourished, the writers who put it into print did not.

All things that rise must fall, and strange fiction fell hard in hard times. The depression took its toll as did World War II and as its great writers began to pass, H.P. Lovecraft in 1937, Robert E. Howard in 1936, E.R. Eddison in 1945, H.G Wells in 1946 and Lord Dunsany in 1957, strange fiction withered into obscurity, becoming remote from the eyes of the common reader. Arkham House printed its books in small runs, usually in no more than three thousand copies due to low demand, and even the great Weird Tales magazine went out of print shutting down its press in 1954.

A resurgence of strange fiction emerged from the shadows in the seventies as a new circle of authors including Stephen King, Robert Bloch, Dean Koontz, Harlan Ellison, Ray Bradbury and others tried to bring the old genre back to prominence with their work. Presses began to reprint strange fiction from the earlier part of the century in cheap paperback in order to make it more accessible to the common reader, and for a moment strange fiction was revived.

Today, strange fiction is back in the darkness where so many of its tales take place, unseen and relatively unknown but still waiting to re-emerge and take the public by storm. It is for this reason, that I so eagerly accepted the task of writing an introduction for Charles Clemons' second collection of strange fiction. Being an enthusiast of strange fiction, I endlessly read unusual fiction from new up-and-coming authors, and in my opinion; Mr. Clemons is one of the best contributors strange fiction has had in many years. His first book, Cosmic Contemplations boldly carried its tales across the vast universes of space creatively pitting man against alien races, extraordinary creatures and man's own imperfections. As I read this book, what intrigued me most was the author's method of character development. His characters were there for one reason, to drive the plot of the story; whether they lived or died, succeeded or failed was of no matter. It is an easy task for an author to take a virtuous character and elicit sympathy from a reader, but it is another to take an immoral character and muster that same support, a feat that this author has achieved in my reading on several occasions.

The collection of work you hold in your hand at this very moment collects a full length novel, three short stories, a play and six poems put to paper by its author for the sole purpose of pleasing the reader. I believe the compilation of prose works and poems you are about to read will do just that. Strange fiction has been waiting for a chance to return to eminence and with new authors such as Charles Clemons that time is on the horizon. Strange has a new name, and it is Charles Clemons!

Mark Grenshaw

Funky Shrooms:

The Amanita muscaria is a slightly poisonous and highly hallucinogenic fungus that grows freely throughout the northern hemisphere. The Celtics considered it the "food of the gods" believing its consumption revealed the secrets of the universe. In rituals to reach the spirit realm through lucid dream, Siberian Koryaks drank the urine of their shamans after their ingestion of fly agaric, an entheogenic mushroom, so to cross the barrier from our world to that beyond. The Norse believed the Amanita muscaria was a gift from the gods, which formed during rainstorms when lightning struck the ground. May this book help you cross over from the mundane to the extraordinary as did the fly agaric to ancient cultures of the past.

Autobiography of a Necromancer

Delamogue leading the dead into battle during the first age of Helminth.

S ome who read this story will find it appalling, others
unbelievable, but everyone will certainly find it strange.
It is the story of my life. I am a necromancer, a
resurrecter of the dead. The previous sentence alone will be enough to
make most people close this book. That is fine. I'm not writing this
biography for anyone's approval. I am writing it for those few people
who find the bizarre appealing or at least interesting. Besides omitting
specific names and locations, what I am about to tell you is verity. I'm
not excluding these details for any reason except legal recourse. What
I have done, though much of it may have been illegal, was in the
name of the black art known as necromancy.

As a child, I was always interested in things that were dark
and forbidden in nature. I frequented cemeteries and other places of
burial as a youth and was seen as an aberrant child. It was this unusual
interest that turned me to the study of demonology, witchcraft,
voodoo, necrophagia, and other practices considered taboo in the
public's eye. Most of my knowledge came from forgotten tomes and

lore such as, the *Necronomicon*, the *Book of Iod*, the *Book of Eibon*, *Neresis* and *Cultes des Goules* to name a few of many. The assembly of such a collection of books came at a great expense to both myself and others.

It was through the art of necromancy that I found it easiest to serve my unusual lust for the unnatural. I became involved in several cults, but found their congregations and rituals to be purely theatrical and had better success while studying on my own. In college, I strayed from the common fields of education and concentrated on subjects that I thought might benefit my desire for forbidden lore. This urge led me to the study of etymology, chemistry, Latin, Arabic, Sumerian, astronomy, religion, history and mathematics, but my mastery of the arcane came from my relentless independent studies.

It was while I was working on my doctorate that I obtained my first breakthrough. I had taken an entry level cytology course to better understand cells and their reactions, when during a lab I successfully resurrected a frog while the professor was performing a dissection! The action of the frog startled him to the point that at first I thought he had swallowed his own tongue! If he had, the emergency medical technicians would have had to carry me out on a stretcher with him. I was so taken back by the hilarity of the situation that I fell out of my chair in laughter. The rest of my classmates did not share my same dark sense of humor.

This minor success in revitalization of the dead is what motivated me to continue on in the art of necromancy. It seemed the more complex the subject the harder it was to successfully perform the rite of resurrection. It wasn't long before I could revive insects and other smaller life forms with ease, but I still had trouble with higher life forms, especially mammals. Small birds and reptiles became the staple of my research and it wasn't long before I had a reasonable mastery of their anatomy. I continued on in grueling research and two long years passed before I successfully resurrected my first mammal. My subject was nothing more than a common field mouse, but it was a major step in my development as a necromancer. After several more successful attempts on mice, I moved on to larger mammals and by the end of that same year I resurrected a small calf.

It was at this time, I began to feel the financial strain of my research. I had not taken a job after college and the expenses associated with my work had depleted what little of my trust fund that remained. It wasn't long before I was evicted from my apartment and while being homeless, my research came to a standstill.

At first I took on a job as a lab assistant at a local pharmaceutical institute to supplement my income, but the mental and physical strain of the everyday workforce began to affect my work and I decided to find another way to finance my studies. It was through communion with the dead that I finally found financial independence.

The next several weeks, I spent my nights roaming graveyards speaking with the spirits of the dead. I still had not developed my skills fully and it showed with my inability to control the conversation. I spent endless hours listening to the dead ramble on about their boring and meaningless past lives gaining nothing of value for myself, until one night my luck changed. I found a spirit that had been the personal secretary to the president of a current prominent worldwide corporation. Their relationship over the years had blossomed beyond that of business causing a dilemma when he failed to follow through with his promise to divorce his wife. After the young lady threatened to bring their affair to light, he had her killed. The next day, I tracked him down and to my delight, found out that he still held the same position. I tried several times to set up an appointment with him in vain. Numerous failed attempts to reach him by phone forced me to go to his office and demand an audience in person. He finally agreed to speak with me, after I left him a simple one word message, Stephanie, the name of the woman from the grave. He had me meet him late one night after work and was willing to accommodate all my demands when I explained to him in detail how the murder was committed.

With my newfound wealth, I moved out of the shabby quarters that I currently occupied and bought myself a small ranch in the country. It wasn't extravagant, but it was secluded and it met the needs of my research. Best of all there was an old confederate graveyard within walking distance of the property! It was from this graveyard that I obtained my first human subjects. My first attempts failed miserably along with all of my subsequent endeavors. I finally came to the conclusion that the condition of my subjects had deteriorated beyond usefulness or at least beyond my meager abilities.

The next day I drove into town with the intentions of getting myself a recently deceased subject for my studies. Being something of a hermit, I rarely went to town and decided to make a day of it. I got myself some coffee, a local newspaper and began to sort through the obituaries.

As I sat at a local cafe, I began to laugh uncontrollably. The man sitting at the next table gave me a furtive glance before continuing on with his business. I assume he concluded that I was reading the funny section. The situation was actually quite comical. I was looking through the obituaries like most people look through the classifieds.

What I needed was a young specimen that had died with minimal physical damage to their body. Obituaries are as deceiving as the classifieds. They are written in a positive light leaving out traces of the negative, especially if that person's death wasn't exactly virtuous in nature. Things such as social diseases, drug overdoses and violent murders tend to be left out. A good indication of such an oversight is when someone dies very young. I circled a few possibilities and with a little research narrowed my prospects down to the best candidate.

He was quite young and had drowned in an unfortunate boating accident. Late that night I slipped into the funeral home where he was being kept. Most funeral homes tend to be very lax on their security so I waited until his family and friends left for the night. I had always pondered the tradition of family members staying with their dead overnight, but now I assume that necromancers of the past had stolen bodies for research. Carrying on in such rich necromantic tradition brought warmth to my black heart.

The two young men who had volunteered to stand watch over the body did a poor job, falling asleep quickly and allowing me to easily sneak out with the corpse of the young man. I had originally toyed with the idea of digging the corpse up after the burial, but digging up a casket in the dead of night wasn't an easy task. This method of obtaining subjects was certainly the easiest, even though the risk was higher. People tend to get upset when one of their family members disappears the night before their funeral.

I spent the next two nights in intense study and preparation for my impending ceremony of resurrection. Everything in such a rite had to be perfect. All it took was one tool of incorrect purity or a mispronounced word and the subject was useless, but this time my arduous efforts did not go unrewarded! It was a night that I will never forget. Not because it was my greatest achievement to date, but because of what my subject did upon resurrection. He rose up from my lab table, looked at me blankly and walked away! In my zealous desire to raise the dead, I had overlooked the importance of yet another craft that I had yet to master, the ability to control one's creation. I tried to detain him with both verbal commands and physical strength, but found my suspect relentless in his desire to leave. Unfortunately, I had to destroy him before he could put my research in jeopardy. What I hadn't realized was that learning to control the dead was a task far greater and more essential than simply raising them. What good are the dead if you can't control them?

I spent the next year in constant study, experimentation and frustration. It was vexing to spend so much time obtaining and resurrecting subjects and then in the end having to destroy what I could not control. It seemed I was constantly confronted with one dilemma after another. If it wasn't the need of a new specimen it was the problem of disposing of one. At first I started burying my failed research subjects on my property, but before long, the area began to look like an Indian burial ground. Empty graves and missing dead began to fuel rumors of occult and demonic activities in the surrounding community, making my research even more difficult.

For the safety of my research, I refrained from further tests on human subjects and began once again with lower and easily obtainable forms of life. Continuous failures forced me to leave the laboratory and return to the arcane matter of my dark books. It was in a single treatise from the little known necromantic book *Neresis* that I discovered the secret of dominating the dead. It was written by and based on the studies of a mid fourteenth century monk who had turned to the study of necromancy after separation with his church during the great black plague. Most of the book was written while in isolation, when society was in turmoil. The sheer magnitude of deaths in Europe at the time provided a limitless supply of subjects, allowing his research to take place in the open without fear of repercussions. Those certainly were the golden days of necromancy! Ah, if only things were as accommodating today!

A fragment of one chapter translates as follows:

> For the dead shall someday return to the great circle of life and become another, but this process can be delayed! If this circle is broken the dead can walk and serve those who wish it, until it is completed once again. Severance, preparation, and consumption of the desired host's tongue before resurrection grants control over its body and all the body's available abilities.

It was after reading this passage that my research broke all of its past limitations and neared its full potential. Within weeks I had dozens of dead slaves who followed my every behest. Under the cover of night, my relentless slaves dug up more dead who rose to dig up even more. In less than six months I had an army of undead at my command! I had the willing corpses dig huge underground caverns to house my research and to hide my undead army during the day. My underground lab would have made a colony of ants jealous. I quickly learned through observation, that the condition of the subjects was usually determined by their abilities. Those who had been dead longer were slower and more fragile than the more recently deceased. Some of my subjects actually broke apart under the strain of hard labor, making them useless, but it was a funny sight. During one such incident, a Civil War veteran broke into pieces right before my eyes when his pickaxe struck a large rock in the ground. I thought I was going to die from laughter alone!

It was during this successful period that disaster struck. I had been up all night directing the actions of the undead and had fallen asleep, when I awoke to a knock at the front door. My heart almost stopped when I opened the door and two police officers were standing on my front doorstep. I put on my best poker face and prepared to put on an academy award performance.

Apparently, two hunters had wandered onto my property early one morning and had seen several suspicious looking characters working in my fields, believing them to be possible illegal aliens. Of course I denied any such doings, but the men claimed that they needed to look around for the sake of procedure. I grudgingly agreed, fearful of what these sudden intruders might discover.

I had little to fear in the search of my home, for I had cleaned it and moved my research underground months ago. It was the search of the grounds that I feared! I could only hope that the efforts of my undead over the last few months would pay off. They had dug up all of my prior failed experiments and carried the wasted corpses below ground, along with anything else that might be incriminating while camouflaging the numerous entrances that led below. I walked with the officers, taking every opportunity to babble about subjects that no one could possibly find interesting, in hopes of ending their search early. I rambled on about my family, the weather, and the year's crop return to appear like nothing more than a lonely old hermit. My constant badgering must have worked, because in less than twenty minutes the men came to the conclusion that everything was on the "up and up". I thanked each one and invited them in for some coffee. I was politely refused as I had hoped and sighed a deep breath of relief as the officers began to leave my property.

I was almost in the clear, when one of the bumbling idiots stepped near one of my hidden doors leading below ground, and a large creak came from below! Both of the men stopped and began walking around the area, making the same creaking sound with the weight of their bodies. One began to ask me sarcastic questions about the odd noise, while the other one began digging with his hands. I had never felt so sick in my life. They thought they had busted a moonshiner or a houser of illegal aliens, but what was really below their feet was beyond their wildest imaginations! Scores of living dead and heaps of failed research that could incriminate me beyond legal defense lay strewn in the hole the officers were about to enter.

Once the door was uncovered, one quickly drew a gun, while the other one went below to see what great crime they had solved. The stench of the dead rose out of the ground like the steam of a recent rain stirred by the rising sun nearly bringing both men to their knees. My act was over and I didn't even pretend the odor affected me. All I could do was stand and wait for an opportunity to gain control over the situation if it presented itself.

The officer holding the gun began shouting at me demanding that I tell them what was below. They wouldn't have believed anything I told them whether it was the truth or not, so I shrugged my shoulders and gave them a blank look. One took out a handkerchief to cover his nose and crawled into the small opening of my underground laboratory. The second officer, who was guarding me, began to get noticeably nervous when his partner didn't immediately return. He took his attention off of me for a second to call out to his colleague. Now I may be old, but years of digging up coffins and carrying around bodies weighing as much as me, had strengthened my muscles and before he could react, I pushed him in along with his companion and slammed the huge earthen door trapping both men below. I screamed the command for my undead to kill. The officers tried to defend themselves by firing their guns, but only dismemberment can stop the dead once the black art of necromancy has its hold upon their body.

I went below once I knew it was safe and found the men in literal pieces strewn throughout the caverns. My dead had literally torn the men apart bone by bone while still alive in a rage to fulfill my command. With the death of the two officers, I knew my time in the country had ended.

I hated having to destroy the ranch and my servants who had served me so well. Except for a few, I commanded my dead to destroy each other in an attempt to cover the tracks of my black art. My few remaining servants burned down the house and every piece of evidence that I could not take with me. It was a disastrous setback in my research and one from which I would never fully recover. I took what remaining money I had, three servants and the bare essentials of a necromancer to start over elsewhere. All I left behind was the scorched earth and the ashes of my work.

I chose a location further north, a bit cold for my taste, but its remoteness catered to the solitary needs of my work. It was around this time that I made another mistake. I took on an apprentice. To this day, I'm still not certain why I did it. Maybe it was because I was lonely or that it was nice to have someone around who appreciated my work. He had a talent and love for necromancy almost equivalent to my own. He was a small man who had a bad case of the short man syndrome, but his worst quality was that he was sadistic. He loved to inflict pain on others, whether it be physical or mental, and perceived things of a violent nature to be hilarious. It was his reckless sense of humor that made him so dangerous. One of his favorite pranks was to send a recently resurrected relative over to his former families' house for dinner. Just the thought of the expression on their faces would cause him to burst into incorrigible laughter. I continued to look the other way, and tolerate his childish behavior for the sake of his company, even though a lot of his antics put my work at risk. That was at least until he stooped to murder.

His victim was a young woman of astounding beauty. He had been enthralled with her since he had first met her at the hardware store in town. She had turned down his advances numerous times, until her father, who was the owner of the hardware store, finally banned him from the premises. When I discovered that he had murdered and resurrected her only to serve his sexual lust, I couldn't ignore his misdeeds anymore.

I'm not going to try to deceive anyone by claiming I'm the best person to make judgments about morality, but I had never resorted to murder unless it had been absolutely necessary. I still to this day regret having to order the death of those two police officers. The situation with my apprentice unfortunately was going to be another murder of such necessity, but I had to be careful because he was younger than I and prone to violence.

I had been working on a new translation for weeks and used it as an excuse to invite him to my quarters. I told him that I had discovered something that been lost from present day necromancy for over a thousand years and that it alone could grant powers beyond imagination. He happily accepted my invitation, as I knew he would, and walked directly into my trap. I had three of my best conditioned undead servants hide in the dark corners of my chambers and commanded the creatures seize him upon entry. He pulled out his knife and gave them the best fight he could, but the dead know nothing of pain and easily dispatched him. I couldn't control his dead minions, so I had them destroyed along with him. I didn't feel it would be appropriate to have him serve me, since he had been my confidant, so I cremated him ensuring that he would never become a servant to his own profession.

Necromancy deals with bringing life to the dead, not taking it. Ordering the death of my colleague is a decision I will have to live with the rest of my life. I have always felt that a man will do what he has to do when it is necessary and that is the only defense I have for the actions I took that night.

The art of necromancy is a lonely one and with the death of my only companion I fell into a deep depression. I spent the next few years in nothing more than a drunken stupor. I believe that everyone goes through a time that can be classified as the lowest point in his or her life and mine was as low as anyone's had ever gotten. My work became meaningless and my progression as a necromancer came to a standstill. My dead, who at one time benefited my work, did little more than run a winery. As soon as they would fill a bottle, I would empty it. My addiction also helped me to drain one more thing, my wealth. Once again I was reverted to the poverty of my post college years. It wasn't long before the toll of my age and my drinking binge, if you can call two years a binge, took an unwholesome effect upon my health. At first I used the inebriating affects of alcohol to ignore the symptoms of my failing health, but my condition finally degraded to the point I couldn't function on a day to day basis and I was forced to see a physician.

Due to my extensive work in human anatomy, I was less than shocked when the doctor diagnosed me with the early stages of cirrhosis of the liver. It was this death sentence that gave me the will and the power to give up the bottle and to return to my only love and hope: the cultivation of the dead.

Up to this point, my knowledge and understanding of necromancy couldn't be classified any higher than mid level. There were still so many things about necromancy that I didn't fully understand. All my powers over the dead were useless in my own battle against death. The only thing that could possibly save me from leaving this world was high necromancy. I kept only a few of my dead as personal servants sending the rest back to the grave and devoted every waking moment to intense study.

I had already exhausted the knowledge of my current resources and turned to the book of *Helminth*, also known as the *Law of the Worm*. There is no book more vital to the art of necromancy. It is an immense volume written in textbook form filled with explicit illustrations and experiments concerning the law of the worm. It was set to paper by a society of necromancers who resided on several small islands between Greece and Turkey. These early cultists cheated death for hundreds of years by turning to the ancient lost art of lichism. These powerful necromancers raised an army of the dead threatening the mainlands of Europe, Asia and Africa for centuries until they were conquered by the Roman Empire who almost completely erased their demonic culture burning every piece of written word by the order of the great Caesar himself. The pages that did survive give remarkably detailed instructions on telepathic control over the dead, mass resurrections, and most importantly lichism. It was through lichism that I intended on cheating the law of the worm. Lichism is the highest and most costly power available through necromancy. One of the many requirements is that the necromancer has to commit suicide, but if he has performed the ritual correctly before his death, along with all the proper components, then he or she will rise from the dead with his previous state of mind and be impervious to the effects of the worm, living forever.

It was this task that I prepared for as it would either save me from death or deliver me to it with open arms. The pages of *Helminth* had been written to be used as a reference, not as a teaching tool, and I had a difficult time interpreting it. The text would frequently refer to rites and rituals that were required to complete the transformation, but it failed to give any particular details to those particular ceremonies. I assume that at the time it was written, these rites were common knowledge to a necromancer and that it wasn't considered necessary to refer to their details. These "unnecessary details" are what stood between my living forever or dying in a few short months.

I searched frantically for any information on these rites, with little success. It seemed that the only thing that survived this culture of necromancers was the little known book *Helminth*. The rest was destroyed nearly a hundred years after the most of the Roman Empire turned to Christianity. I searched frantically from one book to another without success. I couldn't find any kind of historical information on their society and with that, my hopes faded with the lost knowledge of the past.

I returned to drinking to ease both my mental and physical pain and had all but given up, when I ran across an old poem within the pages of the dark *Helminth*. When I had first read it, I had dismissed it as little more than a dedication to Delamogue, a powerful ruler during the first age of Helminth, but during my second reading, I recognized it for what it was: a map to the tomb of Delamogue! In its verses, it gave slight indications of its location and hints to specific landmarks that were near the tomb. I immediately regained my composure and returned to my studies! Not my studies of necromancy, but of my search for the island of the necromancers. Although I knew little of high necromancy, a former ruler of a necromancer society would know all! I did a great deal of historical and geographical research, but I still couldn't pinpoint the exact islet on which Delamogue's crypt was hidden. I did however narrow its location down to a handful of likely possibilities and decided to spend my last days searching for it. I would need a great deal of manpower to accomplish such a dig and nothing was cheaper or more accommodating than the labor of the dead.

I returned once again to the practice of uncovering the dead and resurrecting their corpses to serve my will. It was pleasant to once again have a purpose for my servants, and for the first time since the death of my comrade I felt alive.

My next problem was that such an expedition would be very expensive. Out of desperation, I concocted an elaborate plan to rob a bank using the force of my undead servants. I had every aspect of the caper figured out, or so I thought. Nothing however, went as planned. The appearance of my undead servants sent the people in the bank into a delirium which disabled my ability to control the situation. Everybody began to run about in a panic and no one would listen to my specific demands. I still hadn't mastered the ability to communicate telepathically with the dead, so during all the commotion, my undead without commands stood motionless. I lost most of my servants and barely escaped with my own life. It was a disappointing setback and with the pain of disappointment I began to feel the crucial importance of every moment.

I had so much to accomplish in such a short period and for the first time, it was life not death that drove me on in the name of high necromancy. I revised my robbery plan and began to raise the dead I would need to complete both it and the excavation of Delamogue's tomb. My first attempt had failed because it had been planned out in precise detail using subjects that were not capable of following such detailed commands. I couldn't afford another such failure, so I kept the plans of my second attempt simple and direct. I rented a moving van and loaded it up with as many dead as it could hold. Once I got to the bank, I waited outside and sent thirty dead into the bank with only one command, to kill everything alive. It was a gruesome scene. The bodies of the once living were everywhere. The bank lobby was literally dripping in blood. Red stains covered the walls, counters, chairs and the floor. In the middle of the bank stood my dead servants waiting for their next command. Making such a decision is easy. It is the result that is hard to live with. Once I regained my composure, I began running around scooping up every dollar that was available. I didn't leave one drawer or wallet unturned. Unfortunately, I didn't have enough time to get into the vault, but the money I obtained during the robbery was more than adequate to finance the burden of my planned expedition.

Over the next week, I did nothing but prepare for my long voyage to the Aegean Sea. I used the largest portion of the money for a down payment on a sea vessel that would be appropriate for my purposes. Knowing little of the sea and its ways, I hired a boatman to help me navigate the severe waters of the Atlantic and to save time sailing among the many isles of the Mediterranean. He was hired under the impression that I was an independent archeologist financed by a private institution looking for remnants of a lost Greek civilization. We loaded my equipment and supplies, along with my undead servants in long casket-like crates, and set sail the next morning.

My boatman seemed to understand a great deal about the ocean and its currents, so our journey moved along quite quickly. He was an elderly man, even by my standards, who had spent most of his life on fishing boats along the pacific coast. The two of us had little in common, save for a love of astronomy.

I had studied the stars and their effects on life forms as a youth, while he had used them for more practical navigational purposes throughout his life. He knew the location and story of every constellation within range of the naked eye. During the day he was withdrawn, but at night underneath the stars he became quite outspoken and more interesting. Unfortunately, he had become a little too interested in my work. One night, I caught him below searching through one of my crates. I immediately slammed the crate shut and asked him to leave. It had been very dark and I wasn't sure if he had seen anything or not. I confronted him on the deck above and demanded that he explain himself. He claimed that he had only been looking for some tools to repair a damaged sail. I toyed with the idea of having my undead heave him overboard, but my fear of never finding land again changed my mind. I decided to keep him on board at least until we reached the Mediterranean. From that point on, I studied all of his responsibilities and learned. He constantly looked through a tool called a sextant and kept our course on a chart down in his chamber. I couldn't quite figure how it worked, but I picked up on the rest of his duties very quickly. Within three days I felt that I could competently steer the boat and raise and lower the various sails with little trouble. He had become distant since I had scorned him for looking through my chambers and now I was pretty sure that he had seen something. In response, I unpacked my pistol and kept it with me wherever I went.

One morning, I awoke with the blade of a knife pressed against my neck. My own retainer had picked the lock to my cabin and surprised me in my sleep. He tied me up and began to scramble through my effects in a panic. Once he had finished searching through my cabin, he went below to search through the rest of my things. He returned within the very same hour carrying my pistol. A strange look of disbelief and horror had set into his sea worn face. He began to stroke his little white beard and make his plans out aloud. He decided that taking me ashore to the nearest authorities would be the best. I sighed in relief when I discovered that he was not going to kill me. It was his value of life that allowed me the time to plan his death.

He left me tied to my chair under his own watchful eye and left me alone only to check our bearings and position. This continued on for three more nights, before I made my move. I waited until it was late and he had fallen asleep when I began to scream for my servants below. He jumped to his feet in horror and threatened to shoot me if I didn't stop ranting. I carried on for a few more seconds, hoping my servants had heard my commands and stopped only when I thought I had pushed him to his limit. He began to fidget uncontrollably and my pistol began to rattle in his hands. Sounds of scrapping and scratching began to rise from the hull below. He jumped to his feet once again in fear and in doing so, the color from his face drained away leaving it pallid and lifeless. He stood white as a ghost listening and shaking nervously.

The sounds continued to get louder and louder and I knew that the sounds of my servants freeing themselves were driving him mad! The sounds finally stopped and for a few seconds our boat rocked in silence. He sat gripping the hilt of my pistol with all his might staring at the door in wild anticipation. We sat in utter stillness straining our fear-drenched ears, hoping for two distinct and opposite results. Our fears spawned not from the sounds that came from below, but from the hollow silence that had taken precedence so quickly afterward. Mine was the fear of failure, while his was of the unknown. During that brief moment of silence it was as if time stopped leaving us churning on an open sea. Then in an instant time took hold of us once again. An ominous dragging broke the silence of our little rocking world and every drop of blood drained from my captor's face. If I had cut him at that very moment I swear he would not have bled. His sunken eyes never stopped watching the door that separated our small cabin from the sounds beyond. The clamor continued to get closer until it suddenly stopped outside our door. For a brief moment, we rocked in silence. A banging that almost shattered my eardrums seized the little door we were both concentrating on so intently. The situation catalyzed my captor and he began to fire at the door uncontrollably until the chambers in his gun were empty. The hinges finally gave way to the tenacity of my servants and the door came crashing in at our feet. My captor rushed for the door knocking two of my servants aside and climbed to the deck above. I commanded three of my servants to take pursuit, while another untied my hands. I climbed up to the deck and searched the boat, but the old seaman was nowhere to be found. Whether he jumped or was pushed into the rocky sea, I will never know, for the dead cannot remember anything beyond their previous life.

 I reached the gates of the Mediterranean through little more than trial and error. Even with the blessing of clear weather, my trip through the heart of the Mediterranean went slowly. My failing health and lack of sailing experience continued to plague me throughout my journey. My physical form was in its last stages and it wouldn't be long before I would collapse, but my soul still burnt with a desire for continued life. It wasn't death I was trying to avoid through necromancy, it was the fear of the unknown. What lies beyond the circle of life, as it is put in the fourth book of Neresis? Is it tranquility, punishment, or rebirth? Would those of us who broke the laws of the worm be included? These were some of the answers that I hoped to eschew with the resurrection of Delamogue and his memories.

 I don't know if I had fallen into some type of remission or if was the excitement of being so close to such a great discovery, but I began to feel better once I rounded the tip of the Grecian mainland.

 I sailed from one island to the next looking for geographic landmarks that matched those mentioned in the book of *Helminth*. Its pages gave very few references to the location of Delamogue's tomb and what little it did give were vague, but my resolve to find its location never wavered. I did however fear the fact that things change over time. Yes, even the sturdy terrain of our earth gives way and relinquishes its form to the might of time. Historical references to particular locations had been nebulous to archeologists and historians for centuries. It was the legends and myths of the local people that I depended on in my search. Locations that were considered sacred or haunted were the ones I searched first. I finally narrowed my search to a group of islands that surrounded another island containing the ruins of an ancient Minoan city that had been destroyed by volcanic eruptions during the second millennium BC. What made the discovery of this site so unusual was that the archeologist involved found all the normal remnants of a lost civilization, but none of the remains of its people. Not a single human remain had been found during the excavation. It had been a topic for years since its discovery and historians had amassed dozens of inconclusive theories to what happened. Of course none included necromancy or that they had been stolen to swell the undead army of Helminth in its unsuccessful war against the Roman Empire. From the moment I arrived at the site I could feel the presence of past necromancy. It was too advanced and large a civilization to not have some type of burial grounds. The necromancers of Helminth had used this city as one of their recruiting grounds! The island of the necromancers and the tomb of Delamogue couldn't be far.

I spent the next few weeks exploring the surrounding islands and questioning its people. I listened to every fable and wives' tale the locals were willing to tell, but none ended being of any significance to my search. It was through the acquaintance of a young shepherd that I came upon a breakthrough. He told me about a place where he had lost a goat in some type of sinkhole on the south side of the island. The hole that his goat had fallen into was narrow and between thirty and forty feet deep. I took to exploring the hole immediately and upon returning lied to the boy to keep my discovery a secret. I explained to the boy that what we had found was nothing more than an area slowly sinking into an air pocket below the ground and gave him a few dollars for his trouble.

Later that night I awoke my dead, gathered my supplies and

went to wake the once mighty ruler and necromancer Delamogue. Two of my servants stayed above to guard my apparatus, while I lowered four of my servants and myself into the caverns below. The elaborate network of tunnels I found was astounding. Each tunnel took several different twist and turns, but they always came to a similar dead end. I began to carve away the dirt on one of the walls and found some unusual markings. Each wall, once it was properly uncovered, revealed a large stone door with various writings and signs. I found four such doors. The one thing that they all had in common was that in the center of each door was the royal seal of Delamogue! I couldn't fully understand all the markings, but I chose the one that I felt contained Delamogue himself. It was tedious work in the dusty dark of the cavern and although I had worked the earth all my life to obtain the dead, this time a chill like I had never experienced ran over my body. It was if ominous eyes were staring over my shoulder watching my every move.

The tunnel's walls and ceiling had been etched out centuries ago and even the slightest touch could mean a massive cave in sending tons of earth upon my servants and me, burying them in live animation and ending my struggle forever. Three of my dead dug full time day and night, while the other three disposed of the dirt. Even then, it took two full days to break the immense door free from its century long hold upon the earth.

What I found wasn't the tomb of Delamogue, but a vault used to hold his many wives. I took the time to perform the ceremony of communion and chose to speak with the corpse that according to the location of her burial spot held some sort of significance. Apparently, the women had been sealed up while alive at the time of their husband's death. She knew very little about the ceremonies of the Helminth or the ways of necromancy. All she could tell me were the details of her own life. She had been taken during a war between her city and that of Helminth. She had been forced to marry Delamogue and was sealed up to die, along with his other servants, at the young age of sixteen. The one useful thing she was able to tell me was that Delamogue had died from a strange disease, meaning that he had not turned to lichism himself. After letting her return to her eternal sleep, I began the dig on the next door.

The work on the second door went very smoothly. We sustained only one ceiling collapse and my servant was unharmed after we dug him out. My excitement continued to grow with each load of dirt that was taken out until my head almost burst when the tomb's door finally broke loose. Once inside, I was not disappointed. It was more impressive than I could have ever imagined. The walls were integrity detailed with exquisite carvings and artwork depicting the lifestyle of a Helminth king and his people. Artifacts thousands of years old lay piled neatly in its four corners and in the middle on a pedestal was the sepulcher of Delamogue.

Surrounding it at floor level were five smaller sepulchers connected to Delamogue's by small two-foot high walls forming a large pentagram. I stumbled through my pockets to find a cloth to wipe the dust off my glasses and began to run around taking in every word, picture, and symbol with the excitement of a schoolboy. I had spent an entire lifetime struggling to gather bits and pieces of scarce information to learn what little I knew about necromancy, and then to have it all thrown at me at once was almost more than I could handle.

The carvings and writings etched on the walls surrounding his tomb gave more necromantic lore than I had ever seen or believed possible. Explicit details on how to infect a live being with the little known necromantic disease ghoulism, telepathy over the dead, clairvoyance through the dead, and vampirism were just a few of the rituals that were portrayed upon its walls. I finally calmed myself after hours of intense study of the walls and decided to get on with the task at hand.

I didn't let the clumsy hands of my servants touch the delicately carved sarcophagus of Delamogue; I myself carefully filed away the seal that held his body in place with my diligent but excited hands and let my eyes feast upon the great Delamogue. His small shriveled body, which lay stretched out in a mummified form, had mostly deteriorated over the thousands years that had passed since his death. Little more than a few decomposed bones lay before me, but they would be more than enough to perform a simple communion with the dead. I sat down and prepared to speak with Delamogue. Closing my eyes, I spoke the words of communion punctiliously, as I had done successfully many times before, and was pleased to see his ghost-like form hovering above his remains when I had finished. My delight in my spell changed to fear very quickly. Even though I had cast the incantation before me, I had no control. His eyes and voice radiated anger and before I knew it I was answering to him. He began to call me blasphemous names and quote sacred laws that I had broken, but never heard. I tried to apologize and explain myself, but he continued to interrupt me by quoting the penalties of breaking these unwritten laws. He scorned me like a captious teacher would his pupil, and began speaking in a manner that made no sense. I sat still and began listening to his words. I had never heard most of the ancient words, but they were being chanted much like that of a necromancer chanting a spell! My insides seized in terror! What ancient necromantic curse or spell was being released upon me? Before I could react, a pair of hands wrapped around my neck! The air in my lungs expired and I gasped to fill them again. I grabbed the arms of my strangler and struggled to breathe. The veins in my neck began to bulge trying push blood into my brain and my head began to feel light from lack of oxygen. I pulled my revolver from its holster and emptied it over my shoulder into my attacker's face. The grip loosened and I broke free. I turned around to see the distorted face of one of my own dead. My shots had honeycombed his face and his eyes were hanging from their sockets. It couldn't see me, but still tried to serve its new master Delamogue by grasping at me. The other two servants that I had brought with me had also fallen under his spell and tried to seize me. I took hold of a pickax and planted it into the head of one of my attackers. It didn't kill him, but by holding on to the end of it, I used it to maneuver him away from me and managed to get away. I got to the rope ladder and climbed above. Panting, I pulled up the rope ladder and collapsed in exhaustion. After resting a few minutes, I killed my three servants that remained above by burning their bodies before returning to my boat. I stayed out at sea that night and prepared to clash with him once again.

Delamogue had instilled something in me that I had never known, fear of the dead. It was something I had never felt when dealing with the dead. It wasn't actually a fear of the dead themselves, but fear of losing control. Delamogue's power had such a profound effect upon me that I didn't want to have anything to do with the dead as long as I was within one hundred miles of his tomb. My plans were simple and excluded all aspects of necromancy. The next day, I returned to the pit leading into his tomb and lowered down my rope ladder. I waited several minutes and finally went below when I felt it was safe. I checked the tunnels behind me to ensure that nothing could cut off my escape and began my slow walk toward Delamogue's tomb. All it took was for my flashlight to shine into his chamber and his dead came out in fury to protect him. I ran back to my ladder, climbed above, took hold of my ax and waited. Within minutes a head poked out as one of my ex-servants emerged. I immediately began to chop him into pieces and had finished dismembering him when another one emerged. I began to chop on the second one when a third one emerged. Before I knew it, a fourth and fifth one had climbed above with me. Delamogue had raised his five guards in the sepulchers adjoining his own and sent them above. I began to chop at his dead like a frenzied maniac, but they threatened to overwhelm my position. Body parts were everywhere crawling toward me to get into the fray. His guards were brittle and a single blow usually disabled their decayed bodies, but my own dead were harder to dismember. Teeth sunk into the flesh of my ankle and another managed to bite my arm before I was finished. If I had been anywhere other than in the open terrain where I could move about freely, they would have torn me apart with a rage unknown by the living.

Still fearing Delamogue's power, I burnt the butchered carcasses that quivered and crawled on the ground still struggling to serve their master. Upon reentering his tomb, I found his body and sarcophagus resting as I had originally found them. Summoning up my courage, I sat down in front of his ancient tomb and prepared to speak with him for one last time. His body rose in a haze of smoke with astute eyes examining every corner of his chamber before finally rested upon me. Once again the faint image before me spoke, but this time it was in a low tone of disgust instead of the high pitch of anger. He insisted that I should extend him the professional courtesy he deserved and let his soul rest in peace. I assured him that I would take every necessary step to ensure his eternal rest, once I successfully converted to lichism. What he said next can only be explained in his own words:

"I will fully divulge to you the information you require to complete the stygian ceremony of lichism, but you must understand that lichism does not grant immortality, it simply means you will not be affected by the forces of the universe. The universe is a vast system of objects, acted upon by forces, and forces that act upon objects. One of the most powerful of these forces is life. Our bodies are nothing more than an object being affected by the force of life. When something dies it is simply a separation of the two. This disunion doesn't mean that either of the two is extinct, but that they have returned to their previous states. The body back to the earth, and life back to the ever flowing forces of the universe. Both will either affect or be affected by something else in the future, the body by a reaction of some kind, while the force of life may resurface in the form of a rebirth. All forces flow in a circle, therefore they are complete and perpetual. It is from the circle of life that necromancers derive their power. A necromancer merely bends and manipulates it to satisfy his own agenda, but to bend it too far can break it, leaving a necromancer outside the circle of life. Once you are outside the circle of life, there is no return. The conversion to lichism will break your circle of life," he paused for a moment and finished, "you will become extinct to every force and object in the universe."

The dark chamber we stood in fell silent for only a few moments, before he began to give me complete instructions on the ceremony of lichism. I took precise notes not omitting a single word, taking care to make sure each word was in the correct order and had the proper pronunciation. My notes filled up more than thirteen pages both front and back, and without a doubt carrying out their instructions would be my most difficult necromantic attempt yet. Unfortunately, as in my past necromantic attempts, there would be no room for mistakes.

Later, as I began to prepare for the solitary ritual of lichism, I pondered the words spoken to me by Delamogue. The single word extinct continued to haunt me with my every thought. It is a powerful word that simply means the end of something without continuation. Another concern that kept creeping up during my preparation was the possibility that he might have purposely given me an incorrect procedure. My failure and therefore successful suicide would certainly be in his best interest. How else could he ensure that I would never disturb him again? Once again the cunning and ancient king had reversed the situation and taken control. The only way to find out if the ceremony that he recited was correct was to actually perform it, and if I didn't, then I would die from liver failure within a few short months. It was easy to see how he had been able to rule an actual empire of necromancers. Even in death and defeat, he was in control.

It is here where I am forced to bring this part of my narrative to a close. Whether it will be the end, a continuation or the beginning of something completely different I cannot say for sure. The last month of my life has been spent completing this biography and putting together a compilation of everything I have learned about necromancy from both my life and the tomb of Delamogue. *The Circle of Life and its Necromantic Manipulations* is what I quickly dubbed it and both it and this manuscript will be left behind in the tomb of Delamogue to survive me. I can only hope that if I fail, they will someday help another necromancer succeed.

The End?

The Final Infection

When it came upon the world, it came in epidemic proportions casting a shadow across the globe that brought death to the living and life to the dead.

Chapters

Chapter 1
History of the Infection

When it came upon the world, it came in epidemic proportions casting a shadow across the globe that brought death to the living and life to the dead. The first known case appeared in rural West Africa and before it was identified, it had decimated the entire African continent and had spread into Eastern Europe and the Middle East. It left a wake of destruction in its path that could only be matched by biblical accounts. The infrastructures of man crumbled beneath its weight creating a tide of men, fear and infection that surged from one country to the next. Governments collapsed and ceased to exist. The plague dispersed armies and destroyed entire cultures leaving utter destruction in its wake. The artificial borders of men could not contain it and within two months it had spread from the Atlantic coast of Europe to the Pacific coast of Asia.

In an attempt to stop the pestilence from crossing the oceans, all forms of transportation from Asia, Europe and Africa were terminated leaving the people upon its soil isolated. An unseen war was fought between survivors and the infected, and after three weeks all communication with the world's largest mainlands was lost. The rest of the world waited quietly. Two weeks passed without any new confirmed cases and a new glimmer of hope appeared when the C.D.C. managed to isolate the source on an offshore platform.

The infection was being caused by a highly contagious virus that once it entered its host began to reproduce at an astounding rate and within a matter of hours was present in every tissue in the body.

The first two stages of symptoms started off basically as do other infections, with the first stage consisting of high fever, making its host highly contagious, and the second consisting of body chills, diarrhea and vomiting. The third stage was far more severe and brought extreme body aches and random blood clots. The fourth and what medically should have been the last consisted of an overwhelming numbness of the body, which inevitably led to coma. It was the fifth stage that defied all medical history and made the disease an absolute horror. Shortly after the host went into a coma, every organ in the body except the brain ceased to function. Then at some point, usually within a twenty four hour period after the initial infection, the hosts would regain consciousness, but they were not themselves. Their body organs remained completely dormant save their brain, but they could still function physically as well as they could before they became infected. What was different was their desire for flesh. Once an infected reanimated, it did not remember who it was, nor did it care. It did not reason nor did it communicate; it functioned from instinct alone, an instinct of hunger, murder and to spread its infection.

Two more weeks passed without a confirmed case and for a moment it appeared as if the contagion had been contained and the remaining of the world spared from its wrath. Then it struck again. This time it surfaced in Central America and quickly spread to both North and South America. All activity in the western hemisphere stopped. The stock market shut down having collapsed weeks ago, people walked off their jobs and all forms of entertainment ceased. Strict government curfews took effect turning the north and south continents of the Americas into refuges of hermits as their people closed themselves off from society. Looting became widespread as people stocked up and prepared for the onslaught.

When it came, it came swiftly, smashing entire towns like a mallet would an exposed anthill, causing its occupants to run around in dismay attacking each other and those whom had succumbed to the infection. The majority of the infections came from stage one. As with the flu, most people exposed became infected, and those that didn't were later infected through the attacks of those whom had. Individuals refused to slaughter their own infected relatives and eventually surrendered themselves be it by infection or attack engorging the infected's numbers. Fear of the infection brought on mass hysteria and the trust between men dissolved. Murders became commonplace, whether due to a mistaken infection, robbery, vendettas or self-defense. Law and order withdrew from society and the infected swelled into its void. The war between the inhabitants of the western hemisphere and the infected had begun.

Chapter 2
The Hunt

      Cool dew streamed elegantly along the faces of the broad leaves high above his head, dripping around him in a slow quiet rain. A drop struck his hunting jacket and swiftly rolled down his water resistant sleeve. He felt the coolness of another one that had landed inside his collar falling flat onto his exposed neck. It gathered itself and ran down his back only to disappear as it soaked into his t-shirt. His dirty damp brown hair flipped out from all sides of his bright orange cap. Resting his cheekbone against the wooden stock of his rifle, he stared down its barrel through a dark brown eye and exhaled softly releasing the air from his lungs. Holding his breath to avoid the slightest movement, he slowly squeezed the trigger and awoke the quiet morning with the sound of gunfire. His target stammered backwards as if in shock before collapsing into the weeds surrounding it, disappearing from the crosshairs in his scope. He stood up in his stand, holstered his rifle and crawled down from his perch. His thick boots pounded against the ground and embedded a small depression into the muddy soil. He crossed the long open field between his stand and his kill taking long high steps in an attempt to avoid the long wet blades of grass. His pant legs took on a darker color than the top of his pants as they became soaked with moisture, and by the time he reached his kill it ran up past his knees. Using the barrel of his gun to lower the grass, he walked forward until he stumbled upon the corpse. It was a seven point, a good kill by anyone's standard. He took hold of its antlers and dragged it through the soft wet field. Its body left a long flat trail within the grass that leisurely rose back to its original height as the morning grew older stealing the dew from the grass with the heat of the sun.

He lifted his trophy up into the bed of his truck and slammed the tailgate shut. It lay flat on its side with its one upward eye staring at him blankly. He turned from its lost look and returned to dismantle his tree stand. It came apart quickly as it had many times before and in a few minutes he was sitting behind the wheel of his old truck bouncing down the wooded trail that cut into the quiet forest. The interior of his truck wasn't much to look at as it had cracks from one end of the dash to the other and a crack in the windshield that had threatened to split his window in half for years. His seats were dirty and ripped from the many extended hunting trips it had accompanied him on through the years, but it was tough. It smelled like the fish he had thrown in the back on numerous fishing trips and the gasoline that always poured freely into its carburetor. He knew every squeak it made and if it was a good one or a bad one. It didn't even have a radio in it as it had been stolen years ago and he had never wasted his time getting another. The fact it had gotten stolen didn't make him angry; it was the fact he hadn't caught the person whom had stolen it in the act that made him mad. It would have been worth it to lose his cheap stereo if only he could have caught the damn thief in the act, he thought. It was without a doubt a man's truck and a many a woman had refused to ride in it and that was how he liked it. He didn't have time for an arrogant woman in his life anyway and he used his truck as an initial test. One of his favorite tests on a first date, before his radio had been stolen, was to play the song Closer by Nine Inch Nails, without saying a word while it played. If a woman couldn't handle its lyrics without getting offended or started acting weird, then he knew they didn't have a chance for a relationship.

He had been out on this particular hunting trip for ten days. He had seen three deer quietly pass his stand before he finally pulled the trigger, not willing to waste a shell on either a doe or spike. Besides it was the solitude of hunting that drew him to it, not slaughtering everything that walked, and with the state of society at the moment he needed the break.

When he had left for his trip, people been had been going mad, ranting about some sort of rapture and the end of the world. Nothing was on the television but constant reports about its spread. Every channel was nothing more than a group of scientists, reporters or politicians arguing about it twenty four hours a day, and to his dismay they had even canceled the World Series. At first even he had sat in front of the tube and listened to the reports, but after two weeks nothing changed. They kept talking about the same thing, and from their reports it was obvious they knew no more about it than he. Each report he heard contradicted the next. Some reports claimed that people should isolate themselves so not to spread the infection, while others claimed isolation only made it easier for the infected to overrun an area without resistance. It hadn't taken him long to grow weary of everyone's attempt to prepare for something they knew so little about. Long gas lines, supply hoarding, fear of others and near absolute lawlessness had finally sent him out into the seclusion of the woods to escape it all. He hoped as he drove back toward town that things had gotten better. It was a long drive, especially at the speed he was forced to maintain along the uneven dirt road between the city and the country. His truck rolled side to side as it maneuvered over the bumpy road causing the loose contents in its cab to slide back in forth in the compartment. Every so often a coin or trinket would slide excessively and annoy him to the point that he would catch it in mid slide and toss it into something that would restrain it.

Nearly an hour passed before the dirt road ended and blended into a wider gravel road. Once his truck pulled onto it he increased his speed replacing the earlier rocking of his truck with a smoother ride accompanied with random dings from stray gravel. Streaming a cloud of white dust, he leaned back using his leg to steer, slid the middle window in his truck open and reached into a strategically placed cooler in the bed of his truck. He fished his hand around in the lukewarm water pushing around empty cans until he found a full one. He pulled forth a warm beer and popped the lid. Bubbles spewed out of the can and he quickly stuck its top to his mouth sucking down the foam until it ceased. It might have been warm but it was refreshing he thought.

Two more hours passed before he saw another junction and three more before he finally reached a paved road. He stopped and looked down both stretches of the long highway. There wasn't a car in sight in either direction. He turned left and picked up his speed on the smooth paved road. His truck sped around a long turn and before him extended the main highway. He slammed on his breaks and his truck came to a shaking and skidding stop. He opened his door and stepped out to get a better look. In both directions as far as the eye could see were rows and rows of what appeared to be abandoned cars, trucks, vans and eighteen-wheelers. They were smashed into each other with open doors and hoods as if there had been all been involved in some sort of hundred mile long pile up. If he had had any supplies left, he would have turned around and gone back to the woods at that very moment, but all he had left was about half a pound of jerky and a couple of beers. He was the type of man who could go a long way on such provisions, but knowing he would one day have to return, he got back into his truck and started it up. It rumbled trying to fulfill his command then sputtered to a trembling stop. He cranked it again bringing the truck's engine to full throttle before releasing his foot on the pedal and slowly pulling toward the wake of destruction along the horizon.

Chapter 3
First Encounter

The front of the old truck lumbered up to the edge of the long congested highway rumbling to a stop. A man in hunting clothes stepped out into the sun slamming his door. Before him stood a four-lane highway engorged with vehicles lined bumper to bumper from one horizon to the next. It had been turned into a junkyard of proportions so immense not even a motorcycle could have squeezed through the entanglement. Unsure how he was going to pass through wreckage on such a monstrous scale, the young man turned back toward his truck catching a shadow out of the corner of his eye. A head popped up through the back window of a car a few feet away. It began to bob up and down from behind the back of the seat. Curious, he slowly walked up toward the car and leaned around to look into the front seat. Strapped into the front seat behind the driver's wheel was a man with short black hair in a long sleeved white shirt and a long black tie. He started to reach toward the door when the man's head turned staring into his eyes. Its black eyes although moving seemed dull and lifeless much like those of the deer he had killed earlier that day. When its eyes made contact, the man in the car went berserk. The wild man began to bang and claw at the driver's window while screaming as if in glorious pain. The aggression of the man in the car troubled him and he fell backwards onto the ground. The enraged man started to bang his arms and legs trying to break free, convulsively sounding off his horn and finally shattering the driver's window with his fist. Glass flew on the ground landing around the young hunter, who quickly jumped to his feet. The man in the car began to try and crawl out of his window but was held in check by his seatbelt.

Startled by the strange man, the hunter began to back away from the horrible scene, watching the man fight with the seat beat seemingly too dumb to merely unlatch it, when suddenly two arms wrapped around him from behind and began to tear at his jacket. He spun around and found a crazed woman with long blond hair and dried blood on her chin gnawing at his jacket with her teeth. Had she been tall enough, she would have been able to reach his neck and face and immediately infect him from her bites. She began to bite at his jacket in a frenzy and tear at his exposed face with her hands. Her body jerked quickly as a person does on a VHS tape when fast-forwarded, and he found her assault surprisingly strong for a woman, as he couldn't tear loose from the grip of her long slender fingers and red polished nails. In her aggressive efforts to bite him, she knocked him down onto his back and fell on top of him. He pushed her head up so she could not reach his exposed neck and pulled his hunting knife free. She began to scream and yell like a mad woman possessed for flesh. Her teeth partially tearing through her cheek gnashed like a lawnmower and pinched his skin painfully through his thick hunting jacket. He jabbed the long sharp blade into the side of her neck releasing blood in long squirts as he tried to slow her assault, but the action showed no signs of slowing her attack. Adrenaline flowed through the veins in his muscles bringing on a primordial strength equal to that of his ancient forefathers in a struggle with some wild beast for survival. Bringing the tip of his hunting knife to bear squarely above her head, he swung with all his might, piercing the thick bone of her skull. The blade sank deep within her brain abruptly ending her struggle.

The man trapped in the car near him was still struggling like a madman in an attempt to reach him. The man's arms began to bleed profusely as they ripped across the glass of the broken window as he attempted to somehow break free. The man's leg lodged between the steering wheel and the steering column sounding the car's horn in a long alerting howl. Standing to his feet in shock after killing a person, he looked out toward the highway. In response to the loud horn, heads began to pop up in other vehicles, while bodies began to stand up from within the tall grass along the median and the side of the road.

Upon seeing him, those in cars began to bang their way out as those already free began a mad dash toward him.

"Oh shit!" he screamed running back to his truck.

He fumbled with the keys in his pocket and slammed them into the ignition. The engine turned over with a loud grumble, but didn't crank. He looked down at the gas gauge. It sat near empty.

"Come on God damn it!" he screamed gritting his teeth. "I know you still got some juice in you!"

A huge mob formed down the long highway and several of the crazed people were just moments away. They ran at a frenzied pace, like drunken men on speed shaking in aggressive jerking motions all with vacant stares fixed upon him. He cranked the ignition again and once again the engine turned but didn't start. A red headed man with an eye hanging out from under a torn eyelid leaped up onto the hood of his truck and began to claw at his front window. He began to crank his truck wildly in a panic for his life and it turned over once again but the engine wouldn't start.

Two more frenzied people ran up and began to bang against his truck. Arms began to pound on his window and he instinctively locked his door, although neither tried to use the door handle. The man lying on his hood ripped one of his windshield wipers loose and began to pound it against his windshield. The crack in its glass began to race toward the other end threatening to allow access to the wild man. Another man rushed up to his passenger window and began to shake the truck. He cranked the ignition again and finally the motor came to life with a rumble. His windshield split in half with a crushing blow from the man on his hood and two hands reached in and took hold of his steering wheel. His foot slammed on the gas pedal and his hands spun the vehicle around in a one eighty, all the while beating at the invading hands upon the wheel. The man's hands slipped from the wheel and his body tumbled off the hood onto the road, rolling to a stop as it crashed against a parked car. Using his hand, the driver pushed his windshield out onto the hood causing it to side off the side crashing against the ground. Two more crazed people ran directly at the front of his truck and he bowled over their bodies rocking the truck over toward the passenger's side, causing him to nearly slide out its door. He drove along the grass on the side of the highway leading a train of infected running behind him in a craze for flesh.

Every so often one would dart in front of the truck from behind a car on the highway or try to grab onto his truck as he passed, but he never lifted his foot up from the pedal and crushed them with smooth acceleration. Their bodies would disappear below the hood as if melting away into nothing. He drove on until he had lost all sight of the infected, before pulling over under a tree in the shade.

Leaving his truck running, he pulled open his jacket and looked at his chest. He had bruises in three places where the woman had pinched his skin between her teeth, but the skin had not been broken. He sighed and leaned back to rest for a moment. His fuel gauge still sat near empty and he leaned forward shifting into gear. He drove on slowly along the side of the road as far away from the road as possible. Occasionally he would pass infected who always ran as fast as they could toward him, throwing themselves recklessly at his truck. He avoided them when he could, but when one attacked him from the front, he didn't attempt to swerve around it. He rolled his truck through the tall grass as he crossed an exit ramp, being very careful to avoid anything that might give him a flat tire.

Up the road was an abandoned gas station filled with empty cars and strangely strewn objects. Suitcases, clothes, lawn furniture and car parts were spread all along the highway as if the area had been hit by a twister. He sat still for a moment and watched the station carefully from the safety of his truck. Nothing but loose trash blew around the otherwise motionless and quiet gas station. His truck started up on his first attempt and rolled slowly toward the tranquil station. A vehicle of some sort blocked every pump and he quietly pulled up behind a small dirty white compact car. He pulled his hunting rifle down from his gun rack and loaded a shell into the chamber before stepping out of his truck. His truck made a low grumbling noise as it ran idle and he was mindful to leave his door open in case he needed to make a quick escape. His steps slid slowly across the smooth pavement as he approached the car blocking the pump. He cautiously looked through the vehicles dirty back window and after finding it empty, opened its door and found its keys still in the ignition. He flopped into the driver's seat, discreetly shifted it into neutral and with a slight grunt slowly pushed it out of the way. He quickly ran back to his truck and pulled it up to the pump. His hand hastily unscrewed the gas cap, stuck the fuel nozzle into the gas tank and squeezed the trigger on the pump. The pump had power, but didn't pump fuel. Instead it beeped at him as if scolding his actions. He looked at the pump and saw a large white sign reading: Please prepay before pumping when not using a credit card. He fumbled through his wallet and pulled out his card. He slid it into the slot and waited. The digital screen read: Credit not available please see cashier. He cursed and looked into the dark windows of the convenience store. Its lifelessness loomed over him in a heavy shadow and he lifted up his rifle to reassure himself before methodically walking toward the double glass door. Maybe he could figure how to turn the pump on he thought reassuringly. With the level of people theses places hired, he thought, it couldn't be too difficult.

   The door creaked open slowly and he stepped in out of the sunlight. He jerked his rifle up to bear toward a fat body lying face down on the floor. He walked around it carefully ready to fire at any moment. It was a large white man's body stained in dried blood. He kicked it in the side but nothing more than the fat on his body moved. He rolled it over and saw that the man had been shot in the face. He stood up and walked over to the cash register. A thick bulletproof glass surrounded it, but as he checked it, he found the door unlocked. He stepped inside and began to push every button he could find. Lights came on and others went out before he found one with the same number as his pump. The glass behind him shook with a loud bang and he spun around in horror to see an infected man beating against it. The hysterical man was wearing a shirt with the name "Pump and Go" on it. The wild eyed began to slide along the glass toward the door to the register area in an attempt to reach him. The young hunter ran over to the door and slammed it shut before the infected man could get in with him. The crazed man began to beat at the door furiously causing the hinges to bend unnaturally. The hunter put his boot at the bottom of the door and let the top half squeeze open. The infected man stuck his head and one of his arms through the opening and began to claw and bite at him into the air. He rested the barrel against the decayed head and split it wide open when he pulled the trigger. The man's body collapsed to the floor and wedged in between the door. He grasped the man's shirt and pulled him inside before stepping outside the bulletproof glass. Another load bang came from the front door getting his full attention.

Outside banging on the glass were four more infected individuals trying to get into the small station. Their faces were grotesquely pressed against the glass as young children might do at a candy store, the irony being that he was the intended treat. He ran up to the door and locked it. The sight of him being so close caused the creatures to scream madly while they beat at the door with their bare hands. Dark blood smeared over the thick glass door as it poured from their broken and shattered hands. He ran to the back of the store and stumbled through its small stockroom before finding the back door and kicking it open. An alarm sounded as the door swung open solidly and bounced off the back of the store banging back into him.

He ran around the side of the building and peeked around the corner toward the gasoline pumps, white smoke poured reassuringly from his truck's tailpipes. The blasting alarm resonated around the building alerting other infected in the area. Infected men, women and children began to roam out of the woods and weeds of the surrounding area and deliberately stream toward the small gas station. The young man ducked low and ran across the parking lot toward his awaiting truck. An infected man saw him and began to run after him screaming like a wild Indian. He jumped into his cab and slammed his door shut as an infected woman reached it. She began to claw at his door and several more attacked the front of his truck as he backed out. The gas nozzle hose still sitting in his tank stretched to its limit until it burst loose ripping off his truck's gas lid cover and landing in the face of an infected man, sending him hurtling to the ground. His thick knobby tires boiled across the pavement in reverse crunching an infected boy as he fell beneath its weight. He rode along the roadside again until his pursuers were out of sight and stopped to inspect the damage he had done to his beloved truck.

"Fuck!" he screamed after looking at the damage to his truck.

He banged his fist against his rear fender in frustration. He ought to go back and blow the shit out of those fuckers he thought. God damn them, no one fucked with my truck he thought angrily. The pump nozzle not only had ripped off his gas lid cover, but it had pulled the neck to his fuel tank out and misshaped it to where if he had a gas cap it wouldn't have fitted. He cursed again watching his gas gauge religiously as it hadn't moved in nearly twenty minutes expecting his fuel supply to give out on him at any minute.

Chapter 4
Going Home

His truck sputtered at the edge of the woods near his parent's home until he reluctantly turned the key bringing the old engine to a halt. He stepped outside his cab walked to the back and stuffed a glove into the opening of his gas tank. Pulling his rifle from the back window, he walked through the lush overgrown grass of the back yard. Once he was in the open he bent down into a low crouching run and made the back door of the house without incident. It was locked as he had expected it to be and after fumbling through his key ring, he hastily unlocked it, stepped inside and shut the door quietly. All the curtains were drawn shut forcing him to squint for what little light was available. For as long as he could remember, every piece of furniture in the den had been in the same location and he knew the layout by heart. He navigated the darkness of the den with ease and found the light switch, flicking it on. The light he had expected to illuminate his surroundings never materialized and he stayed emerged in a cold darkness.

He crept over to his old room and slung its door open, it stood empty and as neat as it had always been since he left home. After moving out on his home some years ago, it had been converted into a guestroom. Cautiously he examined his old closet and was relieved to find his childhood junk, which his mother had refused to throw away. Digging deep into the relics of his childhood, he found several of his old knives and he strapped the largest one on his waist. He threw a smaller one into his pocket and smiled upon seeing his old boy scout backpack. It jingled as he lifted it up and he examined its interior. Happily he found his old mess kit still intact…god the pounds of canned chili he had prepared in the thin metal pot he thought lightly.

He threw the old pack onto his back and slowly walked up the stairs toward the kitchen. The door to the kitchen creaked loudly as it had all his life. He had always hated it, because he could never sneak upstairs to get a midnight snack without waking up his mother.

"Do you know how late it is young man?" she would whisper loudly to him so not to wake his father whenever she caught him in the middle of one of his midnight binges.

A freight train bursting through the house wouldn't have awoken his father who slept like a rock, but she still nagged him every single time. He pulled his gun down and walked into kitchen. The sliding glass back door near the dining room was broken and the wind blew in, gently swaying the curtains. The cabinet doors were open and after inspecting them he found each to be strangely empty. His mother's cabinets were never empty and he assumed they must have been emptied by his parents and taken somewhere else or far worse, looted by scavengers.

Gazing up through the dark hallway toward his parent's room, he saw the dim image of their door. Although terrified of what he might find, his curiosity of their whereabouts was too strong to ignore. His large boots made their way up the luxuriant carpeted stairs and within a few moments he found himself at the door of his parent's room. It was closed tightly and he gently placed the palm of his hand on the knob. His heart began to race as he turned the knob in wild anticipation. It turned slightly before it stopped and clicked into the locked position. Having often unlocked every door in their house as a child with ease, he pulled the plastic toothpick from his Swiss army knife and gently slid it into the hole in their doorknob. It clicked as he turned the knob to the right until it stopped. The door creaked open slowly letting light into the dark hall.

A brute force followed by screaming and scratching slammed the door shut and in a panic he fell backwards against the wall. The hinges on the door began to swell outward from the force behind it as it began bending in and out violently. The hunter stumbled down the hall just before the door burst open and two figures landed on the floor on top of the broken door. He looked back quickly over his shoulder and saw the twisted faces of his parents staring at him hungrily. Both scurried to their feet and scrambled down the hall fighting each other in an attempt to reach him first. He darted into the den and locked the door. It began to shake viciously and the screams beyond it struck a horror in his heart such as he had never felt. Both voices were recognizable to him, but they had an excruciating shrill and tortured tone. He fell into the far corner of the den and pulled his knees up to his chest for support. Seeing his parents as the monsters they had become was too much; he gave up and braced for the end as so many others had done before him since the beginning of the infection.

The door at the top of the stairs gave way in a burst of wooden splinters and tumbled down the stairs into the den a few feet away. Suddenly, something deep down within him snapped and a primal instinct to survive overwhelmed his reflexes. His muscles surged wildly as he took a hold of his rifle. First to come into his rifle's sight was the torn and ragged face of what had been his father. It wasn't his father he thought…it wasn't his father. The trigger on his rifle clicked and splattered his father's brains along the wall, covering his high school graduation picture. He instinctively ejected the shell in his rifle's chamber sending it soaring across the room and reached into his pocket fingering another shell. His infected mother ran over the body of his father and leaped into the air. He lifted his rifle up to stop her assault and used it to hold her head away from him as she crashed into his body. Her horribly decayed face snarled at him madly from only inches away.

"Why are you doing this to me!" he screamed crying. "I can't fucking take it!"

Using his leg, he slid out from underneath her to one side and used his weight to flip her over onto her back, pinning her head to the floor with the stock of his rifle. She struggled with him like a wild animal and he had to shift his weight onto her to keep down. Using his knee on her stomach as leverage, he reached up with his right arm and took a hold of one of his father's old bowling trophies. In one brute swing he brought its sharp marble base down upon her skull. It took three vicious blows to smash her skull and stop her struggling. Her blood splattered face fell quiet and he lifted her body onto his lap crying for her loss. He had nothing left in his heart but a desire to kill.

Chapter 5
Moving On

Grasping his father's shotgun and two boxes of shells that he had found in parent's closet, he jumped into the cab of his truck and slammed the old door. It rattled as metal clanked against metal. From the best he could tell from his parent's home, they had locked themselves up in their bedroom in fear of the incoming infection and either one or both had come down with the horrible life-after-death virus. Both cars had been taken by what he assumed must have been looters, but he had found about two gallons of gasoline through siphoning it from the tanks of their push and riding lawnmowers. With two more gallons of gasoline in his truck, he leaned back into his seat and turned the key in the ignition. After just two cranks, it started up with a loud rumble and rolled through his old neighborhood. The damn infection had taken everything he thought angrily, his life, his family…his heart. It was cold, stone cold.

He was heading towards Karl's market in hope of finding enough supplies to go back into hiding deep into the woods he knew so well. It wouldn't take much to sustain him he thought. He wasn't picky and a few basics would be enough. He drove on through the destruction of his childhood neighborhood when he came along side the house of his lifelong and best friend. He caught its pink exterior out of the corner of his eye and unconsciously brought his rumbling truck to a skidding stop. His friend had got a great deal on the old pink house. He always intended to repaint it, but after years of procrastination, he got used to it and it had never changed. He looked around for a moment in deep thought and then before he might change his mind, he turned off his engine and waited quietly. His ears burned in silence and after he felt reasonably sure that he had not been spotted by an infected, he stepped out of his truck holding his rifle.

They had been best friends since the fifth grade, and after his parents moved from the neighborhood his friend had bought his own home on the same block in order to live where he grew up. The house seemed dark and for a moment he stopped and contemplated if he should go in and check or leave while he still had a head. He wasn't sure if he could survive another killing of someone he knew, but after gathering up his strength, he took another step toward the small two-story house and never stopped. Walking around the back of the house, he noticed a group of people clawing at a large tree in the back yard. He quickly counted about eight, but before he could hide, a young infected girl spotted him. She screamed at him as if throwing out some kind of war cry, before running after him fanatically, only to trip on her long yellow dress. Several more of the infected followed her lead and took to the chase stepping all over the young girl in their pursuit. Her face and body sank into the mud beneath her which covered her body leaving the front side of her body brown and her backside yellow. He quickly ran around the side of the house only to find two more infected that had heard the screams standing near his truck. They came after him and cornered him between the infected pursuing him from behind. Thinking quickly, he threw his rifle over his shoulder and scrambled up the side of house using its gutters like a hunted squirrel. Once on top, he pulled the gutter free and kicked it loose so his pursers could not follow. They began to scream all around him and several more infected from around the area began to gather. He stood up on the point of the house and looked out over the neighborhood. They were everywhere, swarming along the streets hunting for those lucky enough not to be infected to convert them to their side.

"Get down or more will come!" yelled a voice.

He dropped down onto the rooftop and looked around to find where the voice came from. He recognized it, but couldn't see from where it originated.

"Where are you?"

"Over here up in the tree," replied the voice.

He looked over at a large tree in the middle of the back yard, and sitting up high in one of its branches was his best friend.

"God damn, Tommy, how long have you been up there?" he said with a small bright smile. Speaking to another human being lightened his heart.

"Three days now," replied the man from the tree. "Man, am I glad to see you! You are the first uninfected person I have seen in two days."

"Thought you said you were up there for three days?"

"I have but about two days ago I saw some lady run down the road with some of these fuckers chasing her. I assume they got her; they were hot on her tail."

"How the hell did you allow yourself to get treed by these things like a raccoon?" asked Chuck from the top of the house.

"Didn't have much choice, one of those things chased me in one side of my house and out the other and then several more cornered me out here. It was either climb up here or jump into their stomachs," he replied. "And every so often another one will wander by, see me and join in on the party. How did you manage to get run up onto that house?"

Chuck nodded as if saying touché before reaching down into his pocket and counting his rifle cartridges. He had twenty one counting the one in the chamber of his rifle. That would be enough he thought, enough to kill them all so they could get down. They would be easy targets at such close range. He lifted his barrel and took aim at an extremely ugly one below in the driveway.

"Don't shoot!" cried Tommy out loud.

He lowered his rifle.

"If you fire that shot we'll have so many down here that you won't be able to count them all. That's what Mr. Riley did."

"The old navy seal guy?"

"Yeah, I sat here and watched the shootout my first night up here."

"I bet that mean old mother fucker got a bunch!" he said in excitement.

"Yeah he got about twelve and the other fifty ate him right out in his front yard," replied Tommy sadly.

His smile left his face and he half-heartedly lowered his rifle to rethink their situation.

"All right," he said forming a new plan, "start making some noise and see if you can't get some of these fuckers' attention. I'll be right there to get you."

Tommy looked at him as if his lifelong friend had lost his mind, but he was willing to try anything to get out the tree he had been perched in for so long. He began to yell at the infected below, but what really got their attention was the dangling of his legs. He dangled one of his legs toward the ones below and the excitement of seeing it so close got the infected into a fervor. They began to scream and hiss at him all the while jumping and frantically trying to scale his tree. Their commotion called the attention of the other infected below the house giving his friend the break he needed to crawl over to the other side of the house unnoticed. He hung over the edge with his hands and dropped down to the grass below. It was a long fall and he felt his knees buckle below him as he collapsed into a roll to reduce his momentum. He jumped up quickly ignoring the pain in his legs, and jumped into the cab of his truck slamming the door shut. He turned the key, fearful of how many cranks it would take to start it. It started in one try and he hooted in excitement while pounding his fist into the top of the cab.

Pulling around the house at full speed, he smashed through the small group of infected below the tree and stopped below his trapped friend. Tommy swung down from his branch and landed into the bed of the truck. An infected man still on his feet attempted to crawl into the bed with him, but Tommy's boot connected directly into his face knocking him down and rolling him onto the ground. The truck sped through the rabble of infected disappearing down the long twisted road of their neighborhood. Once they were out of sight of the infected train they had created, the truck came to a skidding stop and Tommy climbed into the cab on the passenger's side.

"Damn Chuck! I sure am glad you stopped by!" he said happily massaging his thighs.

"Perfect timing uh?"

"No, three days ago would have been perfect timing, but considering… I ain't bitching." He sat quietly for a moment before breaking the silence of their tiny enclosed environment. "I'm fucking famished, you got anything to eat?"

"There's some jerky in the glove box."

Tommy flipped open the glove box, pulled out a zipper bag of dried beef jerky and began to stuff his mouth like it had no limit.

"God damn this shit is good!" he said mumbling through a full mouth. "This is the first thing I have eaten in three days."

"Well chow down while you can. Besides that deer back there," he said while pointing his thumb toward the truck bed, "that's all we got."

"So I guess you've been out on one of your extended hunting trips?"

"Yeah," he replied. "Would you mind telling me exactly how all this shit happened?"

"About a week ago everybody started coming down with the fever and anybody who got near someone infected came down with it too. Every hospital and clinic in the area became overwhelmed and closed down within hours. And the churches, man did they pack out the churches…begging for mercy I guess. But they didn't get it, because within twenty four hours after the fever started these damn things started running around attacking anyone who wasn't infected. It happened so fast…one minute I hear about the fevers setting into the area on the news, the next minute people are eating people in my fuckin' yard. I shut myself in and hid down in my basement until one of those things heard my radio and broke in through a window."

The two sat side by side as different as night and day. Chuck with light brown hair, quick and impulsive and Tommy with dark black hair, slow and observant. Although complete opposites, their friendship had thrived over the years from the mixtures of their contradictory personalities making the two stronger than they could have ever been alone. Without Tommy, Chuck would have died in some rash stunt years ago and Tommy without Chuck wouldn't have done anything out of the norm, but together they were both fearless and cunning, a universal combination for any situation. They drove on in silence crossing open yards and shallow ditches when the road became impassable by rubble or piled up vehicles. An infected lady spotted their truck from the middle of the road and ran toward it with her arms extended out.

"Hey watch out for that bitch," said Tommy pointing.

The old truck's driver turned it toward the screaming woman and gunned the accelerator. The truck hit her in dead center of its hood flinging her body underneath its undercarriage with a loud crunch gobbling up her image. Chuck slammed on the brakes and stopped the huge truck with a long skid in the mud. They could still hear her screaming for their blood while trapped underneath one of their truck's monster tires. He held the brakes down and spun his wheels in the soggy soil burying her beneath it.

"Well that put her under!" said Chuck laughing.

Tommy smiled. Whenever Chuck pulled one of his stunts, like he had done all life, they did one of two things to Tommy. First they pissed him off and secondly they always made him laugh. He had seen him pull so much shit, that each time, he felt sure the next one wouldn't shock him, but they did, they always did.

"So where to now?" asked Tommy.

"To Karl's I guess to get some supplies."

Chapter 6
Stocking Up

The old truck pulled up behind Karl's Market and came to a shaking stop like a bad massage bed in a cheap motel. Tommy took a hold of the shotgun from the gun rack and pulled it free.

"There should be a box of pumpkin balls under the seat," said his friend.

The two men stepped out armed and vigilant of their surroundings. They leaned up against the back wall and hugged it until they reached the back door. It was sealed tight and without an outside handle, it was too strenuous a task for them to remove without literally waking the dead. Tommy motioned to Chuck with his head toward the front of the building. A quick scan of the front parking lot made it appear to be relatively safe and they made the long run around the front of the building to the front door.

"Shit, it's locked!" said Tommy whispering under his breath.

"Move a second," said Chuck.

Tommy stepped back while watching the parking lot anxiously.

The stock of Chuck's rifle came down against the glass door smashing it open with a high pitch crack. He quickly reached in through the hole and unlocked the door from the inside, but was held back from entering by his friend.

"Just one second," he said holding his shoulder. "Let's wait a second and see if anything heard us."

They stood still and listened. Trash shuffled through the parking lot aimlessly blowing up against the market's wall and then rolling on down the sidewalk.

"God it's quiet out here. No cars, no planes… no people," said Tommy sadly.

"Get in before something sees us."

The two rushed in and Tommy quickly locked the door looking out through the dirty glass toward the parking lot one more time. The only light in the store filtered in through the front glass door. Chuck walked around the front registers and took a peek down the aisles. He couldn't see but halfway down their length, but he could see that the shelves were still packed with merchandise.

"Damn this place is still full!" he said in excitement.

Tommy kept his shotgun against his shoulder and moved toward the store's front office with watchful eyes. He found the office door open and timidly peeked around the doorframe's edge to look inside. It was empty. Chuck slung his rifle over his shoulder and pulled a buggy free. The clank startled Tommy and he spun around.

"Shopping spree!" Chuck said with a big smile on his face.

"What about the back?" asked his partner still gripping his weapon tightly with both of his hands.

His friend crammed the buggy back into its hole with the rest of the unused buggies and took hold of his hunting rifle.

"Let's go check it out."

The two walked the dark floor of Karl's market aisle by aisle finding nothing to fear in its many shadows.

"Come here and hold this," said Chuck holding out his backpack.

Tommy came over and held it open with one of his free hands, while his friend loaded it up with fresh batteries from a display.

"Great new flashlights too," he said while tearing them out of their packages and loading them up. A beam jumped out of the first one he loaded and he handed it over to his friend. Then he proceeded in loading another one.

"Once we get stocked up here, we will be on easy street," said Chuck.

"We're not out of the city yet," warned his cautious friend.

"That's where we are headed next," he said trying out his new flashlight in delight. "Ah great, let's go check out the stockroom."

Their lights cut through the darkness of the back half of the store and within moments they found themselves standing in front of the stockroom door. It was a double swinging door with a single round window centered in the top half of each door. Behind the doors loomed an eerie silent blackness.

"God it smells like something is dead in there," said Tommy covering his noise with his shoulder.

"It is," replied his friend calmly. "Back there is where they butchered the meat and without refrigeration everything has spoiled."

The two looked at each other for a moment and Chuck stepped toward the door. Tommy's hand gripped his shoulder once again.

"Man, I don't really want to go in there. The last thing I want to do is fight zombies in the dark."

"Fuck it then," declared Chuck raising his left shoulder. "Let's stay out here and see if anyone comes out.

They began to make noise by banging their feet and whistling out loud. Suddenly two feet appeared at the bottom of the swinging doors as if answering their call.

"Shit!" whispered Chuck fearfully.

"Hey you if you are alive you better say something before we wax you," announced Tommy.

Neither of the feet moved and the two-armed men began to get nervous.

"Fuck him man… he had his chance!" said Chuck before firing his rifle into the door.

The round struck the door and tore through it ripping into a cloud of splinters. The door swung open and a man in a bloody apron with cold dark eyes bore at the men. His mouth opened angrily and he rushed at the two men without restraint. Chuck stepped back behind a display of donuts and reached into his pocket for another round. A loud boom extended from Tommy's shotgun ejecting hot lead that tore the attacking man's head from his shoulders. The headless torso collapsed backwards and spilled blood across the floor spreading back under the stockroom door. A volley of beating and pounding sounds came from the front of the store and the two men quickly ran up to see what was causing the commotion. Dozens of infected were gathered at the front door beating against the glass rattling their weak frames.

"How much time you think we got?" asked Chuck.

"Not long. Let's get what we can."

The two hurried over to the buggies, pulled one free and began to stuff it full of food. They ran around as if in a shopping spree game show cramming anything that caught their eyes into the buggy. They had their buggy heaping with food when they heard the breaking of glass.

"Oh shit, they're in!" screamed Tommy. "Out the back!"

Their buggy skidded around the corner spilling groceries as they rushed toward the stockroom door. Both burst into the dark stockroom frantically shinning their flashlights around.

"Over here! I see the back door!" screamed Chuck.

The maddening sound of ravenous screams and shuffling feet echoed from behind.

"God damn it!" he screamed. "The fucking door is barred shut!"

He began to kick at the door relentlessly. The stout door stood solid deflecting his hysterical kicks. Tommy motioned for his friend to step aside and pointed his shotgun at the lock that held the bar locked forward. He fired and the bottom half of the lock tore off. He reached down and tried to pull it free but the bolt held steady.

"Shiiit!" Tommy screamed in frustration. "The mother fucking lock won't budge."

He kicked it with his heel in an attempt to break it off, but it refused to give way. He quickly fumbled through his pockets with his sweaty hands to retrieve another round. The swinging doors to the stockroom burst open and an infected man ran into the darkness. Chuck focused his right eye into his rifles sight in an attempt to get a good shot.

"Where the fuck did he go?" he screamed after losing his target in the darkness.

Tommy took hold of a shell and loaded it into his gun's chamber with shaking fingers. The infected man leaped out of the darkness and seized Tommy from behind bearing his teeth towards the back of his neck. The infected man's left temple burst wide open, spilling his brains along the stockroom wall. Tommy gripped his ear and bent over.

"Did he bite you?" screamed his friend in fear that he might not have shot the infected man in time.

"No," he answered, "but I think noise from your gun burst my eardrum."

The stockroom doors swung open again, but this time neither one saw what or how many got into the darkness. Chuck ejected the empty shell from his rifle and fumbled to reload it again. Tommy turned toward the door again and fired on the lock again from inches away. This time the lock flew off the locking bar bouncing against the floor with a high-pitched clank. Tommy jerked the bar back and kicked the door open. The bright sunlight from outside engulfed the dark stockroom, sending their pupils into a white blindness. Both shoved the buggy blindly into the light and slammed the door shut staring down as their eyes focused. They leaned against the door and for a moment they stood in the calm quiet wind outside the store. Then the door behind them erupted into an uproar tearing the silence around them apart. They slid their feet further out onto the concrete to gain leverage keeping the rattling door sealed shut. Screams of cannibalistic desires rattled their ears and jolted their bodies. A hand reached outside the side of the door and clawed at Tommy's shoulder tearing a hole in his shirt. He spun around and kicked the door shut catching the roaming hand in it. The bones in the hand made a loud crunching noise as they snapped from the force of the slamming door.

"We're not going to be able to hold them for much longer, go get the truck!" ordered Tommy. "I'll try and hold them."

Chuck took hold of the buggy and ran with it toward his truck. The wheels on the buggy began to shake with his mounting speed threatening to turn over and spill its precious load. He rammed it against the side their truck and with an adrenaline surge powered by primordial fear, he lifted the entire buggy up full of groceries and heaved it into the bed of his truck. It fell into the deep walls of the truck bed with a clank spilling only small part of its contents onto the ground. He spun around quickly and jumped into the cab. His friend had already let go of the back door and was running toward the truck with a mob of enraged infected in pursuit. Chuck quickly put his key into the ignition and once again his truck started on the first crank. He thanked the Lord, shifted into drive and drove toward his friend slowing down enough for him to jump into the back. The infected in pursuit began to leap and hold on to the truck as he sped by, but they lost their grip one by one as he raced across the market's parking lot. The last one to lose his grip finally fell free when the driver's side mirror ripped off into his hands leaving him tumbling on the road. Chuck actually watched the man toss around like a tumbleweed for nearly twenty feet then immediately jump to his feet and continue his chase dragging along his broken body.

Chapter 7
Plan B

Tommy reached through the little window in the middle of the truck's back window and retrieved a bag of chips that had started to float around in the bed of the truck. He ripped the bag open and began to stuff them in his mouth by the handful. His teeth munched on them relentlessly until they were completely gone and then he crumpled the bag up into a small ball and tossed it out the window.

"I guess we can forget that whole keep America beautiful thing," he said laughing.

"I guess what we need to worry about now is keeping America alive," replied Chuck.

"No shit man, that was too close back there!"

The truck's brakes locked up and they skidded to a bumpy halt next to a large yellow house.

"What's up?" asked Tommy concerned.

"I'll be right back."

Chuck jumped out of the running truck and ran through the yard of the yellow house, stopping in front of it. He looked around and after seeing that it was clear pulled his knife from its sheath. When he returned to the truck he was holding part of a garden hose that he had cut into one long four foot piece. He threw it into the floor and slammed his door. The truck grumbled on through the long grass that had grown throughout the city since the infection had struck.

"What's that for?"

"To siphon gas," he replied pointing at their gas gauge.

It was still sitting on empty.

"Oh yeah," replied Tommy.

"We'll stop at the next thing that holds gas and fill up."

They drove on through their neighborhood and stopped at a car that had apparently crashed into the ditch. He backed the truck up so to align their gas tanks, left the truck running and got out with his rifle and piece of garden hose. Looking around calmly he pulled a wadded glove from his gas tank neck, then opened the gas cap door on the abandoned car and pushed one end of the garden hose down into the tank until it stopped before sucking on the other end. His face wrinkled up and he jerked the hose from his mouth spitting out the fuel that had flowed into his mouth. Fuel began to pour onto the ground near his feet and he alertly put the end of the hose into his truck's tank. He held the hose still until he felt the last bit of fuel trickle down into his tank. He filled his tank's hole with his glove and jumped back into the cab.

"Shit!" he said spitting. "My mouth is on fire!"

"I dare you to light up a cigarette," laughed his friend.

He glanced at his fuel gauge. It sat dangerously at an eighth of a tank. The small movement of the little red gauge made him happy.

He drove on with a renewed confidence.

"I know a clear path back to the woods, we just need to cross town and make the highway."

An old lady ran out from a trailer near their truck and began to run toward the road across her yard. Tommy leaned away from his door and held his shotgun ready. Chuck stepped on the accelerator and sped by her inches from her reach. Her screams echoed in their cab as they past, leaving her in their rear view sights clawing at the air in madness. Both men relaxed as she faded from the rearview mirror and slumped back into their seats once the danger had fully past.

"I should have done that bitch a favor and ran over her!"

A clanking sound sprang from under the truck's hood, causing their truck to sputter.

"Shit, what the hell is that?" inquired Chuck.

"I don't know," answered his friend concerned.

The truck stalled and rolled to a stop. Its driver tried to crank the ignition again. It started for a moment but backfired and stalled again.

"God damn it," yelled the truck's owner rubbing the dash with his palm as if petting it, "don't quit on me now baby."

He tried to crank it again but it failed to fulfill the desperate command of his ignition.

"Damn!" he said loudly jumping out of the cab and popping the hood.

His friend stepped out with him and stood guard. Chuck poked his head under the hood and checked all the connections.

"All the fluids are good," he announced from under the hood. "All the wires are connected, what the fuck could be wrong?"

"I hope it's nothing serious," said his friend staring back from where they had came.

Chuck spun the wing nuts on his valve covers and pulled them loose. He had purposely sealed only one side his valve cover gasket to the valve cover so he could easily check underneath it.

"Shit!" he yelled out loud kicking the side of his truck. "One of the valve springs is broken!"

"Won't it run without one?"

"Apparently not!"

They stood next to their two thousand pound problem on wheels with blank stares hoping an easy solution would somehow present itself. Tommy gazed of the roof of their hood and jerked his friend's arm to get his attention.

"Here comes that bitch!" he announced raising his shotgun up.

The old lady they had passed earlier was running down the hill still screaming in pursuit. Her long gray hair flapped behind her spinning wildly around her head. A loud gunshot cracked through the air and the ladies head burst like a melon on her shoulders. Her body collapsed and tumbled forward into a lifeless ball from her momentum.

Tommy looked over at his friend's smoking gun gritting his teeth.

"Haven't you noticed that every time you pull that trigger we end up running?"

"What did you want me to do? Let her come down here and eat us?"

"That lady had to be eighty years old! If we couldn't have handled her, then we are pitiful."

A long moan interrupted their argument and both ducked down against the front of the truck.

"Did you see where that came from?" asked Chuck.

Tommy leaned around the side of the truck and peeked up towards the hill. Four infected had come over the hill and were wandering through the woods moaning. They were scanning the area diligently apparently alerted by their gunshot. Leaves boiled up around them as they slid down the steep hill awkwardly. Tommy ducked back around the truck, leaning up tightly against its grill holding his gun.

"There is a shit load of them headed this way."

"How many?"

"I counted four."

"Ah hell I can cap four no problem," he said rising up with his rifle loaded.

His friend's hands pulled him back down behind the truck's hood.

"If you shoot those four then we might have twenty more down here and on foot we would be fucked."

Tommy leaned back out just enough for his eyes to clear the edge of the truck. Two were wandering off into different directions, but the other two were walking down the hill toward their truck. Chuck leaned down and looked under the truck. Four legs were standing by the bed of his truck moving around to opposite sides. The pressure was too much and gunshot or not, he wasn't going to let one walk up to him and bite him as long as he had a bullet in his chamber. He signaled his friend with a simple nod and stepped to the side of the truck bringing his target in the sight of his gun. The infected man saw him and shrieked in the excitement of seeing a live person on which to feed. The round caught him in the top of his head completely shearing off the hair on top of it, sending him into the shadow of death where he truly belonged. Tommy had seen his friend's motions and had done the same on the other side of the truck using his shotgun to nearly cut the infected man on his side in half. The shot had apparently severed his lower spine disabling his legs, because after he fell, he could not get back up to his feet. Tommy stepped back and watched the infected man drag his half torn body toward him with only the use of his hands. Its teeth gnashed at him vigorously as it crawled slowly across the asphalt. He cracked open his single shot barrel and ejected the shell. Slowly backing up he reloaded it and slapped the barrel shut. He pulled up his barrel and aimed to shoot, only to see his friend bash the creature in the head from behind with the stock of his gun. Its eyes finally shut, resting forever. The other two infected had heard the shots and now were reinforced by half a dozen more zombies who had been alerted to their presence by their gunshots. More began to pile out of the surrounding homes screaming in glee of new prey to feast.

"Hurry, grab whatever you can and let's get out of here," yelled Tommy's friend anxiously.

He jumped into the back of the truck snatching what little he could while Chuck loaded up his backpack hectically. They ran down the road and took cover into a wooded thicket. They ran like madmen at a pace unlike any they had ever run. Branches slapped against their faces and tore against their exposed skin. Chuck glanced behind and saw that the infected had taken pursuit and were running through the brush. He stopped for a moment, took sight on a target and fired. His slug glanced off a small hanging branch missing its target. He turned around and continued running trying to catch up to his friend, who had never broken stride. The muscles in his chest ached with every breath of cold air he inhaled and his heart beat in his throat forcefully pumping blood through his arteries so his legs could carry him farther. They ran aimlessly away from their pursuers stopping at the bank of a swelling creek. Rapids rolled over large smooth rocks and sprayed over the sharp ones that had not yet been filed away by the water's endless current, dispersing a fine damp mist into the cool air. Chuck caught up to Tommy and leaned over, grasping his knees in an attempt to catch his breath.

"The woods are thick with them now," he claimed gasping for air.

Moans and screams came from the woods closing in growing louder with each passing second. Dirty rotten-fleshed faces began to appear from the wood line, trapping the desperate men between it and the rushing creek.

"Go!" screamed Tommy as he leaped immersing himself in the cold water of the rapids.

He tried to hold his shotgun up above his head, but the current of the creek pulled him under bouncing him around like a wet doll. He managed to get control of himself by using his feet and hands against every rock he passed until he finally got across the center of the creek into its slower waters. Chuck came out of the waters onto the bank a few feet ahead drenched from head to toe. More infected came out of the woods and upon seeing the men on the other side of the creek their forms piled into the water. They crashed into the water recklessly and once they lost their footing were swept away with the current bouncing off protruding rocks as they floated away. Their heads and other various body parts bobbed up and down almost ridiculously out of control until they were finally out of sight. Chuck laughed out loud.

"Did you see that?" he said in exhilaration.

"Ain't that a bitch?" laughed his friend back. "I thought we were done for."

"It's like they don't have enough coordination to swim or something," replied Chuck.

"That just gave me a great idea," declared Tommy.

"What?"

"It's going to be hell trying to make it across town on foot with almost no supplies."

"Yeah?"

"Well the marina is just a few miles from here. I think we can make it there through these woods," he said looking up through the trees.

"What, get a boat?"

"If these things can't swim and we commandeer us a boat to get out to an island on the river..."

"Then we are sitting pretty," interrupted Chuck. "When can go ashore, make supply runs to the coast and live large on our own island. Fuck yeah, I like it."

"Cool, then let's get started before one of those things floats over to this side and makes their way back up here to us."

Chapter 8
Piracy

They traveled the rest of the day through tightly woven forest fortunate enough not to encounter more infected. They stayed in the woods for most of their trip crossing only a few small roads, which aided in keeping their direction. Once they found the shore of the river, they stayed along its edge and within a few hours found themselves staring at the marina from across the bay. The docks sat quiet still harboring several boats of various types and sizes.

"What kind do you think we should try and get?" whispered Tommy.

"Well I don't know shit about sail boats, but I guess the major factor will be if there is any gas in it or not."

The men slinked down to the edge of the water like muskrats moving quickly along its shore, using the river's high bank to cover their movement. Two sets of eyes peer over the edge of the docks, watching for movement. Waves crashed against the bank as the two men climbed up onto the creaking wood scurrying along it toward the boats. Pontoon boats, ski boats and gloomy houseboats rocked slowly along with the current.

"Damn!" replied Tommy in a loud whisper to his friend down the dock. "All of these boats are missing their keys and their gas tanks are either empty or gone."

"Same here," his friend whispered back. "Looks like everyone else beat us to this idea."

After inspecting the dock without finding a suitable boat, the men as a last resort decided to search the large and darkly looming houseboats. The insides would be dark and tight, so if they did discover an infected inside, it would be hard to get away from it, increasing their odds of becoming infected. To make matters worse, they didn't have a good close quarter weapon. Save their knives, they would have to fight hand to hand so as not to alert more infected that might be within earshot. A quickly hatched plan would send one of the men inside while the other would wait ready to bash any infected that might pursue the other out. Six houseboats rocked gently in the docks, with four of the six appearing to have not left the safety of the dock in decades. The other two were new and shiny looking worthy of the swift river water. Chuck chose the larger of the two standing before it gathering his courage. The houseboat that rose before him in a slow rocking motion was enormous by anyone's standards.

Chuck opened its back screen door which emitted a long light creak. He fumbled slowly with the glass door handle and brought it down with a small clicking noise. It swung open quietly, exposing the dark interior of the houseboat's vast interior. He waited a moment listening cautiously. A creaking noise came from upstairs and a chill ran down his spine causing his heart to miss a beat. Calming down, he regained his composure forcing himself to step inside with a flashlight leading the way. The light streaked through the darkness bouncing off the walls, striking a mirror and exposing his image. Startled, he staggered backward from his reflection. His heart raced within his chest beating against his breastplate viciously. The interior walls were covered in crooked pictures hinting to what had once been a much happier place.

He tiptoed into the kitchen and found the door to the back deck. An aura of fear washed away from him as he stepped out onto the breezy sunlit deck. He inspected the motor at the stern and was glad to see that next to it was a hefty looking generator. After examining the boat's generator, he walked over to a ladder leading onto the top deck. He took hold of it and climbed up just far enough for his eyes to peek over onto the top deck. The back half of the top deck was wide-open supporting lawn furniture for comfortable sunbathing. The front half, which was the farthest from him, was enclosed.

He stepped up onto the top of the boat and eased his way through the lounge chairs that littered the top deck before opening the door to the enclosed half of the deck. Inside, lying flat on his back, was the body of a slender elderly man. The sight startled Chuck and he jumped back instinctively. The man lay motionless slightly rocking along with the motion of the boat bouncing gently against the floor. Regaining his composure Chuck kneeled down next to the body and touched its leg. He jerked his arm back nearly falling over backwards before catching himself. It remained as motionless as the dead. Carefully he leaned toward it once more and slowly slipped his hand into one of its front pocket. His hand met with a jingle of metal and with one of his fingers he could feel the rough jagged side of a key. The man rose up with an aggravated growl as if to protect his belongings and wrapped his hands around Chuck's neck pulling him toward his open and snapping mouth. The young hunter quickly put his knee on the infected man's chest to keep their bodies separated and began to tear at the hands that gripped so tightly around his neck. He could feel the man's nails digging into his exposed neck and a fear of becoming contaminated struck deep down within his heart, bringing out desperate screams from his lungs as he struggled for his life. Viruses that had already infected billons primed themselves to infect another through the dripping saliva of the elderly man's mouth. Chuck managed to break one hand free from the back of his neck and with every muscle in his right hand, he bent the infected man's fingers back until they snapped and collapsed onto the back of his rotten hand. The man's other hand still held its grip tight around his neck and with a strength that comes from pure hunger it drew him closer until the man's teeth were barely an inch away from his face. A deep thud resounded from within the infected man's head causing him to release his tight grip and the chattering of his teeth to cease. His body stood motionless for a moment before collapsing back into the position it had been found only a few minutes earlier. The tall slender form of his friend holding a claw hammer appeared from behind the fallen man.

"You all right man?" asked his friend holding out his new hammer."

"Yeah," Chuck replied rubbing his neck.

"Found this downstairs," he said looking at it proudly. "I like it…think I'll keep it."

Chuck reached into the dead man's pocket and pulled his keys out.

"Here," he said tossing them to his friend. "See if these work."

"Oh shit," said Tommy in excitement. "They have to be for the boat, they're on a foam key ring!"

Chuck stood up holding his neck and followed his friend down to the lower deck. Tommy went back into the houseboat and began to fumble around the boat's controls, leaving Chuck a moment to lean down to the edge of the water and wash his hands off. He reached around the back of his neck and rubbed the area where he had been attacked and looked at his hand. Blood dripped off the tips of his fingers. It wasn't a lot, but the skin on the back of his neck had been cut. The boat came to a rumble and Chuck jumped up hiding his hand from his friend as he came out onto the deck.

"Shit, this thing has a half a tank of gas!" he said in excitement.

Chuck gave a lack luster response followed by half a forced smile.

"You sure you're all right Chuck?"

"Yeah!" he said lying and wiping his hand clean on the back of his pants. "I'm still just a little shaken from that last attack."

"Well let's get this boat moving," Tommy said happily. "I know where there are a couple of islands up river."

The two men ran around the large houseboat, untying it from its dock before starting up its generator and gently pulling it out into the harbor. It sputtered along slowly, while both young men walked around examining their new home.

"This place is the shit," said Tommy from behind the boat's wheel. "We got a stove and everything."

"Oh my fucking god! This place has a television!" said Chuck from the other side of the boat.

"Turn it on!"

Chuck fumbled with twelve screens of snow.

"Nothing," he said back while shifty the television antennas. "I can't tell if all the stations are out or if the reception on this thing sucks!"

"Hell…we don't need a fucking television anyway. I mean were already stuck in a bad Night of the Living Dead sequel."

The large houseboat sloshed its way up river moving slowly over its gentle rolling currents passing along loudly with the sound of its generator in motion. Its driver peered through heavy eyelids struggling to stay awake as the sun began to set below the tree line along the river.

"Chuck man I'm fading out. I can hardly keep my eyes open."

"How long has it been since you slept?"

"Besides occasional catnaps I haven't really slept in three days."

"Screw it! We don't have to make the islands tonight. We got everything we need here," he announced surrounded by the luxury of a fine houseboat. "Let's drop anchor and crash here."

"Okay, but let's get out of the middle of the river, to make sure our anchor holds…last thing I want to do is wake up in the morning sitting next up against the shore and looking at a bunch of those infected fuckers."

They pulled their boat into the next slough and turned off their generator to conserve fuel. Then they dropped their front and rear anchors in the middle of the small bay before lying down to go to sleep. The sun faded away engulfing the boat in darkness and for the moment, peace.

Chapter 9
Island Paradise

A thin bright line of light rolled over his eyes as it cut through the cracks in the boat's window shades arousing him from his deep slumber. He stared blankly at the off white ceiling and for a moment wondered if he had dreamt it all, but upon feeling the back of his swollen neck he realized all too well that although it wasn't a dream, it was a nightmare that would never truly go away. Lying still, he could hear his friend snoring in the corner catching up on some well needed rest. He sat up quietly so not to disturb Tommy's slumber and began to shuffle through his bag and their meager supplies. He popped open a can of Vienna sausages and shook off the unsightly jelly that clung to the skin of the meat before putting one in his mouth and chewing it up. He ate one after another until they were gone, before getting up and looking into the refrigerator. As soon as he opened it a warm stench engulfed him turning his nose and causing him to slam the door shut quickly.

"Guess that shits broken," he mumbled quietly before returning to his chair.

He reached up behind his neck and gently touched the swelled lump on the back of his neck. A fierce pain shot down his neck, causing him to jerk his hand away quickly. A drop of dark red blood dripped from the tip of his finger onto the shaggy carpeted floor below turning into a menacing black spot. He stared down at the tiny black dot vexingly. A relentless ominous scratching noise rang up from under the boat stealing his attention. Long light scraping noises began to echo through the boat bringing him to his feet in an attempt to discover their origin. The boat must have come loose and they were dragging across bottom he thought. He shuffled to the back door and swung it only to find the boat sitting in the exact same spot they had anchored the night before. A tranquil fog surrounded the boat covering the cool flat surface of the lake making it appear as if they were floating on a cloud. The faint scraping noises he had heard earlier grew louder as he stepped outside on the back deck. Curiously he looked over the side of the boat and down into the green murky water of the lake below the hovering mist. Something moved in and out of the deep water near the edge of the boat and at first he thought they must have run up onto a sand bar and that the scraping noises were coming from the hull bouncing up against it. He reached his hand down into the water to see what was causing the noise when a pale hand seized his hand. Terror streaked directly from the infected man that gripped his hand up his arm and into his heart nearly freezing it in mid-beat.

"Shit!" he screamed ripping his hand free from its ice cold grip.

He stumbled back onto the deck and fell over a lawn chair that sat on its deck flopping onto his back. He jumped up quickly and looked over the side railing again. Below the boat at the bottom of the lagoon were dozens of infected reaching up with their fingertips scratching the bottom of the hull in an attempt to scale up onto boat's deck. Every so often he could see one of their horrible distorted faces engulfed in flowing hair and tangled weeds. He ran over to the sliding glass door and slid it open.

"We've got to get the fuck out of here now!" he screamed to his friend still a sleep onto the couch.

Tommy jumped up from his slumber and stumbled around while finding his bearings.

"They're all around us trying to climb onboard."

His friend ran out onto the deck and looked overboard down into the water.

"God damn!" he replied upon seeing the horror that lurked below water's surface. "Pull up the anchors so we can get into deeper water!"

Chuck ran over to the anchor's rope and tugged on it cumbersomely bringing it up through the water. The anchor was as heavy as any he had ever felt and he had to brace his feet against the deck to get enough leverage to haul it in. Two lime green hands that had ridden up with the anchor came out of the water with the rope and took hold of the boat's deck. Dropping his grip on the anchor's rope, Chuck began to beat at the green hands wildly in an attempt to break their grip, but they held fast. He alertly pulled his hunting knife from its sheath and began to saw at their joints. The sharp blade cut the fingers free from the infected man's hand bouncing the digits onto the deck and sending the pallid form plunging back to the bottom of the lake. Chuck quickly cut the anchor loose so another couldn't climb aboard, leaving it at the bottom of the lake as well. Tommy started up the boat and attempted to pull it out of the small slough. The motor churned through the arms and hands of infected that stood below it and stuttered to a stop. Chuck looked through the inside of the houseboat and saw the form of another infected climbing onboard the front of the boat.

"Tommy there is one on the front of the boat!"

Tommy turned around alertly and ran to the glass door kicking it shut before the man could get inside. The soaking wet infected man began to beat on the glass with his bare fists, causing it to shatter with a loud crash into the boat. Tommy brought his hammer up striking the man directly in the center of his forehead sending him stumbling backwards onto the front deck. Following him through the broken glass door, Tommy kicked the man to the floor and straddled him to hold him down as he beat the man's head to a mushy pulp. Another hand came out of the water gripping onto the front anchor's rope. Tommy quickly untied the rope zipping it off into the water with a deep splash as the infected man plunged back into the depths of the lake.

The boat grumbled to a start once again and churned its way through the infected sputtering as it cut into bone, but it never completely stalled. Once they were out into deeper water, they assessed their situation.

"How's the prop?"

"Two of the blades are chipped and one is split, but I think they are going to be okay," said Tommy examining the motor.

"Damn, man, if we didn't have bad luck we wouldn't have any luck at all!" screamed his friend in frustration.

"I don't know about that. I think we got a lot more luck than most people who I've seen walking around lately."

Chuck nodded in agreement.

"Come on let's get this fucker overboard before he stinks the place up," Tommy said looking through the broken glass door.

The infected man's body hit the water like a sack of potatoes and floated away until it was little more than a speck in the distance as the houseboat churned slowly upstream toward its island paradise. The trip normally would have taken only a few hours, but with their damaged prop, the boat lumbered the day away before the first of the islands came into sight. Both men ran to the front of the boat in excitement when the first line of trees in the middle of the river appeared on the horizon. Their eyes watched the island loom larger until its banks came into view.

"Look," screamed Chuck pointing toward the right side of the island, "there are some boats tied off over there!"

"I knew we couldn't be the only people left!" yelled his friend in excitement.

Their boat chugged on limping through the water as its operator steered it toward the boats docked on the right side of the island. Tommy pulled the front of their boat up near three docked boats and slammed the motor in reverse to stop their forward momentum. After cutting the power to the motor, they sat motionless bouncing slowly in a murky silence.

"Why isn't anyone coming to the shore?" asked Chuck in a whisper.

The sound of rustling undergrowth came up from ahead and through the thick brush a white shirt appeared. Chuck and Tommy watched silently in exuberant anticipation of who or what they would encounter next. The form pushed through the brush and upon seeing them on the deck of their boat, the worn and decayed man began to shriek in wild stimulation. He plummeted into the water toward the boat sinking under the smooth surface into the water's depths. The sound of the infected man's screaming and splashing signaled the entire island and in a matter of moments dozens of infected were teeming into the water toward the waiting boat. Tommy leaped through the broken door and started up the boat's motor switching it into reverse, leaving the cursed island behind in the distance.

"It's like those fuckers don't need to breathe and they just roam the bottom of the lake," said Tommy shaking his head.

"Meaning we can't stay on an island because they will wander up onto it and eat us like they did those other people. Hell, we don't even have anchors… and even if we did we couldn't use them since one of those things might bump into it and climb up with us while we're asleep. And if we don't drop anchor we might run aground while sleeping."

"Where do we go now?" asked Tommy.

"I say we go ashore and back out to the woods," he said pausing, "I didn't see a single infected motherfucker while I was out there."

"I've got nothing… let's go."

Chapter 10
Starting Over

The two refugees unloaded everything of use that they could carry from their houseboat and left the boat tied to a tree along the shore before hiking off into the thick woods along the river's edge. The dense brush gripped and tugged against their clothes and seemed to be almost deliberately attempting to slow their progress. They traversed deep into the thickets fighting its thistles and thorns until they finally came upon a gravel road that sliced through the tall thick trees. The popping and ricocheting sounds of gravel bounced from under their boots as they quickened their pace along the open road. Tommy noticed his friend holding the back of his neck gingerly.

"Chuck you all right?"

"Oh yeah my neck's a little sore… got a crick in my neck from sleeping on that hard ass couch."

"I could tell something was wrong the way you've been walking around like a robot from the neck up."

Chuck reached back and lightly touched the back of his neck after his friend turned his head, but jerked his hand away from the pain that ensued. It has swollen to the point that he could barely twist his head. Suddenly Tommy stopped and dropped face down onto the gravel road. Chuck followed the actions of his friend and dropped face first onto the dusty gravel road, sliding up next to him on his stomach. A white cloud of dust rose as they low-crawled to the road's edge and glanced over it. Down the road barely a hundred feet away was an infected woman walking mindlessly up the road.

"I don't think she saw us."

"I can cap her no problem," whispered Chuck confidently to his friend.

"Go ahead. There shouldn't be that many way out here."

The young hunter shouldered his rifle in a prone firing position and centered his target in his sights. The loud crack of gunfire tore through the quiet air dropping the infected woman lifelessly to the ground ending her haphazard roaming forever. A small bird burst through the trees above their heads fluttering off into the distance, leaving them immersed once again in a deep silence. Their eyes and ears strained through the blaring dead silence that seemed to have suddenly encased them.

"Come on," said Chuck, "let's see if she has anything on her."

They continued cautiously down the long gravel toward the body of the young woman. Her body laid face down into a twisted ball of broken and decayed flesh covered in her long matted blond hair. Using the end of his boot, the young man rolled her bloated and swollen corpse.

"Oh shit, that's Stacy!" he said stunned.

Tommy kneeled down to his knees and examined her jumbled form. Her worn and haggard face had already begun to decompose. The beauty he had once known in her soft blue eyes and gentle complexion had been stolen from her by the same infectious disease that had stolen her life.

"I don't guess you two will be getting back together."

"Shut up," Tommy said rising to his feet and turning his head so to never look at her again.

He tried to push the gruesome image from his mind so he could remember her, as he had known her, sweet and kind. He walked on down the long gravel road remembering how beautiful she was back in high school when he had taken her to their junior prom. She had been his first. His friend stood back staring at her remains for a few more moments before catching up. Several uncomfortable moments of silence passed between the two friends as they walked aimlessly to wherever the rural road led.

"Hey man, I'm sorry for what I said...I wasn't thinking when I said it."

"Forget about it," he replied simply. "It's hard seeing someone you know ending up like that."

They walked for nearly an hour without a word passing between the two, when Chuck saw a small sign up the road that he was more than glad to read out loud.

"Nuclear faculty access road authorized personal only," he read. "Damn, this road leads to the nuclear plant."

"I hope they didn't leave that thing up and running. If so and no one is watching it..."

"Meltdown," replied Chuck quietly under his breath.

Neither spoke another word about it nor did they concern themselves about a situation in which they had no control. If it went up, then it went up. Although it weighed heavy on their minds, they walked on concerning themselves about the things they could control and at the moment that meant merely staying alive. They followed the road as it twisted through the thick forest passing dozens of signs that were duplicates to the one they had seen earlier.

"If we can get around this plant, I think I'll know the way back to the freeway..." said Chuck pausing as he stepped onto a body in the tall grass and fell to his knees, holding up his rifle in defense. "Shit!"

Tommy pulled up his shotgun and took aim at the stagnant body in the grass.

"It has already been shot in the head," Tommy said upon examining it closer.

His friend stood up straightening his clothes.

"Man when I stepped on that fucker it scared the shit out of me!" he said holding his chest.

After observing the body, they walked on wary of the tall grass along the road, mysteriously finding the sides of the road littered with more dead bodies.

"They all have holes in their heads."

"It's like there was some kind of shootout here or something."

"I've counted nine since you stepped on that first one."

They traveled on through the shadows of the wooded road finding dozens of more dead curiously stopping at a clearing. Off into the distance stood two tall cooling towers with white steam rising into the air. The clearing stretched about 100 yards before it ran into a fifteen-foot high chain link fence with a huge double fence gate covered in barbed wire. The grass clearing, which wrapped completely around the complex, was covered with bodies.

"Looks like that place is still up and running."

"I just hope all these bodies are good and dead," said Tommy looking uneasily at the various body parts protruding through the tall grass.

"This place looks like Fort Knox. Wonder if we can get past that gate."

Walking through the tall grass, they headed toward the gate, maneuvering gingerly around dead bodies, when a gunshot struck a tall tree splintering wood into the cool air. Both intuitively dove to the ground for cover. Flopping down on the ground, Tommy landed on top of a dead body, startling himself. The man's eyes, which stared directly into his, were cut in half by a trickle of dried blood that had escaped from the bullet hole in his forehead. Chuck brought his rifle up and began to scan above the grass line in search of their attacker. Another shot rang out zinging past Tommy's head injecting itself into the dirt.

"Hey we're alive!" screamed Tommy. "Don't shoot!"

They lay deep within the swaying grass hiding nervously from the unseen shooter. Chuck scanned along the fence line through his scope, but he couldn't tell where the shot came.

"Stand up!" yelled the voice from behind the fence.

"Let's stand up." Tommy whispered while motioning over to his friend.

"Fuck that," whispered back his friend. "That'll make us an easy target."

Another shot dug into the grass between the two and although he couldn't see his target, Chuck returned fire.

"You stupid fuck!" he screamed while reloading. "Zombies don't shoot back at you!"

"Stand up!" replied the distant voice again.

"Do you have any idea where the shots are coming from?"

"No," replied Tommy hugging the ground.

Another shot cracked through the air throwing dirt into Chuck's face.

"God damn it!" he shouted spitting dirt from his mouth.

"All right!" screamed Tommy. "Don't shoot. I'm standing up!"

His friend watched him with a concern look and Tommy could tell he didn't want him to do it, but he slowly stood up holding his hands high into the air. He stood still sweating nervously in the cold winter air.

"Both of you!" commanded the voice.

The young hunter looked up at his friend standing tall with his hands open, putting himself on the line; and although he loathed being vulnerable in any situation, he stood up in the open and held his hands out. A man in camouflage pants and a brown t-shirt tucked roughly into his beltline stood up from his foxhole keeping his rifle trained on the helpless men. He flicked a cigarette butt through the fence and blew some smoke from his nostrils.

"You are not welcome here, get out of here and don't come back," he said.

"Listen you are the first person live person we've seen in days! Those things are swarming everywhere out here. We just need a safe place to stay," replied Tommy.

"Well I recommend you go and find one because you can't stay here," he replied coldly.

"Hey man what's your fucking problem? You had to know we were alive during those last few shots you took at us!" yelled Chuck.

"I'm not going to argue with you!" he yelled back. "Get out of here before I turn you into a lawn ornament!"

Chuck noticed the man's combat boots, B.T.U.s and M-16 assault in his arms.

"Thought you guys were supposed to be on our side?"

"Hello, did you miss the past couple of weeks? There is no us…there is no United fucking States of America…there is no God damn army and the reason we are still here and not running around trying to eat everyone, is because we don't take outsiders!"

"Do we look sick to you?" asked Tommy.

"Here is the low-down. We've got everything we need. We've got security, supplies and all the power we could ever use. One thing we don't need is you…you're not worth the risk. The slightest bit of fever and we'd all be gone. Now get the fuck out of here! If I ever see you in my sights again, I'll drop you."

"Nice rifle you got there. Isn't that standard military issue?" asked Chuck.

"I don't know," he replied pausing, "would you like me to send a shell your way so you can inspect it?"

"No," he replied walking off calmly. "I just wanted to know if the range on your rifle is as long as mine…it's not."

Although it was a comment that could easily ignite a trigger finger, it was a classic Chuck comment and arguing about it wouldn't change that it had already been said. His friend had only wished it had not been said at such a precarious moment, while they were still at the mercy of the remark's target; but once again, it was the impeccable timing that made it a Chuck comment. Tommy turned around and followed his friend back into the woods from whence they had came, all the while half-expecting a gunshot to strike him from behind. He could tell from his friend's stern face and clinched teeth that their encounter with the soldier had really gotten to him. They hadn't traveled any more than a few hundred feet through the trees when his friend stopped and spun around with an evil determination in his eye. They gleamed maliciously making Tommy uncomfortable. He had seen that look in him before and he knew he was about to pull a stunt.

"Which way now?" asked his friend.

"I'm going to go back and kill that piece of shit!"

"Man forget about him, we've got a long way to go before dark."

"That fucker left us out here to die!"

"Come on," said Tommy trying to soothe his friend's anger. "He's just trying to stay alive like the rest of us. They've found what works for them and are sticking to it."

"I don't give a shit about what works for him!" Chuck replied furiously. "All I care about is that I don't like being shot at!"

"That guy is dug in deep…hell we couldn't see him until after he stood up."

"This rifle has a lot longer range than that piece of shit the army calls an assault rifle. All I got to do is wait him out, next time he gets up to take a shit I'll blow it out of him."

"And then what? Huh?" replied Tommy raising his voice to match the levels of his friend. "What happens after you kill him? Hmm? Think they will invite us to stay with them then? Nothing but bad things can happen if you go back there. I've seen enough dead people already to not want to make anymore."

Chuck stood defiantly still in a decisional crossroad gripping his rifle tight, his mounting rage leaned toward going back and finishing off the cocky soldier, but the sight of his friend walking away without intentions of waiting on his return forced him to swallow his anger and follow reluctantly. He lowered his gun doing just that and chased after his friend down the long gravel road away from the plant's complex. They trekked around the vast compound being wary not to wander within rifle's range and before long came up upon a paved road, which Chuck believed would eventually lead to the main highway cutting between the city and the rural mountains he knew so well. They walked up the side of the two-lane road side by side as they had done all through their childhood together and immediately felt younger from the renewed experience.

"Been about ten years since the two of us have walked this much," said Chuck laughing.

"Back in the day we used to walk everywhere until you got your first car."

"Oh God, was that Duster a crumbling piece of shit! Almost nothing worked on it, including the air conditioner. Man, crap used to fall off it while I drove down the road. And remember the eight-track player?"

"Yeah!" Tommy said with a long smile. "I remember digging through my mom's old tapes up in the attic and finding us a couple of cool ones."

"And the holes in the floor boards! You had to hold the floor mats down with your feet whenever you hit a water puddle."

"Hell, I wish we had it right now."

They continued to talk and laugh of old times and for a moment the death and destruction that had engulfed the entire world faded away and once again they were safe roaming the neighborhoods of their youth.

"I wish we would run up on Angelina Jolie or something, I think right about now, I would have a pretty good chance to score with her," declared Chuck dreaming.

"She's a little too skanky for me," said Tommy. "Now if we happened to rescue Jennifer Garner I'd be here to console her."

"Skanky, you know what skanky is? It is a term coined by women who don't put out on a regular basis to belittle women who do, because they are pissed they enjoy sex like men. Men would fuck twenty four seven if women would let them, yet there are no terms to degrade men who will sleep with anyone, because men don't give a shit."

"Gigolo?"

"That's a compliment in my eyes."

"What if it had been the opposite in that women wanted sex all the time and had to pressure men to do it?"

"I would have been the biggest slut ever!"

Tommy roared in laughter from his friend's comment, "You know all the guys would talk about what a skank you were?"

"I don't give a shit. I would do six chicks a night, three or four times each, they could take advantage of me all they wanted," he said with a smile. "Who the hell is Jennifer Garner anyway?"

"The chick from Daredevil."

"Oh yeah... I'd do her."

A vivid touch of reality brought on by the sight of two infected ripped the young men from the haven of their light conversation and brought them crashing back into their current struggle for life. The two infected noticed the vagrants walking along the road and immediately came running down the hill screaming. Chuck brought up his rifle and took aim. Their forms bounced wildly down the hill in his scope as one tripped and tumbled down the hill in a ball falling behind the other one before it jumped back up and continued its pursuit. His first shot hit its target tearing the first infected man's face in half sending his body tumbling onto the road and spilling blood across the small highway's solid yellow center line. The hunter jerked back the bolt lever on his rifle, ejecting its empty casing recklessly trying to reload. The second infected man ran across the highway's centerline at a frantic pace releasing a high-pitched shriek as it neared its intended target. Another boom burst into the air decapitating the infected man sending his head bowling back across the road. Chuck looked over at Tommy's smoking barrel and sighed before inserting a shell into his rifle clicking it shut.

"Come on, let's get off this highway before we become road kill like these two fucks!" said Tommy.

Chapter 11
Field of Death

The two men slinked along the edge of the highway traveling through its high weeds and unkempt growth for cover. Besides an occasional fence line, the pastures alongside made for easy travel and before long they stood below the ridge of the freeway that separated them from the safety of the deep woods beyond. From down in the fields Chuck could see the tops of the cars jumbled along the road and he reached out to stop his friend's advance.

"Don't go up there," he said. "I've already made that mistake once."

"How else are we going to get across it?"

"I think there's a drainage tunnel a few miles up from here," he replied pointing up ahead.

They began their long march and the longer they walked, the less sure Chuck became about its true existence, until his memory was redeemed with the unmistakable evidence of its presence. It was a small long half circle tunnel that rose up about two feet from the ground. A small trickle of water wiggled through it winding its way to the other side of the immense freeway. Tommy leaned down and looked through the long dark tunnel.

"You sure you would rather crawl through that than run over the top of the freeway?"

"Yes," Chuck replied remembering how he almost died the last time he had been on the freeway. "If we go up there, we will have a shit load of trouble after us."

Two sets of eyes watched intently through the tunnel for possible signs of danger; nothing moved, including the two young men. Tommy looked over at his friend and raised his eyebrows giving him the sign to go first.

It had been an unwritten law with the two since childhood, whoever thought of something first had to do it first, whether it was cliff jumping into an untested location in a lake, a new trick when they were skateboarding, or crawling through a possible death trap.

Slinging his rifle onto his back, Chuck leaned down, dropped to his knees and peered down the long tunnel. A large lump sat motionless in the middle of the tunnel partially blocking the distant sunlight at the tunnel's other end, and after observing it carefully, Chuck slid down onto his belly, slipped his rifle onto his back and began to crawl. Freeing his knife from its sheath, he scooted through the shallow water in a low crawl dragging his body through the soft mud. He continued his long grueling crawl, all the while keeping a relentless stare upon the stationary bump up ahead. As he got closer, he lifted his knife. It glistened in the darkness, reflecting the light from behind lifting his spirits, as would a child's security blanket in the darkness of his room. He crawled up to the lump and reached out to touch it with his free hand. He tugged on it ripping a pair of pants loose from the pile sending a streak of pain through his chest nearly launching his heart free from its cavity within.

He rose up with a small grunt and drove his knife deep into the lump. The sharp blade drove down to the hilt, splattering mud onto his face. Calming down, he reached over and began to sift through the lifeless lump, finding a mound of trash and mud that had piled up against a small rock. He sighed in relief and slithered over it recovering from his scare. He was nearing the halfway point as well as the tunnel's darkest point, when he began to feel the darkness within it close in. He began to crawl faster, nearly out of control, tearing the knees out of his pants and the skin on his knees in an attempt to escape the shadows and reach the safety of sunlight. An aura of fear surrounded him as he madly crawled forward, engulfing his friend in his wake of terror as well. Chuck leaped out into the warm blinding light bending over and huffing heavily from the strain of the frantic crawl. His friend tore out right behind him covering his eyes with the palms of his hands. A long wide flowing field merged before their eyes as the white fog of their blindness faded away.

"We don't have shit in supplies… no matches, no food…hell we don't even have a single beer, but I have never been so glad to see the woods!" Chuck said blissfully with mud and blood caked knees.

"It's going to be some hard living with only a few shells and our wits to go on," replied his friend.

"Yeah, but it's a living."

It was a comment with which no one with a will to live could argue. They began their long ascent into the tall swaying grass never looking back. They were about halfway across when a torso rose up from the tall grass about twenty feet ahead. The worn man looked around strangely as if he had somehow been awakened from a deep slumber.

"Shit, there's one," said Tommy pulling his friend down into the grass.

Their eyes anxiously watched the torso look around above the grass line. The form slowly rose up and began to stumble around clumsily. The grass rustled beneath his feet and suddenly more torsos began to rise. They popped up all around the cowering men in every possible direction one after another as if heeding some strange call.

"Oh man this is bad…this is reeeeeal bad," Tommy whispered beneath his breath.

"What the fuck do you want to do now, start a shootout?" asked Chuck, ready to go down in a blaze of gunfire.

"We are so fucked…we are sooooo fucked," he repeated.

Dozens of infected rose to their feet and began roaming around aimlessly. They were everywhere. It wouldn't be long before one was bound to stumble upon the men raising the alarm and recruiting the two into this undead army's field of death.

"I say we make a run for it before one spots us and they get the jump on us," suggested Chuck. "I think there is an old farmhouse around the edge of those trees."

His friend's eyes followed along his arm and then on into the distance toward the indication of his finger, and the image off an old farmhouse almost materialized in his head.

"You sure there is a house over there? If there isn't these will run us ragged and those will eat us."

"Yeah, I remember seeing it several years back…I think."

"Fuck it, we've got to run somewhere."

Two images appeared above the waist high grass line and took off into a sprint. The tall grass whipped aside from the force of their long strides, swinging behind as waves would behind a churning boat. Droves of infected spotted their flight and took chase with mad screams for their blood. Dozens converged on the men as they ran for their very lives. Tommy raised the wide end of his shotgun's stock and tore through the first line of infected that blocked their path. His stock came under the chin of one breaking its jaw and sending it collapsing into the tall grass out of his way. His friend followed bashing another one in the head as it reached out.

Once they cleared through the first line, more took to the chase and for a moment their path looked clear. Suddenly, the torso of another infected rose up to a sitting position directly in front of Tommy. With catlike reflexes Tommy leaped over the head, which strangely appeared to be floating on the tall grass. His friend, who was watching those pursing rammed headlong into the lifeless head. The infected man grabbed hold of his legs and accomplished a textbook tackle sending him onto the earth headfirst. Hands seized him from the back and began to climb up his body gripping his clothes. He spun over and caught the infected man's head with the tip of his rifle barrel. His trigger clicked and the top half of the man's head shattered into a v-shape, splattering red blood into the tall green grass. Chuck jumped to his feet in a panic and ran after his friend who was a good twenty feet ahead.

Tommy ran on without the knowledge of his fallen friend and came around the tree line, hoping to see the farmhouse his friend had described. It stood staunchly barely two hundred yards away offering a gleam of hope with its door swinging open in the wind. He took a second to look back and saw his friend running toward him with literally dozens of screaming infected in hot pursuit. He turned around and ran with all his might nearly tripping face first onto the porch's steps leading up to the front door. He ran inside and held the door open for his friend who was only a few feet away. Chuck scaled the long stairway in three long gliding strides and leaped into the doorway helping his friend seal it shut. They quickly locked the thick sturdy door's two locks, dangling chain and deadbolt. The infected on the other side hit the door like a ton of bricks, shaking it nearly off its hinges on the first blow. The door recovered and settled back into its original location, promising to hold for at least a few more minutes. Chuck reloaded his rifle and both stepped back from the bowing door. It shook back and forth on its hinges, drawing in light from the outside through its outer edges with each blow.

"That shit isn't going to hold much longer," replied Chuck ready to shoot the first thing that burst through.

Tommy began to look around the living room and leaped back from the window when the shadow of a man cast through the curtains. The glass behind the long curtains shattered into the room splitting open in the center and revealing a pair of cut and slashed arms. Tommy and Chuck ran into kitchen and stopped in an entryway with two open doors, one leading upstairs and another leading down into the basement. The sound of breaking glass forced a quick decision.

"Let's go upstairs!" suggested Chuck.

"If they follow us up there where will we go?"

"We could climb out onto the roof."

"Last thing I want to do is get trapped up high again, besides if they see us up there, we will have hundreds roaming around the house like buzzards waiting for us to die."

"I don't want to go down there," answered Chuck looking down into the dark stairway."

"Come on," he said stepping down into the darkness. "Hurry up before one sees us."

Trusting his friend over his gut, he stepped into the basement, closing the door. A quiet damp blackness engulfed the two as if they were two children hiding in a closet during a game of hide and seek, but in this game there was no "base" and if they were found, the penalty was death.

A loud splintering vibrated from the other side of the flimsy door and both men dropped their bellies onto the cold basements stairs. A wide beam of light projected from the crack under the door onto their faces like a movie projector would onto a movie screen, playing out their story. They watched it intently, to see how it would turn out. A pair of feet shuffled by the door into the kitchen and then out of sight, rattling dishes that had fallen onto the floor. Several more followed, all going into the same direction. They looked at each other with worried faces and watched on as another set of feet stopped at the edge of the door with the toes of its feet pointing squarely into their eyes. The door shook, rattling the two men as well as the door's old frame and then it stopped. Neither took a breath, it was as if time froze and they no longer needed to breathe. They waited with guns ready whatever the outcome as the feet shuffled on. The desire to breathe once again returned, and quietly they sucked the musty air of the basement into their lungs. Tommy looked down into the pitch-black darkness of the basement below and wondered what was resting in the dark.

"Man let's see if there is anything down there," he said uncomfortably, "I don't like having my back turned to it not knowing if there is anything down there or not."

"Be real quiet, if there is anything down there, it won't move unless it knows we are here. We'll have to wait until it's clear out there before we can check it out. If we had to fight something, it might get a little noisy, and the ones out there might bust in here with us, making a literal sandwich of us."

Two hours had passed before Tommy's eyes reopened in the unfamiliar darkness of the basement stairwell. His shoulder, side and leg throbbed from lying against the jagged edge of the basement stairway. He leaned over and shook his friend's shoulder, waking him. Chuck jumped up in a daze nearly rolling backwards down the dark stairwell. Tommy reached over and grabbed his shirt, saving him a rough tumble. They watched underneath the door for several more minutes before deciding it was as safe as it ever would be and then prepared to check down below. They clicked on their flashlights and pointed their light rays down the dark twisting stairwell, but the stingy darkness seemed to almost swallow up their beams, not allowing either to see beyond the end of the stairs. They walked down the stairs which groaned slowly from supporting their weight, causing the men to flinch with every creak the old boards made until their feet touched the solid concrete of the basement's floor.

It was a large area, having the same floor space as the house itself and extended off into the darkness in all four directions. Their lights cautiously explored every corner bouncing off tables, boxes and an old rusty water heater.

"Thank God it's clear," said Chuck relieved. "I was sure we were going to find one of those fuckers down here and have to fight it in the dark."

Tommy still unsure, continued to walk around and inspect his surroundings. He kicked over a stack of boxes knocking them across the floor.

"Shhh!" said Chuck pointing up at the ceiling. "There still might be some up there."

Tommy kneeled down and began to sort through the rubble for anything that might be of use. Chuck walked over to what appeared to be some kind of workbench and shuffled through its drawers.

"Nothing but a bunch of toys and clothes over here," said Tommy.

"Oh shit!" said Chuck holding up a shiny hand axe. "I just found a nice toy over here."

Tommy looked over at his friend with a smile. Chuck swung the sharp edge of the axe down onto the wooden workbench. Its sharp blade sunk in deep splitting the wood several inches in both directions as well as splitting his mouth open into a wide smile in the process.

"It seems pretty safe down here," said Tommy looking around. "I say we stack some boxes up and down the stairs to warn us if anything comes down and sleep here tonight."

"Sounds good, I think if we crawl through the weeds in the morning we can make the woods without being seen."

Tommy agreed and after lining the stairs with every trinket they could find, they stretched out on the hard concrete floor and slept as soundly as they would have on a plush mattress with silk sheets.

Chapter 12
Christmas Comes Early

Tommy leaned over the couch, carefully parted the curtains and looked nervously outside over the front porch. Long unkempt grass swayed quietly in the wind hiding countless dangers to their lives.

"It looks clear," he said leaning back.

"All right, let's go out the back door."

Chuck checked out through the small window in the kitchen's back door and slowly turned the door's rusted knob. It gave away with a loud click and the two men slid along the back of the house as if they were part of an assault team dropping into the tall grass disappearing. They low-crawled on their bellies, parting the grass with their bodies, while moving through the field toward an old barn which lay halfway between the house that had saved them and the forest that they hoped would. The thick grass split open effortlessly as Chuck crept along slithering through its shadow, never allowing him more than a few inches of vision. Tommy crawled behind, using his elbows to drag him along the trail that had been laid before him. Chuck continued on quickly trying to make the barn as fast as he could, stopping upon the appearance of a leg that penetrated the grass. He stopped crawling. He stopped doing everything, not even daring to take a breath. Tommy dragged up behind, bumping into the back of his friend, nearly knocking him over onto the object he dared not awaken. They sat frozen like two statues misplaced in an overgrown field staring at the motionless leg. The old dirty shoe protruded through the tall grass blocking their way. Moving quietly, Chuck pulled his new axe from his belt and motioned for his friend to part the grass over the body. Tommy pulled up the barrel of his shotgun and split the tall grass exposing the body of an old man with a potbelly wearing dirty overhauls. Chuck swung the axe down bringing it deep into the man's forehead and split it as he had the workbench in the basement the day before. The man never moved, until Chuck pulled the axe free from his head. He wasn't sure if the man had even been alive, but he really didn't care. He had done what needed to be done. Tommy checked the man's pockets and found a money clip full of bills, a key ring and a lighter. He took the only item of value out of the three, pocketing the cheap plastic lighter.

They finished their crawl to the barn and rolled up against the building's old double door. Chuck motioned for his friend to take position on the other side of the door and pulled open the door with one hand while holding his axe with the other. Tommy gripped the handle to his hammer tightly and rushed into the shadows of the barn. Sunlight dripped in through the barn's old roof sending shadows crawling along the walls like spiders hampering the two young men's eyes by not allowing their pupils to adjust to the contrasting lights. They scrambled around walking in a large circle covering each other's back. A chain dangling from the ceiling swung in small circles casting the shadow of a wiggling snake across the barn's earthen floor, while the old boards of the barn moaned against the force of the wind. They walked around ready for anything, all the while hoping for nothing.

"Oh my," said Chuck walking slowly toward one of the barn's stalls.

Tommy followed up behind him to see what had gotten his friend's undivided attention. Parked in the stall was a shiny blue four wheel all terrain vehicle.

"Thank you God!" bellowed Chuck while looking up into the roof of the barn as if he might actually see God watching them receive his generous gift.

He ran his finger along it as he studied it from one end to the other.

"This thing looks brand fucking new!" he proclaimed in excitement. "You know how much these things run?"

"I don't know, with the current economy…free?"

"Before everything went to hell, one of these babies ran about seven grand. Man this thing can go anywhere," he said as if in a trance like a little boy staring at presents under the tree on Christmas morning.

He fumbled all around it and shuffled through its small storage compartment under the seat.

"There aren't any keys," he said disappointed.

"Hey!" said Tommy in a revelation. "That old guy you butchered in the field had a set of keys in his pocket."

Chuck's eyes nearly popped out of his head when he saw two full tanks of gas sitting in the corner of the stall.

"Shit man we hit the mother load!" he said lifting the tanks into the air proudly.

Tommy smiled and laughed at their change of luck.

"We're traveling in style now," he said happily. "I'll be right back, I'm going to get those keys and see if they work."

Chuck nodded to his friend and popped off the four-wheeler's gas cap. The tank was half full and he carefully topped it off, treating every drop of fuel as if as precious as their very lives. A few drops dribbled out onto the side of the can and ran down the side of the tank, causing him to winch as if they were his own drops of blood.

Tommy came back into the barn holding the keys up into the air, jiggling them proudly. Chuck held his hands out and Tommy tossed them into the air. They spun through the air turning in a spiral until they came to rest in the palm of Chuck's hands with a sweet jingle. He flipped through the key ring trying each key in the ignition, until one slid in perfectly. They both smiled as Chuck shifted the four-wheeler into neutral and rolled its shiny blue frame into the center of the barn, tying both of the fuel tanks onto the back rack.

"Is there going to be enough room for both of us?"

"Not with the extra gas," Chuck replied callously.

"What the fuck am I suppose to do?"

"There's another one over there."

Tommy skeptically walked over to the stall that Chuck had just pushed the four-wheeler from and saw a small dirty red four-wheeler parked in the corner.

"That's for a little kid!"

"No man those things are tough…it'll carry you, no problem."

"Why do you get the good one?"

"We'll take turns."

Tommy pushed the small A.T.V. out into the open and plopped on top of it, nearly knocking himself out with his own knees. Both men begin to roll with laughter at the sight of his lanky body on the tiny vehicle.

"You think this thing will be able to go fast enough with me on it to outrun hungry zombies?" he asked rubbing away the water created in his eyes from laughter.

"I doubt they will able to keep up for all the laughter!" Chuck said roaring while holding his stomach.

"Yeah," he said dryly, "besides if they do, I'll just drive between their legs."

They had a good laugh like they use to as kids right after they had pulled a prank on some unknowing soul, but once the laughter stopped, they returned to the business at hand and prepared to make a run for the hills. Their largest fear was that one or both of the A.T.V.s wouldn't start, alerting infected in the surrounding fields leaving the two trapped in a raggedy old barn. The last thing either wanted was to recreate the Alamo's last stand in an old barn.

Tommy kick cranked the small four-wheeler and it stalled with a long grinding squeal, sending chills down their spines. The race was on to get it started before they were discovered by infected and he re-cranked it making the same loud faltering start. Chuck sat tensely on top of his four-wheeler waiting to make sure his friend's vehicle would start before trying his own. A long moan seeped in through the wide cracks in between the boards of the barn's walls. Tommy began to crank his four-wheeler faster as a slow moving shadow walked along the exterior of the barn. Chuck watched it intently as it circled the barn moving toward the crack between the barn's wide front doors. A high pitch whine came from underneath Tommy's legs and for a moment he didn't realize that his youth size four-wheeler had started. Twisting its handle to feed it fuel, it jumped forward nearly toppling him off the back of it, signaling Chuck to start his own four-wheeler. It started up on his first attempt and he led the way out through the front of the barn bursting through it knocking the doors wide open. The smaller four-wheeler took chase and burst out into the open following the wake in the grass created by his friend's larger wheelbase. An infected man reached out to grab Chuck as he rode out the barn, but the rider alertly ducked, missing its outreached and decayed arms. Tommy's small four-wheeler zipped right by the awkward creature behind Chuck's leaving the lumbering zombie chasing after the two in vain.

Both vehicles zipped through the long field avoiding numerous infected, as they seemed to come back to life, rising from the tall grass and taking pursuit of the loud motor vehicles. The riders rode side by side at full throttle on an adrenaline run to freedom. Chuck could see a break in the tree line ahead where the trail to its interior began. He pointed toward their distant image so to make his friend aware of their destination and steered toward it. Tommy sped up so not to get too far behind, when his small knobby tires struck an unsuspected lump on the ground sending his four-wheeler soaring into the air tumbling forward. The two small tires struck against the ground first flipping the four-wheeler on top of its driver and spinning out of control into the grass. Chuck barely noticed the accident through the corner of his eye. He quickly spun around to help his friend slamming on his breaks. Tommy rose up slightly dazed, but with enough awareness to flip over his toppled four-wheeler and plop on top of it. It failed to start on his first attempt and Chuck pulled up next to his friend carefully watching the huge mass of undead running in their direction. He had never seen so many at once. There had to be nearly forty, black, white, male, female, old and young it seemed the infected had no prejudices. A small whine came from under Tommy's A.T.V. and Chuck was about to turn around when something caught his eye. A young man had burst out the back door of the farmhouse they had hid in overnight and jumped off the deck waving a white shirt in an attempt to signal the two riders. Several more infected burst out the house in pursuit of the man leaping off the deck in chase. They clumsily fell to the ground in a jumble of arms and legs before getting back to their feet and surging after him. The poor man was trapped in between the infected of the house and field.

"You all right?" asked Chuck.

"Yeah," replied Tommy rubbing his arm.

"Go, I'll catch you up the trail. This thing is twice as fast as that piece of shit. I'll go and get that guy."

Tommy looked back at the horde he intended on trying to outmaneuver and rolled his eyes as his friend sped toward the waiting horde.

Chuck's four-wheeler raced through the tall grass crashing through the first crowd of undead spinning them around backwards and changing their focus toward him. The young man ran toward him in a sprint with only few dozen feet behind him and a mass of raging infected. The big blue four-wheeler spun sideways and skidded to a stop rumbling wildly in front of the wide-eyed man.

"Get on!" said its rider.

The man quickly tried to throw his leg over the back, but there wasn't enough room for the tied on gas tanks. An infected man ran up toward the two only to collapse backwards when his head nearly disintegrated off his shoulders with a loud boom. Tommy sat on his mini wheeler with smoke coming from the barrel of his shotgun.

"Rip the tanks off!" screamed Tommy reloading his single shotgun.

Chuck looked at the tanks and sighed before slinging them off. The two tanks bounced against the hard ground tumbling out of sight into the tall surrounding weeds. The young man hopped on the back of the four-wheeler sinking its frame toward the ground with the addition of his weight. The four-wheeler locked in its gears nearly knocking the new passenger off as it propelled forward in a wheelie. They swiftly rode around the swarm of infected and raced off into the woods down a wide-open trail. The four-wheelers drove on for nearly twenty minutes of ear numbing noise before their drivers stopped along the trail and cut the engines. All three men stood up and stretched the tightened muscles in their legs.

"Nice to meet you," said Chuck holding out his hand to the man he had been with for the last thirty minutes, but had never spoken.

"You too," the man said happily. "Thanks for coming back to get me back there."

"No problem."

Tommy stood stiffly with his right arm hanging limp at his side, while holding it with his other.

"You okay man?" asked Chuck.

"I can't move my right arm," he said. "I fucked it up back there or something."

"Is it broke?" asked the newest member of their party.

"I don't think so. I could move it fine right after I wrecked. I think my shoulder is swollen up or something."

Chuck walked over and looked at it for a moment.

"I'm no doctor, but I bet you pinched a nerve somewhere or maybe dislocated it," he said confidently. "Can you use it at all?"

"Just my fingers," he said slightly wiggling them.

"You…" paused Chuck realizing he didn't know the name of the man he had just saved, "what's your name?"

"Oh sorry," he said. "Jeff."

"Can you ride?"

"Shit!" he said. "Since I was six!"

"All right you got the midget mobile. We don't have a lot of fuel, just what's in the tanks. So let's ride them out."

Two four-wheelers pointed toward the heart of the forest and disappeared into its depth with the grind of gasoline engines winding into the distance.

Chapter 13
A New Enemy Falls?

The young men marched in line along the thin trail that twisted through thick trees, brush and rocks as if to never end. The four-wheelers' tanks had run out of fuel two days ago, forcing the fleeing men to abandon the useless hunks of metal and plastic where they had stopped and to carry what meager supplies they had left on their backs. Tommy's arm had gotten slightly better with each passing day and now was nearly one hundred percent. Small flakes of white snow were starting to fall, gently cooling the already cold hard ground beneath their feet. None of the men were properly dressed for the cold weather they were about to face and save for Chuck's thick jacket, they looked more like they were ready to go to the mall than into the mountains during the frigid month of February. Jeff had only been wearing a t-shirt when he had been rescued, but during their first night out, a liner donation from Chuck's jacket made the weather bearable, but barely.

"It's starting to get dark," said Chuck looking up at the sky. "We better set up camp and gather up some fire wood."

The three men began to scour the immediate area for anything that would burn and before long a huge pile of sticks, twigs and logs to build a fire appeared from their labor. Using dry leaves, one of their two lighters and some extra oxygen from their lungs, a small fire crackled, radiating a comfortable heat. The three freezing men settled down next to the fire, where they prepared to bed down for the rest of the night.

"Jeff," said Tommy, "you never told us how you happened to be in that house."

Jeff threw a stick onto the fire and leaned back against a tree getting as cozy as the elements of the forest would allow.

"That house belonged to my fiancé's father. Six of us held out there for about a week after everything got turned upside down, until those zombies overran it and killed everyone but me. My fiancé and I got separated during the commotion as we were chased upstairs...I managed to get up into the attic and pull up the stairs," he said reliving the experience. "They had blood in their eyes. I'd never seen such hatred. All I could do was lie up in the attic and listen to her screams as they ate her. I wanted to go down and save her, but I knew it was too late. It got warm up there, that's why I wasn't wearing any heavy clothes. To make a long story short, I laid in the attic until I heard your four-wheelers."

"Didn't you hear us downstairs the previous day?" asked Chuck from across the fire. "I know we made a shit load of noise down there."

"I heard some glass breaking... I assumed one of those clumsy fucks bumped up against the china cabinet or something.

"You took a hell of chance running out into that swarm of undead," declared Tommy sitting on a log. "If we hadn't seen you or not came back for you, you would have been torn apart."

"Hell, I have always believed when it's your time to go, there ain't a fucking thing you can do to change it."

"If that is true, I guess it was time for just about everybody," said Chuck.

"All I know is, when it's my time to go," announced Tommy, "I don't want it to be by the teeth of some fucking zombie."

"Ah!" said Jeff. "There are worse ways to die."

"I'd like to hear what you would consider worse," challenged Tommy.

"I knew this guy, and I went to his funeral, so this isn't some bullshit urban legend I'm going to tell you about. One night this guy gets a call from nature to go and drain the ole lizard. Well... not thinking much about the rain, he goes to the can and takes a piss while standing up, about the same time a thunderstorm rolls into the area. While he is doing this, a bolt of lightning strikes a tree in his yard and travels down its trunk into its roots, which happened to be touching one of his water lines. Then the lightning bolt travels down his water pipes, into his toilet and straight up his piss right into his dick, bursting it into flames. Fortunately for him, if the word fortunate can even appropriately be used in this story, it didn't kill him… it just turned his dick to ashes. Well the guy falls back into the tub almost completely paralyzed from being electrocuted and all he can do is lay there and hold his crotch where his cock used to be."

"Damn!" said Chuck. "That's some fucked up shit."

"So he died?" asked Tommy curiously.

"Yes, but not from electrocution," replied Jeff finishing the story. "After seeing he didn't have a dick, he crawled to the cabinet beneath the sink and drank a full container of Drāno to finish off the job."

"I have to admit that's pretty hard," said Tommy gritting his teeth from behind the glare of an open fire.

Chuck passed out the last of their jerky and the three chewed on it silently below a light snow as they continued to chitchat.

"Do you think passing out a piece of shriveled meat after that story is appropriate?" joked Jeff.

"The three of us might get to see how bad starvation is, if we don't get some food soon," said Chuck in mid chew. "That's the last of it."

"How many shots you got for that rifle there?" asked Jeff nodding toward the rifle leaning up against Chuck's stretched out body.

"Eleven."

The two young men across from him flinched in response as if they had been pinched.

"I've got twenty three shells left," said Tommy after counting the shells in his pocket.

"Don't let me get off on the wrong foot here or anything, because I really appreciate how you two saved my life, but what exactly is the plan here?"

"To go somewhere where we can get away from the infection, I knew it would be clear way out here."

"But how are we going to live through the winter with no supplies?" asked Jeff curiously.

"I don't know… how were we going to survive back in the city?" debated Chuck. "Eventually we would have been overwhelmed no matter what we did or where we stayed. This seemed like our best hope."

"Shouldn't we go back and steal some more supplies? Like maybe some winter clothes, food and ammo?" suggested Jeff.

"I know these woods. We can hunt and fish. Besides there are some caves a few days hike further north from here. They stay a constant fifty through sixty degrees inside year around."

"You got any fishing line?" asked Jeff.

"I don't want to be rude or anything," said Tommy interrupting, "but you don't have to follow us anywhere."

The young man got an irritated look on his face, but quickly dropped it as fast as it had appeared.

"You're right. It's not my place to question plans you two had before I joined in, I'm just glad to be here."

The three sat quietly for several uncomfortable moments before Chuck stood up and broke the cold silence that had gripped their primitive camp.

"Guess I'm going to get some sleep," he said feeding the fire.

Its flames rose higher into the dark chilly air and a new wave of heat came over their cold faces.

When Tommy's eyes opened early the next morning, it was to a fresh fall of thick snow. He dusted the cold snow that had collected on his body overnight and stood up shivering. The flames from their fire had died down long ago and he quickly gripped a stick with numb hands and stirred its coals hoping to rekindle its previous glory. The stirring awakened deep red embers in the center of the fire and the young man fumbled through their firewood reserves and tossed a hand full of twigs and sticks onto it resurrecting its flames. The man's joints ached as if actually frozen crackling with their movement. New warmth came from within the circle of fire and the young man quickly extended his fingers out toward the flames nearly burning them before his nerves transmitted the pain of heat.

"Guys!" shouted Tommy loudly. "Get up!"

Two long lumps of snow began to wiggle around until two men finally emerged from their white and frozen cocoons.

"God damn, it's cold!" said Chuck through chattering teeth.

"I can't feel my hands or my feet," declared Jeff trembling next to the fire. "What I wouldn't give for a sleeping bag."

"Looks like we got about four inches last night," announced Tommy standing up to fuel the flames.

Sparks jumped away from the flames as he tossed a handful of brush into fire. The bright yellow and red flames brought welcome warmth to their blood and revived their spirits. After warming up and exhausting their fire's provisions, the three men put out the fire with a lump of snow and took back to the trail. They marched on vigorously to keep their bodies warm from exertion and to limit the amount of cold nights they would have to spend under the stars before they reached the shelter of the caves. Snow continued to mount on the ground throughout the rest of the day becoming a new and overwhelming enemy. Their feet shuffled through the cold snow brushing it aside tangling their shoelaces into frozen knots.

"Will we make the caves before tonight?" asked Jeff puffing hot breath into his exposed hands.

"No," announced Chuck in the lead, "but we should make them by tomorrow."

"I don't know about you guys, but I am not looking forward to another night out in the open," commented Jeff.

"Since we know it is going to be cold, we will pick a better campsite, like in a depression or something to block the wind," replied Chuck.

"Okay, boss man."

"I am not the boss man," retorted Chuck defensively. "Tommy and I been best friends since kids and we have always been a pair with equal input, not a leader and a follower."

"Sorry," said Jeff realizing he had touched a nerve. "It seems since I have been with you two, you have been the one leading us around and stuff."

"That's because I know these woods better than Tommy...and that's all."

Tommy recognized the slight suggestion of a possible power struggle between the three men, but if that was what Jeff was intending to do, he didn't realize what he was up against. The two trusted each other entirely. As boys they had sat stone cold in front of teachers and parents alike never folding under pressure or selling the other out, even in guilt. There was too much loyalty for him to wedge a split thought Tommy. Although their friendship had certain rules, such as never dating the same girl, whether the other was currently involved or not, it had been the team concept that primarily had been the successful component between the two friends since they were children. Neither had ever had the desire to see who was stronger, smarter or faster, as did most boys. Although they had been in numerous arguments over the years, they had never physically fought and every one of their disagreements had always ended without hard feelings.

Of the three, only Chuck was even remotely dressed for the monumental task that lay ahead. Their thin clothing did little to harness their heat and the two who were wearing tennis shoes were in constant threat of slipping to the cold hard ground. They traveled without stopping until the distant sunlight faded below the tip of the mountains and the bitter night took hold once again. The darkness swiftly engulfed their surroundings almost instantaneously leaving the group alone in a thick blackness with only the heat of a fire to help them struggle through the long night.

A heavy snow fell throughout the night never letting up on the three men and their makeshift camp. Sleeping in itself was a difficult task, being in conflict with the pain of their nearly frozen extremities. They slept in shifts with one man staying awake on a two hour shift to constantly excavate wood from its frozen and snow covered blanket to keep their fire fed, almost as if it was a newborn child needing constant nurturing.

As the night grew older and the temperature continued to drop, the three men instinctively edged closer to the fire as its heat seemed to shrink away until they were nearly sleeping in the fire. A ceremonial sunrise finally appeared stubbornly at the edge of the sky and reflected off the bright white snow revealing three weary, cold and weather worn men. They dusted the snow off with deadened hands, broke camp, and then quickly took to the trail, chasing the promise of a better night. Although it never actually got warmer through the day, they all felt better from the exertion of the hike and remained cheerful through the day, carrying on in playful conversation along the way.

"Man I can't wait to make those caves," remarked Jeff enthusiastically.

"It's not going to be like the Marriott," said Chuck trying to keep his expectations in check.

"Any place where I can lay down and not be covered in snow sounds good to me," he replied. "I hope we don't run into some zombified group of spelunkers."

"Hell, try and think positive about it," said Tommy. "They should be pretty easy to kill and they might have some shit we could use."

"Well," he remarked with a big smile, "if I'm going to think positive about it, I am going to think about something better than some crappy spelunker gear," said Jeff laughing.

"Oh yeah," asked Chuck playfully. "What would you wish for?"

"How about if we got up there and found some helpless triplets living in our cave," Jeff said following a substantial laugh, "with perfect bodies and big ass tits!"

The comment made Chuck laugh out loud and brought a huge smile to Tommy's face.

"I would have to concur on that one, but why not just three hot chicks?" asked Tommy curiously.

"Are you fucking kidding me?" he responded. "Nothing is hotter or sexier than good looking twins or triplets! Besides, it alleviates the problem of who gets the best looking chick. You know how when you usually meet two or three chicks at once… there is always one super hot chick and then some lame one that some guy has to take so everyone else can score."

"That is one hell of a day dream you are having over there," replied Tommy enjoying a conversation for once that wasn't gloomy.

"But how would you choose which chick went with which guy?" asked Chuck.

"Did you listen to what I just said? I said triplets, meaning they're identical."

"No, I mean like their personalities, you can't go switching up mates later down the road because the one you chose had a sucky personality."

"Hey if they suck that's even better!"

"You know what I mean, what if one is smarter than the other?" inquired Chuck.

"We'd have to draw straws and the loser would get stuck with the smart one I guess," joked Tommy.

"There are no smart identical twins or triplets period!" Jeff declared boldly. "See… there is only so much intelligence to pass out per egg, twins are only half as smart and triplets are only a third as smart, because they have to split it up, unlike the rest of us who came from single eggs."

"What?" asked Tommy.

"After that stupid ass comment I'm going to have to assume you're a quintuplet," said Chuck.

"All right smart guy. Can you name one twin or triplet that has done anything exceptional?"

"Hmmm," mumbled Chuck thinking, "just because I can't think of one, doesn't mean there wasn't one."

"You can't think of any, because there hasn't been any. No Noble Peace Prize winners, no great leaders, no scientists, no philosophers… no anything. You think throughout history there would be at least one," he said defending his earlier comment. "But tell you what Chuck, if we get up there and find two hot twins and some ugly smart chick, you can have the smart chick so you two can contemplate the universe together, while Tommy and I fuck like rabbits!"

"Fuck you," said Chuck through a wide smile.

"Well all I know is if we don't stop talking about this shit, I am going to have make a pit stop at the next bush for a quick jack off," Tommy said in jest.

All three laughed and continued drudging up the snow-besieged mountain in good spirits, finally stopping with huge smiles.

"The caves are up on those cliffs," declared Chuck pointing at some distant rock formations.

Chapter 14
Mountain Man

The three ill equipped men had difficulty scaling the ice-covered cliffs slipping and sliding most of the way up the rocky formation. Thick frozen snow covered the ground, making it difficult for Chuck to remember the exact location of the cave's entrance. It took diligent eyes to spot the hidden cavern and nearly thirty minutes using wet sticks and bare hands to clear a hole large enough for the three to slide into the mouth of their new home. The cave that Chuck had chosen was nearly forty feet high from its floor to ceiling and nearly sixty feet wide, with ten foot tall tunnels leading off into two different directions. The floor was covered in hard red mud, but was fairly dry and surprisingly warm. Tommy walked over toward the entrance of one of the tunnels and clicked on his flashlight shooting a weak beam down its long twisted corridor.

"Where do these lead?" he asked.

"The one behind you leads to some underground lake about three or four hundred feet down, the other one goes on forever, I've never explored it to its end."

"Can we build a fire in here?" asked Jeff.

"Not unless you want to smoke us out. This cave's doesn't have enough draft to draw the smoke away. We can make any fire we need for cooking or to dry off outside."

"Isn't it going to get as cold as shit in here at night without a fire?" Jeff asked, concerned.

"No, all we got to do is go down one of these corridors a few hundred feet and the temperature stays constant."

"What about the entrance?" asked Tommy. "Won't it get covered up in snow tonight?"

"If it does, then all the better, it will help to block out the cold weather."

"Won't we smother in here?" asked Jeff unsure of their new dwelling.

"I'm not a chemist, so I really can't be sure if oxygen passes through snow or not, but I doubt the three of us could exhaust all the air in this cave network in one night."

The three men began to wander around their new residence with a heightened curiosity about their new environment until they all agreed on an area suitable for their base camp.

"Man, this fucking floor is going to be as hard as hell," said Jeff trying to find a comfortable spot to spend the night.

Chuck took off his jacket and rolled it up to make himself a primitive pillow. Tommy leaned back against the wall and pulled his shoes off.

"I wouldn't do that if I were you," said Chuck looking at his friend's socks.

"What?"

"Take your shoes off."

"Why not?"

"There are a few small bats in here and I hear they like to suck on people's toes."

"Bullshit!" said Jeff sitting up.

Chuck laughed, "I just said that to fuck with you guys. There are bats here, but I don't think they suck blood."

Tommy flipped up his collar tightly against his neck and quietly slid his shoes back on, hoping no one would notice before he went to sleep.

Over the next week, using their cave as a base of operation, Chuck got two good deer kills, both does. He laughed at the excitement he felt from killing a doe out of season. It was something he normally wouldn't have ever done, but of all his kills in life, he wasn't any prouder than as he was of these two. All of his past kills, although he had used their meat, had been primarily for sport, while these had been for survival. Each shell in his pocket was precious and he had gotten two good kills with only two shots. With their newly caught meat, they feasted the first night and ate until their stomachs nearly burst, with plenty to spare. They were also able to enlist the snow as their ally and use it for water and to refrigerate their excess meat. Tommy examined his new deer coat poncho, which he had made by cutting a slit in the middle of it and slipping over his head, before holding it closed at the bottom with his belt. Jeff stood next to him modeling his deer poncho replica.

"Now we look like real cavemen!" he said looking at it proudly.

"No," said Tommy correcting him, "you look like Fred Flintstone and I look Barney Rubble."

With full stomachs and furs to stay warm, their lives became bearable, but with each shell they fired, they drew closer to the day when they would be forced to survive without the technology of man and not one of the men wanted to face the cruelty of nature without it. They continued on in this matter for three more weeks postponing the inevitable, living for only the moment happy to be fed and warm, until Chuck returned from one of his hunting trips empty handed, but full of excitement.

"I found something you two are going to want to see!"

His friends followed him through the woods for nearly an hour before he dropped to one knee on a hillside and pointed into the valley below. A small cabin sat deep in the center of it with a long gray stream of smoke bellowing from its chimney.

The old wooden door stood stoutly before the half frozen men separating the icy mountain winter from the warmth of the cabin's interior and the three men from whoever inhabited the small cabin. A frozen hand reached out and rattled the door with three loud knocks. They stood quiet in the white silence that blanketed the mountain valley and waited in anticipation of who or what would answer. Without discussion, the men assumed from the smoke coming out of the chimney that it wouldn't be a zombie that answered the door, but whether it would be a family, an individual, or triplets they were unsure. After several long moments without an answer, they knocked again only to receive the same lack of response. Chuck leaned forward and tried to push the door open, only to find it securely locked. His fist came down upon the door again rattling it in its place and sending a deafening hollow thump through the interior of the small cabin. For another long moment it stood deadly still with the audience of six eyes intently fixed upon it, until it suddenly clanked and slowly cracked open to expose the face of an elderly man with a short white scruffy beard.

"Hi," said the dumbfounded man.

"Hi," said all three of the men almost in unison.

"Can I do something for you?" asked the old man through the crack.

"Mind if we come in?" asked Chuck.

"Umm… sure," he said hesitantly, "Come on in."

The old man pulled the thick stubborn door inward so to let in the unexpected visitors and then quickly shoved it closed behind the last of the three. The interior of the cabin was small, consisting of one large room with a fireplace that churned out a warm dry heat that almost instantly thawed their frozen exteriors from the outside in. The room was jumbled with crude furniture including a thickly fur lined bed, a solid oak table and tall wooden chairs, which the men had come to know as mere luxuries during their time in the mountains. Hanging over the last half of the room was a crooked loft that looked as if it was about to collapse. In all, the cabin was quite basic in appearance and function, but to its three new visitors it was a palace.

"Sorry about my manners there," he said apologetically, "but I don't get visitors up here this time of the year."

"No worries," said Tommy unzipping his coat to fully enjoy the cabin's cozy environment.

"You three look as if you have come upon hard times," he said eyeing their raw and weather-beaten appearance.

"The whole world has," said Chuck sharply.

"The world finally cave in on itself? It was just a matter of time I guess," said the man calmly. "That's why I live way up here away from everyone and just about everything… couldn't stomach anymore of the violence and greed."

"You sure got quite a set up out here," said Jeff impressed. "Di you bring all this stuff up here by yourself?"

"Ah!" he replied humbly, "piece by piece over the years."

"How long have you been up here?" asked Chuck.

"Somewhere around twenty two years give or take a season."

"Do you know anything about all the shit that has been going on?" asked Tommy amazed.

"What, did someone start another world war or something?"

"You could say that!" said Jeff laughing at the man's ignorance of current events.

"You mean you have no idea about the infection?" asked Chuck.

"No," answered the man plainly. "I only go down twice a year, once in the spring and once in the fall for supplies and even then I don't listen too much about what's been going on. I try and stay out of world's business and it stays out of mine."

"This is one piece of business that isn't going to stay out of yours, about everyone is gone."

"Something like small pox?"

"More like walking small pox," interjected Jeff.

"It's kind of hard to explain," said Chuck finding it difficult to find the appropriate words, "but it's a highly infectious disease that always kills its host."

"Oh and don't forget to tell him how they come back to life and start eating everyone," said Jeff interrupting.

The man's thick white eyebrows lifted up on his forehead and he rested his chin in rough hands that bore more resemblance to bark than skin.

"Listen, whatever you three have done, is none of my business, I don't want any trouble."

"I know it sounds crazy," said Tommy reassuring the suspicious man, "but they are telling the truth."

"So what is left?" he asked.

"Nothing, we barely made it up here with what little we have," stated Chuck.

The old man kindly invited the three orphans of a lost society to stay in his home passing the night away as they explained to him in detail everything over the past few weeks that he had been fortunate enough to miss. Their host listened intently, gripped with concern.

Chapter 15
A New Discovery

The four men spent the next snow-ridden month in what would be considered by modern standards as poverty, but to the downtrodden it was one of pure luxury. Surrounded by tall temperate trees providing limitless fuel for warm fires and a log cab to hold in heat as well as keep them dry, there was little room for complaint and even if there were, there was no one left to hear. Their hunting skills provided fresh meat to complement the old mountain man's skimpy provisions and although their future seemed far from secure, it appeared somewhat hopeful. Their daily routines consisted of the constant chore of chopping firewood, hunting and all night long card games next to a hulking fire. Both Chuck and Tommy enjoyed the company of their two new roommates and discovered through their daily mannerisms that each of the two men came from the opposite sides of the spectrum. Their host on one side was a very quiet and hospitable man, while Jeff on the other side was boomingly loud and opinionated. It was the latter that worried the two the most, although neither ever spoke about it; they had learned over the years to see each other's thoughts through their facial expressions. A hand on the neck or a crinkle in the cheek told one everything the other felt about a situation. Jeff had a mean streak that secretly worried both to the point that they weren't sure if they could keep the peace between the four men bunched together.

"Come on old man," yelled Jeff. "We need a fourth for spades."

"I don't know how to play that," he replied softly.

"Don't be so unsocial," replied Jeff shuffling a deck of old tattered cards. "You can be my partner and I'll carry you until you catch on."

"No thanks."

"Come on!"

"Hey if he doesn't want to play, it's cool," said Tommy.

"I'm sick of rummy."

"We can play three man spades," offered Chuck.

"Fuck that, I want to play real spades! We have been here with this guy for over a month now and I don't think he has said more than ten words."

"I'm not much for idle words," stated the man faintly.

"Really…" said Jeff patronizing their host, "what a news flash!"

"Do you ever shut up?" asked the mountain man from his rocking chair.

Jeff stood up with an aggravated look in his eye.

"Do you want to try and make me?"

The man stared back into his eyes with a slight squint flipping over the blanket lying on his lap exposing an old revolver pointed toward Jeff.

The young man stared into the darkness of its barrel without fear, "Go ahead, old man. Pull that trigger because I'm not going to shut up."

Chuck and Tommy stood up grabbing a hold of his shoulder.

"Man," said Chuck into his ear, "what are you trying to do?"

"Get this guy to loosen up!"

"He's going to loosen up that trigger and then it's going to get weird in here," warned Chuck.

"Chill out," pronounced Tommy, "if he doesn't want to play, he doesn't want to play. All you are doing is stirring up a bunch of shit over a card game."

Jeff sat down with a rumble and start dealing out cards into four distinct piles. The men across from him saw what he was doing and Chuck quickly put in to an end to it by pushing them all together and declaring he was done for the night.

The next day lit up with the bright sun's reflection off a crystallized world, chilling the three men standing out in it nearly to the bone.

"I asked you two to meet me out here so I could tell you something. I am a man of few words and I don't really have the words to say this properly."

"Hey if it's about Jeff, I apologize about last night and it won't happen again," replied Tommy.

"No it's not that…" he said pausing, "I'm an old man who doesn't care much for people. Not that I don't like you guys, but getting away from everything is the reason I came out here nearly a quarter of a century ago. After everything you have told me, it appears to be the best decision I ever made."

"What are you saying Joe?" asked Chuck curiously.

He fumbled with his hands clumsily and reluctantly finished what he was saying.

"I hate to ask it, because I know you guys have had a hard one, but if I don't, we will all have it hard."

"You're asking us to leave?" said Tommy verifying the man's wishes.

He didn't have to say a word the two men could see it in his face.

"I'm sorry, but from what you guys have told me, I can't go back and get more supplies in the spring. The only thing I am going to have is what I've got left. With one, I can ration it out for a long time, but with four, we won't make it through the next winter."

"We can stock up this summer, by hunting, fishing and gathering up nuts and shit," said Chuck.

"You know we can't store any meat through the summer. These creeks don't have any fish worthwhile and there aren't enough nuts and berries around here to feed four men through a winter. You even said yourself you guys are almost out of ammo."

The three stood silent and for that moment they could actually hear the snow crash against the ground.

"I don't mean to push you out in the dead of winter; hell I wouldn't do that to a rat. You three can stay until the frost breaks, so to prepare for the next winter up here."

"No Joe, you're right, us being up here with you has put a hardship on you," rebutted Tommy.

"No, I'm thinking about the future."

"We will get our stuff together and be out of here tomorrow," stated Tommy.

"Don't jump the gun boy. I don't expect you to leave in all this."

"Every day we stay, the less you are going to have, if you could spare a few minor things to help us along, we can trade some of our meat as payment," conferred Tommy.

"Sure fellas, let me know what you need."

The two young men kept their host's request to themselves for the moment and let Jeff sleep in, saving the precarious confrontation until later that evening. They decided it would be best to break the news somewhere away from their host Joe, so as not to stir up another altercation. The two escorted Jeff out on what was supposed to be a quick hunting trip, but in reality it was nothing more than a facsimile to get him in an environment where they could minimize his reaction.

"Why the hell would you want to leave right now?" he asked surprised at their intentions to leave early the next morning.

"It's for the best," replied Chuck coolly.

"Going back into that damp dark cave in the middle of winter is for the best?"

"Yeah we've been eating this guy out of house and home," replied Tommy.

"Did that old fucker asked us to leave?"

"Yeah, but not right away, I figured since we are a hardship on him we should go out on our own as soon as possible," said Chuck.

"That was big of you."

"Yes it was," he said back quickly, "we are not going to force ourselves upon him."

"Man, fuck etiquette! This is survival! I saw some of the shit that old man had hidden under the floorboards. He had all kinds of flour, sugar and canned goods!" he screamed back. "I'll be damned if I am going to sit out here in this freezer and starve to death while he sits in that cabin and eats high on the hog!"

"We are not going to rob this guy," said Tommy furious at Jeff's suggestion.

"No we're not, we're going to make it on our own, just like our forefathers before us. I spoke with Joe and he is willing to lend us some of his tools so we can build our own cabin this summer and we can trade with him."

Jeff made a motion with his hands as if he didn't want anything to do with their new plan and walked off in frustration.

"You think he will try anything?" asked Tommy.

"I don't know him well enough to guess, but let's keep an eye on him."

"What are we going to hunt with once we run out of ammo?"

"I don't know, I guess the same way the Indians did hundreds of years ago, with bows, arrows... spears and shit."

"You've watched too many hours of the history channel," said Tommy amused.

"Anything is better than running from those ugly things, besides we might not have to stay up here too long."

"What do you mean?"

"I've been thinking a little about it and theoretically those things can't go on forever. I mean they're dead, surely they will eventually start falling apart from decay."

"Or starve and then we would have the run of the world... that doesn't sound too bad."

"Best scenario I can come up with at the moment."

The three men hiked back to their desolate cave and dug in for the long deathly cold night ahead. They had become spoiled from their previous nights in the old man's snug cabin and suffered through the icy night waking up to the morning's bitter frost with stiff joints. Their bodies ached from the combination of rime, bad nutrition and fatigue as they drudged through the day collecting firewood, foraging and building a lean-to tent to guard the entrance to their cave from the harsh winds that blew in from the mountain's peaks. Once their lean-to stood over the cave's entrance, a small inconspicuous smile came to their faces, but faded away as quickly as did their body heat drifting away through their thin outer clothing. In an attempt to build up their food stocks, while conserving what little ammunition they had left, the three men decided to try fishing down at a nearby creek before nightfall.

"You sure this is going to work?" asked Tommy skeptically.

"It's how they always do it in the movies when they don't have any fishing line," he said walking by his friend sharpening a long branch with his knife.

"I saw that movie and this place is a little colder than the Blue Lagoon."

They continued to walk along the river looking for a suitable place to slip down from the height of their trail's ledge to the base of the small swift creek below, when a cloud of snow swelled up around the men. Having lost his footing, Jeff slipped over the edge and began to slide down the rough hillside feet first as a child would on a sled. His two companions slipped down after him as fast as they could with their hands and feet to guide them down the steep snowy slope. Using his feet to guide him, Jeff leaned back to avoid a low branch and unwilling launched into the air off a hump soaring nearing six feet up into air before landing hard into the snow below and finally skidding to a stop.

"You okay Jeff?" yelled one of his friends following in his snow wake.

"Yeah, I think so," he said sitting up and checking his arms and legs for injuries.

Everything appeared to be in good order when he stood up and slipped back down to the ground coming face to face with a set of cold piercing eyes.

"Shit!" he screamed sitting up frightened.

They were a deep ice blue and gazed at him eerily from underneath frozen eyelids. Tommy was the first to reach Jeff and he quickly raised his shotgun toward the frozen and partiality exposed body. Jeff jumped up quickly so not to be within reach of the iceman. The man's eyes intently followed his movement.

"Oh shit!" yelled Tommy. "It's alive!"

Jeff pulled out a long stick he had fashioned as a crude club and raised it to end its miserable existence.

"Wait!" screamed Chuck. "Don't you get it…it's frozen solid."

"So?"

"Ever noticed that sometimes when we shoot these fuckers that their blood spatters like its dry?"

"Yeah," said Tommy.

"I don't think that blood pumps through their veins or arteries, meaning they can't keep themselves warm!"

"They're like reptiles!" said Tommy coming to the same hypothesis as his friend.

"How cold do you think it is?" asked Chuck to his friends forming a plan.

"I don't know but from where my nuts are hanging I would guess around ten," said Jeff sarcastically.

"And how cold do you think it is down in the city?"

A gleam came to each of their eyes as their minds aligned with the same theory.

"I don't know for sure," said Tommy, "but it's got to be below freezing!"

"Meaning those fucks down there could be like this guy, or at least as slow as slugs!" said Chuck finishing his friend's thoughts.

"Then let's go take it back!" said Jeff in excitement.

"What if it slipped down the hill like you did and broke its neck?"

"Tommy why do you always have to screw up my foolproof plans with a question?"

"I don't know… maybe cause they're not foolproof and I like to stay alive."

Chuck stood still staring back at the horrid creature watching the men helplessly and though out their latest options.

"We've got to know if he is really frozen or not before we go back down there with those things," said Chuck in concentration. "The last thing I want to do is be chased around by those bastards again."

"How the hell are we going to do that?" asked Jeff curiously.

"I guess we need to warm him up a bit."

"Who?" asked Jeff.

"Him," Chuck said pointing to the frozen body. "Let's get him back to camp."

Tommy looked at his friend as if he had lost his mind for making such a suggestion, but after seeing the stern look in his eyes he knew he meant to do just that.

Chuck took a hold of his arms while Tommy and Jeff reluctantly took a hold of one leg each dragging the infected corpse back to camp.

"Can we drop this fucker a sec and turn him over? I can't stand how he is watching me," asked Jeff.

"What are you bitching about?" replied Chuck never looking back. "If he wakes up he is going to bite my ass not yours."

"It is a little creepy," said Tommy in Jeff's defense.

"Okay, everybody stop looking at everybody back there," Chuck said joking, "because if I have to pull over everybody is going to be sorry."

The two men following smiled from the pun, but the constant stare of the man they were carrying swiftly brought back to reality the bizarre situation in which they were involved.

The young fire flickered, as it got stronger with each passing moment illuminating and warming their camp and the frozen man lying next to it. Three armed men stared back at the creature ready to end its existence with the slightest sign of movement.

"I think we should have tied him up," said Jeff.

"With what our ass hairs?" replied Chuck.

"I don't know, maybe a vine or something."

"This isn't the jungle."

Tommy held his shotgun ready ignoring the argument between his two friends and stared back into the man's eyes unblinkingly. There was nothing else in the world but those two eyes he thought, absolutely nothing. The two other men continued to argue about the best way to handle their circumstances, as Tommy held steady. The heat from the fire continued to grow and a bead of sweat formed on his forehead rolling down his face, but the paralyzed man never moved. Another drop of sweat swelled from his hair and rolled down into his eye. Tommy's eyes blinked from the sting of salt as the man roared to life assaulting the quarrelling men like an un-caged beast. The defrosted corpse's hands took hold of Jeff's neck and knocked him to the ground falling on top of his body bearing its teeth for the infection. A shot rang out from the tip of a barrel ripping the man's jaws from his face sending his teeth splintering into a nearby tree. The man's body flew to the side and Jeff used his feet to lift the man backwards into the air and squarely into the raging fire. The man crawled out of the tall flames with black scorched skin and ran toward his victim on fire only to have his skull collapsed by Jeff's heavy club.

"Damn Tommy that was one hell of a shot! That fucker's teeth are sticking out of this god damn tree… Woo!" screamed Chuck.

"Thanks Tommy," said Jeff stunned. "I didn't realize you were such a good shot."

"I'm not. I had sweat in my shooting eye, so I just pulled the trigger."

Chuck tried in several vain attempts to make another comment but neither of two men could understand him from his uncontrollable laughter.

"No one could duplicate that shot again in a million years and you did it without even looking!" he screamed in a roaring cackle with tears in his eyes. "Damn, Jeff, do you realize how close you came to biting it… how close you came to it biting you?"

Jeff's face got as pale as the moon above their heads and he sat down on a nearby log silent and visibly shaken.

Chuck held up his Boy Scout canteen and made a symbolic toast with a swig of water.

"Boys let's take back our city!"

Chapter 16
The Key to the City

Three sets of eyes stared through the brush fixed on the house they had so narrowly escaped a few weeks ago. The back door continued to swing back and forth banging against the wall as if it were in some perpetually recorded hypnotic loop beating away what otherwise would have been a dead silence. A light layer of snow barely half an inch deep covered the open ground, leaving a dangerously tattered and mingled field of tall brown grass crystallized haphazardly. Each set of eyes was well aware of how many infected were probably still lying in the suburban jungle ready to reincarnate at the slightest sound or movement.

"I hope it's cold enough," whispered Chuck.

"It's not near as cold as it was in the mountains, but it's still pretty fucking cold," said Tommy shivering.

"If we get out in the middle of that and it's just one degree too warm, then we are going to be nothing more than lunch," commented Chuck. "How are they hangin now Jeff?"

"Bout half way."

"Guess they can't make a decision either."

"Why should all three of us go?" asked Jeff. "It's pretty stupid for all of us to go, isn't it? At least this way if the shit hits the fan, only one would die."

"Sure knock yourself out hero," said Chuck nonchalantly. "Hell if you are feeling that brave, go ahead and kick one in the ass while you're at it and see what happens."

"Fuck you, I was trying to think of a way so all of us don't have to put our asses out on the line."

"How do you propose we pick which one of us runs interference?" Chuck replied.

"I don't know… draw straws?"

"We've got a better method than that," whispered Tommy. "The guy who brings up the plan is the one who puts it into motion, kind of cuts out really stupid ideas all together."

Jeff stood up with determination in his chin, walked out into the open and began a slow wary descent into the mouth of the field. Tommy stood up to stop him, but was held back by his lifelong friend.

"Let's see what he does."

The entangled grass broke apart with stiff resistance crunching like thin blades of glass underneath the soles of his feet. His feet sunk deeper with each step he took toward the house until he was waist deep in frozen grass and thirty some odd feet from the hauntingly inviting door. Lying on its deck slumped up against the wall was a partially decayed woman staring down between her legs. The old deck creaked loudly from the pressure of his foot sending a chill up his spine that escaped through his mouth in a shudder. He tiptoed up toward the slouched woman's body blanketing her in his tall slender shadow. His fingers sunk deep into her tangled dirty brown hair exposing her pale white face and sunken cheeks. Her flesh was rotted down to the bone exposing bloodstained teeth and a set of sunken eyes that rolled upwards to greet his own. They watched him longingly. He dropped her head and raised his leg back landing a deep kick directly into rear butt cheek rolling her over into an upside down heap.

"Hell has finally frozen over!" screamed Jeff with outstretched arms.

Tommy and Chuck jumped out from behind their hiding place hooting and hollering in excitement, and so began the largest shopping spree in American history.

The three men passed thousands of stiff zombies strapped in cars, lying on the ground and slumped over wherever the cold had overwhelmed their bodily tissues. Each man marched with a renewed spring in their step energized with an enthusiasm of condemned men who had narrowly avoided a last minute death sentence.

They walked from one side of town to the other before picking out a brand new truck straight off the lot. Their truck rolled from one location to another gathering up supplies, food, extra fuel, weapons and ammunition, until their bellies and truck bed were completely full.

"That old fuckin geezer kicking us out was the best thing that could have happened to us!" said Jeff mumbling through a mouth full of food.

"Shit, I had almost forgot about that poor old man," said Tommy in revelation, "and after what we told him about what was going on down here, he will starve up there before he comes back down."

"Serves him right," said Jeff.

"Where do you guys want to spend the night?" asked Chuck from behind the wheel ignoring Jeff's last comment.

"Let's stay down at the Marriott… in the presidential suite!" suggested Jeff in excitement.

"I just want to stay somewhere cold," said Tommy.

"What about Mrs. Criteon's place?" asked Chuck.

"The real estate lady?"

"Yeah, that old lady's place is a mansion with a giant ten foot high gate completely surrounding it."

"Hmm… sounds like the perfect combination of luxury and security," commented Jeff from the back of the truck cab.

Two bright beams of light uncovered the image of a tall double gate looming up from the surrounding fog and darkness.

"I'd rather not search the place during the dead of night," said Tommy from the comfort of their warm cab.

"We've got brand new assault rifles!" bragged Jeff. "We can handle anything that old bitch can throw at us!"

"Looks like the gate is locked anyway," said Chuck. "Let's bed down here tonight and check the place out in the morning."

Jeff argued his point for several more minutes, but in the end they locked up their truck and spent the remainder of the night parked in the entrance of Mrs. Criteon's driveway holding their rifles in their laps as children would teddy bears. The next morning Chuck awoke to a frozen windshield and the sounds of two men snoring so loudly that he had actually dreamed he had cut firewood with a chainsaw most of the night. He leaned forward with joints stiff from being crammed in their overcrowded truck, turned the key in the ignition and cranked up the heat. The sound of the truck's engine and the blast of warm air awoke the other two sleeping men.

"Who the hell farted all last night?" mumbled Tommy while rubbing the crust from his eyes.

"It was Chuck man," declared Jeff throwing a small bag of peanuts at the truck's driver. "I told him to lay off the chili yesterday."

Chuck blocked the flying bag of nuts with his arm while presenting a long uncontrollable smile, admitting his guilt to the other members of his party. The three men stepped out of the truck in their new winter coats and stood in single file examining the tall gate.

"Yeah real tight," said Chuck after shaking it and it failed to budge, "and it's going to be a bitch to climb it too, since the rails go straight up and there isn't anything to get a good footing."

"Let's drive right through it," suggested Jeff.

"Give me just a minute before you destroy our ride," answered Chuck concentrating on the structure of the gate. "Give me that rope we got back at the army surplus store."

Having passed over the security of the estate's gate, the men stood in a looming shadow cast down by the giant three-story home.

"Shit dude this place is a fucking palace!" said Jeff.

"Let's go sweep us out a palace," said Chuck, tired of sleeping in trucks, tents, caves and under the stars.

They found every single door and window on the ground floor to be locked tight and after much debate decided to break a small window so to gain entrance. Chuck was the first to step in finding himself in what was apparently the servant's dining area. The floor was littered with broken dishes and loose utensils, but the first thing that got his attention was that the interior of the immense home wasn't cold. Tommy and Jeff slipped in sliding over the kitchen sink and began to search around quietly. Dark dried blood was smeared across the kitchen table and down one wall in five long streaks as if put there by someone's or something's hand. No one spoke, but the movement of their heads and eyes communicated wholly their plans and intended direction. They quietly slipped out the small kitchen's door and moved down a long hall in a crouching walk. As they moved further in toward the center of the home the natural light from outside gradually faded away forcing them to rely on the unnatural yellow light of their flashlights. Their hands began to sweat against the stocks of their guns and they apprehensively noticed that they could no longer see their own breaths. The first room was vast den without windows that extended far out into the darkness. At the far end of it was an empty fireplace with a deer head hanging over the mantle.

"Why the hell is it so hot in here?" asked Jeff in a cautious whisper.

Chuck wiped the sweat from his forehead with his sleeve.

"I don't know," he said looking around the dark room for answers, "it doesn't make since that the heat would still be working. The power is out and surely if they got gas heat that shit would be down too."

"I don't like this at all," commented Tommy uneasily.

They searched around the room and after finding nothing to clue the group in on the home's strangely warm condition, they moved on down the hall toward a beam of light streaming from the end of the hall. Their forms faded away into the dark shadows of the long hallway as if they were ghosts until their material forms burst from the darkness into the bright light at the end of the hallway. They found themselves standing in the center of an enormous circular room with a high vaulted glass ceiling and four arched entries symmetrically surrounding its center. In the center of the room was an elegantly adorned fountain stagnantly quiet surrounded by marble pots housing dark green shrubs, trees and hanging plants. The light of the sun sparkled through the clear glass above feeding the room with enriching light, creating a near tropical heat.

"This place has a greenhouse!" said Jeff captivated by its beauty.

"It's a solarium. That's where the heat is coming from," said Tommy pointing toward the ceiling. "The sun shines into this room, creating heat that escapes through these four open doorways, heating the house.

"I'm glad you two find this place so great, because I don't find this architectural phenomenon so comforting…"

Chuck stopped in mid sentence interrupted by a shadow that glided up next to his feet and stopped cold. A dark figure dressed in a blood stained suit with a horribly deformed mouth and protruding teeth stood in the doorway watching him intently with evil eyes. A drop of infection fell from the tip of its front tooth falling and splashing quietly to the floor. The man leaped at Chuck with outstretched arms sending their two bodies sliding across the slick granite floor crashing into the base of the fountain. Chuck's reaction had been slower than his attacker's, but he had managed to get the barrel of his rifle between the two and centered on the crazed man's forehead. The shot spilled the man's brains out a huge cavity in the back of his head, spraying it across the polished granite floor. The shot echoed through the vast home from one room to another as if some part of a minor sonic boom, before tapering into a deadly silence. Not one of the three moved as they strained their ears through the ghastly silence that followed. Suddenly screams rang from up stairs, followed by the shuffling of feet and the scratching of hands dragging along the walls.

"Oh shit!" said Tommy in a troubled voice.

"Back outside!" screamed Chuck.

He leaped to his feet and rushed down the dark hallway recklessly leading the way back to the servant's kitchen. He kicked the swinging door open to find three figures in servant's uniforms standing with eyes fixed upon his entrance. He pulled the door shut and spun around bracing the door against the onslaught of their attack. Hands reached around the opening of the door trying to pull him in.

"Go back!" he screamed leaning against the door.

He held the door as long as he could before using it to propel himself down the hall toward his friends. The door slammed open sending small streaks of lights past his pursuers illuminating the long hallway enough for Chuck to see its end. A crowd of silhouettes plugged the doorway to the solarium blocking the light from its ceiling leaving the three trapped in utter darkness. Small balls of light flashed from the tip of Jeff's assault rifle sending metal slugs tearing through the scampering swarm of bodies rushing down the hall. The rounds struck the infected that charged down the hall tearing into their torsos, barely slowing the bloodthirsty horde of zombies.

"In here!" cried Tommy holding open the door to the den they had explored earlier.

Jeff was the first one to squeeze into the den, followed by Tommy and Chuck who led the mob of infected by only a few feet. They crashed against the door as Tommy slammed it in their faces holding it firmly with his shoulder. The three men desperately worked together to get the door sealed and bolted shut. The door shook cracking near its hinges partially splintering and sending shards of wood onto the floor. The three men frantically began to move furniture and any object that would move in front of the door until they were standing in a windowless room completely empty save the pile of junk they had piled near the rooms only door.

"Reload now," ordered Chuck thinking of the only thing they could do to better a near hopeless situation.

The fanatic creatures continued to beat at the door until it crumbled apart into a splintered pile exposing a host of infected creatures with wild eyes. They frantically swarmed over the pile of furniture hysterically racing to be the first of their multitude to pass on their infection. The three men set loose a volley of fire that lit up the dark room in wild flashes ripping into their targets and sending them spinning to the floors in all directions. Blood poured onto the floor from open wounds turning the room into a hellish slip and slide. More infected swarmed into the room like angry ants, crawling over the bodies of those that had fallen, more than willing to suffer the same fate for an opportunity to taste their flesh. Shots split heads and tore open cavities in the bodies of the oncoming dead bouncing them off the walls into neatly makeshift piles until there was nothing left but a jumble of torn bodies and oozing blood. Tommy stood in amazement on how many bodies were strewn on the floor.

"God damn, how many people lived in this house?"

"Mrs. Criteon lives here alone…I think we waxed the help."

Jeff kicked away the hand of an infected man that had fallen a few inches short from the tip of his shoe.

"Now they're true working stiffs," he said.

"Well, where the hell is she?" asked Tommy. "I've seen her rich ass mug on billboards all over town and not one of these is it."

They kicked through the pile of dead bodies failing to find a face that looked even remotely similar to the face they had all seen advertised on her many for sale signs around the city. Three sets of eyes looked upon each other with trepidation for a task not yet complete. Vigilantly, they entered the long dark hallway once again leaving behind the mound of death they had so desperately created. They walked through the warm solarium and into a wide-open vestibule layered in white marble, rich dark wood railings and the home's huge double front door, which had been bolted shut from the inside. Gripped along the wall of the large open room was a long winding stairwell leading upstairs to an extensive balcony lined with doors. They inaudibly walked up the deep stairway stopping at the balcony's first door. Chuck and Jeff stood to each side of the door, while Tommy held ready with his rifle. Chuck's hand took hold of the door's handle and after a small jiggle and a nod he slung it open. Tommy stood firm gripping the trigger on his gun ready to unleash its fury at a moment's notice. Only silence leaped at him and for the moment he held his finger steady. They moved from room to room, auspiciously finding each to be unlocked and empty until they reached the final door. It stood alone at end of the balcony resting quietly at its dead end holding the last secret of the colossal home. Chuck reached over and pushed the door's curved gold handle down feeling it come to a jolting halt as it banged against the door's stiff bolt. He rattled the thick varnished door, but it held steady in place. The sound of light ruffling came from behind the door seizing the three men's undivided attention. Chuck nodded to Tommy to take up his position. Not having the door's actual key, Chuck stepped back and prepared to use his boot as a universal key, only to be interrupted by a hand signal from Tommy.

"One sec while I switch to the shotgun… it has more kick."

Tommy slung his rifle onto his back and cradled his single barrel shotgun. Chuck stomped the door squarely in its center, but its broad construction absorbed the entire blow showing no signs of structural failure. A short moment of silence surrounded their small world before being awoken by the strange rustling they had heard earlier. Chuck eyed the door in frustration before pulling his hand axe from his belt. He raised it high above his head and brought its blunt end down in a swift arc upon the door's long handle. A spark leaped instantly from the point of contact between the two compositions of metal, sending the handle ricocheting to the floor and down onto the floor below. The door, no longer held in place by its deadbolt, swung open releasing a bright light from the room's massive back window engulfing the men in its blinding energy. A small withered shadow rushed out of the sun's radiation effectively eclipsing it into a black void. Tommy pointed his shotgun at its head and pulled the trigger at point blank range launching a burst of shot peeling the beings skin and hair from its skull. The small skinless headed frame flew headlong into Tommy knocking him backwards and over the balcony's railing. Jeff alertly took aim and fired his rifle into the back of the creature's glistening bonehead shattering it into flying shards of bone, brain and blood. Chuck ran over to the railing with wide eyes staring down at the distant marble floor. Five slender fingers held tightly around the base of a paling supporting the dangling body of his friend swinging some fifteen odd feet from the hard unforgiving floor below. A hand gripped the hanging man's arm and pulled him back up onto the balcony.

"What the hell was that?" asked Chuck in anger.

"What was what?" answered Tommy bewildered at his friend's sudden anger.

"That wasn't a fucking pumpkin ball you shot at that scrawny bitch!"

Tommy looked down at his shotgun with a confused look and ejected the shotgun shell from its chamber. A large red plastic shell casing flung from it smartly landing right into Jeff's outstretched hand. A thin curly stream of gray smoke streamed from his fingers, as if he had just lit a cigarette.

"That's squirrel shot," said his friend looking at it dryly.

"Shit, I forgot to switch back to a slug after hunting for those squirrels yesterday."

This time Jeff burst into an uncontrollable laughter, mimicking the similar laugh fest Chuck had burst into at the campfire when he had almost gotten infected.

"Nice shot there," said Tommy with a grateful gulp.

"Nah," said Jeff tossing the shell to Tommy, "the sun was in my eyes, I couldn't see shit, so I just let one rip. Let's call it even."

Chuck began to laugh along with Jeff at the irony of the situation, only Tommy stood without laughing gripping an empty squirrel shell.

Chapter 17
The Easy Life

Once they had successfully cleared out the old real estate tycoon's mansion, they dragged out its many dead occupants and fueled a huge bonfire off the property to rid the home of the corpses and the wretched stench of death that radiated out of their pores, ears and eyes as would a pungent scent from a patch of wild flowers. Fearing contamination, they stood up wind from a distance and watched the mangled bodies burn madly on into the night.

"I don't think we should have used so much diesel," said Chuck, fearful the fire might spread out of control.

Jeff took a long slurp from his beer before responding; "The heat is on…" he took another slurp from his cold can, "we'd better start stocking up while we can."

The men spent the next two weeks from sunup till sundown hoarding everything they could find, from absolute essentials to pure luxuries.

The three stood in the kitchen filling their cupboard with canned, boxed and bagged food.

"This is fucking great," said Tommy hungrily eyeing each can he shoved into the overcrowded cabinets. "We've got so much good stuff I don't know what to eat first."

"That idea of yours for each one of us to get a truck, so we could bring in three loads at a time instead of just one was fucking brilliant!" declared Chuck giving his friend kudos.

"I still can't believe we went all the way downtown to get you a dumb ass comic book!" said Jeff.

"Are you fucking kidding me?" said Chuck holding up the comic book with pride. "Spider-man number one, I have wanted this damn thing ever since I was old enough to look at a cartoon!"

"We had to cross three medians and dodge all that wreckage… not to mention the store owner who tried to eat us all for a freakin comic book!"

"Spider-man number one!"

"Sorry… Spider-man number wun!" said Jeff sarcastically. "That thing isn't worth the paper I wipe my ass on now."

"Hey, I didn't bitch when we took you to the pro golf shop to get you a new set of Cobra clubs."

"Golf!" screamed Jeff. "There is no greater game than golf!"

"Golf is a pussy's game," retorted Chuck.

"Golf is a real man's game," replied Jeff jokingly.

"A man's game my ass… my grandma played it until she was eighty."

"Then your grandma was one hell of a man."

Chuck stopped for a second while Tommy laughed; he had been burnt and he knew it, but he hadn't lost the argument yet.

"If you want to talk about a man's game then start talking about football."

"What, soccer?"

"Where the hell are you from Europe? No, American football."

"Football is for dumb-asses."

"They all have a college education."

"Don't go there," said Jeff laughing while pointing toward his debater. "Those guys all got free rides through college because of how fast they could run, not for their level of intelligence."

"Hockey kicks the shit out of both those sports. Golfers dress like bitches and make the crowd be quiet so they can concentrate, while football makes players wear helmets and allows pussy positions like kickers to control the game," said Tommy interrupting. "So why don't both of you quit arguing about meaningless crap and help me put all this shit up?"

"At least I could put a hole into a zombie's head if need be…I'd like to see you do that with your crappy comic book," said Jeff holding up one of his new clubs.

"Don't have to," said Chuck brandishing a shiny three fifty seven magnum pistol, "I've got this!"

Tommy shook his head from his feeble attempt to end their endless bickering, but it quickly fizzled out on its own.

Jeff walked over to the back door and pulled it open with a loud click letting the cold winter air rush into their cozy warm kitchen.

"Where are you going?" asked Tommy.

"You said you wanted help unloading all this stuff, so I'm going to start unloading truck number two," he said while holding up two fingers.

The door shut with a clank and the small room slowly warmed up once again from the power of the sun and the fires they kept burning all night and day in the mansion's three fireplaces. The room echoed with the clatter of shifting cans and bagged food being shuffled into the kitchen's deep cabinets.

"He's not so bad," said Tommy to break the silence.

"I know," replied Chuck decisively. "Hell, I enjoy arguing with him… spices things up a bit."

"Well don't make it so spicy around here that we can't stomach it any longer."

The small kitchen door swung open quickly banging against the tile wall startling the two men standing within it. Snow blew in from behind the shadowed figure standing in the doorway blocking off the bright sunlight.

"Look at what I found!" screamed Jeff.

"Good god you scared the shit out of me!" said Chuck slipping his pistol back into the holster on his hip.

He stood in the door with a look of exhilaration as if he had somehow discovered some great new secret. In his hand was a long skinny pole topped with a yellow triangle shaped flag embroidered with a white number one in the center of it.

The three men stood on the t-box in the cold winter wind looking out over the long stretch of snow-covered grass.

"Can you believe it?" asked Jeff in exhilaration. "This place has a par three hole!"

"It's covered in snow. How are you going to see the ball?" asked Chuck without the same excitement Jeff had about the discovery.

"You can't putt on snow, so I'll have to clear the green, but when it comes to seeing the ball all I have to do is use a yellow ball."

"So I assume we are going back to the pro shop in the morning?" asked Chuck confirming his intuition.

"Yep."

Over the next two months the three men lived in as much luxury as their city could support. Although they worked hard during the light of day chopping wood, hoarding supplies and hunting game, they spent their nights in extravagance. They brought power to their mansion through the use of generators, cooked the fresh meat of their kills outside on a propane grill, watched their vast DVD collection on their new high definition entertainment center and soaked away the aches of their muscles in a hot bubbling tub. They spent entire nights drinking, smoking, playing cards and laughing at whatever could still bring smiles to their faces, knowing all the while that harder times were to come. The cue ball came to a spinning stop passing on its energy to the number six ball, sending it with a clunk into its called corner pocket.

"I love this table even though it took us nearly an entire day to lug it up here."

Chuck walked around the table pulling his cigar from his mouth and in a puff of smoke called his next shot.

"What bothers me is that after some twenty odd trips into town, we haven't seen a single sign of another live soul out there," he said while taking a shot. "You'd think with all the zombies frozen more people would be out."

"Who says there is anyone else?" asked Jeff leaning against his pool stick.

"Come on, we can't be the only ones left," replied Chuck.

The eight ball sank into the side pocket.

"You're up Tommy," announced Jeff.

Tommy got up and took hold of the stick as Jeff passed it on to him in an admission of defeat and crashed onto the couch to watch the impending game.

"There are more people out there," said Tommy racking up the balls. "If a bunch of rabble like us made it, I know someone with preparation like, scientists, government officials, military installations survived."

The balls crashed together and ricocheted around the table bouncing against its soft walls, but not one found a home in the table's deep pockets. Chuck leaned back and watched Tommy line up a shot and call stripes. It dropped and the game was on.

"Those guys might be book smart," said Chuck comfortably buzzing from the alcohol content in his blood, "but what the hell do they know about survival?"

"That's true," said Tommy in agreement, "but the government had weeks to prepare before the infection struck and they had to have secured some type of research facilities or bomb shelters that could weather all this."

"Whether they did or not, I doubt they are stocked with as much beer as we have!" said Jeff in a toast.

The three men cheered in ignorant bliss through the dark cold night in the warmth of their new home and played pool until the sunlight broke without a care. Each one had taken a room upstairs and made it his own by filling it with whatever comfort he saw fit. As the sun rose, they slowly made their way toward their room shuffling through the large house. Tommy walked to the end of the hall past his two friends and stood in front of the doorway to the master bedroom. He had won the right to it in a late night poker game with the three and ever since, walking past the two down that long hallway brought a long smile to his face. They all fell asleep under the warmth of their plush covered beds and snoozed under the light of dawn.

"Good morning," replied Jeff to his roommate in the hall.

"Hey man, seen Tommy? He's not in his room."

"He went downstairs to start up a fire. You ready to go?"

"Yeah I'm ready," he replied rubbing his stomach.

They both walked down the stairs and slipped on their heavy coats to be ready for their daily scavenging trip into town. Nothing raised their spirits as much as stealing loot from the dead to benefit the living, namely themselves. They stepped outside and buttoned up their jackets to stave off the sharp cold wind.

"Where to today Tommy?" asked Chuck.

"Kinda figured we'd hit the north mall," said Tommy flipping sausage links carefully on the grill so they would not fall through onto the hot coals below.

"Cool, I want to get a down blanket and some satin sheets for my bed," replied Jeff.

"What the hell are you…the ladies man?"

"No but that shit is comfortable."

"As long as you don't start walking around the place in a smoking jacket."

The three sat in the lukewarm kitchen and ate breakfast before driving off in their small convoy of three trucks toward the north mall, dodging wrecked cars and rubble along the road. They pulled up toward the mall's south parking lot and cut the rumble of their engines long enough to inspect the mall's back entrance. The lot was filled with debris, broken light posts, scattered vehicles and stiff bodies of both the dead and undead, a truly chaotic scene frozen in time by the frost of winter. They pulled their trucks up to the back entrance and kicked open the giant doors wide enough to drive into the mall's wide walkway. Tommy opened the driver's side door to his truck, but froze when he felt something cold drop onto the top of his head. He raised his head up and watched another drop of water fall from a long icicle hanging from the edge of the mall's roof. It spiraled through the air glistening in the sun before ending its long plunge with a splash on his arm.

"Guys come have a look at this."

The two other men stopped their labor with the mall's doors and came over to stand next to him, then following the suit of their friend's actions, they both looked up toward the mall's roofline.

"I don't see shit," replied Jeff.

"The ice on the roof is melting."

"That's just the sun," he responded, "it will refreeze tonight."

Chuck reached over and touched a shaded part of the mall's wall, the ice on it was wet, instead of dry, as he had hoped.

"The frost is breaking," he stated sternly. "The fun is about over."

"That's it," declared Tommy, "no more bullshit, unless we need it we don't get it."

"Yeah," agreed his long time friend, "let's concentrate on fuel, ammo, food, propane and crap."

They jumped into their truck and sat in it silently with heavy thoughts. Each one knew that this moment had loomed on the horizon for weeks and was bound to arrive, but it still hit them with a new grave realization of an unsure future. The truck drove into the shadows of the dark powerless mall to start the rush of their last shopping sprees.

"I'm still getting that new blanket and sheets for my bed," said Jeff defiantly to himself.

They spent the next week in the confines of their mansion living up the last days of winter. Jeff spent every waking moment from sunup till sundown playing golf, while Tommy and Chuck spent most of their daytime hours shooting hoops. At night all three converged on the pool table to put away some beers, shoot the breeze and sink a few rocks. Jeff unrolled a small sandwich bag from his pocket and flopped it carelessly onto his lap. The two other men froze in thought and actions as their eyes converged onto the bag lying still on his leg.

"Is that what I think it is?" asked Tommy.

"The shit that killed Elvis! One full ounce… I've got six more where that came from," he replied smugly.

"Where did you get?" asked Chuck in excitement.

"Remember that house I said was my cousins the other day? It was really my main connection. I knew he would have a shit load. I just didn't say anything, since I didn't know if you guys were down or not."

"Man we spent most of our high school years being down… hell that shit is the reason I never graduated from college!" declared Chuck.

Jeff pulled a packet of rolling papers from another pocket and proceeded to roll a tight white stick. A lighter lit its tip and began the pass around. Tommy took a long puff and passed the number to Chuck who put it up to his lips and brought its tip to a bright red glow.

"Doesn't it bother you guys that we're doing nothing more than scavenging from the city of the dead?" said Tommy exhaling a creamy haze.

Chuck held his breath for moment pausing the conversation before letting a stream of smoke escape from his nostrils.

"Hell they don't need it," commented Chuck in a cloud of smoke. "Their brain cells are already dead!"

The cue ball lightly struck the number four ball, sending it into a slow roll across the table where it sat still for a moment at the corner pocket before it rolled in with a small clank.

"What do you want us to do, starve?" asked Jeff gripping the small joint between his thumb and index finger.

"You going to eat that wide screen and that DVD player we dragged in the other day?" asked Tommy.

"No," said Jeff coughing, "but if we're going to hold up here, we might as well be comfortable."

"When spring rolls around and those things thaw out, it's not going to be so comfortable in here."

"What do you think we should do?" asked Chuck while eyeing his next shot.

"I think we should fill up the three trucks with as much as they can hold and head back up into the mountains before it's too late."

"No fucking way, I am not going back up into those mountains and slowly starve to death with Jeremiah Johnson," said Jeff commenting on the mountain man they had met.

"We won't starve. This time we have the right equipment. Tents, kerosene heaters… and every winter we could come back and stock up."

"Come on, look at this place! None of us had it this good before the infection hit!"

"Tommy," said Chuck reassuringly, "Jeff's right, that gate is pretty secure. We're not going to find anything better than this. All we got to do is hold up here through the summer and go on another winter shopping binge."

"Then what? When does it all ever end?"

"I don't know, but it's living; and these things just might decay away in a few seasons and we can start over, go out and find other people. I know there have to be other people out there besides those assholes back at the nuclear plant."

"There better be," said Jeff, "because if we don't find any chicks, our hands sure are going to get tired over the years."

"Hey… Moo Jeff Shoo if you can see through those Chinese eyes rack em up."

"Roger that Wang Chuck Chang."

Chapter 18
Death Springs

A new season took hold, beget by the warm winds that churned from the earth's rotation upon its axis as it tilted closer to the sun, bringing forth new life and revitalizing the dead. Flowers sprang from the soil in bright colors decorating the surrounding woods of their compound, only to be trampled back into the mud by the rising dead. Three straight days of temperatures above freezing brought the first of many to the outside of their home's tall outer barrier. The dead crowded against it in force pushing each other, as would a mad riot, all the while watching every movement of those inside intently with hungry wild eyes. Three forms lay still on the top of the vast mansion's roofline observing the ever-increasing danger that continued to converge around the property line. The dead moaned and shook the gates from all sides blocking any possibility of escape while clawing at the fence's thick bars in an attempt to get through.

"That one in the blue vest," suggested Jeff acting as a spotter.

Chuck looked through the scope on his tripod sniper rifle and observed the recommended target.

"Man… that guy worked at Wally World," he said defensively. "He worked harder and made less than anybody out there."

He paused a moment searching the crowd of berserk dead for a more suitable target, stopping the crosshairs of his scope on the center of one's head.

"That fucker right there," he said pointing. "The one in the three-piece suit."

"Looks like a lawyer to me," replied Jeff.

"I bet he made a shit load of money off of other people's misery, doing divorces and estate planning and shit," said Chuck in disgust.

The other two men brought up their binoculars and brought his intended target into their sights.

"That's a long shot," said Jeff in response. "I bet you don't get the round through the gate."

A loud boom resonated from the tip of the rifle echoing off the home's multi level roof cracking the air above their heads and screaming off into the distance. The round hit the man wearing the blue vest dead center in his nose collapsing his face into the back of his skull and driving his body backwards into the mob of dead clawing at the gate.

"God damn, you were so far off you hit the guy next to him," screamed Jeff.

Tommy pulled down his binoculars. He had seen his friend pull off shots with far more difficultly through dense trees.

"He didn't miss."

"I thought you said you were going to cut him a break?" asked Jeff.

"I did, I figured I would let that rich fucker suffer instead."

"Well I'll be dammed," said Jeff softly. "That is one bad ass rifle."

"Don't you two realize that every shot you make kills one and brings six more?"

"We're trying to do our part in controlling the dead population. Don't forget to have your local zombie spayed or neutered," replied Jeff. "Hey Chuck, let me have a crack at that bad boy."

Chuck handed it over and Jeff set it up eagerly eyeing through its sight looking for his first target.

"So who are you going to take a shot at?" asked Chuck eyeing all the possibilities in the distance.

"That little ankle-biter in the blue shirt over there. Seeing little kids as those things creeps me out."

Another explosion echoed off in the distance startling the few birds that had not been scared off from their earlier shots. Their wings carried them safely into air away from any danger that the dead could possibly pose. A dazzling spark leaped from one of the gate's long bars, ricocheting the slug away from its intended target and sinking into the chest of a large lady knocking her to the ground. The fat decaying form disappeared into the crowd for a moment before it leaped back up to its feet and continue its fight against the gate as if it hadn't been injured at all.

"Guess it's the man that's bad ass and not the rifle," said Chuck slyly.

The dim light illuminating the room flickered from the connection to the outside generators barely breaking the dark shadows that hovered in the corners of the large room. A warm fire held back those dark cold corners, comforting them only slightly. Cries of pain and hunger coming from the dead could be heard plainly from within the thick walls of their fortified mansion.

"God, do those things ever shut up? I mean they haven't seen hide or tail of us in eight hours!" commented Jeff from the comfort of his lavish armchair.

"I can't think of a world more fucked up than one where the living can't sleep for the noise of the dead," commented Tommy.

"They know we are in here," said Chuck while chewing. "They're not going to leave until we either kill them or they kill us."

"I vote we kill them," said Jeff.

"Fat chance of that… three against an entire city of roughly a million," inserted Tommy.

"One thing is for sure we can't go outside anymore," stated Chuck. "Tomorrow night after it gets too dark for them to see us, we can load the trucks up in case we need to make a break for it."

"Have you seen how many that are out there? There is no way we could break through that. I think we should stock everything we need upstairs and knock the stairs out so they can't get up," declared Jeff.

"Let's do both," said Tommy calmly appeasing both parties involved. "That way we have options, but one thing is for sure we can't go outside anymore not even for golf."

"What?" replied Jeff surprised. "Now that all the snow is gone I can actually play with a white ball."

"It gets them too excited."

"I've got to keep playing to keep up my skills. Hell, I might be the best in the world, considering Tiger is a zombie now."

"He could still kick your ass in a round of golf... zombie or not," joked Tommy.

"Shit, I shot a 53 yesterday."

"You shot a par three eighteen times," laughed Tommy. "It doesn't count."

"Dude, fuck off and take off your shoes." replied Jeff aggravated that his friend always kept them on since the dead had arrived. "Stay a while."

"Screw that! I'm going sleep in them as long as those things are out there... with the laces double knotted, just in case."

Chuck laughed between shoveling peanuts into his mouth.

"You're going to get athlete's foot," predicted Jeff.

"Guess I'll just have to scratch my feet after you're dead."

The three men laughed in an almost grizzly humor, for it was the only comedy left on earth, at least any earth known to the three. They went to bed early that night tormented by the cries of those that hungered for live flesh, but although they lay still with their eyes closed, no one rested, especially the dead.

The next night, they moved the trucks in the darkness of a moonless sky without the aid of the trucks' lights and parked the vehicles by the back kitchen door. They packed the trucks with everything that would be essential to a fresh start, in case they had to make a quick exit. The first truck was loaded with clothes, food and camping provisions, while the second was packed down with nothing but fuel and ammunition, a volatile but necessary combination. Then they concentrated on the conversational remodel of their home from that of a luxurious palace to a crude but modern fortress. They stocked the upstairs portion of the home with all their major supplies and then with the use of sledgehammers, sweat, muscle and a little blood tore down the long marble and oak-wooding staircase that was the only way upstairs and boarded up every window and door in the home, save for the kitchen door. For it, they had made a long flat board-like wall with stilts sliding out from it so that it could slide up against the door and nailed to it and the floor making it a formidable barrier. A long homemade rope ladder was the only way upstairs and it was never left hanging unless no one was upstairs. Once every imaginable preparation had been made, the men finally rested and did the only thing there was left to do, wait.

A loud cracking noise awoke the three men from their light slumber bringing the three stumbling out of their rooms into the upstairs' catwalk. They looked at each other in bewilderment still drugged under the adverse effects of being awakened in the middle of the night.

"What the fuck was that?" whispered Chuck in case something or someone was in earshot.

They could hear loud screams and moans coming from outside, much too loud for their comfort.

"I don't know, but it sounded like a tree falling or something," retorted Jeff.

Chuck slung the rope ladder over the railing and dropped down to the first floor.

"Where the hell are you going?" asked Tommy from above.

"To see what the hell that was."

The other two men followed and began to peer out of the home's bottom floor windows.

"The front gate is fine," reported Chuck.

"So is this side," yelled Jeff.

Tommy ran to the other side of the house and peeked through a crack in the boards over the window. A dark figure stood was standing outside the window looking around unemotionally in the yard. Their eyes met and in a flash the dull quiet moment exploded with the glass between Tommy and the shadow. Shards bounced against the window's wooden barrier sending Tommy backwards, while covering his eyes. Fingers gripped and tugged at the cracks between the boards, bowing them outward slightly, but they rebounded quickly and held firm. Chuck and Jeff bolted into the room with their guns drawn in response to all the commotion.

"The east fence is down!" screamed Tommy.

"The kitchen door!" yelled Chuck running toward the kitchen.

The three men ran down the long dark hall toward the kitchen as if trying to outrun time itself in an attempt to seal it off before it was too late. The sounds of breaking glass came from all around the house hastening their pace into the kitchen. The three hectic men burst onto the kitchen's smooth tile floor sliding across and crashing into the farthest cabinet. Arms had burst through the kitchen door's small windows and were struggling to get inside. Jeff pulled a machete from his belt holster and began to chop at the flopping arms gashing deep cuts into the exposed flesh, but failing to deter their movement. Tommy and Chuck took hold of their makeshift barrier and slid it up against the door ramming it into the shifting arms crushing the wiggling limbs in between the door and the wide board. Jeff ran over to the counter drawer and pulled out a bag of long nails and a hammer. Chuck leaned his back against the barrier holding it in place against the door as it rocked back and forth from the force of the two struggling sides.

"What are you doing?" he asked.

"Nailing this damn thing down."

"How the hell are we supposed to get out of here?"

"I'm not getting out of here," he argued. "I'm not going anywhere near those things out there."

"How long do you think a few boards and nails are going to hold, "he screamed back, "till next winter?"

"No, but long enough for us to get upstairs!"

"If you want to climb up there and be part a living zoo on display for the dead the next seven months be my guest, but I'm not going to be trapped by hundreds of walking dead without anywhere to go!"

"Are you fucking crazy?" shouted Jeff. "Because if you're talking about going out into the dark with that army of walking pus, then you have lost your fucking mind!"

The sounds of shattering glass came from down the hall near the front door, followed by the high-pitched noise of creaking wood.

"You can stay here in this death trap if you want and we will leave you like we found you, trapped all alone in the top of some house."

Jeff looked over at Tommy and he could see in his face that he was going too. He pulled up his assault rifle and nodded.

"Fine, I'll go out with you, but when those things are eating us I am going to tell you… told you so."

The crashing sound of splintering wood swept down the hall from the front of the house like a rushing flood of panic drenching the three in fear. Each knew they didn't have long before the thin defense they had constructed would crumble under the weight of dead and soon fill the house with their lust for flesh.

"Tommy and I will take the first truck, Jeff you take the second."

"Sure I'll take the one full of bullets and flammable diesel."

"You want me to take it?" asked Chuck frantically.

"No, but if I crash those fucks are going to get a rip roaring barbeque."

Chuck pulled out two pistols from his belt and held them up to both sides of his face.

"Time to dance with the dead," he said dryly.

The men pulled back the barrier and unlocked the kitchen door, letting in a flurry of dead that fell in a volley of gunfire. The men burst out in the back yard in the dark of night with their guns blazing. A barrage of bullets cleared a path to their trucks bursting heads wide open from the force of gunshots from only a few feet away. The red truck beeped on command from the control in Chuck's hand, unlocking the doors and signaling the roaming dead with flashing lights. Tommy hurdled over the driver's side into the passenger's seat in one broad leap and landed squarely in it. Chuck flew into the cab right behind him and tried to shut the door, but it bounced back open. His hand caught the handle on it before it could swing wide open exposing the truck's innards to the mass of dead clawing at the truck from the outside. He looked down to see what was stopping the door from closing. A large black hand had somehow reached in the cab and had a tight grip on his seatbelt strap. He began to slam the door repeatedly as hard as he could in an attempt to break its grip, but failed. The dead began to swarm around the truck and in an attempt to break in were rocking the truck it back and forth, threatening to turn it over. Tommy hysterically crawled into the backseat and took hold of the driver's side door handle holding it shut.

"I got it! Go! Go! Go!" he yelled.

Chuck looked back at the truck behind him and saw Jeff's truck lights flash. Squealing tires pushed the lead truck forward slinging grass in all directions as it bowled over the mob of creatures dragging the one holding onto his seatbelt along. Dead began to chase the trucks through the yard recklessly throwing themselves in the vehicle's paths. One bounced onto the hood, rolled over the roof and landed into the bed of the truck. It rose up onto it knees and began to pound on the truck's flimsy back window. Tommy spun around startled by the beating on the window above his head and while still holding the door shut with one hand, raised a pistol. The shot rang out nearly bursting the small cab's occupant's eardrums raining a shower of glass shards into the cab. The slug struck the infected man directly in the forehead sending his body backwards and out of sight into the back of the truck. The two trucks picked up speed and headed straight towards the front gate. It stood stoutly locked defying the force of dead still pushing against it from outside the compound.

"Get ready, we're going through!" yelled Chuck.

He stomped on the accelerator forcing it all the way to the floor and subconsciously closed his eyes. The truck burst into the gates dead center splitting them open in a burst of sparks and broken metal. The gates sprung open dividing the dead standing behind them with a swinging force that crushed the mob against the stone entrance. White smoke bellowed out of the truck's crumpled hood engulfing the entire front of the truck and completely obscuring the driver's view. Going by feel, the driver spun the steering wheel to the left and sped down the road blindly through a cloud of white smoke. He quickly rolled down his window and stuck his head out in an attempt to see where he was going, but was overwhelmed by the smoke that began to flow into the cab. The truck raced down the road erratically dragging loose pieces of metal, plastic and the dead. The temperature gauge in the dashboard shot into the red and after a high winding from the engine, the vehicle shut down to a slow roll stopping in a ditch. Chuck swung open the driver's door and placed his foot on the neck of the infected man that had continued to hold on the entire time.

"Let go you stupid fuck!" he shouted in frustration.

He fired his pistol at it from point blank range splattering skull and brains across the road. The second truck pulled up squealing to a skidding stop.

"Hurry up, they're coming!" screamed Jeff.

Vaguely illuminated by the red taillights of Jeff's truck was a horde of infected scurrying up the road toward the two trucks in the darkness emitting dreadful screams into the night. Tommy and Chuck began to seize everything they could from the wreckage in a frenzied race to save as much as possible. They slung bags and sacks of supplies from one truck to another as if they were being fast forwarded on a video with fire in their blood. They grabbed every last possible bag that time allowed and leaped into the truck making a quick getaway with only seconds to spare.

"So what's next?" asked Jeff staring over the hood of their truck into the dark foggy night.

"Well, after much consideration and recent events, I've come to the conclusion that Tommy's plan is the best one."

"Man, fuck you," replied Tommy lightly. "And why are you laughing? Hundreds of people trying to eat us during a high speed chase isn't funny."

"I know," he agreed while smiling. "I'm just glad to be alive right now."

"Oh shit!" said Tommy shifting through the many bags in the cab. "We didn't get either one of the tents!"

"Damn!" said Jeff frustrated.

Chuck began to shift through jumble of bags, but came up with the same disappointing results. In the hectic shuffling of bags from one truck to the other they had left both of the tents.

"I'm not going to go back and sleep in that damp old cave," declared Jeff from behind the wheel.

"Calm down, we'll make a quick pit stop and pick up some new ones on the way," said Chuck calmly.

"Those things are running all over the city," replied Tommy.

The truck swerved, sending Chuck and Tommy crashing into the side the truck.

"What the…" asked Chuck rubbing the side of his head.

"One of those things was standing in the middle of the road."

The two men quickly clicked their seatbelts into the locked position.

"Well, slow down, they can't run forty miles an hour."

"Let's find a quiet out of the way place to get through the night and in the morning we can get a few things and head into the mountains until next winter."

"Sounds good… so where to?" asked the driver.

"Pinky's Point."

"Hey, I like you guys, but not like that."

"Yeah, yeah…. just head that way, you whore."

Every youth and everyone who had ever been young in their city knew about Pinky's Point. It was rural wooded spot far out of the way from the city. A shiny blue truck pulled up toward the bluff and came to a rumbling stop, cutting its engine and lights leaving the small clearing in a silent gloom. Worn from the long night, they leaned back in their seats and fell asleep in the cold dark without saying a word.

A long horizontal beam of light broke over the bluff and sparkled through the dew-covered window of the damp truck's exterior waking its driver. He leaned up and rubbed the sleep out of his eyes so to better see the area. He had been to the point several times himself as an adolescent, but he had never seen it during the light of day. Somehow it seemed much smaller than he remembered. His door opened quietly on its new hinges letting in a cool damp breeze that gave him a chill. He zipped up his coat and quietly closed the door shutting himself off from the warmth of the truck's cab and placing himself in a state of isolation. He lit a cigarette and stood at the edge of the cliff overlooking a calm vast lake. A still fog hung over the smooth water. The head of his cigarette glowed bright red as his lungs drew enriching oxygen through its long paper cylinder. An infected man wandering through the woods saw the small intense flame shoot from the man's hand and his hunger grew to an insatiable level. Running through sharp thorns, the man tore through the rough underbrush screaming in the anticipation of sharing his curse of living death. Jeff, although startled, drew a pistol from his belt and shot the man three times before he launched off the cliff, disappearing into the treetops below. Tommy and Chuck leaped out of the truck stumbling in disarray with their guns drawn.

"Good morning guys," said Jeff still puffing on his cigarette.

"Did you use that gun to light your cigarette or did you actually shoot something?" Chuck asked looking around aggravated.

"We had a visitor, but he had a flight to catch."

Chuck and Tommy rubbed their heads too confused before their first cup of coffee to ask any further questions. The men made some coffee and ate some boxed donuts before hitting the road again.

"So where to?" asked Jeff from behind the wheel.

"The sporting goods store near fifth. They should have some nice tents," said Chuck from the backseat. "There is a wooded area behind it. We can park on the other side of it and walk right up to it, without being out in the open."

"You know we don't have to have a tent," replied the driver. "We could always make a lean-to tent from the tarp we got covering up the back."

"No fucking way man, we're going to be up there all summer. The bugs will eat us alive. And if I have to scratch my nuts all summer long, I want it to be because I'm comfortable not because some chigger has burrowed in it."

"You know you like it."

"Interspecies sex baby," replied Chuck from the backseat.

"Well they do say opposites attract," commented Tommy.

"If you mean opposites as in a dick and pussy, yeah then opposites attract."

"What about your fiancé? Didn't you two have something else between you besides sex?"

"I loved her more than anything, but I'll tell you right now I wouldn't have gotten engaged, or even gotten to know her, if she hadn't had a snatch."

"I'll admit that when I'm with a chick and it's not serious, sex is what I'm after, but when it comes to a long-term relationship, there has to be more than just sex."

"More is just icing on the cake, but without sex there's no cake. Just think about it, all marriages are based on sex. Shit why the hell would you marry a chick if there weren't any sex involved?"

"Kids maybe?"

"Oh yeah," laughed Jeff, "like you're going to live with some woman for sixty years without sex to have a kid. What are you going to do with her once the kid moves off? If there was no such thing as sex, would you spend your entire life with some bitchy woman or with your friends who have the same interest?"

"Damn, the quintuplet has a point," said Chuck.

Laughter echoed through the truck's small cab, followed by a few more randomly innocent insults.

The truck pulled quietly through the thick brush dragging deep unsightly scratches into its shiny new clear coat finish coming to a stop a few feet from the edge of the tree thicket. They exited the sides of the truck as if part of a swat team, all wearing empty backpacks and running from tree to tree so as not to seen. They ran across the small clearing between the thicket and the back of the shopping center swinging their rifles in their hands in an uncomfortable low run. The bright morning sun cast a long dark shadow along the back of the building concealing their movement along it. A head poked out of the shadows and peered around the side of the building, which radiated a slow heat from its hours of direct exposure to the sun's rays.

"Looks clear," said Chuck turning his head towards his friends. "Let's move in and out real quick."

The three men ran along the brightly sunlit parking lot that looked more like a junkyard than a shopping center with jumbled cars and piles of trash. They had made it nearly halfway across when they stopped at the sight of six men dressed in camouflage. They were all carrying rifles and whispering to each other in good humor as they came around the side of a building heading toward the same sporting goods store. Chuck and Tommy recognized one of the men as the soldier that had run them off with gunshots a few months back at the nuclear plant.

"Hey over here!" yelled Jeff excited that they had finally found someone else.

Tommy tried to warn Jeff diving toward him, but before he could, Jeff's words had already rung out across the parking lot. Burst of gunfire tore through the cool morning breeze awakening everything. Jeff's hand was still extended high into the air signaling the men, when he jolted backwards from the force of a round collapsing his chest, falling into Tommy's outstretched arms. Tommy fell onto his backside holding his friend in his lap. Blood gushed from his chest covering his entire front side soaking into his clothes and running onto the pavement. Chuck leaned down behind a parked car and returned fire forcing the soldiers to take cover around the side of the building.

"How is he?" yelled Chuck.

"He's gone," said Tommy holding the body of his dead friend.

"God damn it!" screamed Chuck. "I'm going to kill every one of those fuckers!"

Tommy sat still staring at the torn body of his friend in a trance.

Gunfire burst into the car in front of him, but dazed by the loss of his friend, Tommy never flinched. A hand tugged at his shoulder.

"Come on!" screamed the clouded voice. "We've got to get out of here!"

Tommy looked up in a reverie toward the commanding voice and saw that it was coming from the hazy image of his lifelong friend. Suddenly more gunshots ripped into the car covering the two men jerking it slightly with loud thuds. The strange mist around him cleared and abruptly he found himself back in the war torn parking lot holding a dead body in the middle of a gunfight.

"Leave him! We've got to get out of here."

Tommy slid out from under the blood-covered corpse and leaned up against the car in a low crouch. More shots hit the car behind him ricocheting into its interior shattering the glass window above his head.

"Go, I'll cover you to the next car!"

Chuck rose up over the bullet riddled car's trunk and returned fire successfully pinning the men down behind another car about a hundred yards away. Tommy made the next car and emptied a clip into the car covering the opposing soldiers giving Chuck enough time to roll up beside him. Chuck in turn took over firing upon the men effectively beginning a leapfrog for the two men until they made the side of the large building near their truck.

Chuck stood at its corner and fired into the parking lot.

"They're moving up on us."

A bombardment of gunfire hit the corner of the building shattering a piece of the block wall into flying shards and concrete smoke. Chuck spun his head around and held his cheek in pain, smearing a small trickle of blood across it.

"Go, we've got to make the truck."

They ran for their lives across the small grass area between the back of the building and the wooded area concealing their truck. If the soldiers got to the back of the building before they made the safety of the trees they would be easy targets, targets easy enough for even a greenhorn to hit. Both breathed a small sigh once they reached the shade of the trees and the sight of their truck's blue exterior. Shots began to rip the bark off trees as leaves fell from their perch and danced around in a twirling flutter. Chuck leaned up next to a tree and looked over his shoulder through the thickets of trees toward the building. Through the hanging brush he could see four of the soldiers running through the small grass clearing, while two more stood at the end of the building firing into the woods.

"They're still coming!" screamed Chuck in a sprint.

Tommy had never stopped running and made the truck first. He impulsively reached into his pockets to retrieve the key, but found them empty. He had not driven, he thought quickly. Jeff had been the driver.

"Shit!" he screamed at the top of his lungs. "Jeff has the keys!"

"Ah… fuck!" replied his friend huffing and puffing from the long sprint.

Tommy pulled up the barrel of his rifle and fired directly into the driver's side window shattering it into thousands of pieces, before reaching inside and pulling out a bag full of ammunition. Chuck followed suit and slung a bag over his shoulder before sprinting off behind his friend. They made their old neighborhood and hid in a network of drainage tunnels they had played in as children.

"I remember these things being much larger as a kid," commented Chuck crawling down the long round tunnel no more than three feet in circumference.

"No kidding, I haven't been in these things since I was twelve when we used to go tunneling almost every day."

"Remember how we used to crawl through them and name them like they were roller coasters?"

"Yeah," said Tommy trying to keep his knees dry from the small trickle of water that flowed down the center of the small tunnel. "This one was the snake I think."

"That little room should be up ahead."

When they crawled into the underground room, both immediately noticed how right he had been in describing it as little, as it stood no more than four feet tall and five feet wide in dimensions. A clutter of sticks and leaves littered the center of its base. They leaned up in opposite corners as they had as children and once again hid from the world.

"God, I remember when we talked that chubby kid Jason to come down and ride the snake, he cried the whole way through," said Chuck reminiscing.

"He was in jail last I heard. Shit, he might still be alive in there, I can't think of many places more secure than that."

"He was a pussy, so I'm sure he became a hood ornament for some big nigger's dick anyway."

They paused a moment and let their hearts slow down.

"So, what's the plan now that we've lost everything?"

"These two bags of ammo are our ticket to anything we want."

"Back to the mountains then?"

"Yep, but I want to settle a little score first."

"Going back there is only going to settle one thing… and that's us."

"You're telling me that after what they did to Jeff you're going to just let it slide?"

"I want to blow the shit out of the fuckers as much as you do, but I don't think getting ourselves killed is going to teach them a lesson."

"Jeff was one of us and they blew him wide open for no reason! That could have been one of us lying out there in that parking lot!"

"We barely got out of there alive and you want to go back for more? I counted six back there… and I know they didn't leave their base unguarded."

"Don't puss out on me now! If that had been me that got shot out there, would you be telling Jeff the same thing right now?"

"I'm not pussing out you stupid shit! I'm just not into suicide pacts! How the hell are two guys on foot going to successfully attack a military compound full of soldiers while they're trying to dodge zombies?"

"I've got a plan," said Chuck coolly.

"Oh, you've got a plan? Well that changes things, now I know I'm out."

As friends, the two had been through literally hundreds of his plans and every one had a certain element of risk, an element of risk that was usually too high for Tommy's own interest of self-preservation.

"You may have talked me out of it last time, but this time I'm going after them with or without you!"

Tommy sat in his dark corner without answering and the two of sat in quiet for several moments before he finally broke his silence.

"What's your plan?"

A wicked look oozed from his eyes from across their small dark concrete shelter.

"We're going to open up the gates of hell on these mother fuckers. Ever hear the saying the enemy of my enemy is my friend?"

Chapter 19
A War within a War

The two men sat high upon the hill kneeling low in its swaying grass observing the tall cooling towers with the assistance of binoculars. They waited patiently and watched the actions of the men in the compound for three days noting their actions and the timing of their routines with their wristwatches. They wanted revenge, but were in no rush, as they wanted a complete and final retaliation. The soldiers worked on four hour guard shifts, both day and night with one man stationed in the foxhole at the main gate with the duty of picking off infected and another that walked the perimeter looking for stragglers that found their way up against the fence line. On several occasions during their stakeout, an infected would wander within the range of one of the guards and to Chuck and Tommy's delight, whether it took one shot or three to drop the creature, no one came out to see what the shooting was all about.

"They're too comfortable with their situation," replied Chuck after watching the soldier in the foxhole rise up and kill an infected woman with two shots.

"I noticed that," said Tommy from behind his binoculars. "The other guy on shift didn't even come to see what was up."

"Their complacency evens the odds a bit."

Tommy's keen eyes focused down upon the secured compound eyeing the situation subjectively, "Knocks them up a couple of notches from impossible."

"Thirty minutes after the first evening shift, it begins. That way it will be dark by the time we get back with the party."

Chuck lay down, putting his hands behind his head disappearing into the tall grass, staring into the clear blue sky through the eyes of a prisoner on a dead planet.

"Did you ever think about how fucked up all this is?" asked Tommy still observing the compound below.

"It's hard not to, especially since about everyone I meet tries to eat me," said the voice from within the grass.

"I know but I mean about how this damn disease nearly wiped everyone out, but instead of uniting against it, here we are warring against each other like independent tribes or something."

"I'm all for live and let live, but these fuckers stirred up my belief in kill before being killed; besides did you ever think that this was what was supposed to happen? That this epidemic is nothing more than the final part of some big picture, some great plan that won't allow anything or anybody to get too powerful? Hell, if anything has gotten out of control, it's man. We cut everything down, pollute our surroundings and create weapons powerful enough to destroy everything. Maybe this is the natural order of things... maybe this is nature's way of cleansing herself of us. Everything has its rise and fall, the Romans, the dinosaurs, the fucking dodo. How the fuck do we know that this isn't what destroyed the dinosaurs?"

"Zombie dinosaurs?"

"Yeah they fucking get infected, eat each other and boom they're extinct and we come along build up and bang, it happens all over again. Maybe you and I are resisting destiny… maybe we're just fighting against the natural order of things."

"Maybe I don't give a shit about destiny."

The men laughed breaking the hard silence that had dominated the past three days. A cool wind swept down the slopes of the mountains racing across the valley below, swallowing the two men in a tidal wave of swishing air and cutting into every exposed part of their body, making an already uncomfortable situation even more unnerving. They waited until the men in the compound switched shifts, and they did so on the minute. The two shifts chatted together and burst into laughter before going separate ways and leaving the compound under its scheduled guard pattern. Chuck put his eye gently against the rim of his scope and brought it to bear on his target. The man stood still chewing tobacco and watching the long wide field that lay broken in half by the main gravel road leading up to the plant's main gate. The crosshairs sat squarely in the center of the man's head hovering directly on his ear. This was the most important shot of his life he thought, one he couldn't afford to miss. Their entire plan's success depended on being able to make two perfect shots. If either failed, so would their plan and his vengeance. His rifle jiggled a bit from the pressure of such a long shot. He paused and pulled back his eye to regain his composure. A deep brown eye bent on seeing the task through returned itself to the scope and set the target. He had shot many an animal and infected in his time, but this was different somehow. He could feel it in the pit of his stomach; it churned uncomfortably as if he had eaten something bad. It was no different than a deer, for it was alive too he thought, it was no different than killing a deer, but he knew it was a lie as he gently squeezed the trigger. The man's body went limp and slumped down into the foxhole out of sight. They watched the foxhole through their binoculars in quiet anticipation, but the man never rose. Chuck quickly turned his rifle over to his left and waited for his second target to come into view.

The man walked up along the fence line casually smoking a cigarette. His second shot would be far more difficult, not only because his target was moving, but also because he only had a small window of opportunity for a clear shot over the fence. Otherwise he would have to try and make the shot through the fencing before he came around and was alerted by the body of his partner. The dark form of the man's head came into view slightly protruding over the top of the fence. His eyes peered through the tightly linked fence on the lookout for infected. Chuck slid the cross hairs over the man's face and calmly squeezed the trigger. The man's body flipped backwards into an unnatural arc collapsing into a limp heap. The two men on the hill sighed in relief. They had successfully completed the first part of their plan.

"I'm going down to cut the chain on the front gate. Pick me up down the road," said Chuck. "Then we can go round us up a posse."

Their truck drove through the surrounding neighborhoods blasting its horn waking the dead and summoning infected from every home, ditch and yard along the way. They began to run behind the slow moving truck flailing their arms in an attempt to catch it while ranting and raving in feral screams and grunts.

"Look out!" pointed Chuck.

The truck's driver swerved to the left in an attempt to miss an infected man, but caught him on the corner of the right front quarter panel sending him into a roll down the side of the truck. His head hit the passenger's window with a loud thud before he tumbled onto the road, disappearing underneath the feet of the crowd of infected in pursuit.

"How many we got back there?"

Chuck leaned back looking through the back window.

"Looks like about thirty or so, but I want at least three times that."

"I feel like a demented version of the pied piper. Think those things can keep up all the way to the plant?"

"Sure... if I see them start getting tired, I'll throw in a little motivation."

Chuck rolled down his window, stretched his torso out and began to scream while pounding his chest, "Ding ding ding... dinnertime! Come on you slow fucks if you want some of this... you're going to have to work harder than that!"

"Want me to put in the theme song from Rocky?"

"Yeah you got it?" asked Chuck poking his head back into the truck.

"Oh shit! They're coming from everywhere!" he yelled while trying to dodge the numerous infected that were coming toward the truck from all directions. "I'm starting to get a little uneasy about this man; I kinda feel like we're starting up something we might not be able to finish."

"We're the icy man for zombies dude. Look at them running after us like kids. Just don't get a flat and we'll be fine."

"Oh God that would suck."

"Hey go up that way... there's lots of more houses up there."

The truck turned, beaming its headlights up a dark curvy road leading a surging mob that continued to grow as they honked their horn and hummed the theme song to the movie Rocky.

"I think that will be enough," replied the passenger.

"You think so, what tipped you off, the fact that you can't see the road behind us anymore?"

"Hey, this is going to be a party… the more the merrier."

The truck drove slowly along the road toward the plant so not to lose the multitude of shifting infected following behind like a swarming train. The long winding gravel road finally gave way to the image of the fence's tall gate under the exposure of their truck's bright headlights.

"I hope they didn't find the guys you capped."

"If they had, we would already be under fire."

The truck sat still, held in check by a patient foot on its brake pedal as four eyes watched a blank reflection in the rear view mirror. Seconds ticked with long slow clicks converting into full agonizing minutes as the two men waited anxiously for their reinforcements. Another minute passed without their tired image and both of the men began to get noticeably nervous.

"What the fuck?" said Chuck confused. "They were just behind us."

"I think we might have given them the slip."

"God damn it," screamed Chuck spinning his head around, "let's go back and get the dumb asses."

Tommy spun the steering wheel around as far as it could go and was about to slam his foot onto the gas pedal, when the image of hundreds of bouncing heads, arms and legs poured from around the bend and up the road towards their stationary truck.

"It's on like Donkey Kong," said Tommy upon their appearance.

The truck's tires spun, fishtailing through the gravel toward its objective. Its engine growled as it accelerated down the long gravel road bursting open the unlocked gates in a torrent of sparks and bent metal. Infected swelled into the compound as would water through a broken dam running between its many buildings and guard shacks. The blue truck raced recklessly between the small buildings trying to put as much distance between themselves and the horde of flesh eating zombies as possible. The loud crash against the gate and the screaming hunger of the dead outside alerted the occupants of the nuclear plant and they began to come of the buildings. Although armed, most were immediately torn apart as the swarming dead overwhelmed them in the form of a frenzied mob out for blood.

Gunshots vainly rang out around the compound in its defense, but were unable to slow down its attackers. Chuck's eyes lit up with the image of the soldier under the truck's bright lights that had taken pot shots with his rifle when they had first wandered up upon the nuclear plant. He pointed his pistol at the man as they drove by, firing directly into his abdomen. The man fell forward onto the ground grasping his stomach in the fetal position. Infected converged upon the helpless man tearing his flesh from his body with bared teeth and hands consuming him alive. Another soldier took a shot at the truck shattering its rear window before he was taken down and mauled into pieces by dozens of infected. They tugged and pulled at his body with such force that they tore his limbs apart from his body and began to feast upon them in glee. The two men instinctively ducked when the round struck the truck, showering them in tiny sparking shards of glass. Tommy rose back up and looked over his steering wheel, only to see the figure of a woman frozen like a statue in the beam of his headlights. He jerked the wheel narrowly missing her before crashing into a row of garbage cans and skidding to a stop inches from a concrete wall.

"Hurry, back up before they get here!" yelled Chuck.

His eyes illuminated in fear of the infected mob that was coming toward the truck in the dark. Tommy looked back in his rear view mirror and saw the figure of the woman he had missed standing in the path of the oncoming horde of dead motionless. He sifted the gears in the truck and backed up stopping a few feet behind her.

"Come on get in!" he yelled.

She stood still as if a statue.

"Dude forget her!" screamed his friend sitting helplessly in the passenger seat. "Get us out of here!"

Tommy jumped out of the truck's cab and spun the girl around. Her eyes looked at him blankly, while her body stood static in a paralyzed state.

"Shit don't leave the wheel!" screamed Chuck desperately.

Chuck frantically crawled over the truck's console hurdling the shifter before taking hold of its controls and speeding up backwards next to his friend.

"Get in now!"

Tommy picked up the frightened woman and in an adrenaline surge tossed her into the backseat as if she were little more than a rag doll, before diving in after her.

The truck's tires spun out slinging loose gravel in an attempt to quickly gain traction and sped forward. Infected began to beat at its sides and tug at its trunk bed in an attempt to tear it open as it slugged forward under the shifting gravel beneath its wide tires. Finally the tires came in contact with hard ground and jerked forward leaving behind the crowd of frenzied dead.

"Which way out?" asked Tommy anxiously.

"I don't know. Maybe if we circle around along the fence, we can make it back out the front gate."

The truck barreled around the corner of a building and sped along the backside of the large compound circling around the mob. They made a tight turn and began to drive along the fence line at a high speed toward the front gate. An infected women and man came around the side of a building and upon sight of the racing truck ran directly in its path. Seeing them, but not willing or able to stop, Chuck lowered his head and crashed into their bodies at full speed throwing them underneath the truck, nearly turning the vehicle over as it bounced on its massive inflated tires. They raced through the wide open front gates and never looked back.

"Is she going to be okay?" asked Chuck looking into the rear view mirror.

"I guess, it's like she is paralyzed or something."

"Paralyzed people don't stand in the middle of a nuclear plant… she must be in shock."

She had long straight raven black hair and smooth natural tanned skin. He stared at her looking for any signs of life save her heavy breathing. As far as he could tell, she was a little older than he, maybe in the middle to late thirties he thought. After a few moments her eyes opened in the darkly lit area of the truck's backseat and looked into his own.

"What happened?" she asked sitting up disorientated.

"Are you all right?" asked Tommy in a concerned tone.

"How far you want us to go back," replied Chuck, "to when the infection first hit?"

She responded politely, "How did all those things get into the compound like that?"

"We don't know either," said Chuck covering. "We were driving by when we saw it all going down… we just swung in to try and help."

Tommy's wide eyes met his in the rear view mirror. It was a look the two knew well, when to hold a lie."

"But there were so many."

"Who knows… maybe the remnants of some marching band that happened to march by your plant? Those things are running around out there like packs of rapid wolves now."

"How many people were in there with you?" asked Tommy curiously.

"Sixty two," she said sadly.

Tommy's heart sank, they had thought through the plan, but not through the consequences.

"What were you guys doing there?" asked Chuck.

"When the infection first began to spread widely across Europe and Asia, the United States Government began assigning small cells of scientists and doctors around the country to various military compounds and research facilities, in case the infection made the shores of North America and got out of control. My husband and I got the orders to be stationed here, a few weeks before the infection struck."

"So you're a doctor?" asked Tommy.

"A general practitioner, but my husband was the one that got us stationed here, he's a surgeon."

"Oh my god, my husband! We have to go back for Brian!"

"Were not going back to that buffet, in case you didn't notice we were the main course," decreed Chuck boldly.

"Please, he might have gotten away or bolted himself in somewhere!"

"Or he might be dead… or he might not be dead but contagious… or we might get killed," interrupted Chuck.

She covered her face with her hands and began to sob out loudly from the realization of her husband's fate. Tommy considered consoling her, but he held back his emotions, fearing his actions might be inappropriate considering what she had been put through. A weight like a boulder set into the pit of his stomach as tears welled up his eyes. The guilt of his involvement began to play upon him like a master would his puppet and he clandestinely shared a small part of her pain. Chuck drove on with a free conscience, content in his retribution.

"What about all those military dudes we saw running around?" he asked trying to change the subject.

She cried for a few more moments then wiped her eyes dry regaining some of her composure.

"Oh those brutes? Every cell was appointed a group of soldiers to keep the area secure from looters, infected and so on."

"Who was in charge?"

"Well initially it was Doctor Werner, but after things started getting bad and it began to appear that we were on our own, Captain Hauser took over… he was a real asshole too. Whatever he said went, and since we weren't armed there was nothing we could do but try to discover some sort of cure."

"I assume you haven't found one yet?" asked the driver smartly.

"No not an outright treatment, but we did learn a lot from our studies of it and from other cell's research."

"You were in contact with the other cells?" asked Tommy surprised.

"Through the use of satellite radio we were able to stay in contact with all of the cells at first, but as the infection spread we started to lose contact one by one as they succumbed to the infection. That's when Captain Hauser took over and closed off all contact with us from the outside world, even the use of the radio, but my husband and Doctor Werner set up another receiver and in secret we were able to kept contact with a few remaining cells."

"I'm not a scientist or anything, but I think it's a little too late for a solution now, especially since about all the damage that can be done has already been done," said Chuck concentrating on the dark road ahead.

"That may be true if you are a pessimist and you are concerned only with the past, but with a little optimism there may be hope for the future."

"I hate to break it to you, but have a look around… the pessimists were right."

"Let's take a break from this argument," interrupted Tommy, "we don't even know each other's names."

"Oh I'm sorry," she said sniffing. "My name is Laurie."

"Hi Laurie, I'm Tommy and this dick goes by the name Chuck."

"Hey," he said.

"I'm sorry I guess I should be thanking you two for saving me instead of arguing with you…I'm not myself right now… after everything that's happened."

Tommy not knowing how to handle her misguided gratitude dropped his head and leaned back tormented by his conscience. Free from such anguish, his friend milked the moment in jest as he had all their life and poured salt on the wound of his agonizing friend having effectively two different conversations in one, with both recipients hearing two completely different meanings from the exact same words.

"Well it was my idea to head down toward the plant so you can give most of the thanks to me for us finding you."

"You can give him all the credit," said his friend softly, "without him we would have never met you."

They drove on through town using back roads so not to attract much attention and besides having to avoid a few stragglers they made the edge of the woods with little difficulty. They drove up the trail for nearly an hour before no one, including the driver, could keep their eyes open before pulling over into a secluded spot and locking things down to go to sleep.

Chapter 20
A Different Direction

The sunlight slowly crawled across the wet hood of their truck gently drying it as the sun crept up from behind the mountain immersing it in the surrounding brilliance of the morning light. It bore directly on Chuck's face awakening him gently in a warm glow. He opened his eyes in a squint to protect them from the bright light and looked around to familiarize himself with the area he had driven into late last night. He reached back and tugged on his friend's arm to wake him and then stepped outside into the chilly air. He stomped his boots onto the ground so to relieve the tingles in his legs brought on by being crammed into a small cab without being able to stretch out. His leg dragged behind him in an odd limp as he walked to the back of the truck and fished through their supplies with a few dings and clanks before finding a small propane stove. Then after finding a suitable flat spot, he set it up and began to brew some coffee. There were only a few bags left, but he felt unusually tired and this morning he felt he deserved a kick-start. Tommy limped out of the truck a few minutes later scratching his head and zipping up his coat.

"Mornin."

"Mornin."

His friend reached down deep into an inner pocket of his jacket and pulled free a small plastic cup with a tiny handle and filled it up with steaming coffee. He took a big gulp and then spit it out.

"What the hell did you do, piss in it first?"

"No the last filter we got broke, it's a little crunchy but it's got some kick."

"It needs to be kicked right into the dirt," he said slinging the rest of it out of his cup.

"Whoa, whoa, that shit is precious, don't throw it away!"

Tommy sat down across from his friend and looked at him seriously.

"We got enough supplies for the three of us?"

"We'll be fine until next winter up there, and then we can come back and load up again. Figured we'd stop by and say hello to Joe too, you know set up a trade with him like we planned the first time."

"Sounds good," said Tommy with a straight forced smile.

The truck's rear cab door swung open revealing another set of legs.

"Whew, it's cold this morning," commented their newest member.

"Got some hot coffee here just off the press," offered Chuck.

"If you dare," warned Tommy.

Chuck handed her a cup and both men watched curiously for her reaction.

"Just like I like it… strong as hell."

Chuck burst into laughter, "Most pussies can't handle it."

Tommy leaned back a bit embarrassed, but after a moment he gave away to a small but noticeable grin.

"I know I'm just tagging along here," said the woman brushing her long hair aside, "but where are we going?"

"To get out of the city," said Chuck with a long slurp, "go somewhere where they're aren't so many of those things running around."

"So that's it? We're going to run?"

"No, I figured we might walk some too," said Chuck deviously.

"Then what?"

"Does not getting eaten alive sound good for starters?"

"You can't run forever. Eventually you will get caught," she cautioned.

"Oh are you some sort of psychic, because if you can communicate with the dead, that would be really useful right about now."

"It might be tomorrow, it might be ten years from now, but it will eventually happen, all running will do is stall the inevitable."

"I never said we were going to run forever, just until we die of old age…it's a foolproof plan if you ask me," Chuck said blowing off her warning

"We've got a lot more to worry about than getting killed by infected. I have done a lot of research on this virus and its gestation cycle is similar to that of the common flu, meaning it alters its genetic code ever so slightly from season to season as a defense mechanism against the immune system.

"What other options are there?" interjected Tommy. "There are too many of them to stay in the city."

"This virus has contagious qualities similar to that of the common flu, meaning it is going to come back year after year until one of us comes down with it."

"You don't know shit about this virus and if you didn't notice, the laboratory in our truck is a little inadequate. If we get away from all this, how are we going to catch it?"

"Once this virus enters its host, it begins to attack and infect every cell in the human body at a rapid rate… the heart, the liver, the muscles… and finally the brain, eventually clinically killing its host. The most incredible part is that although it kills the other organs in the body save the muscles, the brain actually stays alive being dormant of all activity but its most primitive functions, violence, hatred and hunger. It is like it triggers these emotions for self-preservation, using the death of its host as an instrument to spread itself further."

"What does all that mean?" inquired Chuck unimpressed with her knowledge.

"It means that although the host walks around, no blood is pumping through its body, meaning it is still decaying, infecting the soil, the water anything it comes in contact and in our studies the virus had begun to alter its genetic code, to where it might be able to infect cells from other species."

"Other species?" asked Tommy.

"Other living organisms," she replied deprecatingly.

"Great, as if things weren't bad enough already now we're going to have to contend with rabid man eating squirrels and rabbits."

"I'm not exactly sure that's what will happen, but it does mean that the next animal you eat or the next drink of water you take might be your last. We have to find an inoculation before it's too late."

"Well shit," said Chuck slinging his prized coffee into the dirt. "I can't believe it… she has actually scared me."

"I wanted my mommy when she got to the rapid rodents. Now we can't even supplement our diet by hunting or fishing. With what little we've got, we'll be close to starving by winter."

"I do have a little good news," she said lightly.

"What it's airborne too?" replied Chuck weary of more morbid news.

"Just before all this occurred Brian was in contact with another scientist from the CDC that claims to have discovered a serum."

The two men's eye sprung wide open as if soaking in her voice.

"A little late don't you think?" replied Chuck.

"Who?" asked Tommy ignoring Chuck's remark.

"Doctor Ledbetter in Atlanta."

"We're not going to Atlanta," declared Chuck.

"This might be our last chance to find a cure," she said with enthusiasm, "an opportunity to stop the spread of this infection!"

"Do you know how many people lived in Atlanta? Last I heard it was something like five million people. Do you know how many people live there now?"

He paused a second pretending to give her time to answer, but interrupted her just before she could speak.

"Don't bother answering, because I can tell you right now it is close to like five. Besides finding a cure now is like getting the answers to the test after you've already failed it."

"It doesn't matter how many are alive, without that vaccination we don't have a future."

"It matters if you have the other four million nine hundred ninety nine thousand nine hundred ninety five chasing you through Atlanta."

"I don't know, Chuck, I think she has a point, it sounds like our only hope."

"Our only hope? This isn't Star Wars man. If we go in there we'll never make it out alive."

"Hey," she said kindly, "I know I'm the new guy here and that I'm trying to change all your plans, but I really feel that this is our only practical option."

"Great, what's your plan for getting through the streets of Atlanta? Oh forget that, that's the easy part," he said mocking her. "Just how do you plan on getting there, with it being hundreds of miles away? I'll tell you right now you can't take the highway."

"Is that all you do, criticize everything? Have you ever thought of trying to be constructive and help out?"

"I am helping out... helping to keep us alive."

"It's easy to sit around and shoot holes into people's ideas. The real challenge is being productive. Go ahead tell me what you think we should do?"

"You know my plan," said Chuck. "Don't try and be cute."

"Really, do you have enough bottled water in that truck to last all three of us through the summer?" she said on the attack. "Because if you don't, we are going to have to wonder after every drink we take if we are infected or not. What about food, got enough sealed food to last us until next winter? Every time one of us eats something, we'll have to worry about wanting to eat each other later. You better think about these things before you disappear into the mountains."

They sat around the small stove in an uncomfortable silence and waited out their argument as if it had somehow gone into halftime resting up for the second half, when one team threw in the towel.

"If you two think that going toward the highest concentration of infected in the region instead of away from it is a good idea, then I'll bite my lip and shoot as many as I can along the way."

Tommy smiled in relief. He had never seen anyone change his friend's mind so quickly. There was something special about this woman he thought, something really special if she could persuade someone so stubborn.

"Besides I think I know how we can get to Atlanta."

Their truck rolled through the sparse woods trails coming to the edge of a long tree bordered field. They ran across the field warily and kneeled down behind a small bush line that had grown along a barbed wire fence separating two nearly identical fields. Their eyes peered through the small openings in the overgrown fence and watched in amazement.

"They're beautiful," she said mesmerized.

Grazing peacefully in the middle of the next field, as if the infection had never occurred, were dozens of multicolored horses. A dove sprung out of the grass cooing stridently as it took to flight startling the horses into a light trollop.

"I use to drive by these beauties every morning on the way to work, wishing I was riding instead. Damn that saying, be careful what you wish for is prophetic," said Chuck. "Come on the barn is over this way."

It was an old barn with red weathered paint and large cracks in its walls from where the planks had shrunk away from one another with age. Its door stood wide open creaking back and forth slowly with the wind. They walked in slowly with guns drawn examining its interior with wary eyes and bodies covered in wide sunlit stripes.

The tall frame of the barn groaned as it slightly rocked above their heads withstanding the force of gravity and the wind as it had done since its construction decades ago. Seeing a saddle straddling the side of a stable stall, Tommy walked over and touched its ripened leather with the palm of his hand. Its smooth worn exterior had seen many hours of riding since its stretching. Chuck followed Tommy over to the stall and began to shift through a pile of objects sitting in its back corner. Laurie stood in the center of the barn holding a pistol as the two men continued to scavenge for items they would need for their trip.

A tangled pile of hay shifted giving birth to worn infested head with a shaggy beard rising up from its base. The man's eyes absorbed the image of the woman's back standing in the center of the barn, triggering every muscle in its body. The creature screamed in excitement upon seeing her and leaped to its feet. Laurie spun around distressed by the scream and instinctively began to fire into the charging man. Bullets tore through his soiled shirt and sank deep within his chest jerking him backwards nearly knocking him off his feet, but doing nothing to stop his attack. Chuck and Tommy spun around, but were unable to fire on him in fear of hitting Laurie. The two forms collided and slid across the floor. Chuck lifted up his rifle to fire into the back of the man's head, but pulled back when his friend ran in front of him to seize the man on top of Laurie. One of his hands took hold of a thick wad of the man's shirt, while the other seized a tangle of his matted hair. He tugged against the crazed man with all of his might lifting him off his screaming victim before throwing him against the side of the barn. His head hit a loose board splitting it in two jagged pieces before crashing through to the other side. The man began to push against the wall with both of his hands and feet ripping his head back through the splintered wood. He turned around hissing and gnashing his teeth with long splinters protruding out of his torn and bleeding neck. Chuck took aim and fired his rifle splattering the man's head against the wall like an impressionist artist would modern art. Blood began to trickle slowly down the wall as the man's body slumped down on top a pile of hay. Tommy ran over to Laurie and held her head in his hands consoling her loud cries.

"Are you all right?" he asked concerned. "Did he hurt you?"

"I don't think so," she cried hysterically.

"Shhh…" said Chuck. "There could be more around."

She continued to sob holding Tommy, who turned his eyes toward his friend with an annoyed look. Chuck saw the irritation in his eye, and although he felt justified in his request, he knew continuing to argue his point would do nothing to better their current situation. Once Laurie calmed down, they took to courting four horses for their long impending trip, three for riding and the fourth as a pack animal to carry their supplies.

They traveled from sunup till sundown following the freeway in order not to get lost, while staying as far away from it as their vision would allow for safety's sake. It was a long grueling trip that could be broken down into small journeys from field to field. Each field carried its own challenge almost always ending in some type of fence line, bringing their travel to a complete stop until they made a breach, a task that was little more than a nuisance, until it became a death race.

Numerous pockets of undead had chased the small group along the way, but with the swiftness of their horses, they had escaped with little difficulty. Chuck rode up front, pulling along their packhorse with watchful eyes. He gazed over the acres of swaying weeds and grass mindful of any unusual movement. He caught the creature out of the corner of his eye, but before he could pull his pistol free from his hip holster, it had startled his horse and unsaddled him. His body tumbled into the tall plush pasture as if swallowed up by it vanishing from sight. The high grass did little to break his fall and he landed solidly onto his back. A bright shiny pistol ripped from his holster pointing straight up into the air. Fearful of who or what he might hit, he fought his primal instinct to blindly fire through the waving blades of grass above his head. Gunshots began to resound through the field as he sprung to his feet holding his pistol out in extended arms. The tip of his pistol hit the forehead of an infected man with a thud and came to rest flatly against it. Their eyes met for a split second before the man's eyes faded away in a cloud of smoke and fire. Dozens of dead began to rise out of the surrounding grass and pile over a small fence that separated the field from a highway that looked like more like a junkyard than an expressway. They came from all directions screaming madly as they put on an all-out ambush that couldn't have been better prepared by an elite covert operation. Tommy and Laurie began to fire their pistols on top of their saddles aiming at the closet of their assaulters, horribly missing their bobbing targets upon their rousing horses. Still dazed from his fall, Chuck spun around unaware that both of his mounts had run off during the scuffle, spooked by the screaming and gunfire. An arm stretched out toward him and he took hold of it using it to sling himself onto the back of Tommy's horse. The two horses bolted upon command and ran through a small group of dead. Hands gripped their legs, their saddle and the harness of their horses nearly bringing their horses to a final standstill. Tommy kicked the sides of his horse encouraging his horse to break free, as Chuck fired his pistol into the sea of heads trying to overtake them. Teeth gnashed at their legs and for a moment their horse almost went down, before it broke free with a loud snarl and made the open field. Laurie's horse had not done as well and in the turmoil it had bolted in the opposite direction toward the highway and a wave on oncoming dead. Upon seeing the approaching mob, it reared back onto it hind legs nearly throwing its rider. Already having lost control of the horse, Laurie froze letting go of her pistol as well as the horse's reins and held on with all her might. The horse spun around doing an effortless one eighty digging its hoofs into the soil and springing away from the onslaught carrying its helpless rider along. Tommy rode hard toward the next overgrown fence line oblivious to Laurie's dilemma. His horse came to a stop a few feet away from the brush and weeds that had swallowed up the long barbed wire barrier that stretched between two separate properties. Chuck ran up to it tearing away at the foliage frantically looking for anything metal to cut with his wire cutters. The tense wires coiled back with a high pitch sound as they snapped in two racing back toward their respective posts. Tommy leaned down next to his friend pulling at the hardy gnarled weeds concealing their only path to freedom. His hands ripped and yanked mercilessly shredding them from their grasp upon the fence and exposing its long rusty twisted wires. The last wire snapped in two curling backwards revealing a six foot wide escape route. The two men's faces erupted in excitement of having cheated death at least one last time, until Tommy's came crashing down as quickly as it had risen upon seeing that they had been separated from Laurie. He could see her stiff body lying face down upon the back of the horse sliding from side to side as it ran back and forth like a pinball trying to avoid its many pursuers. Without thinking, Tommy swung back on top of his horse and turned it towards her. Chuck could see the intentions of his friend and grasped the thick leather reins with his left hand.

"Don't, there are too many! All three of us don't have to die!"

Tommy turned his head toward him and their eyes met. He didn't know the man on the horse next to him; it wasn't the Tommy he had known most of his life, for his eyes burned suicidal. He let go and the crazed man charged across the field with no concern for his own self, crashing into the dead that barred his way to Laurie.

The infected ran around in a frenzy of excitement chasing the woman's horse around the field as if taking part in some demented county fair. Left on foot, Chuck dared not to risk a run out into the open and slid down into the weeds besides the fence with feral eyes. Tommy's horse nimbly dodged the assailants swerving through them like a snake would a cornfield. He rode up to Laurie's horse and grasped hold of its reins calming the animal and turning Laurie's eyes directly into his own. They bore into his through a glassy haze unaware of the mayhem she had been a part. Tommy kicked the side of his horse with his heels and brought his horse to full gallop toward the broken fence line with Laurie's horse in tow. The two horses ran in a wild panic side by side effortlessly darting by their pursuers and breaking back into the open. Chuck stood out from the tall brush and leaped onto the back of Laurie's horse reaching around her and taking control.

The next field stretched into the horizon allowing the two to use the speed of their horses to fade the images of the dead like mist in the wind. Tommy's horse grunted from the long grueling forced march that had been placed on it as its rider stepped down to give it a break. A loud clash of thunder crackled above their heads followed by cool slow drizzle that hung in the hot summer twilight like a wall of fog. They slid down against the trunk of a large single oak tree that had somehow avoided being cut down, although it stood in the center of a immense rolling green field, perhaps from the sentimental mercy of a previous land owner.

"I don't think it's such a good idea to be hiding under a tree during a lightning storm," said Tommy.

"Lightning is the least of our problems right now, besides do you want to run across that field leading these horses under that wrath of God?"

Laurie lay under the tree with her knees pressed up against her chest without saying a word.

"I don't know about you two, but I've had enough of God's wrath to fill a lifetime," finished Chuck.

The tall dense tree stood stoutly shadowing the downtrodden group with its protective foliage holding off the ensuing downpour only to tease them with large arbitrary drops of rain. The rainfall continued to descend throughout the night while three figures curled up against the tree's large trunk and slept a hard night.

A ray of sunshine streaked over the mountaintops streaking down the valley, illuminating the wet field below as would a lighthouse the ocean on a calm morning. The slight rise in temperature awoke one of the sleeping wet bundles beneath the tree and brought it to its feet. Tommy hobbled around from sore and aching joints beget from the previous day's rough ride. An eye popped open peering over the top of a jacket collar watching Tommy work out his pain.

"Aerobics?" asked the voice from behind the large jacket.

"I feel old as shit and I've got saddle sores from Hell."

"I know what you mean," said Chuck standing up gingerly, "I was walking around all bowlegged, like a genuine cowboy yesterday."

Tommy sniggered as he sifted through a small saddlebag on his horse in search of a lighter.

"About yesterday man, that wasn't too cool how you hung me out to dry in the middle of that field without a ride," said Chuck boldly confronting his lifelong friend.

Tommy's head turned around slowly exposing a face seized in annoyance.

"What the hell are you complaining about, all three of us are breathing aren't we?"

"You left me there without any way of getting away, had I been spotted."

"What should have I done, left her?"

"I'm not saying that, I'm saying I don't like being put into situations like that."

"Oh come on," said Tommy angrily, "like you haven't put my ass in jeopardy over the years!"

"I haven't."

"Bullshit! What about the mansion? Hmm... didn't I say that we should leave before things thawed out? But oh no you wanted to stay and we ended up having to break out through an army of those fuckers. So don't act so almighty, I came back for you."

"What about this little excursion into Atlanta? Is that going to put us into any jeopardy?"

"You heard what she said! We don't have a future without a cure."

"What cure? What future? How do we know that she is not taking us there to link up with an old flame of hers?"

"She's married..." Tommy paused a second after noticing his error of words. "She was married."

"Oh and no one married has ever had an affair."

The two men bumped into each other in wild anger and clinched with tight fists. They scuffled for a moment and then froze when they realized what was occurring. The two men stepped apart ashamed by what had almost occurred. They had never raised their fist against each other, not once.

"All right we both said what we feel," said Chuck ending it.

Laurie aroused from all the commotion, stood up and pretended to have missed the entire encounter. She shuffled between the two men and broke the silence that had overcome them after she awoke.

"Anyone start any coffee yet?"

"Not unless someone else found our pack horse out there and started some," said Chuck sarcastically.

"Hmm," she said running her fingers through her hair in frustration, "what else did we lose?"

"The tent, the sleeping bags, most of our food…" said Chuck.

"Nothing we can't do without," said Tommy interrupting his friend. "We just passed exit 296, so we should make Atlanta in the next couple days."

Chuck saw the determination in his friend's eyes and he knew nothing would alter their crusade into the city of the dead short of death or far worse, the eternal grip of infection.

Chapter 21
City of the Dead

Three slender shadows rode drearily upon horseback in the fading dawn ever so slowly trudging toward the tall skyscrapers piercing the horizon. No one uttered a syllable when the lead rider pulled up on his horse's reins ending the day's long forced march. Their horses, beat from the hot summer sun and the weight of their loads, stood complacent as if locked in some invisible stall. The three dark figures collapsed into the tall plush grass disappearing into transparent voices.

"I can't ride another inch… my ass hurts in places I never knew existed," said the feminine voice.

"Well the sight of those buildings has answered your prayers," said the deeper voice of Chuck. "We're going to have to go into the city on foot."

"Couldn't we move faster on horseback," said the third voice, "in case we are spotted."

"If we can even hope to make it in or out alive, we're going to have to do it without being spotted or heard and we can't do that if those big lug's huffs are clanking against pavement."

"So are we leaving in the morning?" asked the female's voice curiously.

"No, tomorrow night."

"When it's dark?"

"These things, besides being dead, are no different from you or me, meaning they can't see or hear any better than anyone of us. So if they don't hear us, or see us, then as far as they are concerned, we're not there."

The figure of Tommy sat up from the tall weeds and dug through his backpack distributing out dinner, "I hope the CDC stocked up on food, because this is the last of it."

"More fucking trail mix?" said Chuck shifting through his share. "And why the hell do I always get a shit load of almonds, I hate almonds.

"I'm so fucking hungry right now. I'd eat a raw rat's ass while it was shitting so if you don't want them I'll take the fuckers."

"Fuck you. I'll trade them for cashews."

"Are you crazy, the cashew is like the most desirable nut. It's as good as cash, that's why they call them cash-ews. The fucking almond is at the bottom of the nut list."

"I didn't mean nut for nut, but a trade based on value."

"You two are the nuts," said Laurie interrupting their dispute.

"Okay, I'll give you one cashew for every five almonds you produce," said the voice ignoring her comment.

"Bullshit, I'll give you two per, but not five."

"No way, the cashew taste good, while the almond hardly has any taste at all."

"I'm not debating that the cashew doesn't taste better, but that you are underestimating the value of the almond. Considering our current situation and lack of nourishment, the almond's value is higher than usual based purely on substance. It's larger and at the moment, what's more important taste or fulfillment?"

"I'll give you one cashew for four almonds but that's it."

"Come on bro, I'm starving here and besides I'm not entirely sure since you dealt out the mix, that I got a fair cut."

"I dealt it out purely by weight, nothing else."

"Look at all the cashews your bag has, hell I don't think I got more than six, besides almonds weigh more so I really got screwed on the nut count."

"Fine, I'll go as low as one cashew for three almonds, but that is my final offer."

"Done, but they better be whole cashews, not halves or pieces."

Nuts changed hands as cash would during a monetary conversion.

"Good now eat your nuts before I bust them," said Laurie.

All three laughed, before continuing on with small talk that quickly led to sleep under the cover of weeds and the watchful light of the stars.

The three passed the light of the next day lying hidden beneath the tall grass in casual conversation, all the while dreading the fall of night and the magnitude of their next undertaking.

"I don't understand why whatever it was that gave us life, did so only to end it every time with death. No matter what you do or how long you live, it will all eventually be wiped out and forgotten under the cover of death. Just think about it, three hundred years ago, three other people might have lain in this very spot contemplating the universe, but it might as well have never happened, since they are dead, and there is no one left to remember them," whispered Tommy, "Man went too far again and God decided to wipe the earth clean of their presence. The first time he used water, this time he used the dead… I'd rather have been there when the water hit."

"I guess the moral of the story is, to enjoy the moment because it's the only thing that really matters when it's all said and done. Forget the past, live for the moment and don't waste your time thinking about the future, since there really isn't one," replied Chuck.

"How can anyone live with such an outlook on life, knowing it's all for naught?" asked Laurie.

"I don't know; if you think about things too much you'll just fuck it up."

"That's the attitude that drives scientists and research doctors mad, everything we do is for the future and then people without the foresight beyond the next quarter come and cut or eliminate our research budget because it's not profitable enough… you have the same attitude as of those soldiers back there."

The pressure in Chuck's veins swelled with anger upon his comparison to the soldiers from the nuclear plant, although her assessment was far closer to the truth than he would ever admit.

"I know you think I am an asshole, but you're only half right, because I am a mean asshole who doesn't plan on ending up dead anytime soon and what you call lack of foresight, I call the instinct of survival!"

"If everyone thought like you, we would still be living in the Stone Age!" she declared.

"At least if we were still in the Stone Age, we would be killing each other with spears and shit and instead of all of those brilliant bombs your scientist friends invented!"

Tommy had hoped the argument between his best friend and Laurie, whom he wasn't entirely sure what she was to him, was going to fizzle out on its own, but it continued to escalate out of control and he grudgingly spoke up to stop its escalation.

"Guys… look at where we are at. We're not in the Stone Age and we don't have bombs to drop on anybody," he said playing the role of diplomat, "what we do have is each other."

The two verbal combatants settled down once Tommy had taken the air out of their sails and went silent, as would a sailboat on a windless sea. The sun lowered below the horizon, leaving them mere shadows in the faded light of dusk. Their minds churned on the undertaking ahead as they glided through the tall grass as shades toward the blackened skyscrapers in the distance determined to invade the city of the dead at all cost. Somber but resolute faces carried them single file through the dark and nearly indiscernible brush covered in the invisibility of night. Chuck dreaded what they were doing and in his heart he felt it would be their end. Had it been anyone else besides Tommy, he would have let them go in and die alone without the slightest remorse. He had always believed that if you made a bad decision you lived with it, even if it killed you, but not when it came to his friend. He was the hunter. He knew how to move unseen, unheard; if there was any chance of getting in and out alive, it would be up to him.

"One thing we know about these things," he said in a whisper, "is that their senses are no better than ours, meaning if we can't see, than neither can they. As humans our sense of smell isn't a concern and our hearing is subpar at best, so if we move quietly in the dark we won't draw any attention beyond what we walk up upon."

He walked quietly leading the way pausing his advice, pushing the grass aside with long unwavering strides, while pulling an axe from his belt, "And anything we find we kill silently. No guns unless it is our only option and I promise you if you use a gun it will be our last option… it will be our last everything."

No moon hung in the black sky, only the stars shown to prove it was even a sky at all and the three faded from each other's view within the distance of only a few feet. They walked closely together in line towards the gray cloud that spread like a plague with the absence of the sun cloaking the city in invisibility without the service of its once abundant lighting.

"Do you know exactly where the CDC is, Laurie?" asked Tommy bringing up the rear.

"Sixteen hundred Clifton Road," she whispered into the darkness.

"Have you ever been there?" asked Chuck.

"Yes, several times."

Chuck stopped and she bumped into him clumsily.

"Well lead the way, the only thing in Atlanta I've ever been to is a Brave's game," he said holding out his hand.

"I've only gone there directly from the airport in a car and I never drove."

"What, you don't know where it is?" asked Chuck astonished.

"No, I've never walked to Atlanta! Do you know where the ballpark is?" she said in defense.

Chuck stepped back angrily; he never liked the plan and he couldn't help but to try and shoot holes into it, exposing its weaknesses; "You brought us all the way down here with only an address? Well shit, let me get out my map! Oh yeah that's right we didn't bring one of those either!"

"Chuck calm down, you can't expect her or anyone to walk into an unlighted city in the middle of the night and find anything," said Tommy defending Laurie.

"We are going to end up wandering around that place all night until we get surrounded and eaten."

"If we can get within a few blocks of it I'm sure I'll catch my bearings," she said.

Chuck walked off out of sight livid about their situation not only because he thought it was too dangerous, but also because they had chosen her idea over his own.

"Come on, Chuck, this doesn't change a thing. Without a cure we don't have a future," said Tommy following after him. "Man I've never seen you back down from anything… not once."

He stepped up through the darkness and his pale face came out of it as if he had poked it through a hole in a black wall. His eyes bore into Tommy and for a moment they had a stare down.

"It's not because you are afraid is it?" asked Tommy. "All those years everything we did, they were always your ideas, weren't they? Good ole Tommy will do anything you say, but when someone else has a plan you don't want anything to do with it do you?"

Chuck stared at him silently not saying a word.

"At some point we are going to have to risk our lives to have one and this is the time," said Laurie hoping to separate the two.

Chuck walked off toward the city disappearing from the eyes of his two companions, "Destination 1600 Clifton Road," he said.

Tall buildings ripped up beyond the few feet of their limited sight and vanished into the sky. Their feet gently scraped against the broken and crumbled pavement below making only the slightest of sounds that tore into their eardrums as if they were at a loud concert sending chills down their spine with every graze of their feet. They skulked from one road sign to the next with their pistols holstered away. Their fingers clutched tightly around more brutal melee weapons as they stalked aimlessly through the dark with squinted eyes. Not a word was spoken and although not one knew any form of true sign language they spoke through silent hand, eye, neck and mouth movements. The strangest part of their invasion was not that there were no cars moving or lights shining, but that after peripatetically roaming nearly eight blocks they had not seen a single infected or dead person.

Heat stored within the pavement from earlier in the day steamed up into the cool night air opening the pores of their flesh in a hot muggy ambiance. Anguish embedded in rolling sweat steamed down their faces soaking their garments and biting into their vision with a sharp sting. Tommy wiped away the perspiration from his brow diligently so as not to lose more than a blink of sight. They sank deeper and deeper into the blanket of darkness, metal, glass and concrete until the three were noticeably lost and confused. Chuck eyed the compass in his hand again as if it were lying. They had followed it south whenever possible, but the continued near identical surroundings of what appeared to be the largest junkyard on earth, left them uncertain of their progress. After crossing several smaller roads they came upon what appeared to be some sort of major causeway. With three nods they began to move up it only to come to a stop at the edge of an immense pile up. Cars were stacked up upon each other nearly two high cutting off the possibility of easy passage. Chuck crawled up onto one of the cars and looked over to see if he could see an end. The thin metal hood beneath his foot crept from the weight of his body into a shallow, but noticeable dent. It creaked slowly in a low pitch and carried off into the humid air disappearing quickly. His muscles contracted upon hearing the dreadful noise, standing motionless as if posing for some sort of last portrait. Laurie stood on edge as the hairs on her arms rose, as if conducting the very fear from her heart. Chuck slowly lifted his foot under the watchful eyes of his two friends and for a moment the indention held in silence, then it happened. It sprung back with a pop that rang their ears and echoed away into the night bouncing off broken down cars, as would a rock skipping across water finally sinking away. A long lingering creak answered the echo bringing every muscle in their bodies to a halt including their hearts. Something moaned on the other side of the causeway and all three of their heads spun vainly trying to make out from where in came in the black night. It was dark… so dark that Laurie could barely see she thought nervously. Her mind raced out of control and her limbs began to tighten up… if only there was some light, just enough for her see beyond her hands she would be all right she murmured to herself quietly.

Long sluggish footsteps dragged in the daunting darkness. A ghostly white face emerged from the darkness piercing into three sets of terror stricken eyes. Laurie froze in a paralyzed state as she had when she had first met Tommy and Chuck and stood helpless. The calm serene face twisted sadistically forming into a screaming attack as it saw the uninfected. A long black metal wedge sank into the center of its face splitting its nose in half embedding into its skull and coming to rest in the soft tissue of its brain. The body slumped to the ground where Tommy placed his foot on its head and shook his axe back and forth until it came free from its hold. The sounds of more footsteps and moans began to pierce through the nocturnal void of darkness.

"Let's gets out of here now," Chuck said slinking off into the darkness.

Tommy stepped forth ready to follow, but stopped upon noticing Laurie's state. She hadn't moved since the attack, standing with clinched muscles and wide unblinking eyes. He ran up to her and coddled her face in his hands speaking to her gently.

"Come on, we've got to move before more come," he whispered barely an inch from her face.

Her complexion had lost all of its natural color as if it had drained out her pores and she stood like a tormented ghost. He grabbed her hand and tugged her off into the darkness. She began to run with him and within a few moments she recovered from one blackout only to merge into another as the black night cloaked her eyes.

"Chuck," yelled Tommy in a quiet raspy voice, "where are you?"

The sound of a distant scream bellowed from a desperate infected and the reverberation of some type of scuffle in the dark distance rang into Tommy's straining ears. He pulled Laurie into the direction of the commotion, only to stop when the pounding of countless footsteps surrounded the two in the black steamy night. An infected man leaped out of the darkness seizing Tommy, brining Laurie's lungs to peak capacity in a long shrill. Using his leg to trip the man, Tommy slung him flat onto his back and implanted the edge of his axe into his head swiftly ending the struggle. Another form tore out of the darkness and tackled Tommy from behind taking him to the ground. Tommy spun around onto his back and gripped the man between his legs using his hips to pull his face away from his own. The man's teeth began to chomp at his arms and chest like a piranha trying to infect his flesh. Having lost his grip on his axe, Tommy pulled his pistol free and fire into the man's face evaporating it from his view in a spurt of fire, smoke and worst of all sound. The body flipped backwards with a shove from Tommy's foot freeing him from its weight.

More gunshots rang out in the distance and Tommy pulled Laurie toward the direction from which they came. They ran through the darkness at a maddening pace twisting through infected that were running around haphazardly in search of the three like a crazed crowd of the blind. They bumped into a tall gray-haired infected man knocking him into the darkness as they dashed by. A tattered hand reached out and ripped Laurie's shirt as she ran by, nearly tearing it completely off her shoulders. Tommy rose up his pistol and fired into the back of a woman's head bursting it off into the darkness. A wide wall appeared before their eyes and the two crashed up against it hard.

Blood poured from Tommy's nose and dripped onto his shirt turning it as black as the night in which they found themselves trapped. The sounds of tortured moans and scampering feet rang around the two as they slid frantically along the wall to its end. Another hand reached out from the black cloud of night and gripped Laurie's shoulder spinning her around. Tommy swung the tip of his pistol around and shoved it into the face that came out of the darkness clinching the trigger in a slow cock.

"Shit man," whispered Chuck, "where the fuck have you two been?"

Tommy sighed, lowered his pistol and released the trigger gently bringing the hammer to rest. He had come within a hair of pulling the trigger.

"Come on this way," Chuck whispered.

The three ran around the wall and across the street stumbling blindly into an infected man who in the obscurity of the night seemed to appear from thin air. The sudden encounter surprised all involved and for a moment the four stared at each other motionless. Chuck's pistol ignited the darkness dropping the man in one shot, but in the flash of gunfire dozens of eyes flashed in dull green sparkle before fading out of view as would a firecracker late at night.

"Oh my God!" said Tommy weakly predicting their doom.

Their pistols burned the night as they fired into the swarming mob that leaped recklessly toward them. Hands tore at their clothes and flesh as they ran through the throng of infected that tried to pull them down into a ferocity of rabid teeth and dirty nails. Tommy slung open a door at the side of building and the three hectic survivors ran in slamming the old door. It immediately began to rattle from the force behind it nearly coming off its hinges. Tommy propped up against the opening and held it still with the weight of his body, frantically trying to latch the lock. His form bounced back and forth against the door while he tried to latch the vibrating lock in vain.

"God damn it, I can't get it!"

"Forget it, up the stairs!" screamed Chuck.

A long dark staircase ascended up into a black stairwell disappearing into a dark void. Tommy's eyes got uneasy from its eerie appearance and he really didn't want to run upstairs into the unknown, but the shaking door behind him left him little choice. He let go of the door and sprinted up the stairs behind his two friends hurdling three steps at a time. The thud of the wooden door smashing into shreds below hastened their paces until they reached the top of the stairs and utter darkness. A darkness known only in the caves of the earth and the pits of Hell engulfed the three, leaving them unable to see each other. Feet stumbled maladroitly from the darkness below chasing after them mindlessly through the dark. Chuck lifted his hands and began to feel through the darkness until his palms came in contact with a wall. His fingers skimmed along its smooth surface piloting him through the darkness. His fingertips ran across the scattered indentions of doorframes and small light fixtures leading the group through the long cluttered apartment hallway. Their feet bumped into unidentifiable lumps and piles of matter that inspired the worst of images in their imaginations.

Screams and loud bumps came from the top of the stairs as infected scrambled through the darkness into the shrouded hallway. Their wild bodies crashed into the walls blindly charging in the direction their prey had run, scratching and tearing at each other selfishly trying to be the first to impregnate the infection. The hysterical shrieking injected the three living soul's veins with an almost liquefied terror that seized their blood and sent them into a blind rush. They began to run down the hall without inhibitions unaware of their course or any objects that might stand in their path. Chuck stumbled and slid to the floor face first coming to rest against a soft object. Both Tommy and Laurie, still running at full speed and oblivious to his fall, accidentally stepped onto his back and legs and tumbled to the floor past him. A hand reached out and grasped Chuck's wrist in the darkness.

"Tommy?" asked Chuck curiously.

Teeth sank into the bare skin on the top of his hand grinding against the bone. He screamed in both shock and pain as sharp teeth masticated the bone, flesh and veins of his hand. His free hand began to beat at the head latched onto his other hand with the butt of his pistol in continuous deep thuds. He spun the gun around in his hand effortlessly.

"Get the fuck off me you fucking piece of shit!" he screamed gnashing his teeth and pulling the trigger on his pistol.

A spark of light from the tip of the barrel revealed a set of feral bloodshot eyes and grinding teeth clamped onto his hand tightly. He clicked the hammer back again and again until it clicked empty, echoing high-pitched clanks down the narrow hall. The short brutal lights that sparked from the tip of his pistol revealed the body of the infected man as well as those that were in pursuit hysterically crawling over each other down the hall in short flashes like an old film that was running slowly enough to expose each frame. The infected man's hand went limp from its grip on his wrist and slipped down his arm hitting the floor with a thud. Tommy reached down through the darkness guided by memory of their places and grasped his injured friend underneath his arms. Chuck rose up under assistance and stood to his feet in the black void of the apartment hallway clinching his hand. He wasn't sure how bad it was, but it was wet, slippery and numb.

"Run Laurie," screamed Tommy into the darkness frantically, "we're coming!"

Panicking from the situation and the terrifying sound of Tommy's plea, Laurie ran headlong down the cluttered hallway leading their escape from the infected scraping along the walls from behind. Her body suddenly ricocheted into a hard barrier sending her backwards with a jolt on her backside. She ignored the spark that shot up her spine as her tailbone struck the floor leaping back to her feet fondling the walls with her hands wildly searching for an exit, door or another hallway. Her hands came in contact with a door knob and she twisted it without concern for what might be on the other side; nothing could hold the terror of what chased her through the darkness. After she stepped in, the floor dropped six inches and she lost her footing, tumbling down a flight of stairs. Her head came down hard against the wall at the end of the stairs sending stars across her vision in the dark stairwell. Two more forms stumbled down the stairs after her stopping just short of her glassy eyes. The slightest radiance of starlight emitted through a dirty door window exposing the shadowed image of Tommy and Chuck. Tommy lifted her slumping body to her feet and slung her arm over his shoulder and neck holding it in a firm, but kind grip. Chuck opened the door with his good hand and they found themselves back outside in the open streets of Atlanta.

They ran down the road to escape the infected mob that eventually swelled out of the apartment complex alerting other inactive dead in the area. Screams in vain reached them through the darkness and to regain their composure they held up in a small abandoned corner store. Tommy pulled a gate across the glass door and collapsed into a dark corner out of site from the street. In the dark hallway during all the commotion, Laurie had not become aware of the nature of Chuck's injury and neither he nor Tommy spoke a word about it. To ignore the situation at least allowed the two friends to forgo the realization of Chuck's ultimate demise. Avoiding subjects over which they had no control was something the two not only preached, but strictly practiced.

"We'll give it an hour or so to let things calm down out there before we move out," whispered Tommy.

Chuck knew they had to move soon before daylight improved everyone's vision, possibly revealing their presence, taking away the cover of darkness that had just allowed them to escape. They wouldn't escape again as they had under the rays of the warm sun. The heat would make the putrefied bodies of the infected faster and it didn't have to be said what the sight of three uninfected would do to their desire to infect. Another ghastly thought burrowed its way into his worn and weary mind; he would have to leave Tommy and Laurie before he spread the infection and what would he do during that time before he changed and he was all alone? He took a firm grip on the hilt of his pistol wondering if he would wait it out and join the ranks of the living dead or stop it by taking his own life. He tried to shake the thought from his mind, but the wound on his hand reinserted it with each throb.

"Let's move before we lose any more of the night," proclaimed Tommy rising to his feet.

Laurie got up still shaken from her fall but ready to move, Chuck's leg protruded from behind a box motionless. A lump instantly formed in Tommy's throat as he swallowed his words and went mute. His eyes stared at the still leg desperately longing to see it move, for it to come to life in motion. He wasn't ready to lose his friend yet.

"I'm not coming," said the voice slowly.

"What?" said Laurie bewildered. "What do you mean?"

He didn't reply and Tommy stood helpless unable to respond.

"I can't believe you're going to walk out on us when we need you most," said Laurie walking over to confront him.

His shadowed form lay hunched over holding a bloodstained hand.

Their eyes met, "Oh my God!" she gasped stepping away from him.

She slowly backed up until she bumped in Tommy who stood hypnotized by the image of his friend's still leg. Laurie's fear stricken eyes spun to meet Tommy's only to find them lost, unaware of her presence. Her hands caressed his checks and pulled his eyes away from their fixation.

"Tommy," she said gently, "we have to go now before it's too late."

He stood quiet without saying a word and although his eyes stared into to hers, he didn't acknowledge her.

"Listen to me; if he is not already contagious he will be in a few hours."

Her words sank into his heart like a huge stone landing in a tranquil pool disturbing it to its base. Survival meant he had to leave the very friend whom had saved him from the perch in his yard.

"I won't do it," he replied.

"This infection can become highly contagious in a matter of only a few hours. It won't do us any good to stay together and join him."

"A few days back when you got separated from us on your horse, he wanted me to abandon you and I didn't. I didn't leave you for him and I won't leave him for you."

"He won't hold it against you. He knows we don't have any other choice."

"What about the CDC, the whole reason we came here is for a cure!"

"That's right a vaccine... something to prevent infection, not reverse it."

"He came here for a cure and I'll be damned if I am not going to try and get it for him."

"Remember when I first met you and I wanted to go back for my husband, but he wouldn't go back because the risk was too high? This is no different!"

"Listen to her," said the cheerless voice. "It's what I would do. I might agonize about it, but I'd do it."

"Well you're one lucky son of a bitch that I'm not an asshole like you," declared Tommy firmly.

He walked over to his lifelong friend and helped him to his feet, "I don't want to hear it, either you help me or we literally rot here."

Chuck stepped back to stand on his own and began to wheeze in a long deep cough. His injured hand hung limp at his side and his face had begun to take on an unnatural color under the cover of shadows. The sight of their devotion drove the fear of infection out of her heart, inspiring compassion. She went over to the two men and while staring into Tommy's eyes began to wrap his friend's injured from a piece of her own shirt. She nodded for Tommy to lead the way and he slid over toward the door to keep watch.

"It's clear."

They stumbled out back into the street and shuffled clumsily away from the groans that echoed in torment. They crossed silently through the dark city coveting its shadows and using its blocks to measure their progress.

Piercing dead eyes leaped from a swell of darkness guiding out stretched arms and a searing scream that emerged from rotten teeth. Tommy fired his pistol into the scurrying body dropping it with three loud shots. More eyes focused on the group from outside the darkness bringing on an all-out assault of infected. The trio circled like covered wagons and threw back the onslaught that came in upon them in a fury of gun smoke and fire. Pale faces continued to appear from the surrounding darkness threatening to overwhelm the three and devour them in a surge of infected. Tommy frantically holstered his empty pistol and cradled his assault rifle using its power to rip through the crowd.

"Run!" screamed Tommy.

He forged a spearhead into the mass of swirling arms and rabid teeth cutting the mob down viciously. Laurie seized Chuck's arm dragging him through the crowd stepping over the bodies of the fallen. A haze came over Chuck's eyes and although he ran in pursuit, he couldn't have cared had they left him in that crowd or not. He continued to shoot carelessly as their eyes came into the focus of his own placing a slug of metal in between those that got too close as would an expert sniper, not necessarily because he wanted to, but because he still could.

"Emory University!" said Laurie in excitement. "I think I know the way now!"

They took off through the darkness zigzagging between buildings confusing those that pursued losing the majority of the infected in the dark alleys, but as they ran their pursuer's screams awoke more dead that took passionately to the chase. She saw the building up ahead and began to run like she had never run before, ruffling the black night through her dark hair until they merged into one with no beginning or end. Her heart pumped blood through her veins giving life to her muscles that injected force into her steps like that of a champion in the final lap of the big race. She left nothing in reserve and collapsed up against the door beating at it fiercely with limp limbs. The flesh and bone of her arms crashed against the solid framework of the door until they went numb with sensory overload. She spun around and began to pound at it with her heels before suddenly stopping. In her frantic run to the door, she had lost her two friends… she was alone. Her eyes widened toward the darkness from hence she had run in both hope and fear of what might appear.

"Tommy! Chuck! I am over here!" she screamed in desperation. "Please I am over here!"

She slid down to the base of the door and sat ready to accept her fate… the fate meant for all of man. Long and sporadic groans filtered through the darkness, but they were far away, isolating her even further. Had she heard gunshots or even that of infected, then she would have had some hope, but she had outrun her friends and now she stood alone… forlorn. She dropped the clip from her pistol and loaded her last one faithfully following the directions that Tommy had given her a few days back when he had coached her step by step how to load the pistol. It weighed heavily in her hand fully loaded, and she contemplated what it felt like to be shot in the head. Would you feel anything she wondered… was this earth all there was to their existence or was there more? Shadows came out of the darkness and ran up upon her seizing her in fear.

"Laurie," said the cloudy voice, "wake up, we need you."

She turned her head toward the voice that tunneled towards her subconscious, but it faded before reaching her conscious.

"I can't get through to her," said Tommy rising up from her slouched body.

Chuck leaned over a railing and began to vomit uncontrollably. Tommy could see it in his friend's eyes and lazy mannerisms… he was going fast. It wouldn't be long before he would have to make a decision to kill his friend or let him kill him.

Infected began to appear from the darkness in the corner of Tommy's eye and he spun around shooting one in the head barely six feet away. Chuck began to fire his pistol at any movement he saw, but through haphazard coughing he missed his targets until his gun clicked empty. Unable to reload it, he dropped the gun to his side where it clanked off the sidewalk and disappeared into the brush through the railings. Tommy quickly reached back and freed the loaded pistol from Laurie's horrified grip and handled it to him, saying something he thought he would never say.

"Wait until they get real close before you shoot; you can't hit the side of a barn."

Chuck nodded wiping blood from his mouth using the wall to brace himself while he watched with tired eyes and a shaky pistol. They came at the door in a rage with piercing red blood shot eyes soaking in hot metal rounds audaciously dropping for the opportunity to spread their infection. Tommy reloaded his rifle with lightning reflexes spraying rounds into those that ran up the ramp, dropping the assaulters like they were part of some carnival turkey shoot. The barrel of his rifle turned ash white and clicked heavily jamming a round into its chamber interrupting his fire.

"Shit," yelled Tommy hysterically jerking the lever on his rifle in a mad attempt to eject the round, "it's jammed!"

Chuck dragged himself along the railing and stood in front of him holding his pistol straight out toward the shadowed forms crawling over the mound of dead toward their position. Light ripped from its tip hitting both the dead and infected in random motion as its wielder swayed in fever. A hand took a hold of Tommy from behind and he jerked around half expecting to see Laurie's face, probably for the last time, but instead the gaze of a distinct looking older gentleman in a long white lab coat met him. The older man took hold of Laurie's petrified form and dragged it through the door that she had so greatly desired to enter before blacking out. Tommy grabbed Chuck's stiff body and pulled him through the opening before the man in the coat slammed it shut. The man quickly sealed the door with a long lever and turned around to Tommy.

"Don't worry, they can't get through that. Hurry, we don't have much time, if any."

Chapter 22
The Cure

Two men dragged slumping bodies down a long white hallway vaguely lit by emergency lights spaced just far enough apart to fade the darkness but not enough to expose the pallor of light. They passed through a multitude of sealed doors before finally arriving in what appeared to some type of surgical room. Long metal tables covered with white sheets circled the room like a sterile Stonehenge bringing attention to its bare center. The doctor looked over at the hapless man Tommy was dragging and frowned with concern.

"Get him up on the table so I can start his treatments. I'm not sure if they will be in enough time… from the look, he is close to turning… every second is going to count."

Tommy quickly lifted his friend up on the surgical slab and rolled him over onto his back. The man in the lab coat came over holding a stainless steel tray with an array of syringes and scalpels. He lifted up a needle to the dim lights hanging above and brought its tip down to a swelled blue vein protruding from the patient's arm. A hand literally rose from the dead seizing his wrist with such unanticipated speed that neither Tommy nor the doctor were prepared for such a reaction. Tommy seized the cold hand unable to break its determined grip.

"What the hell are you putting into me?" asked the pale green form lying on the table.

Tommy continued to struggle with the horrid creature all the while reminding himself whom he was struggling with… or at least who it used to be.

"My boy, what I hold in my hand is the only hope you've got left," said the doctor regaining his composure.

The hand loosened its grip and fell back to the table with a lifeless thud.

"Don't let me come back! Do you hear me Tommy?" screamed the voice from the pallid green face. "You do me right fucking here if I come back! Do you hear me?"

"As God as my witness… I swear I will spread your brains across this room if you come back."

"Thanks man, you're a true friend. I knew I could rely on you! It's this piece of shit right here that I don't know if I can trust or not," he said pointing at the doctor shakily.

He had never trusted doctors.

"Please use those straps to restrain him," ordered the doctor.

Chuck lay still and closed his eyes as the needle pierced his skin releasing the yellow serum into his bloodstream, hardly caring if he lived or not; anything to end the way he felt at the moment was fine with him, even if it meant death.

"Will he make it?" asked Tommy in a whisper.

"I can't guarantee anything. He's pretty far along."

"Will he turn?" asked Tommy nervously wondering if he would have to keep his promise to his friend.

"I am the only one who has taken the vaccine… it has never been tested on a subject so far along. I assume the inoculation I gave him will destroy the infection within him and if he turns to the infection before it completes the cycle, then he will die along with it or at least for our sake I hope so," he said looking at him frankly. "You two have quite a fight ahead of yourselves too."

Tommy looked at him queerly.

"Both of you two are infected as well… you'll probably make it, but you are in for one hell of a long night."

Tommy and Laurie spent the next thirty six hours with chills, body aches, vomiting and body temperatures that were up and down the thermometer like a child's yoyo. They passed back and forth through the world of sleep and reality until Tommy awoke to the delicate features of Laurie's face and soft lips.

"Hey tiger, you up for something to eat that won't fit through a tube?"

"You got a thick cut steak and a beer in your pocket?"

"Come on let's see what we can find to eat around here."

"Wait!" said Tommy half awake from his morbid dream sleep. "Where is Chuck?"

Doctor Ledbetter stood with his back toward the door blocking the view of his patient stretched out on the surgical table. He heard the door click open and turned around to greet his visitors.

"Welcome back to the world of the living, what little there is left of it," he commented.

Tommy ignored his dry comment and walked up to the still form of his old friend. His face showed the signs of the struggle he was fighting from within, twisting erratically with quick jerks and short grunts.

"I've done everything I could with what training I have and the tools available. I put him on a ventilator after he quit breathing on his own."

"Is he going to make it?" asked Tommy.

"He's already a miracle surviving death twice on this table. I had a hell of a time getting his heart started again, but for the moment it's faintly beating on its own."

"Doctor," asked Laurie, "are you the only one here?"

"Yes I am afraid so, my child. Infection spread through the facility several days before I had completed the vaccination."

"But how did you…"

"How did I survive?" he said interrupting her. "I stayed away from everyone, treated myself kind of like a computer; if it's not on-line or you don't share data, then you cannot be infected by a virus. So, I sealed myself off from everyone else as soon as I heard that someone was sick. They are still over there right now staring through the glass in the door."

"But how did you know that everyone was infected?"

"I didn't… I was too close to a breakthrough to risk any possible failure."

"Don't you think that's a little fucked up?" asked Tommy.

"If I hadn't done what I did, then all of us including myself, would have fallen to the infection as well and the world would be without hope, but now we have hope, the chance for a new future!"

Laurie and Tommy stood silent as the doctor revealed his success with a look of almost absolute madness.

"You two must be starving. I don't have anything more than a limitless supply of MREs left here by the National Guard unit detached to us, but you are welcome to as many as you want," he said noticing their hesitation. "There is nothing you can do for him right now. I'll keep an eye on your friend. The food is down the hall to your left."

They tentatively left the room shutting it before following his directions.

"I don't trust Doctor Kevorkian back there."

"I know he is a little eccentric, but he is obviously a genius," she stopped before continuing. "He saved us and he is trying to save Chuck. His condition is beyond my expertise, Tommy. Without Doctor Ledbetter he is as good as dead… we have no choice but to trust him."

They found the room with little trouble and once inside, sat down ready to eat surrounded by a heap of scattered boxes. All were of the same shape and size bundled by two white straps each. Tommy opened one up and poured its contents onto the floor. Light brown plastic sealed ready to eat meals spilled between the two displayed as a 3D menu on the hard polished floor.

"So my lady," said Tommy in a horrible English accent, "on what shall you dine tonight? We have twelve selections all fresh and expertly prepared by some dehydrator several years ago."

She laughed, "Hmm… I'm feeling a little spicy. I'll have the chicken with salsa."

"A fine selection and the cook will have country captain chicken."

Over the next few minutes the two dug through the contents of their little tan bags and ate as if it were an elegant seven course meal.

"Why did you come with us even after you knew he was infected?"

"It seemed right at the time. I guess that is what the rest of the world thought when their loved ones became infected, and instead of abandoning them to the infection, they held them until they joined them too. Compassion… it's the only thing that separates us from the beast of the earth. The infection took that in to account I think, it knew our weaknesses."

"Not every one of us shows compassion," he said nodding back toward the doctor.

The only defense for the doctor that Laurie could muster was silence. Tommy chewed on a cracker and watched her intently from across the room, digesting his meal, but all the while his secret continued to digest him. He had to tell her before he could ever hope to have any true relationship with her he thought. His thoughts drifted off away from their tiny dark room way above all the mess of the infection and came to rest on some mountaintop safe from the reach of the dead. He held her and they laughed carelessly with nothing but hope and aspirations for the future. How wonderful that would be he thought slowly drifting off to sleep nestled in between a pile of boxes.

Two eyes awoke to the smooth round tip of a black pistol barrel listlessly shining under the fluorescent lights.

"Say something before I keep my promise and spread your brains across this room."

"Something," said the voice faintly.

"God damn I knew it couldn't keep you down, you mother fucker! You are the first to ever come back!" screamed his friend wildly as if he was drunk at some frat party. "Tough as nails man, you are tough as nails."

"I sure feel like I got hammered all right," he said half conscious.

His continued good sense of humor through such a trial lightened the room tremendously, and even the dry demeanor of the doctor shifted into that of a wry smile.

"Welcome back young man, you were on the doorstep to reanimation… you have given medical science hope."

The small group spent the next week huddled in the city of the dead safely locked away from its inhabitants as the three recovered physically from their exposure to the infection. Within three weeks, not one showed any signs of being sick, except for a few minor skin discolorations similar to bruises, symptoms that Doctor Ledbetter claimed would pass as the blood that had clotted in their tissues cleared. A safe place to rest with plenty of food did the trio good and before long Tommy and Chuck were their old selves arguing the meaningless of matters, while Laurie and Doctor Ledbetter mulled over the success of his miracle cure.

"It was my passion to understand this virus, not just to stop it, that aided my achievement in discovering a cure. This virus is really a miraculous step in the evolution of the most basic form of life," said Doctor Ledbetter to an attentive Laurie, whom saw him as a living genius.

"How do you mean?" she asked.

"This particular virus is interesting on so many levels that it nearly boggles the mind with all the fail safe measures it includes in its DNA, almost as if it were genetically engineered by something not of this earth. The cells it infects go through an accelerated cycle of mitosis and cytokinesis nearly one hundred times that of normal cell division until it overwhelms the host and takes control of its central nervous system, which in turn it uses to transmit motor signals directly to the somatic nervous system. It contaminates the brain tissue, deteriorating all of the body's sensory neurons apart from the cranial nerves, so its host will not be susceptible to pain but still be able to use its olfactory, optic and auditory systems," he said excited. "The manner in how its hosts have such an inexorable desire to infect everyone of its species, the way the hosts go into a hibernation mode to save energy when there are no suitable capsules to contaminate are unparalleled in the known history of disease. Other diseases simply depend on random exposure to survive; this one ensures it."

On the other side of the room Chuck and Tommy were having an entirely different and far less technical conversation.

"I'm telling you weight lifting is for pussies," said Chuck

"Arnold Schwarzenegger?"

"Pussy."

"Lou Ferrigno?"

"Gimp."

"I doubt you would be saying that if they were here standing next to us."

"The easiest fights I ever got into were with weight lifters, I'm telling you they are bunch of chumps."

"When did you ever get into a fight with a weight lifter? I've known you since you were ten and if you had ever kicked the shit out of some weight lifter I would have heard about it."

The conversation had gotten so farfetched that it had gained the attention of Laurie and Doctor Ledbetter from across the room as well.

"For your information I was eight and he was twelve on the school weight team. He was such a puss it wasn't worth mentioning," he declared with a sly smile.

"That wasn't even a good lie. They don't even have weight lifting teams at twelve."

"Seriously, what does lifting weights do for you besides compensate for low self-esteem? When the hell do you ever need to be strong enough to lift perfectly balanced three hundred pound objects with no slip handles? If something weighs that much and you need to move it, it comes with wheels or they made shit like dollies and forklifts to move it."

Tommy reached up to the top of his head as if he were wearing an invisible hat and tipped it toward his friend across the table.

"We have a winner! It is official. All weight lifters are pussies."

"Thank you sir, for listening to reason."

"A compelling conversation," said Doctor Ledbetter under his breath to Laurie.

She laughed at their youthful charm ignoring her colleague's remark.

"Gentlemen," he said interrupting the two, "there has been something I have been meaning to talk to you about, but I thought it would be best to wait until all of you were of sound mind and body."

"So you've given up on the sound mind thing eh?" joked Chuck.

"This is serious," he said a bit frustrated.

"More serious than the five million zombies outside the door?"

"It will have an immediate effect upon our current state of affairs."

"Sorry Doctor Ledbetter we were just joking around," said Tommy once again making peace for his friend.

"I have been sending transmissions via satellite feeds since the beginning of the infection, receiving little more than a few scattered responses from other lone research facilities across the country," he said pacing across the room, "but once I started broadcasting about the successful development of a vaccine, I received a very interesting response from our government."

"We have a government?" asked Chuck with a new interest.

"Weeks prior to the arrival of the infection into North America, the President, Congress, the Supreme Court and other components of our government went to the air to avoid contracting the virus."

"Where are they now?" asked Laurie.

"Our government has relocated itself in its entirety to the distant islands of Hawaii."

"So we are not alone," said Tommy relieved.

"Damn, of all the people I hoped had died in this shit, the President was at the top of my list," stated Chuck.

"Separated by the vast Pacific Ocean, the infection has not found its way to its shores yet and by executive order all travel to the islands is strictly prohibited, but with the word of our new discovery, this executive order has been temporarily waived!"

"Once your immunization is duplicated there won't any need for such a restriction," commented Laurie happily.

"Yes, that is precisely why we need to prepare to leave as soon as possible."

"Wait a minute," said Laurie astounded, "you mean you haven't given them the formula to your vaccine yet?"

"Of course not my dear, without it we are worthless."

"What about all the other research cells out there at risk to the infection every second of the day, research facilities like mine... like yours."

"You must understand my research is our only bargaining chip. If I broadcast it on open frequencies then we have no more value than four hicks hopelessly locked up in a basement. Once they get it, do you think they will send a rescue team into a city with millions of infected for four people?"

"Have you gone crazy, you are a doctor?" she screamed angrily. "You took an oath to help those in need."

"We're in need," said Chuck.

"Shut up!" she screamed. "Every second you hold back millions of lives are placed in peril."

"You are thinking irrationally. Rational thought is why I am still alive, why all of you are alive, rational thought is why we have a cure. If we do not use this as leverage, we will be left here to rot," said Doctor Ledbetter.

"I don't believe you. Our government would not abandon us once we gave them the cure."

"Who the fuck is your government?" said Chuck. "Because I know my old government would sell me down river for one barrel of crude oil."

Laurie walked over to Chuck gritting her teeth and turned his chair over backwards in a rage sending him flat on his back with his feet protruding upwards into the air, before stomping out of the room.

Tommy burst into laughter.

"Shit, I really pissed her off this time," said Chuck's voice from under the table.

Tommy got up from his chair and followed her into the hallway. He chased her around the corner and spun her around, bringing their eyes together. Hazel pools peered out her swollen lids leaking tears out their corners onto flushed cheeks.

"You can't bring him back," he said soothingly.

"No but maybe I can save someone else's Brian!" she declared emotionally.

Tommy held her close without the words to say he was sorry. He wanted desperately to reveal his sin, his crime toward such a lovely soul. Tears of his own swelled painfully in his eyes dripping down onto her shoulders as he held her tight.

"I can't believe you of all people are siding with those two," she said as if the two men they had left in the room were monsters.

"Do you see me in there with them? If it were my cure I would broadcast it out to everyone from the rooftop if I had to, but it's not mine to give. Hell, I wouldn't know what it was if I was holding it in my hand right now. He researched it. It is his to do what he wants with it… right or wrong."

"Not at the expense of mankind," she cried. "Not at the expense of mankind."

"We owe him our life Laurie. I can't go in there and beat it out of him, the best thing we can do for now is get to Hawaii as fast as possible, so they can get the cure… so we all can have a future."

"A future at the expense of others is a future without me!" she screamed before tearing away and disappearing around the corner.

Tommy let her go and quickly dried his eyes before going back into the room with his friend and Doctor Ledbetter. Chuck saw the red in his eyes, quickly averting his own gaze from that of Tommy.

"Women make rash scientists, but good ones. She'll come around," commented Dr. Ledbetter.

"What about our government, when are they going to come around for us and the old cure?" asked Chuck.

"They're not," he said queerly.

The two men sitting calmly froze with wide unbelieving eyes and dumbfounded facades struck like stone by his response. He saw their puzzled features and elaborated.

"I'm not entirely sure if they completely believed my claim of having a cure, so we are not worth the risk for a pickup in Atlanta, but they were curious enough to give us a thirty day window."

"This invitation… does it apply to all of us?" asked Tommy. "I mean you're the miracle man, the rest of us are expendable."

"It doesn't matter, it can't be done. There is no way we can make it to Hawaii in thirty days. We'd be lucky to make it out of the city."

"We don't have to go all the way to Hawaii. Our government has agreed to meet us halfway. We've got to reach a set of coordinates near the southernmost tip of Monterey Bay National Marine Sanctuary in thirty days for pick up. I'm an old man and you three have proven you can travel across country. They may not need you, but I do."

"Still can't be done, California is too far away. We can't walk it in time, the roads are clogged, they might as well as told you to shove that cure right up your ass," declared Chuck.

"We can make it by air," said Laurie stepping back into the room fully composed.

"Forget that we don't have a plane at the moment, where are we going to get a pilot?" asked Chuck.

"You worry about the plane, I'll worry about the pilot," she said confidently.

"You're a pilot?" asked Tommy surprised.

"My dad was a Colonel in the Air Force."

"Why the hell didn't you tell us this on our way to Atlanta?" asked Chuck.

"You never asked."

"Okay, that is a talent that in our current situation we should know about, i.e. you can read tarot cards, you're a masseuse, hello I can fly a plane!"

"What type of plane can you fly?" asked Doctor Ledbetter weighing their options methodically.

"Personal aircraft, I was trained on a Cessna one eighty two."

"So you really have a pilot's license, daddy didn't let you hold the wheel for a few seconds or something?" asked Chuck warily.

"He let me hold it for a few hundred hours."

"Hot damn," said Tommy in excitement. "We're goin down to Cali."

"Where are supposed to get a plane?" asked Chuck contemplating the most important part of the puzzle.

"I have a road atlas that might help us locate an airport where we can commandeer such a plane," said Doctor Ledbetter.

Chapter 23
Escaping Atlanta

The rest of the day was spent in preparation for their departure from the CDC research facility. Once again they would attempt to travel through the infested streets of Atlanta at night in hopes of clearing it before sunrise. Laurie and Doctor Ledbetter prepared his vaccine and all the documentation they would need to easily transfer his accomplishment to Hawaii, while Tommy and Chuck did the grunt work of organizing the gear and supplies they would need to cross from one coast of the continental United States to the other. The four worked relentlessly through the night and then slept most of the next day resting up for when they would leave the following night. Each one lay stretched out on the floor uncomfortably with butterflies in their stomachs as they waited for the moment at hand. Their eyes watched the second hand on the clock click loudly from one second to the next dragging time along drearily as if it were the only way to know that time had not stopped. The long hand slid quietly over the six at the bottom of the clock, bringing Chuck to his feet.

"Well it's ten thirty…" he said only slightly motivated. "It's not going to get any darker than it is right now."

Everyone got up reluctantly, loaded up their gear and walked slowly down the long hall they had traveled while suffering from the infection after barely escaping from the inhabitants of Atlanta a few weeks earlier. A dull white haze gleamed softly from vacant labs simmering an off white mist around their silhouettes from the reflection of the hallway's off-white tiles. Chuck and Tommy stopped at the huge bolted door and looked at each other with concern. They knew their job, Doctor Ledbetter's expertise and breakthrough had gotten them an invitation to somewhere untouched by the black death of the infection, while Laurie's talents as a pilot were indispensable, leaving the difficult task of escaping Atlanta up to them.

"Nobody says shit unless it's absolutely necessary, and do not pull a trigger unless Tommy and I have done so already or we're dead. Either way you're probably going to die," said Chuck in a stern warning. "Pay attention and don't get left behind, I'm not going back for anybody, cure, pilot or not."

He unlatched the door and a damp stench poured into the hallway, turning their stomachs upside down. Chuck poked his head out the door's slight opening and peered out into the darkness. The buzz of flies rippled past his head in a swirling swarm of black fatality. Bodies of infected dead that had attempted to slaughter them the night they made a near final stand outside the door to the CDC lay in heaps all along the sidewalk and railings feeding the frenzy of bloodthirsty flies. Chuck pulled out his pistol gripping it with one hand, while using his other to cover his nose and mouth. The small group tiptoed through the mass of littered and torn bodies holding back their bodies' natural urge to vomit from the smell and sight of such a horrid scene. They scurried away from the large complex in a close huddle edging through the shadows quietly. Their blackened images flattened up against the wall as Doctor Ledbetter consulted his GPS hand-held unit for the best direction to clear the city. Chuck had never seen such a unit before and although he was old fashioned and not an advocate of new technology, he felt better about their situation with it in hand. Doctor Ledbetter pointed into the dark, signaling Tommy and Chuck to where they should go. They took his heed shuffling from the cover of one building to the next leapfrogging through the city like thieves in the night, except their goal was to steal their very lives. With the four leaning flat against the wall Doctor Ledbetter took another reading from the GPS.

"That is Georgia four hundred," he said whispering in a low tone. "We've got to cross it."

A hand reached up through the darkness and seized Doctor Ledbetter's ankle griping it tightly. Startled, he let out a yelp and began to frantically try and break free from its cold grip. Chuck's stout palm alertly muffled his lips, as would a kidnapper to a victim, silencing his scream. A black boot began to stomp on the dirty face protruding from the darkness turning it to mushy stain on the concrete. The cold hand slipped from the doctor's nervously shaking leg flopping to the ground with a small thud. Tommy stepped back and scuffed the bottom of his soles across the ground drying the blood from his soles leaving a long wide red streak. Cautious eyes and strained ears soaked in the dim night air that shrouded the city anxiously waiting to see if anything had been awakened. The night remained still and quiet without a stir bringing forth silent sighs of relief from the recoiling group. Chuck's eyes watched the still shadows upon the car-jumbled highway warily. It had been on a highway where he had first encountered the horde of the infection, barely escaping from it with his life.

"Let's cross," he said gathering up his courage, "stay low… below the car windows."

Shadowed forms scurried from the darkness like roaches racing for food running in a low crouch toward the crumbled cars parked along the highway. Chuck cautiously slid over the highway barrier landing onto the road's shoulder with his pistol in hand. Three other shapes dropped over and followed his lead. He crept in a low duck walk along the cars slipping between the wrecked vehicles without raising himself into the view of possible infected hibernating within. Leading the pack, Chuck straddled the median and slid over to the other side of the highway with the agility of a cat. Doctor Ledbetter followed the others landing awkwardly onto his side while gripping his precious briefcase with all his might. If something happened to Doctor Ledbetter, its contents could hold the last hope for mankind. He held onto it as fervently as would a mother her newborn baby, following the other three around parked cars and into the brush along the side of the highway. The tall unkempt weeds and brush covered their slow global-guided march through the dark city from highway to highway. They had encountered only one infected since their departure from the research center and each person cautiously thanked whatever forces, power or luck that allowed such a miracle to transpire upon their small group.

"This should be four-o-seven," said Doctor Ledbetter quietly to the trio.

Chuck signaled for him to be quiet, before cautiously moving with alert eyes onto the overpass. Oil and antifreeze stained the pavement having drained slowly from the wrecked cars creating a slick sludge on its surface that glistened eerily in the moonlight. He squatted down slowly dipping his fingertips into the industrial ooze to keep his balance on the pavement's slimy surface. They waddled single file through the wreckage soiling their knees to avoid the sight of nearby infected. Leaning up against an overturned tractor-trailer the four regrouped and rested their lungs in the hot night.

A cadence of nods signaled the point man of their small group that they were ready and he quickly retook the front. He slipped to his belly and slid up near the end of the truck, coming eye to eye with an infected man's upper torso protruding out from under the over turned truck. The entire lower half of its body from the waist down had been crushed underneath the truck's weight pinning the being beneath the highway's rubble since the infection had first hit Atlanta, but it still lived to spread the infection it served. Its hands began to claw fiercely at the pavement in a feeble attempt to free itself, tearing the flesh from its fingertips to the pasty white of splintered bone. Distressed screams of frustration ripped through the still night at it struggled to reach its objective in vain. Chuck quickly pulled a hatchet free from the holster on his belt and began to strike at it missing it by only a few inches.

"Shit Tommy, see if you can reach it!" said Chuck anxiously. "It's too far away for me!"

Tommy threw his hammer at it with all his might in vague hope that it might strike its target and silence it forever. It missed bouncing off the truck with a spark landing harmlessly next to its intended target. The horrid creature continued to screech wildly howling at the men, as would a wolf at the moon threatening to awake many more of its brethren. Desperate to end the horrible noise, Chuck drew his pistol, taking aim at the horrible screaming nightmare. He focused the gun's sights on the center of its head tensely squeezing the trigger and lifting the hammer away from the pistol. His mind told him that it was the wrong thing to do, but it felt right in his heart to destroy such a ghastly creature. It was the calm hand of his friend lowering the tip of his pistol that helped him to reason once again with his head instead of his heart.

"Let's get as far away as we can from this thing," said Tommy desperately.

They rose to their feet, running through the debris toward the edge of the highway, when it happened. Something in the night broke loose surrounding the small band unwillingly within its dark grip of fear. Pale ghostly faces appeared hovering in the night peering through the darkness out of dirty broken windows with intent gazes. Hungry pupils swelled quietly as if they were not sure if what they saw was real or not. Chuck took hold of his rifle and began to fire at those that appeared from the obscurity first. He sprayed a group of converging infected flinging their bodies to the ground as more seemed to materialize out of thin air.

"Run your ass off and shoot anything that gets into the way," said Chuck lifting up his rifle.

Fire ripped from the tip of his rifle throwing an infected woman over the shoulder fading her image into the thick foliage alongside the road. The other two members of the group began to fire their guns too, while Doctor Ledbetter cowered in between, holding his briefcase tightly against his chest. More infected began to appear from over the sides of the highway blocking any escape along it successfully herding the four within its borders. Unsure where to run, but knowing it was their only hope, Chuck ran up the highway clearing away infected the best he could with a bobbing pistol. A blaze of gunfire followed him up the road dropping infected like flies in a haze of poison. Ahead the vague silhouette of a bridge caught his attention calling his legs to move faster, so that the night seemed to streak by with the blurred faces of infected that took to the chase. The four runners made the edge of the bridge that spanned the muddy Chattahoochee clearing the infected on it with a barrage of gunfire. Infected began to swell onto the bridge from both sides closing in with an insatiable hunger for their blood. Below in the darkness raged the rough brown swirling waters of the Chattahoochee reflecting the shimmering image of a half moon.

Chuck stood up on the edge of the bridge, stared down and offered what might be his last advice, "Cross your legs and your arms and look out at the horizon when you jump."

And with that he disappeared over the edge. His body plunged into the water like a harpoon sinking deep below the river's surface which engulfed him in its black current. Doctor Ledbetter jumped last, not by the will of his courage, but by the fear of being eaten alive, squeezing his briefcase against his chest as would a mother her baby. His body hit the surface perpendicularly ripping his precious briefcase from his arms like a rocket. He unconsciously gasped as it slipped from his fingers and his lungs filled with cool muddy water. A crack of light from the moon struck his eye through the murky water guiding his way to the surface. He desperately reached up toward the light struggling to breathe within the depths as would a fish smothering from the inside out. He made one final frantic grunt and then went silent swirling limply underneath the river's current. Three heads bobbed above the surface panting in the hot summer night rushing down the river out of control. Bodies of the infected began to crash into the water from above raining from the bridge like heavy concrete blocks. The dark forms plunged below the river's surface disappearing beneath it dragging along the bottom of the river like dead weights.

"Where is everyone?" yelled Laurie in a near panic.

"I'm here," answered Chuck swimming toward the bank.

"Where is Doctor Ledbetter?" asked Tommy looking around in the dark.

"Doctor Ledbetter!" screamed Laurie into the swirling dark.

"Shut up!" replied Chuck. "You will wake up more infected."

"We can't leave him!" she replied quietly.

"We're not leaving him, let's get to the bank and regroup."

Three tired bodies crawled into a tangle of small intertwined trees, weeds and bushes, flopping backwards on the river's shore like waterlogged rats.

"Do you see him?" she asked breathing heavily.

"I don't see anything out there," said Tommy staring at the glow from the moon on the river's surface.

"He landed right next to us, but never came back up," said Chuck lying down and holding his side exhausted with closed eyes.

"Oh my God, without him, we have lost the cure," she exclaimed.

"Do you know anything about it?"

"No!" she said frantically. "He was so damned afraid someone would steal it, he wouldn't tell me anything."

"His briefcase!" said Tommy with hope. "It has the cure in it."

"It's gone too," said Chuck.

"We've got to try and find it," said Laurie desperate to rescue the secret of the cure.

"We'll never find a black briefcase at night. This river goes on for miles and when the sun rises, our cover is gone," said Chuck.

"What about the rendezvous?" asked Tommy curiously. "The only reason they are picking us up is because of the cure."

"They don't know we don't have it and they don't know that one of us isn't Doctor Ledbetter. All we have to do is show up for the pick up on time."

"We are so close to the cure, we have to look for it," proclaimed Laurie looking along the shore like a child on a desperate Easter egg hunt.

"What if we find some fishermen that fell to the infection along the shore? We don't have another bridge to jump off."

"You would let mankind perish to save your own skin," she said disgusted.

"Yes I would," said Chuck sitting up. "When I rank myself against mankind, I'm on the top every time!"

"Shh… be quiet," ordered Tommy.

"I got news for you… you selfish son of a bitch!" she said with no intention of being quiet. "I am the only pilot you got and I will not fly us out of here until after we have tried to find that briefcase!"

A twist of fury seized Chuck's face and he drew his gun pointing it at her, "You will fly that fucking plane or I swear to God I will blow you away right here."

"Do it you stupid fucker!" she yelled back at him defiantly. "Let's see if you got the balls you are always flaunting around."

Chuck pulled back the gun's hammer clicking it with determination before Tommy stepped in the way.

"Get out of the way Tommy," he ordered half crazed.

"If we die it's going to be at the hands of a zombie not from the hands of each other. Let's search the banks for a few hundred feet on both sides and if we don't find it we go straight to the airport."

Chuck lowered his gun and holstered it in frustration. They quietly searched both sides of the river for nearly an hour without any signs of Doctor Ledbetter or his precious briefcase finally forcing even the reluctant Laurie to concede its loss. Although they had lost their GPS unit with the disappearance of Doctor Ledbetter, Tommy had managed to dry off a map he had in his pack enough to plot a crude course toward the airport. They followed in the shadows of highway seventy-five huffing and puffing along it in a slow jog in hopes of reaching their goal before daylight. Laurie led the pace with a smooth stride followed by two gasping young men.

"I guess you've jogged before?" asked Tommy holding his side in an attempt to ease its pain.

"I ran the New York Marathon," she said in a whisper back toward the struggling men.

"I think my heart stopped ten minutes ago," said Chuck trying to ignore the pain.

"Come on boys, we've got a flight to catch."

They jogged on and off stopping only to check their progress on Tommy's deteriorating map or to let the two exhausted men catch their breath. It was a long haul carrying everything they owned and all were glad to finally come to rest at the airport's outer fence line.

"There it is, Cobb County airport," she said peering through links in the fence.

"I don't see any planes," said Tommy disappointed.

"If there are any," she said with hope, "they will be in the hangars."

Chuck pulled out a pair of wire cutters and began to cut through the thin wire fence, "These things about beat my hip to death running here, but I knew they would come in handy."

Chuck carefully crawled through the small hole he made in the fence and ran across the airport's wide-open field in a low trot, coming to rest up against the side of one of its hangars. He slid around the corner peering down toward its runway, which was clear and void of any objects including aircraft. Further down on the building's wall, his eyes spotted a slightly cracked open door. An inner blackness that diminished the open air's darkness seeped from it spreading fear into their hearts and the night like an oozing black tar. An eye peered into the darkness cautiously searching for any image that might give a mental picture of what the hangar contained. Three forms slipped into the hangar sealing out the moonlight with a clank of a door. It was only from the slight sound of their breathing that each one knew that they were not alone. A striking sound leaped from Tommy's hand exploding an intense orb of red light into the dark hangar illuminating the hangar's shadowed interior in a dull ruby glow. The image of a vast open internal building appeared to their compromised vision sheltering two small private aircraft. Laurie reached out with her hand caressing the one closest to her, peeling dust from its smooth exterior.

"A Cessna Skylane five seventeen E," she said while inspecting it. "Someone dropped some cash on this one. It can land in fields and everything."

The door clicked open gently revealing four plush leather seats.

"All the whistles and bells," she whispered in excitement.

"Great let's fuel it up and get the hell out of here while the getting is good," said Chuck ready to get away from the millions of infected in Atlanta.

Tommy's flare died out closing the darkness in on the three like a blanket.

"Shit," said a voice from somewhere in the darkness.

Bright beams of light shot forth from their hands like light sabers drawing sharp circles of light against the barriers of the hangar. Tommy's flashlight spun upon the chin of Laurie revealing the distressed look in her eyes.

"What's wrong?" he asked concerned.

"I've never flown at night," she said.

"You mean we are going to have to try and fly out of here in broad daylight?" asked Chuck suddenly filled with concern of his own.

"I could try and take us up at night, but I've never done it before."

"Shit, I bet that mother fucker makes a hell of a lot of noise too," he said while studying their situation. "We could push it out as soon as daybreak and by the time anything hears us we should be up in the air."

"Cool let's get her loaded up," said Tommy. "What else do we need to do before morning to be flight ready?"

"We need to top it off with fuel and find an aeronautical chart," she said.

The three worked with the quick steps of purpose filling up the small plane's luggage compartment with anything they could find of value. Tommy walked up to the plane carrying another can of gasoline.

"Where is Laurie?" asked Chuck.

"Back in the office over there. Since she has to fly tomorrow, I figured she could use some rest. If she nods off up there we might come down hard."

"Yeah no shit."

Tommy finished pouring the contents of his fuel can into the plane's tank before sitting down to take a break.

"I think I am going to tell her," he said out of the blue.

"About the nuclear plant?'

"Yeah."

"Can't you wait until after we make the flight to California?" he asked. "I don't want to become a part of some unwilling suicide pact into the side of a mountain along the way, because once we're up in the air, we are at her mercy. Shit…" he said remembering who he was talking about, "she has enough balls to leave us."

"Not now, once we make Hawaii."

"I think it's a bad idea. If she turned us in, they might even try us for war crimes or something. Wouldn't that be the shit, getting hanged on an island paradise?"

"She told me she loved me. I don't think I can keep it from her much longer"

"And if she dumps you, are you and the truth going to snuggle up on a beach in Hawaii?

"We caused the death of sixty two people!"

"Sixty one, you forget we saved one."

"Somehow I don't think that makes up for it."

"What are you bitching about? If we hadn't done what we did you wouldn't have ever met her."

"This is not some fucking prank we pulled as kids!"

"This shit is really eating you, isn't it?"

"It's tearing me up, I care about Laurie, but every time I look at her I feel like I stole her from her husband, like I killed him."

"It was those fucking zombies that killed him! They signed their own death warrant when they killed Jeff!"

"No one forced us to do it. We did it because we wanted to… Laurie's husband wasn't one of those soldiers."

"What can we do, man? It might have been wrong, but it's done. No matter how bad you want to take it back you can't. So you have to either live with it or tell her and then live with that. Besides every successful relationship has a secret or two."

"Really? What about your mom and dad? Did they have any secrets?"

"How the hell should I know? Do you think that if someone were holding a lifelong secret from their spouse they would blab it to their kid? But if I had to guess, I'm sure they had a few. I doubt my mom told my dad about every bill or credit card she had and I seriously doubt my dad confessed about every chick he nailed before they got married."

"What about us, man? You got any secrets?"

He looked at him with a sly glance, "Remember Cindy Bullard?"

Tommy nodded.

"Well once when you were still dating her, she put her hands down my pants and tried to give me a hand job during a field trip."

"Man, you are so full of shit!"

"No seriously, when I pulled her hand away she punched me in the nuts."

"I know you are full of shit because there is no way you would ever turn down a hand job from a hot chick like Cindy."

"All right... All right if you can't handle the truth," he said laughing.

Tommy sat still with a tint of annoyance in his eye, which he gleamed at Chuck mercilessly.

"Oh come on, you have to have at least one secret you've kept from me."

"Yeah that I think you are an asshole!" Tommy said getting up.

"Come on she was the one who put the moves on me."

"Do you think I am pissed off about a slut who is more than likely a zombie right now? What is pissing me off is that I was trying to talk to you about a real problem and all you can do is joke around about hand jobs. The secret that you contributed to the death of someone's spouse is not the same as a hidden credit card bill."

"You've got something good going on here, if you tell her you're gonna blow it. Take a look around, how many eligible babes have we ran across since the outbreak? Just one," he said answering his own question, "and you got her, so don't fuck it up. You might end up fucking your hand for the rest of your life."

"You don't get it! It's not like that, I love her and I don't know if I can keep such a secret from her."

"I've never heard you say that about a chick before."

"I've never felt this way about someone before."

Tommy sat down on the other side of the hangar and slid down into a corner, disappearing into the shadows. A long period of silence passed between the friends unlike any they had encountered since they had met over twenty years ago.

"You think this will keep us out of heaven?" said Tommy trying to lighten the conversation.

"I sure hope so. I don't want to go down there all alone.

Chapter 24
Air Across America

Chuck and Tommy stood next to the plane ready to jump in once they opened the hangar door.

"Now do I have to like turn the propeller and yell contact once we're ready to fly?" asked Chuck.

"Just get in unless you want to look like Tattoo waving at the plane as we fly off," the pilot said in good forced spirit.

He nodded and began to lift up the thin metal door. A beam of morning sunlight slid in under the door slowly rising up onto the plane engulfing it in a warm radiance. Laurie looked at the instrument panel and fumbled nervously through the checklist in her mind that her father had beat into her memory as a child.

"You have to check everything twice," he would tell her twice every time to get his point across. "You have to check everything twice. It's not like a car that if something goes wrong you can pull over on the side of the road."

She looked at the two square screens in front of her with concern. She could fly and had a license; what she had failed to tell the two men with her was that it had expired and that she had not been up in the air as a pilot since her father's death nearly six years ago. A flood of memories rushed into her mind as she touched the wheel. It was as if he were sitting next to her at that moment watching and critiquing her every move. The door came to rest fully open swallowing the dark interior of the hangar in a bright tidal wave of light. The two men crawled into their seats and buckled themselves in nervously, with Tommy sitting in the front and Chuck in the back alone. Tommy's hands impulsively slid onto the copilot's wheel alarming his friend in the back.

"Oh hell no," said Chuck seeing his hands on the wheel.

"What?" shrilled Laurie.

"I'm not going up into the air with his hands on the wheel," answered Chuck. "I know he can't fly."

Tommy took his hands off the wheel; "I was only checking it out man. Calm down."

"Will you two shut up!" yelled Laurie. "I am trying to think."

The two men quieted down leaving the small cockpit dead silent. The engine started up on Laurie's first attempt, humming loudly as it sputtered cutting gently through the morning air. The plane slowly pulled out of the hangar exposing it and its passengers to the full brunt of the morning sun. An infected man rose out of the bushes awakened from its departure and clawed at the outside gates in an attempt to reach the runway. More infected began to rise out of the field next to the small airport running toward the runway waving their arms as if to signal their prey. Chuck and Tommy's eyes watched around the airport intently as more infected began to appear from the surrounding buildings. Laurie's eyes never left the airstrip or the plane's control panel. She took a deep breath and accelerated to take off speed. The small plane began to rattle as it drove down the unmaintained runway breaking twigs, pinecones and other rubble in its path, seriously unnerving its two inexperienced flight passengers. An infected woman had somehow made the center of the runway and was running toward the outgoing plane in effect creating a strange game of chicken. Everyone in the plane knew this challenger would not yield. Laurie's eyes never blinked as she lifted the plane airborne inches over the outreached arms of the infected woman. The small compartment went from bumpy to smooth as it climbed.

"Can we speak now?" asked Chuck from the backseat like a child asking permission.

"Yes," said Laurie laughing.

"I was checking since you bit our heads off back there."

"I was nervous and you two were acting like kids."

"What's your point?"

"Sorry, I snapped at you two."

"Ah, it's already forgotten. I'm just glad to be off the ground," said Tommy.

"Are we there yet?" asked Chuck in jest.

"All right now, don't start that," she replied with a smile not only from the pun, but also from the feel of the plane under her command.

"Everything is so little from up here. It's like we are flying over a train model or something," said Tommy peering down below.

"It's amazing isn't it?" she said smiling from the rush of flying again. "There's something special about having the freedom of a bird. My father loved it. Even when he was alive, he wasn't truly alive unless he was in the air. I guess a little of his love for it spilled over into to me."

The small plane passed blindly through a low cloud formation, disappearing into a white void before reemerging into a clear blue sky. The rhythmic hum of the plane's engine soothed its occupants instilling a sense of harmony in their souls. Chuck leaned back into his double seat and pulled his hat down over his eyes shielding his retinas from the sun. Although they were up in the air in danger of crashing at any minute in his mind, he had never felt more secure since his first encounter with the infection. He slipped behind the wall of sleep for the first time in over a year without fear of infected trying to tear through the walls around him and shred him apart. While he slept Laurie and Tommy talked with a renewed hope about the future, about their own future. They talked about everything, their childhood, the basics of flying a plane and even the loss of her husband. It was the talk about her past husband that made Tommy uncomfortable. A heavy shroud of guilt came over him, so heavy that he felt as if he might fall through the bottom of the plane from its weight, crashing to his own death, a death he rightfully deserved.

"Chuck, wake up. We're going to make a pit stop."

Chuck's eyes cracked open revealing the back of Tommy's head peering out the front of the plane as if he were actually flying the plane.

"What's up?"

"There's a small rural airport up ahead, Laurie wants to see if it looks safe enough to land and fuel up."

"How long have I been out?" asked Chuck clearing the sleep from his eyes.

"You've been snoring for three hours. You didn't even wake up when Laurie let me fly this thing some."

"Thank God I was out for that. Want me to take over so you two can catch some zs?"

"No thanks," said Laurie. "I'll use that mental image to stay wide awake."

The small airplane made a low pass screeching along the single runway before lifting back up into the sky. Infected began to swarm out from buildings and a nearby tree line roaming in and around the small airport all with eyes locked onto the tiny passing aircraft.

"There is a shit load of them down there. I think we should go on to the next one," suggested Tommy.

"We got enough fuel to make the next airport?" asked Chuck.

"Sure, want to leave?" asked the pilot.

"Let's go on then," said Tommy.

"We can't be sure the next airport won't have more infected or have any fuel at all," said Chuck seriously eyeing the mob below.

"What the hell do you suggest then?" asked Tommy unbelievably.

"It doesn't look like there are more than thirty or so down there."

"Are you saying we should try and clear the place out?"

"If we land on the other side of that field, we can pick them off as they run across it."

"I'm not sure man, sounds risky to me," said Tommy trying to avoid another one of Chuck's wild plans.

"If they get too close, we won't be able to take off either," warned Laurie.

"I can do it, no problem. It will be a turkey shoot," he said confidently.

The plane made another crossing over the airport to line up with the long field next to the airport and came down to a bumpy but uneventful landing. The infected took chase immediately, running toward the plane as if they were the finish line to some cross-country sprint, going through, over and under a straggly fence that separated the airport from the field. Chuck jumped out of the plane as soon as the plane came to a stop and shouldered his rifle. The first to line up in his sights was a young man whose youth had allowed him to outrun the others, making himself a clear and unobstructed target. A loud boom exploded from Chuck's rifle bursting the head of his target some three hundred yards out. One burst of booming gunpowder after another dropped his approaching targets, as the numbers seemed to swell unnaturally in a rush to overcome the uninfected. Men, women, children, black and white were all killed indiscriminately as he attempted to eliminate the all-out assault.

"There are too many," said Laurie to Tommy in the cockpit.

She started up the plane's propeller blending the three blades of the sputtering prop into one smooth swirling circle. Chuck ignored the sound of the plane starting up next to him and continued to pick off his targets as fast as he could between reloads. The plane began to roll forward through the grass, threatening to leave him if he didn't get aboard.

"Can you make it?" asked Tommy.

"I don't think I can clear them in time on a rough field," she answered staring out at the mob running at the plane.

Tommy looked out his window at his friend unflinchingly firing at the oncoming horde of infected, "He needs help."

The plane's prop continued to spin as its pilot and last passenger crawled down onto the field. Tommy ran around to the baggage door and pulled out two assault rifles, passing the first one to Laurie.

"Shoot at the head and don't shoot until you can see the pupils in their eyes, because if you miss they will overwhelm us."

The infected continued to run across the field in a spread suicide formation dropping down one in number with each gunshot. Chuck began to sweat as he frantically picked his targets, slowly squeezing the trigger with excellent marksmanship skills. He had underestimated their numbers and now the three would suffer whatever consequences their frenzied assaulters could inflict. Out of shells and time, he dropped his trusty hunting rifle, which he had managed to hold on to since the beginning of the infection and pulled his pistol free. Tommy and Laurie stood firm next to him holding their rifles, standing ready for the final fight. It would be messy for there were a dozen or more left. They stood quietly in the wind as the feet of infected stormed toward their formation with gnashing teeth and angry fixated eyes. Laurie's chest muscles seized up tensing tightly like twisted knots and she could feel herself about to black out from the stress. Her eyes went glassy and the rifle in her arms dropped down to her side frozen. She pushed the cloudy wall in her mind back not allowing it to engulf her consciousness. They needed her she thought; she was responsible for her own well-being! Her mind cleared and the infected that had churned before her eyes in slow motion, sped up to full speed and swarmed in among the small armed group. Tommy's rifle was the first to fire bursting the head of the first assailant dropping him face first into the grass a few feet away. Chuck's pistol exploded next knocking down a slender woman, whose face had somehow been torn half off her head to expose an oozing skull. Laurie's rifle exploded last in full automatic tearing into two infected throwing their bodies backwards into the tall swaying meadow. One of Chuck's shots glanced off the head of an infected man cutting his flesh and grazing the bone of his skull, but failing to stop him. The man grabbed hold of Chuck's extended arm and tore into the bare flesh on his hand with clamped teeth. A sharp elbow from Chuck's left arm caught the infected man directly on the side of his head breaking the grip his teeth bore upon his hand ripping a long strip of flesh. The pistol in Chuck's other hand spun backwards as if on a swivel bringing up the heavy butt of the pistol allowing him to pistol beat the man to the ground, The force of the weapon sank the beast's head into the soil of the pasture still clamping its teeth before finally going silent as would a toy with dying batteries. The last of the attackers was an infected child who ran into a volley of fire from Laurie's rifle without any regard for its own well-being. It fell to the ground seeming almost peaceful. Chuck rose up from the man he had beaten to death with wild eyes, nearly as wild as those with the infection in their blood holding a bloody pistol.

"See I told you I could do it," he said with a sly smile.

Their plane lifted back up into the air with full tanks and all three of its passengers. Chuck slouched down into the back holding onto his bandaged hand. It throbbed mercilessly keeping him awake like an annoying alarm clock without a snooze or off button. They flew on through the rest of the day landing at another airport late that evening. After clearing it of straggling infected, they found a suitable hangar and shut themselves in for the night.

"I can't believe that none of these airports are out of fuel," commented Tommy in appeasement.

"Once the infection hit, the most you could fill up were the ones already there. From the looks of it, not many people made it to the private airports, and if they did, where were they to go?" said Laurie looking over the plane doing the after flight inspection her father had taught her as a girl.

"I'm going to get some rest; at this rate we will all be twiddling our thumbs at the coast waiting out the rest of the thirty days."

"Yeah sweetie, you need to get some rest, since it will be all up to you again tomorrow," suggested Tommy.

"I'll be right there," she said inspecting the tires.

Tommy went back into the farthest corner of the hangar and crawled under the covers of a pallet he had prepared earlier. His backpack covered by his jacket served humbly as his pillow breaking the fall of his head as it collapsed into it softly so not to bang against any hard objects inside. Chuck threw his jacket over his shoulder walking over toward an opposite corner scratching his crotch vigorously. Laurie caught his image in the corner of her eye.

"You all right?" she said across the open hangar."

"Who me?" asked Chuck from over his shoulder. "I'm fine, going over here to give you two some privacy."

"I mean your itching, not that I've been watching or anything but over the past few days it has been hard not to notice."

"Oh yeah, just straightening up the ole package."

"Are you sure, I'm a doctor you know."

Chuck stopped and turned around looking back at her through the shadows.

"I've had this itching and burning sensation in my groin for the past few weeks that won't go away and I don't mean that in any derogatory way."

She smiled, "Let me see it."

"See what?"

"The area where you are itching."

"Hey that's not a bad line, but I'm not up for it at the moment."

"Listen," she said, "I know we haven't always seen things eye to eye, but we are in this together."

He leaned up toward her whispering, "This is kind of embarrassing."

"I can't make a diagnosis unless I see it."

"What's going on over here?" asked Tommy appearing from out of the darkness.

"He has an infection, but he is too stubborn to let me look at it," she declared loudly.

"Dude, she's a doctor. Let her have a look at it."

"It's my crotch!" he declared back loudly.

"Oh shit, you got a fucking STD or something?" he asked bewildered.

"I haven't had real sex since all this shit started, so unless you can get one from your imagination, I think we can rule that one out."

"I really need to look to make sure it's not some side effect of the cure you undertook or a reaction to the bite on your hand. All of us were lab rats for Doctor Ledbetter's serum."

"Fine, if I show you my slong will you be satisfied?"

He reached down and began to unbutton his pants.

"Just remember it's a little cold in here."

"Ah man, I don't want to see this," said Tommy walking away.

She candidly reached down and shifted his penis to the left looking at it intently. His looked away with a silent sigh, hoping the humiliation would end soon.

"Tinea Cruris," she stated blankly.

"What the hell is that?" he said curiously while quickly buttoning up his pants.

"You have a severe case of Jock Itch."

"What can I do?"

"Not much," she replied, "it's a fungal infection and without medication about all you can do is keep it dry as possible and hope for the best."

"Damn, sometimes I feel like scratching it off."

"It's understandable, since we can't take showers daily or even change our clothes on a regular basis"

"Thanks doctor, I feel a lot better now."

"Just hold out, I'm sure they have pharmacies in Hawaii."

"Heeh, too bad Doctor Ledbetter didn't put a little something for fungus in that serum of his," he said in banter with a slow bow-legged stride toward his corner.

"You two done over there?" asked Tommy.

Laurie sat down beside him, removing her outer shirt before sliding under the covers next to him.

"Does it bother you if I treat people? You know if you get involved with a doctor they are eventually going to treat people of the opposite sex."

"I know that, but sometimes it's hard to think of somebody you are close to as anything but a lover."

"Oh is it now?"

"Come here," he said pulling her over.

She straddled him sliding her leg over his waistline peering down into his eyes. Her long hair dangled onto his chest as he pulled her closer and kissed her on the lips working his way down her neck.

"What about Chuck?"

"I'm not into that," he said kissing her bare breast.

"No," she said shocked at his comment, "won't he hear us?"

"Honey, he knows we have sex. The only person who doesn't know that he knows is you."

She giggled slightly and quickly covered her mouth so to suppress the noise. Her thin curved body rose outward as she slipped of her t-shirt exposing her firm bare breast. Tommy reached up with his hands gently sliding his palms up her flat abdomen over her chest bringing them to rest on the small of her back. He pressed her naked body down against his crashing into her lips with his own in a deep kiss. She came willingly.

Chapter 25
California or Bust

The small plane lifted up into the air once again and took to the freedom of the wide-open sky safely beyond the reach of the infected. Humming securely in the skies the three passengers of the swiftly moving plane joked happily about their future for the first time since the infection had struck.

"Dude, in about three weeks we are going to be lying on a beach in Hawaii soaking up the sun and filtering alcohol though our liver," said Chuck smiling in the backseat like a child on his way to Disney World. "I wonder if pot will grow in Hawaii?"

"Man, pot will grow anywhere," said Tommy confidently. "Remember that time we pulled those seeds from that bag and planted them in Miss Rettberg's back yard to see if they would grow?"

"Oh yeah and one grew up about five feet tall right next to her back window."

"Man were we bummed when we got out of school one day and found out she had cut it down, thinking that it was a weed and burned it with the rest of her brush."

Chuck began to laugh uncontrollably.

"It was a weed all right," he said laughing so hard his eyes began to cry, "she got so high."

"Hell I know she did. Remember her inviting us in for pie, her eyes were all bloodshot and she kept saying that she wasn't sure why she was in such a mood to bake pies, being the only one in the house and all. Remember that? She had baked like three big ass pies. She ate like half a pie by herself."

Both began to laugh hysterically at the impression of her actions from their memories finally spilling the laughter over into Laurie although she didn't find the story all that funny.

"You know once we get there without a cure they may not have room for us," she said recomposing herself.

"I don't give a shit, I will build a little bamboo hut on the shore and finally realize my lifelong goal of being a beach bum," declared Chuck.

"No, I mean without the cure they might deem us too high a risk to take."

"What do you mean too high a risk?" asked Tommy curiously. "We are immune to the infection."

"We are, but they are not, we could be classified as possible carriers of the disease and therefore high risk. Doctor Ledbetter might have known what he was talking about, without the cure we are worthless."

"That's why we play it cool," said Chuck scheming. "The next stop we make, get a pad or something and start writing a whole bunch of medical bullshit in it. Make up a cure or something that no one less than a good doctor can dispute from a glance. You are Mrs. Ledbetter as far as anyone knows."

"But Doctor Ledbetter was a male, they have to know that," she argued.

"Ah yes, but you are his wife and although we lost him on the trip here, you know everything about his work."

"Think it will work?" asked Tommy wary of the plan concocted by his friend.

"I don't see why not and by the time they figure it out we will already be in Hawaii."

"I don't know how long that story will float," she said concerned.

"If we all act dumb and play along like we don't know any better, it will work at least until they get your phony formula to some type of expert."

The two front passengers moaned as if in disapproval.

"If either one of you two get a better idea that doesn't involve the truth along the way let me know," he said leaning back content with his plan.

And just like that another one of his madcap schemes was put into motion enacting a puppetry upon the three in an attempt to fool what would be a shrewd audience. The next three days was spent leaving behind the coniferous and broadleaf forest of Georgia, Alabama and Mississippi, passing over the Prairies and Steppes of Texas and bringing into sight the vast Deserts of New Mexico and the immense splendor of the monstrous Rocky Mountains. The sight of their high peaks took the breath from everyone in the plane, including the pilot who had never seen their massive brilliance with her own two eyes.

"I've never seen a mountain without trees on it before."

Although an avid outdoorsman, he had been born and raised as a southern boy, never having desired to romp past the deep woodlands of the Eastern United States. The vast open space and rich colors of the earth ripping out of the soil thousands of feet into the air left a mark of their own insignificance in his mind as they hovered above in a small tiny contraption only a dozen or so feet long.

"They do look a little bare," replied Tommy.

"I think they are capital," said Laurie enthralled by their natural beauty.

"We would have never gotten over them without you," conceded Chuck.

"Thank you," she said recognizing the first compliment, however small, he had paid her, "but let's get over them before we begin to celebrate."

The jagged peaks passed below guiding their path, serving almost as an immense bulletin board tracking their progress toward the coast. The small plane leveled out its wings as it passed over a sprawling neighborhood bearing toward a tiny airstrip huddled in its nucleus. Infected began to rise out of the bushes and nearby homes, awakened by the sound of the small passing aircraft.

"Here comes the local welcoming committee," said Chuck peering down through his tiny window.

The plane's three wheels came down in contact with the landing strip skidding gently as the craft came down to a slow roll. A shell sign barely recognizable through the dirt and dust that covered its yellow markings sat in the distance. Laurie steered toward it rolling along the runway and coming to a stop next to one of its pumps. Infected began to mass out from the surrounding neighborhood banging and shaking the airfield's fence. An older man came running out of a nearby hangar only to collapse against the runway spilling blood out from his neck where his head once sat. Chuck reloaded his rifle.

"We are going to have to get out of here as soon as possible," said Tommy nervously watching the hundreds of eyes staring hungrily.

"I hate to say this, but I'm about out of ammo. That last airport we cleared wiped me out."

"But it's going to be dark in about two hours," she declared, "and if I can't see, I don't fly."

"Well there is no way we can clear this place and that fence isn't going to hold long," stated Chuck watching it sway from the masses pressing against it.

More men, women and children began to run up to the fence beating at it with their hands and gnashing at it wildly with their teeth.

"Let's just fill it up and get out of here. This is the desert, surely we can find a flat place to land not far from here," said Chuck anxiously.

More infected came from the neighborhood pounding up against the fence almost as if some type of an alarm had been sounded, bringing the entire community to mass to serve the only purpose they now knew, to spread their infection or in this case, destroy those immune to it. A loud clank came from the far side of the airport as one of the gates buckled under the weight of the infected pushing against it, collapsing it to the ground and releasing a tide of infected. The dead jumped to their feet and with a clear sight of their objective ran at full speed, knocking each other out of the way as if they couldn't see anything but the three by the plane.

"Oh shit!" screamed Chuck, alerted by the sound and the sight of a rushing crowd of infected.

"Time to go, honey bunny," replied Tommy grabbing Laurie while she was pumping fuel.

The sight of the bloodthirsty mob seized her muscles in terror paralyzing them in a dull numbness. The sheer weight of panic that swelled up within her shut down her mind and she stood motionless like a displayed mummy. It was a problem that she had lived with since a child, a comma-like state that her mind would revert to in times of extreme duress. Her father had taken her to a psychiatrist as child after she had helplessly witnessed her older sister drown in a lake near their home. Her sister had taken her along with some friends to a local swimming hole that the neighborhood children frequented during the summertime. A long rope hung high from a cliff overhanging the water of the lake. Her sister, always the bravest one of the two, went first, slipping and hitting her head before falling into the water to her death. The fear of the height of the cliff alone and the sight of her sister's death had put her into a comma for three days before she regained consciousness. The psychiatrist explained to her parents that the comatose states she endured were a way of protecting herself during times of extreme stress. After years of therapy as a child without any signs of progress, she quit her therapy as an adult and had lived with the disorder ever since. Now it had returned like a bad nightmare during a time when they needed her most. Tommy noticed the blank look in her eyes and he tried to bring her back.

"Honey, can you hear me?" he asked gently shaking her face. "It's me sweetie, you've got to wake up."

Chuck pulled up the sight of his rifle closing his left eye staring down the barrel with his right. A shifting crowd of targets ran towards him, all worthless shots he thought… not one was worth the shell in his rifle. He never took a worthless shot. He pulled his rifle down and ran back to the plane.

"Time to roll!" he sounded in retreat.

Tommy, still holding Laurie in his arms, screamed back, "Chuck man, she is out!"

"What do you mean out?" he yelled over the screeching incoming crowd. "There is no time for out!"

"I can't get through to her!" he screamed back.

"Get her into the plane, you're going to fly us out of here, I'd rather die in a fiery crash than by the teeth of some fucking zombie!"

He turned around using the sight of their pursuers to motivate him to continue on with their wild and near hopeless escape, leaping into the back of the plane. Laurie lay slumped over in the passenger's seat out cold with glassy lost eyes adding to the desperation of their latest circumstances. Tommy sat down in the pilot's seat shaking nervously while trying to remember how he had seen Laurie start the plane.

"Come on let's go!" screamed Chuck.

"I'm trying! I think it's this," he said flipping a switch.

"No it's this," interrupted Laurie.

"Oh thank fucking God you are back," said Chuck feeling as if a one-ton weight was just lifted off his chest.

"Sorry about the little break boys," she said calmly starting up the plane and turning its noise towards a clear runway.

The small plane streaked down the open runway rising gently into the air and turning the rapid oncoming mob into little more than helpless spectators as they faded way into the sky. All three of the passengers burst into excitement handing out high fives and loud cheers as they managed to outwit the grip of infection once again. The sun beamed a deep orange hue ominously fading into a darkening twilight. A long shadow cast across the face of the pilot stealing her smile like a thief in the night leaving behind a hard face set with concern. Her hands began to tremble nervously as the predatory darkness loomed hungrily from behind the mountains as if preparing to spring forth and engulf the tiny aircraft. The fear of flying blind crept down her limbs and into the steering, rattling its passengers as the plane began to shake vigorously.

"Good lord, are we hitting more turbulence?" asked the backseat passenger holding on for dear life.

"It's getting dark," she said. "I will not fly in the dark."

"Let's head straight to the next airport then," he suggested from the back.

"It's too far away and the landing strip won't have lights."

"Calm down dear," said Tommy.

"We'll see how calm you two are when it gets dark and I black out again."

"Can we fly on through the night without landing?" asked Chuck trying to be constructive.

"Even with a full tank we would run out of fuel before the light of morning."

Both Tommy and Chuck's eyes swelled open in a quiet unspoken terror so as not to contribute to the nervous breakdown of their one and only pilot.

"Can't we land somewhere else?" asked Tommy.

"If we can find a flat area large enough to take back off from."

"This is the fucking desert; isn't it suppose to be flat?" he commented looking down at the rough inhospitable terrain below.

"What about over there?" pointed Tommy toward what appeared to a long patch of flat earth.

The small plane veered to the right, diving into a tilted turn toward the long flat patch buzzing it at only a few dozen feet.

"That's perfect," stated Chuck, "it's flat as hell and out in the middle of nowhere."

"I don't know," said Laurie concerned. "That grass is awful tall, I'm not sure if I will be able to get us back off the ground."

"Just get us down, I'll clear that shit," he said confidently.

Chapter 26
Two Become one

A hard dry wind blew the tall grass mercilessly against the trio's small makeshift camp swirling around viciously swallowing it deep within the bowels of the cold desert night.

"It's chilly out here, can't we make a small fire?" asked Laurie shivering.

"No telling what the sight of a flickering flame might bring in on us under the cover of darkness," said Chuck. "Besides I doubt we could find enough wood out here to support much of one anyway."

"Let's tough it through the night, we should make the coast in a couple of more days," said Tommy sliding up under a heap of blankets, jackets and spare clothes.

"What about you Chuck?" asked Laurie.

"What?" he asked.

"Aren't you going to get some rest?"

"Oh no, I slept in that backseat most of the day. I'm going to sit up a little bit...watch the stars or something," he said walking off from the camp.

He sat down in the dirt gazing at the vast cosmos as had men before him contemplating his place in its machinery. Now that most of man had changed and no longer used technology, the loss of artificial light blanketed the earth in darkness presenting the stars in clarity unseen by the naked eyes of man in over two hundred years. He pondered their quiet sparkle and watched a shooting star streak from one side of the sky to the other before traveling beyond the power of the naked eye. Only on the surface of a distant planet could a man ever escape the threat of infection. No matter where humans went, they would never be completely safe. If man hadn't always been so greedy throughout history being more concerned with profit than accomplishments, he believed man could have already advanced his technology enough to sustain himself on other planets, distancing himself from extinction. No barriers on this planet could hold back the infection and he knew it; no wall or any amount of water would stop it, the infection had already proven it could overcome any manmade or natural barrier. Only the vacuum of space would suffice. Greed had brought man down, his desire for something that wasn't even real, money.

"Hey man, what are you doing way over here sitting in the dark?" said Tommy startling his thoughts.

Chuck jumped reaching for his pistol in a jolt before sitting back down after seeing his friend.

"Fuck you man, you shouldn't sneak up on an armed man like that."

"Sorry about that," said Tommy laughing.

It wasn't very often that he got to see his friend lose his cool.

"Having a hard time sleeping?"

"I've never seen the stars so bright," he said staring into the sky. "What's got you up so late?"

"Ah… I can't sleep."

"The Laurie thing?"

He nodded as if blowing it off.

"Dude, the way this shit is eating you up, I wish the fuck we hadn't done that, but of course if we hadn't you two wouldn't be together. Isn't that a good plot for a Twilight Zone episode?"

He crouched down near his friend covering his head with his hands, "I have to tell her dude. I can't go on like this, I can't sleep, I can't eat… I feel like shit all the time."

"I don't know why you let shit like that bother you. It wouldn't faze me a bit."

"I know."

"I've never seen you so happy with anyone before. Ninety nine percent of the world is fucking zombies and every time you are around her you are smiling like an idiot. You're going to blow it with her if you're not careful

"What's he going to blow with me?" asked Laurie coming out of the dark.

Both men seized up with white faces as if they had just been busted by their mom for smoking pot. Being a far better liar than his friend and having far more experience at it, Chuck spoke up first, knowing from past experience that a quick response added to the legitimacy of any lie.

"He's going to blow it with you if he doesn't ask you to marry him."

"Marry?" she asked, stunned by the mere suggestion.

Tommy, unsure of what to do or say once confronted with the possible revelation of his dark secret, stood motionless unable to speak.

"He just asked me if I thought it was inappropriate for him to ask you to marry him so soon."

She stepped back placing her hand on her breast as if physically stunned, "I don't know what to say. Technically I'm still married to Brian, I don't know if it would be right or not."

"What's there to be right? There aren't any laws anymore... there isn't any legal way to annul your past marriage, and spending the rest of your life alone isn't going to bring him back. At some point you are going to have to realize it's over with him and move on."

Tommy walked off in a combination of frustration and humiliation unsure if he should come out with the truth or continue on with the lie he had fabricated like a shadow to cover their relationship from the awful truth of his guilt. Laurie began to walk after him, but Chuck stopped her by standing in her way.

"Get out of my way! I want to talk to Tommy!"

"After the way you just slapped him in the face, I'd give him a few moments."

"What are you talking about?"

"The way you just ripped his heart out."

"I didn't do any such thing."

"Oh come on! The guy is about to pour his heart out and ask you to marry him and the first word that comes out of your mouth is Brian! Talking about a low blow!"

"Oh God, I didn't think about that!" she said. "I didn't mean it that way, it's just… I'm not sure if I am completely ready for it to be over yet. If I get remarried, then it means he's gone forever."

"I got news for you honey. I was in that compound, if he's walking around, it's as a zombie."

Her eyes turned red and she began to weep uncontrollably.

"You think I don't know that! With all the running we've been doing, I haven't had the time to stop and think, let alone to come to terms with his loss."

"If it feels right," he said getting up, "then do it, that's what I always done and I'm doing better than most."

"I know, but I'm not that way. I try to reason things out first."

"Fine, but don't think about it too long, there might not be anything left by the time you are done," he said walking away.

She sat in the dark lowering her head between her knees and began to cry.

Chuck ran off in the direction he had seen Tommy go, quickly finding his form in the darkness.

"Hey man it's all fixed up," he said proudly. "I spun the whole thing around making her feel like shit for bringing up his name. You're in the clear now."

"What the fuck is your problem?" he yelled back. "I'll never get this shit straight, because every time I am about to come clean, you pull me back in with more shit to cover up the first fucking lie you told to cover up how we helped to murder those people!"

"Hey don't fucking get all high and mighty with me, when you should be on your knees thanking me for saving your ass back there."

"You didn't save my ass back there, you buried me."

"Buried you? You won't be happy until you fuck this thing up will you? I don't think you realize how good this thing is. She might be the best chick left on the planet!"

Tommy shrugged him off and turned around as if ignoring him.

"Think about it, number one she is a doctor, hello free medical coverage!" he said with one finger up.

Tommy laughed slightly.

"Number two she is a pilot!" he said with a second finger extended up. "Think how much money that will save you on your vacations."

Tommy turned around trying not to smile.

"Number three she is hot as hell! I know I don't have to tell what that is good for! Number four and most important of all, she is not a fucking zombie!" he said holding up four fingers. "The only good thing that can come out of telling her is a clear conscience and if you ask me when it comes to having a clear conscience or a hot chick… I'll take the hot chick every time!"

"Thank you, Doctor Phil."

"Forgotten?" he said holding out his hand.

"Forgotten," said Tommy clasping it tightly, acknowledging there were no hard feelings between the two.

"Now you better go find her, I left her pretty tore up."

"Nah, I think I'll let her have some peace and quiet, she's due for some."

The two settled down separately underneath their thin insufficient blankets leaving Laurie the time she so direly needed to think things through. Tommy's eyes awoke to the gentle warmth of the desert sun beating down upon him through the cool morning air. He instinctively rolled over to touch Laurie, but his fingers met nothing but the lifeless cold sand. He quickly sat up as if awakening from a nightmare, shocked to not find her near the camp. Chuck snored loudly from underneath a tiny blanket that was barely long enough to cover the lower half of his body.

"Chuck where's Laurie?" he said jumping to his feet in a daze.

"How the hell should I know, I've been a sleep," he said shivering.

"Get off your lazy ass and help me find her, she didn't come back last night."

Tommy ran over to the plane and opened the door only to find it dreadfully empty. Chuck sat up and began to slip on his boots while his friend ran through the grass and sand in his socks around the camp yelling for Laurie. The slightest darkening graced the corner of Tommy's keen eye projecting ever so slightly over the tall swaying grass almost blending in under the glaring blaze of the desert sun. The muscles in his legs sprang into action carrying him toward the dark unknown speck in the distance. Chuck seized his rifle and chased after Tommy who had already began a reckless sprint without shoes toward the small distant silhouette. He ran toward it unarmed and unprepared because the alternative to him was unthinkable. Chuck, unable to keep up with his friend, stopped to catch his breath after running nearly three hundred yards without stopping and fumbled with his rifle. He brought up his sight and zeroed it in on his target, but it was still too far away to tell if it was Laurie, someone else or far worse something else. If it was an infected and it had gotten Laurie, he knew Tommy would not be able to forgive himself. Tommy screamed for Laurie, but the form either didn't hear him, or for some reason it did not respond. Chuck lifted up his sight, placed it on the center of its head and set his stance, as Tommy ran up to the dark form blackened out from his vision by the sun. He closed his left eye, staring down the barrel of his rifle ready to pull the trigger as Tommy ran up to the undistinguishable form and stopped. Her eyes were swelled a deep red and her hair lay flat unkempt against her face as she looked up toward him.

"The answer is yes," she said.

His arms wrapped around her shivering body pulling her up against his chest tightly to still her shaking body. She collapsed into his warm embrace finally allowing the loss of her sister, father, mother and her marriage to Brian to escape her heart in the form of tears. It was a long hard cry that Tommy didn't interrupt with inept words. He held her under the cool morning air shielding her from its icy grip giving her the time she so desperately needed, and although he never said a word, she understood exactly how he felt. Chuck lowered the long barrel in his hands gently laying it on the ground next to him and crawled back under the scanty warmth of his tiny blanket, making the bitter chill in the air easier to bear underneath the cover of slumber. When his eyes reopened, an ever-rising sun had already beaten away the cool morning air forming a small bead of sweat upon his forehead. He wiped it clean with the palm of his hand leaving a small patch of sand residing in its wake. Still dazed, he turned around to find the fuzzy image of Tommy and Laurie sitting casually next to the plane playing cards.

"What fucking time is it?" he asked confused.

"It is like eleven thirty you sleepy head," said Laurie.

"What the hell… why didn't anyone wake me up? Shouldn't we already be up in the air?"

"Nah, we're going to make the coast with a couple of weeks to spare so we decided to take a day off," said Tommy.

"Take the day off and do what?"

"And rest, even God rested on the seventh day," claimed Laurie while playing cards.

He couldn't argue with that he thought especially since the government probably wouldn't show up until the last day if they showed up at all. He watched the two cheerfully play a game of rummy smiling at each other as if there were no other people on earth save themselves and although a cliché, it was almost true. He was proud of what he had done he thought to himself, proud of how he had convinced the two to commit to a relationship as serious as marriage, when neither were considering it at all. He had done it simply to stop Tommy from screwing everything up with the truth. He had never had trouble with the truth, he had always been able to tell a lie to anybody for any reason no matter how big or how small, without feeling any guilt, but Tommy was a far different story. Ever since Chuck had met him, he always wrestled with either doing the right thing or suffering through the misery of guilt if he had not. Honesty had always been one of his character faults he thought, but at least he knew he could always trust him. If Tommy couldn't lie to cover up what they had done, he would be more than glad to do it for him; it was the least he could do. Except for marksmanship, telling a good lie was one of his only natural assets.

"So did you two work everything out?"

"Yes," she said happily, "we've worked through it."

"So are we going to do it today or are you two going to continue living on in sin?"

"What are you talking about?" asked Tommy.

"Getting married."

Both Tommy and Laurie laughed from the mere suggestion of such impossibility.

"How are we supposed to do that?" she asked curiously. "We don't have a priest.

"I can do it."

"Man, you are no priest."

"I beg your pardon," he said standing up. "I can do the Lord's work as well as any man."

"No you can't," said Tommy clearly.

"How did people get married before there were ministers? At some point someone had to appoint themselves as one."

"Yeah, but they were probably law abiding citizens or something, not some guy who has been driving on a revoked driver's license for three years."

"Do you two think that because there are no ordained priests that God doesn't want people to get married?"

"No, but I don't think he would chose you to do it."

"You can't marry yourself, besides the sanctity of the marriage is dependent on those in it, not the guy who performs it."

"Don't give me all this religious crap, you don't believe in it anyway."

"What a minute, I think he has a point," interrupted Laurie.

"Thank you Laurie."

"Wait a minute, now you two are going to start agreeing with each other? That's a first."

"He's making a lot of sense, if we want to get married, then why can't we? In the eyes of God and in our own hearts it would be as real as any piece of paper could ever warrant."

"You really want to do this?"

"Yes," she said in excitement, "I do!"

They threw down their cards and embraced in a long kiss.

"You two happen to be in luck, because reverend Chuck is at your service. Please hold hands."

They stood side by side holding each other's hands under the gentle warm desert wind.

"Wait, what about a ring?" asked Tommy.

"It's okay I don't need a ring," she said.

"Yes you do," he said pulling a ring from his right hand.

His mother had given it to him after his father's death. It had been his father's high school ring and he had worn it faithfully every day since to honor his memory. He placed it in her palm and she quickly pulled her old wedding ring from her finger, placing the new ring loosely onto her thin finger. It slid around her finger swaying upside down heavily.

"It's all I have," he said seeing that it was several sizes too big.

"It's all I'll ever want," she said with tears.

"Dear God in Heaven, you have shown the world your fury through the spread of infection, now we ask you to show us love through the bond of these two people. For whatever reason you chose to spare the three of us over the billions you did not, we are grateful and can only hope that we will one day fulfill that purpose whatever it may be. I am not a religious man, but when I see two people who care for each other, as do these two, I cannot but for once feel that there might be some hope left in this world for men. Tommy," he said looking at him, "are you willing to forgive Laurie and yourself for mistakes that the two of you might have made in the past, so the two of you might begin with a clean slate today and build a future together as husband and wife?"

Tommy looked at his friend with a queer look. He couldn't believe the words he was hearing from his friend, they were kind and articulate, unfamiliar to what he had become accustomed. He expected him to burst out in laughter at any moment as if this were the punch line to some joke.

"This is where you say yes or no," stated Chuck.

"Oh… yes," he said stunned.

"And do you Laurie forsake all others for Tommy, leaving the past in the past, so to live today with him as your lawfully wedded husband?"

"I do," she said gently.

"Then with the power invested in me as one of the few people left on Earth, I pronounce you as husband and wife. You may kiss the bride."

They kissed.

"I know I didn't get it all perfect and everything, but it should suffice."

"I think you did just wonderful," said Laurie. "Today I think I saw a different side of you."

"Don't expect to see too much more of it."

"Oh I won't," she said as the ice between the two slightly melted.

"Guess I'll go on a long hike and see if I can find anything interesting and give you two a little time alone. Just don't leave without me."

"We won't," she said hugging Tommy.

He smiled and walked off dragging his feet through the thick sand smiling toward the horizon so not to expose his goofy grin. It had been a long time since he had done something nice for somebody and he felt good for it. So did the two people he left holding each other dearly, as two became one.

Chapter 27
A Hard Landing

The next morning husband, wife and friend stared out over the long field eyeing the long swaying grass with concern.

"The sand and grass are going to slow us down," said Laurie uneasily. "I don't know if we are going to be able to get up enough speed."

"I'll take care of the grass, don't you worry about that," Chuck said confidently. "I can't do much about the sand, so worry about that."

She looked at him like he was crazy, "Just how are you going to that, with a lawn mower?"

"Kinda," he said pulling a lighter out of his pocket, "I call it God's lawn mower."

A flicker leapt forth from the small hand held lighter quickly spreading to the tall dry grass bursting into a field of flame. A cloud of black smoke rose up billowing into the sky out of control racing off into every direction.

"Oh my God, the plane!" screamed Laurie.

Flames leaped up biting at their legs as they tried to stomp out the grass swaying near the plane's undercarriage. Their faces glowed a sparkling yellow as they watched Hell literally rise up from the ground spreading its wrath before their eyes.

"Keep it off the tires," she warned running to their defense.

Fire crawled up from the grass sliding gently onto its tires burning ominously. The flames, undaunted by the attempts to thwart them, burned red hot under the desert sun alarming the three with its relentless fury, only to die out and spread away with the loss of sufficient fuel, leaving the three standing peacefully over smoldering ashes. Chuck wheezed and coughed from the black smoke that had filled his lungs.

"That worked out pretty well," he said calmly as if his plan had gone flawlessly.

"Better than most of your plans," said Tommy with smoke rising from the melted soles on his boots.

Their plane lifted off the black scorched earth rising through the black cloud streaming off the fires below, emerging safely into the vast sky. Huge black lines of smoke roared into the distance unchecked by man and free to burn until ultimately satisfied or foiled by nature herself.

"Well, now you are an arsonist," said Tommy.

"I'm absolutely burning up," he said blowing off the tips of his fingers.

Laurie laughed glad to be in the air once again underneath the warm morning sun. They traveled on through the day cheerfully discussing their hopes and desires for the future. The safety of three thousand feet above sea level did well for their morale as they traveled toward the coast with ease.

"First thing I am going to do once we get to Hawaii, is get hold of one of those hula chicks," said Chuck from the backseat.

"Better be on the lookout for her big ass Samoan husband or he might get a hold of you," joked Tommy.

"Chuck's not afraid of one of those guys, are you?" said Laurie carrying on the conversation now a completely accepted member of the group.

"Shit, one of those fat fucks couldn't catch me," he bragged.

"You better run, because if one of those sumo wrestlers does get his hands on you, don't expect any help from me... I'll be like Chuck who?"

The plane buzzed through the open air effortlessly cutting through it, finally passing a small deserted airport a few hundred miles from the coast of the Pacific Ocean. A pair of planes lied smoldered together at the center of the runway, apparently part of some botched escape attempt which left the runway impassable. They passed it one more time to get a better feel of the situation.

"It looks deserted with no signs of infected," reported Chuck peering through the small side window.

"What about the planes on the runway? Can you still land?" asked Tommy.

"Maybe," she said, "if I land hard it might slow us down enough so we can drive around the wreckage."

"It's up to you, boss lady," said Chuck.

"I don't see how we have much choice," she said turning the plane around for a final pass over the runway. "We're about out of fuel."

The plane came down slightly angled with its tail down and wings up cutting against the wind which shook it roughly. Both Chuck and Tommy quickly strapped on their seatbelts during the commotion and held on for dear life. The plane's tires squealed as if in pain when they struck the flat runway creating smoke from its coarse surface. Laurie slammed on the breaks so as not to add to the collage of crashed planes sitting in the middle of the runway. Under her command, the wheels locked tight, fishtailing the plane wildly under the duress of such a forced landing. Skidding wildly, she began to pump the breaks trying to regain control, as the rubble of planes loomed larger with every second. A strange phenomenon overtook the three as if they suddenly had torn through the threads of time slowing down tremendously as seconds ticked ominously by like minutes. Their plane continued to skid, bumping up and down violently as they slid toward the rubble helplessly. Laurie put one last effort into the brakes, closed her eyes and turned the steering wheel hard to the left. Suddenly, the front and left rear tires blew out, creating a barrage of sparks and fire in the air as metal dragged across concrete crippling the plane and turning it sideways into a frictional tailspin. Part of the prop broke off shattering the front window as it ricocheted into the cabin spinning past Chuck's eyes in slow motion before disappearing through the backseat and landing with a thud into the rear cargo compartment. All three of the passengers crashed up against the inside of the plane as it flipped over onto its side ripping off the left wing and skidding to a stop inches from the wreck they had so desperately tried to avoid.

"Is everyone all right?" asked Tommy hanging by his seat belt above the rest of the group.

Chuck reached down unlatching his seat belt and fell down to the left side of the plane which now rested firmly on the ground. Laurie nodded to Tommy hanging directly above her in the passenger's seat unfastening her own seat belt to free herself from its suspension. Tommy flipped open the side door above his head and braced his feet against part of the plane's control panel before undoing his own seat belt. He crawled out kneeling down on its side and reached back down inside to help Laurie and Chuck out onto the landing strip. Amazingly they had all survived the crash landing without injury and Chuck walked around to survey the damage. The propellers on the prop had broken completely off flying away in all directions, leaving the plane a handful of inches from the wreck in the middle of the runway.

"Well, at least you managed to miss it," said Chuck nonchalantly as if the crash they had just endured was not a big deal.

Laurie walked around looking at the rubble stunned from its appearance. Even though she had been in the accident, it looked far worse than she could have imagined. It appeared as if it had merely dropped from the sky as a metal ball.

"She told you she could do it," commented Tommy.

Chuck actually began to laugh as if he had actually gone over the edge of insanity that most people had accused him of crossing years ago. The sound of his friend laughing at such an inappropriate brought him to laughter as well as they surveyed the latest mess they found themselves.

"What is so funny?" said Laurie aggravated. "There is nothing amusing about a wrecked plane. We could have been killed."

"You're right," agreed Tommy, "but did you see Chuck's eyes after that propeller blade shot right by his head?"

"Did you see that thing shoot by?" he asked. "It practically gave me a shave."

"I give up on you two," she said in frustration. "Pot has melted your brains. I'm going to look for another plane."

"Wait!" said Tommy straightening up. "I'll go with you just in case."

"Yeah try and find one with two wings," yelled Chuck as she stomped off toward the airport's small hangars.

A foul smoke rose up from the wreckage blowing into his lungs as he breathed the swift wind cutting across the small airport. Chuck walked over to the other side of the plane with squinted eyes and examined the extent of the damage. The luggage door laid face down on the pavement trapping what remained of their gear and supplies. He tried to open it unsuccessfully and in annoyance kicked the top of the plane. He walked back around the front of the plane and out of the corner of his eye he saw what appeared to be hair slightly above the window in one of the tangled planes. He pulled his pistol from his side holster and stood next to the pilot's door. His free hand slowly slid onto the door's handle clicking it back gently. It clicked with a thud and the form of a man leaped out onto the ground below. Chuck stepped back startled by the commotion and the image of a decayed face covered in maggots and buzzing flies. He stepped back further nearly gagging from the sight turning his head to avoid the horrid stench.

Tommy's form stepped out from one of the airport's hangar, "Chuck, over here!" he screamed.

Chuck ran over to him stepping inside out of the bright desert sun.

"Well we found another plane," said Laurie proudly.

His eyes were still blackened from the change of extreme light of the desert to the shadows of the dark hangar leaving him sunblind. A small beam of light slowly widened within his pupils as they adjusted to the light change revealing an old rusty looking plane, a far cry from the beauty they had just totaled. He walked around it finding running rust spots that looked like unfinished perpendicular racing stripes and peeling decals.

"I don't know anything about planes," he admitted, "but will it fly?"

"I think so," she commented in good spirit, "it looks like someone was in the middle of restoring it, it's a one seventy two just like my father trained me on."

"How old is it?" he asked curiously.

"About thirty years I guess, it has had better days, but so have we," she said happily eyeing it from a distance. "Just give me a little time to check it out."

"While you're doing that, I'm going to go see if I can get our stuff out of the back of the wreckage."

"Need some help?" asked Tommy.

Chuck nodded and Tommy stepped forward as if to leave, but stopped, feeling a responsibility to protect Laurie.

"I better hang around here to be safe," he said apologizing to his friend.

"No problem. I can get it," he said.

"Go ahead and help him," she said. "I'll be fine."

"You sure?"

"I'm just going to make sure this thing will fire up. I'll holler if I need you."

"We'll be right back," he said leaving the hangar.

Laurie's hand skimmed along the worn exterior of the old plane collecting dust as she remembered how much larger the small aircraft had loomed upon her as a child. Her days down at the airport with her father had been magical to her as a young girl. While most other girls her age were hanging out at the mall with their friends, she had spent almost every hour of her weekends as a youth with her father hanging around the airport's many pilots learning all about their aircraft as she herself eventually became a pilot, a talent which was now paying off in huge dividends.

As she slowly walked the exterior of the plane looking for defects, a small closet door in the corner of the hangar popped open revealing a tiny dirty hand under the gloom of the internal hangar's dim illumination. A small round face covered in mold with short black pigtails and blood soaked eyes nudged out of the small opening focusing in upon the woman inspecting the plane. The front of the little girl's neck had nearly worn away from decay exposing her spinal cord as her mouth lifted open in exhilaration of newly discovered prey. An overwhelming desire to shred the woman's flesh apart infused itself irresistibly within every tissue of the little girl as she ran across the smooth hangar floor. Laurie stood with her back to the infected girl unaware of her presence as she inspected the old plane.

The sound of little footsteps running echoed ever so gently off the walls of the small hangar resonating throughout its spacious interior. The slight sound reached Laurie's internal ear awakening her curiosity to its whereabouts. She turned around and met the vision of the little girl's as she barreled toward her with extended arms and snarling teeth. She impulsively turned to the side barely avoiding the outreach of the little girl as she leaped by her and slid underneath the plane. Unable to scream, the little girl growled as she spun around standing back onto her feet. She quickly ran back underneath the plane's belly and seized Laurie's ankle as she tried to crawl into the plane. Her putrefied face rose up from below the plane looking at Laurie hungrily as she tried to sink her teeth into her exposed ankle. Laurie tugged her leg as hard as she could to break free from the girl's unyielding grip, all the while kicking her in the face with her other foot. She finally broke free from the little girl and with a hard stomp to her head; the little girl fell to the hangar floor disappearing from her sight.

Laurie reached over and tried to pull the pilot's door closed in vain, as two little hands clutched the edge of the door starting a tug of war between the two as one represented life and the other death. She pulled it frantically as the little girl's head reappeared into the compartment through the crack in the door. The sight of her bloody face startled Laurie and she lost her grip upon the door falling onto her back. Two hands made the edge of the pilot's seat as Laurie scrambled to free the pistol from her side. Cold hard hands tugged at her legs as the infected girl's body drug up onto of her while she struggled with her holster. The little girl's tangled hair rose into her vision, followed by mad eyes dripping with blood. White teeth bared themselves before coming down toward her face as she pulled the trigger blowing the little girl's head apart. Collated blood splattered like wet paper across the interior of the plane with a loud boom. Laurie shoved the little girl's headless body out of the plane and began to wipe the blood from her face and hands with her jacket as she cried.

The door to the hangar ripped open as Tommy and Chuck ran in with weapons drawn. The body of a little black girl sprawled out onto the floor slowly streaming clumpy blood met their eyes injecting terror into both of their hearts. The sight of the plane's windows dripping with blood added to their fears as Tommy ran toward the plane in a panic. He stopped and reached out toward the door handle pausing for a moment afraid of what he might find inside. She had to be all right, he thought, he couldn't take another devastating blow as to lose her now. He wouldn't go on if something had happened to her. Cries from within the plane's compartment reinvigorated his actions and he slung the door open to find Laurie covered in blood streaking down her checks behind tears. He pulled her to him gripping her in a hug as tight as they both could endure realizing how close he came to losing her.

"I'll never leave you alone again," he cried into her ear.

She gripped him tighter and they held each other as she cried recomposed herself. Chuck being dry to tender moments walked around the corpse of the young girl eyeing what had transpired curiously. He looked around the hangar stopping at the sight of the open door in the corner. He raised his pistol and pulled a small flashlight out of his pocket, before cautiously walking toward the door to investigate. A dark musty shadow seeped from the cool dark closet as the tiny beam from his flashlight cut through the darkness like a scalpel revealing a small doll whose head had been chewed off. He picked up the doll to examine it further and took it back with him to the plane.

"It looks like someone put her in that closet to protect her from the infection," he said throwing the doll down beside the girl's body.

"She was somebody's little girl," said Laurie suddenly finding it difficult to catch her breath after the scuffle. "She was no different than I was when I came to the airport with my daddy."

"That wasn't a little girl," said Tommy consoling her in his arms. "She was lost to this world a long time ago."

"You two set up shop in the office back there, I'll hang around here and keep an eye out for her momma," Chuck said.

Tommy took Laurie back to an office in the corner of the hangar and locked the door as she settled down in the corner.

"Damn!" complained Chuck to himself after looking at the mess inside the plane. "Did you have to blow her away inside the plane? It's going to take forever to clean all this shit up."

He slammed the plane's door and kicked the little girl's headless doll across the hangar in frustration. It spun across the floor skidding across its smooth pavement ricocheting out of the corner into a tight spin suddenly coming to a dead stop marking him with its hand. He eyed it curiously pondering the odds of such a shot, before lowering the hangar door and locking it for the night.

Chapter 28
Small Town America

Nine hours later the hangar door slid open with a bang bleaching the two young men's faces under the bright illumination of the warm morning sun. Refreshed from a long uneventful night, they walked out onto the wide runway examining the wreckage that blocked its usage.

"How the hell are we going to move that pile of rubble?" asked Tommy.

"I'm not sure, but if we don't move it, it's not going to matter if Laurie can get that thing in there to fly or not."

"It'll take a dozer or a tank."

"Or a relative facsimile thereof," Chuck said thinking. "Let's slip into town and see what we can find."

"Let me get Laurie," Tommy said running back to the hangar.

He found her hanging inside the engine compartment mulling it over. Her thin curved body slid ever so lightly across the outer shell of the engine compartment.

"We're going into town to see if we can find anything to move those planes around."

She stepped down from the small ladder wiping her hands partially clean with a rag.

"Flying one and working on one are two entirely different things," she said. "I really don't know what I am doing, but whoever was working on this thing did. I think it will fly… I just wanted to make sure they hadn't left something simple undone, like top off the fluids, finish all the plugs and wires."

"Damn you really pull off the dirty sexy mechanic fantasy," he said eyeing her in her tight shirt and oily hands.

"Really?" she said playing along. "Do you have something you need me to fix baby?"

She embraced him with a firm kiss griping his butt with her two hands securely.

"Honey you're getting oil all over my ass," he complained playfully.

"You have to get dirty sometimes to have a little fun," she said nibbling on his ear.

"I want you to come with us," he said seriously.

She looked into his eyes and stepped away from his stare. She needed to stay to work on the plane; she needed to prove to herself that she could stay alone.

"You two go on without me, I've got a few more things I need to do here so we can take off as soon as possible," she said walking away toward the plane.

"I don't want to leave you alone after what happened yesterday."

"Did you notice what happened to me yesterday?" she said raising her voice.

"Yes you almost got killed by a little girl."

"No!" she said resolutely. "For the first time in my entire life, I didn't need somebody else to take care of me! I took care of myself!" she said turning back toward him. "I didn't freeze up... I didn't black out. I was in total control of myself for the first time since my sister's death. It's as if I had never forgiven myself for her death, but that night out in the desert before we got married, I let it all go... her death, the death of my father and Brian. I'm free from them all... I am finally free from the guilt of their deaths. I don't have to block them out anymore!"

She rushed up to him and hugged him tightly.

"I owe it all to you for saving me back at the nuclear plant and showing me what true love really is! I never knew I could be so happy! I thought I loved Brian at the time, but now after being with you I realize now that we were never really more than colleagues held together by similar career interest. It had to have been destiny for you to come up upon the nuclear plant when you and Chuck did. It is too much of a coincidence for it not to be."

Tommy held her in his arms feeling an immeasurable weight of guilt fall down upon his soul as if the guilt she had somehow lost had transferred itself to him. He wanted to come clean with her about that night, so that he too could feel the freedom that she now felt, but the pain of possibly losing her held his secret yawning deep within his guts eating at him like a parasite.

"Now you two go on without me. I'm a big girl and I can take care of myself now," she said happily holding up a shiny pistol. "Just be careful! I don't want to lose you after finding you."

He kissed her goodbye and walked back out onto the sunny runway completely blinded, but not from the effects of the sun. He stumbled up toward Chuck and bumped him with his shoulder.

"Let's roll," he said unemotionally.

"Where is Laurie?" asked Chuck confused.

"She's not coming," he said dryly.

Chuck stood still dumbfounded not sure what to do.

"Hurry up! So we can get back in time to leave today."

Not quite sure what was going on, he followed Tommy out of the airport in silence. He could tell there was something wrong with his friend from his cold demeanor, but instead of trying to pry it out of him he let it be, so to better focus on their mission. They stalked through the small town from building to building fading from one shadow to the next so to avoid the detection of unwanted eyes. They ran across the street slamming flat against a house pausing for a moment to catch their breath. Their hearts beat within their chests pumping fresh blood through their body spreading oxygen to the tissues in their extremities slowing rebuilding their strength. Tommy edged down to the end of the wall and peeked around the corner carefully. The streets were deserted as they were in Atlanta, but he knew all too well how quickly a mob of infected could form. Chuck rotated his position taking the lead by running past the wall up against a neighboring house. He slid up against the garage door and peeked in through its dirty window. His eyes swelled open, before he quietly signaled for Tommy to follow. Tommy ran across the yard landing up against the wall next to his friend. Chuck pointed at a long sleek purple Cadillac parked in the garage.

"I think that qualifies as a tank," he said in a whisper.

He reached down grasping the garage door's handle tugging on it gently to open it quietly, but it didn't budge.

"Locked," he whispered, "inside."

Tommy ran up to front door taking position to the left side so not to cast an image thorough the door's long glass window. Chuck came up to rest against the right side of the door holding up a pistol tightly.

"How are you on ammo?" Chuck asked from the other side of the door.

"I've got a pocket full of shells."

They were about out of ammunition for every gun they possessed. Clearing out airports across the country had taken its toll upon their once hefty stockpile. If they ran into another mob of infected, they wouldn't have enough ammunition to fight their way out. Chuck jingled the shells in his pocket. He had about half a clip for his assault rifle and was down to only nine more shells for his pistol. Their only option would be to run and the last thing either one wanted to do was to lead a streaming horde of infected back to the airport. Tommy stepped back forcefully shattering the glass in the center of the door with the sole of his boot. Shards spun into the foyer sliding across the hardwood flooring into the living room coming to a silent halt under the grip of friction. The two men cautiously stepped into the darkness leading with extended pistols and wary eyes.

The foyer flowed into a sunken living area with plush couches and chairs angled toward a huge fireplace centered into the far wall. With the darkness that descended from the shadows of the drawn curtains, the spacious room gave the appearance of some sort of home theatre, with a long burned out fireplace standing as its main feature. To the right extended a long hallway that passed an open kitchen disappearing with a hard left into the darkness beyond, while to the left inside the airy living room twisted a stairway up into the black void above. Heat seeped in through the walls from the relentless desert sun outside making the dark home hot and uncomfortable for its new guests. Sweat trickled through their hair rolling down their foreheads, neck and chest. Tommy pointed toward the hallway to his left using his pistol as a pointer signaling his intentions. Chuck nodded, following his friend through the sweltering darkness with squinted eyes. Tommy walked up to the edge of the open kitchen before slowly peering around the corner. In its center was a huge tiled island with thick black kettles and iron skillets dangling from a rack hanging inferiorly to the ceiling. A pistol barrel poked around the island followed by two wide eyes. Tommy sighed upon finding the shadows vacant. They rummaged quietly through the kitchen's drawers finding nothing worth carrying back.

Chuck signaled Tommy with his eyes toward a door that appeared to lead off toward the garage. Both men stood at the door slowly opening it with a long piercing creak revealing a shadowed image of a long gleaming purple car. They edged around the car inaudibly upon the smooth hard concrete checking every corner, including the garbage can before slightly easing their guard.

Chuck's fingers ran across the shiny speckled paintjob from the rear taillight all the way up to its front emblems. Thick dust mounted onto the tips of his fingers breaking away gently into the air softly floating away behind the force of one quick breath.

"A Cadillac Eldorado," he said in an excited but raspy voice, "I guarantee you these people were black."

"What makes you say that?" asked Tommy quietly.

"Come on, this house had to cost three or four hundred thousand. No self-respecting white person with that kind of money is going to own a purple Cadillac with gold rims."

"Maybe Latino?" said Tommy suggesting another probability.

Chuck rose up his head slightly in agreement surprised he hadn't thought of such a prospect. He lifted up on the door handle breaking into a slight smile as the door came open freely. He looked into the back of the car and into the floorboard before sliding into its lavish yellow leather seating. Its interior supported green shag carpet and a custom yellow dash with a motionless dancing hula girl in its center. He fumbled through the console, under the seats and through the glove box, but found nothing of use.

"No keys," he said visibly disappointed. "Guess we'll have to check the rest of the house."

Tommy turned around looking back at the dark hole leading into the living room. A hot black heat radiated from it dauntingly challenging them to search its haphazard obscurity. They walked up toward the door stopping short of its frame. Tommy paused as if to give his friend the opportunity to pass him and take the lead, but after turning around and finding his friend standing trapped from the enclosed walls, he turned around and stepped through into the darkness instead of forcing his friend to squeeze by him and openly broadcast his fear.

He pulled up his pistol gripping its trigger tightly, slightly lifting its hammer as he walked past the kitchen fading out of his friend's sight into the total darkness of the distant hall. His eyes refocused in the dimness in an attempt to decipher the resolution of blurred images deep down its long center. The hall promptly turned left sealing off its passage from the slight natural light from the curtains blanketing it in a sweltering shroud of impenetrable darkness.

He slowly lifted out his free hand reaching out into the black void cloaking his eyes while slowly walking forward blindly. A tiny shaft of light soared past his shoulder forcing the thick black abyss to retreat underneath two doors at the end of the long hallway. His eyes acted in negative feedback against the tiny light contracting quickly into tight pupils to use the new light source more efficiently. He spun around unaware of where the light had come, finding Chuck holding out a small penlight. He took it from him quietly focusing its beam on the door. He stopped at the outside of the door and looked down at its doorknob. He deftly placed the small pen light in his mouth so as to free his left hand and not to hamper his other, which firmly held his pistol. The knob turned freely clicking into open position. He held it firmly not sure if finding it unlocked was a good or bad thing before precariously creaking it open to expose a small white tiled bathroom.

A large crystallized window sat at the top of the back wall distorting the sunlight it filtered into the bathroom covering the surrounding walls in small bright shivering prisms. Just a few feet away hung a dirty white shower curtain pulled closed entirely covering the bathtub. The sunlight from above shimmered down behind the curtain projecting the dark image of a motionless silhouette. His heart restricted tightly beating deeper within his chest as an impulse ran down his nervous system instantaneously signaling the finger that rested upon the trigger on his gun. He fought the reaction locking his finger tightly.

The figure stayed motionless as sweat ran down profusely across Tommy's face. He had to know for sure before he could pull the trigger, a murder accidental or not, was something he couldn't bear to wear on his conscience. It was heavy enough at the moment already.

He dropped the light from his mouth into his free hand, catching it perfectly before shining it onto the curtain. Before he could blink the curtain hanging over the shower ripped loose ricocheting shower curtain rings off the walls with loud clanks. The infected woman leaped onto Tommy knocking him into Chuck, pushing all three back into the dark hallway onto the hardwood floor. The woman's teeth and hands gashed at Tommy from behind the curtain beating at him in a rage to reach his flesh. Using both of his hands, he quickly wrapped the plastic curtain around her head using it as a handle to lift her up. She continued to struggle toward him as his knee collapsed into her stomach bashing her back into the bathroom and into the base of the bathtub. Her head banged against the wall streaming clumped blood down the white tiles as it slid down into the tub out of sight. The two stood in shock of the sudden attack.

"What the fuck?" asked Chuck frustrated. "Why didn't you shoot the bitch?"

"I didn't want to wake the neighborhood," he replied in defense of his actions.

Suddenly the black woman leaped back out of the tub recovering from being temporarily knocked unconscious assaulting them once again. Both men stepped back out into the hall slamming the door shut. The door rattled on its hinges, but held tight. Chuck lifted up his pistol.

"Let that ho out."

"No, that will make too much noise. Follow my lead," he said quickly slinging open the door.

His foot caught her directly in the chest sending her flying back into the tub once again, but this time Tommy ran after her wrapping her up in the shower curtain, while holding her down with his foot.

"Hold her down a second," he ordered to Chuck.

His friend looked at him like he was crazy, but he did so by putting the base of his boot down upon her neck. She seized it with her hand and began to bite into it with her teeth.

"Hurry up man this bitch is eating my boots."

Tommy came back from the toilet holding up a heavy porcelain lid above his head. Chuck leaped back tearing his foot free from the woman's grip. The heavy lid crashed against her head crushing it into silence.

After beating her into an unrecognizable heap, he dropped it to the floor shattering it into pieces. Blood swelled into the shower curtain pouring out its ends swirling into the drain.

"See I told you they were black," said Chuck exhaling out with a deep breath. "If they had been Hispanic we would have seen a bunch of catholic crosses and pictures of the Virgin Mary everywhere."

Tommy hurriedly flipped through the medicine cabinet, under the sink and through the drawers in the cabinets for the outside chance of finding the keys, so they could ride out of town in style. He stood up with a frustrated look, not because he actually expected to find the key in the bathroom, but because he knew what not finding them meant.

It meant they would have to search even deeper into the darkness that hung outside the bathroom. He tossed the penlight to his friend Chuck, who grasped it along with the hint he threw with it. A tiny light shined around the corner parting the darkness revealing the way to yet another closed door. He stopped up at the base of the door placing the small light under his chin before trying the knob with his off hand. This time he found it to be locked, which presented the gentlemen a whole new challenge. Should they break it open with force running into the darkness with guns drawn or should they try and pry it open as quietly as possible? His head twisted back and gave his friend a look that said it all. He was going in his way. The door's dead bolt ripped through the thin wood frame launching splinters into the darkness of the room beyond. Chuck leaped in with his gun drawn ready to fire on anything that moved, regardless if it were infected or not. His tiny penlight flashed around the room searching every corner, as would a searchlight during a prison raid. In the center of the large bedroom was a huge king size canopy bed with thick lush blankets and giant plush throw pillows. The two men meticulously searched the dark room.

"Damn that looks like Jeff's old bed," said Tommy in a low whisper.

Chuck nodded in agreement of an old pleasant memory. He walked around the imposing bed searching the rest of the room finally focusing the point of his light and his undivided attention upon a closet door. Its dark image immediately instigated a disturbing feeling that churned deeply within the core of his gut bringing a long chill that tingled up his neck into his hair. He abruptly rubbed the back of his head to stop the sensation in mid tingle before coming to a tentative standoff with the thin barrier. He gripped its handle and slung it open. A long dust broom handle fell out of the darkness hitting him square in the face. He instinctively fumbled with it throwing it back into the dark closet startled by its quick decent. He swiped his face with his hand to try and subconsciously erase the embarrassment of getting cold cocked by a broom handle.

"I about shot that damn thing."

Tommy turned around proudly holding up a set of shiny keys. He jingled them to get his friends attention.

"Is that them?"

"They have a Cadillac emblem right on them; let's get out of here."

They entered the dark hallway for one last time quietly walking toward the distant light at its end. Once in the kitchen, they went straight to the garage door when in the corner of his eye, Chuck saw a door off in the corner of the kitchen that he hadn't noticed before. The first thing that came to his mind was that it might be a cupboard full of food. He walked over to it and swung it open.

"Wonder what's in here?" he asked to himself and Tommy.

The door opened, but instead of being a cupboard full of can and bag food, there were stairs leading down into what appeared to be the basement. At the bottom of the stairs in its shadows were white eyes, teeth and black faces, lots of black faces. He quickly slammed the door.

"Time to go!" he said running toward Tommy.

Tommy, unaware of what he had seen, stood still holding the handle to the door leading into the garage. Seeing fear flowing from his friend's eyes sent impulses through his nervous system straight to his heart. The sounds of footsteps echoed in the kitchen from below shaking the dishes in the cabinets.

"Go!" screamed Chuck.

The door to the garage slung open bashing up against the wall as the two men leaped down the half dozen steps into the garage. Tommy ran up to the car while Chuck alertly slammed the kitchen door closed. Black hands with white palms flattened against the door's window before it shattered from the force of many sending glass fragments down into the garage onto Chuck. Tommy slid into the driver's door ready to start the car, only to be pushed over by Chuck frantically jumping into the driver's seat as well. Without time to argue, he passed the keys over to Chuck who slid them into the ignition. The door from the kitchen collapsed sliding down the stairs giving the infected behind it a dry sled run into the garage. Two infected men landed right next to the driver's door apparently slightly dazed by the bumpy ride.

"Let's hope they didn't have two Cadillacs," said Chuck while turning the key.

The radio blasted on with a deep beat as the engine turned overpowered by juice from the battery failing to start on the first attempt. Tommy reached over flicking knobs on the radio in an attempt to turn off the noise so he could think. The two infected men upon reorienting themselves began to beat onto the car as more infected began to pile onto it from the kitchen. Black angry faces pressed against the car's windows as clinched and open hands beat against the car's thin glass and metal literally trying to rip through the heavy car. Tommy finally found the power to the radio as the engine started, being a luxury car in its time. It ran smooth as silk without a hitch as he pulled it into reverse. Smoke boiled off the back tires gripping fiercely at the smooth pavement below launching the heavy car, its passengers and the infected hanging all over it through the garage door. The door crumpled underneath the weight breaking apart into a shamble of metal, wood and glass tumbling all over the driveway. Unable to see through any window, Chuck drove straight back into the street crashing into the neighbor's mailbox. The collision caused a few of the infected to slide off the car's smooth exterior tumbling into the yard across the street. The car then spread smoke across the concrete once again as it shifted into drive and began to boil down the road still carrying four infected on its top and sides. Chuck struggled seeing the road around the man still hanging onto the hood looking in at them hungrily. Another infected slid off the back disappearing as she flopped down the road with arms and legs slinging into the distance. A second and a third one fell off as he began to shake the car by wiggling the steering wheel back and forth violently. The fourth and final infected man proved to be more difficult and after several failed attempts to shake him, Chuck got frustrated.

"Just shoot the fucker!"

Tommy's pistol clanked against the windshield directly across from the center of the man's forehead. A loud boom resonated through the interior of the car as the man finally lost his grip and fell off to the side of the car disappearing underneath the driver side front and rear tires. The car tilted over to its right coming down bouncing nearly out of control.

"Thanks."

"No problem," said Tommy wiggling his finger in his ear. "I guess they didn't care for a couple of honkies stealing their ride."

Infected began to appear from homes, back yards and parked cars chasing after the purple Cadillac as it cruised through the neighborhood toward the airport.

"Turn that shit up," said Chuck.

"What?"

"Turn that radio back on; somehow it seems appropriate at the moment," he said leaning back peering over the car's large steering wheel.

"Just don't try and talk black," Tommy responded, "damn white boy."

His fingers gripped the radio's power button clicking it on. A rich base resonated through the car's cabin rattling everything that wasn't firmly attached to the car. Their heads bounced up and down with the beat as they drove through, around and over the residents of the small neighborhood before taking the long way back to the airport driving out into the desert to lose their pursuers. The purple Cadillac glistened on the runway as it pulled up and parked outside the hangar.

Laurie's thin form emerged from the shadows of the hangar standing on the runway with her hands on her hips, "Where the hell have you two been? I could hear you from a mile away."

"Sorry about that sugar booger, things got a little crazy. How's it goin' with the plane?"

"Not being a mechanic, I've done everything I know to do. I checked all the connections and as far as I can tell everything seems to be in order. I didn't want to try starting it until you two got back."

"Let me get all this crap out of the way in case we have to make a forced take off," said Chuck jumping back behind the wheel of the long purple car.

Its heavy weight and powerful engine moved the lighter aircraft off the runway with ease, breaking them apart as they scraped along the pavement. After about thirty minutes of clean up, Chuck stood proudly observing the runway he had cleared for takeoff.

Tommy and Laurie judiciously loaded up the plane hoping it was not all for naught. Laurie climbed up into the pilot's seat quickly running through a mental checklist before attempting to start the plane. It sputtered for a moment and then shut itself off faltering with a loud backfire. She tried it again with the same result. No one spoke a word, fearing a word of either positive or negative nature might permanently jinx their situation. She tried it a third time but this time with far worse results. The engine began to rumble loudly coming to a screeching halt erupting into a cloud of smoke. She jumped out from the pilot's seat and quickly lifted up the cover to the engine compartment clearing the smoke away with her hand. The smell of burnt rubber rushed into their nasal passages stinging their lungs.

"I think I found it. Pass me that electrical tape over there."

Tommy grabbed the small dirty black roll and handed it to her as would a nurse pass a medical instrument to a doctor in surgery. She peeled it back tearing it with her teeth and wrapped it around an exposed wire.

"That should do it," she said jumping back into the plane.

Tommy and Chuck looked at each other with wide uneasy eyes as she jumped back into the plane. Neither of the men had much confidence in the old plane. It stammered roughly once again, but this time instead of stalling out, it eased up and continued to run choppily.

"It's ready!" she said hoping out of the plane with a grin.

The two men stood silent not sure what to say. She noticed their quiet hesitation.

"Come on let's go while we got some daylight left."

"Umm… yeah about that, I've been thinking and I think the old Cadillac could make the run to California no problem."

"What," she said over the loud noise behind her, "are you kidding? You were the very one that said we couldn't make it there in a car!"

"We'll to be fair to him,' said Tommy, "there's really no rush. We have plenty of time to make the coast."

She was proud of her accomplishment on getting the old plane up and running and she wasn't about to bow down to fear again.

She had spent her entire life prey to fear and today it was going to stop forever.

"You pussies!" she said angrily. "I can't believe what I am hearing from you two! Trying to drive across a country swarming with undead is stupid and you both know it! I am going to go get in that plane and fly out of here, if you two are in it great, if not then a hui hou!"

She stomped off and jumped into the plane closing the door tightly.

"What the fuck does that mean?" asked Chuck unsure what hui hou meant.

The plane began to slowly roll forward through the hangar door.

"I don't know but it looks like if we don't get in we'll never know!" said Tommy running after the plane.

The two men climbed into the plane next to a pilot whose stone face obliterated any doubt in the men's minds if she had been bluffing or not. The plane rolled out into the bright noon sunshine turning ever so slowly toward the long open runway. All three of its passengers held their breath as it nudged forward into a headlong run with the wide-open sky. The small plane shook and rattled as it rolled down the runway and for a moment it felt as if it was going to crumble away beneath their feet leaving the three tumbling down the runway. Finally it lifted into the air rising up and down gently until it finally rose above the lower air stream and settled down into a smooth flight. The old plane hummed loudly, but reassuringly, for as long as it functioned their plane could keep itself high in the air safe from the infection and from plummeting violently against the earth.

"So sweetie peetie, you weren't really going to leave us back there were you?" asked Tommy curiously.

"Only if you hadn't gotten into the plane. I'm tired of letting fear run my life… never again," she stated firmly.

The plane's engine sputtered, stalling for a second, then started back up running roughly for a second before humming smoothly again.

"What the hell was that?" asked Tommy nervously.

"I don't know," said Laurie looking at the dashboard with a perplexed look.

Chuck leaned up into the front of the plane, "I'm not afraid to tell you two, I'm so scared I'm about to pee in my pants."

The plane's engine sputtered again going silent for an instant, but to its passengers it seemed an eternity. The noise of the once running engine leaked out of the interior of the plane leaving an eerie hush behind as it whistled through the air in a glided freefall. The engine engaged breaking the horrible silence that had engulfed the terror-stricken trio lifting the plane level with the horizon once again.

"Shit this is bad," said Tommy griping the sides of his seat firmly.

"That's what fear is for," said Chuck from the backseat, "to keep you from doing stupid things."

"Second guessing is not going to help us here, be quiet for one moment so I can think."

"We're really way up too," said Chuck pressing his face up to the side window. "Shouldn't we drop down some in case we have to make an emergency landing?"

"Altitude is our friend. You don't make emergency landings in personal aircraft; you make emergency crashes and hope they aren't too bad."

"I miss the Cadillac," said Chuck leaning back nervously.

"Me too," admitted Laurie in a raspy voice, "but I think it's going to be all right. It sounds pretty good now."

Almost before she could get the words out of her mouth the engine sputtered and stopped with a loud whine. The strange silence quickly returned but this time the engine did not restart leaving the passengers engulfed within its strange void. The propeller sputtered as the plane slightly dipped its nose toward the ground. The steering wheel began to shake fiercely in Laurie's hands as she held on to it with all her might trying to level out the soaring aircraft.

"I guess you don't parachute from personal aircraft either?" asked Chuck curiously.

"No," said the pilot quickly.

"Why not?" he asked uneasily. "I would think the safety code would require all planes to have parachutes under the seats or something."

"I don't know, you just don't," she screamed back at him as they lost altitude.

The nose continued to sink down raising the sky up above the top line of the front windshield. Laurie stomped onto the floorboard and tugged against the steering wheel in an attempt to decrease their descent. The ground began to race up toward the craft looming larger with every second. She gritted her teeth tightly and continued to fight against the wheel. Bluish green veins popped up on the top of her hands and on the sides of her neck as she pulled with every muscle in her body. Suddenly the engine started back up turning the propeller into a solid shifting circle leveling out their plunge. Tommy fell back his seat in a cold sweat, while Chuck thanked a god he didn't even believe in. Laurie inhaled and exhaled out a long breath, breathing once again.

"I say we find a place to land and walk it out," suggested Chuck rolling in sweat.

"I second that," said Tommy in support of his lifelong friend, "all this starting and stopping is going to give me a stroke."

Laurie, shaken by the experience, had lost her initial confidence in the old plane and she gladly agreed with a simple nod. There was a fine line between bravery and stupidity and she had no intention of crossing if she could chose not to do so. She veered off to right bringing the rough terrain below up close and began to search along it for a safe place to land. Before long, they found a small field touching down upon it without trouble. All three of its passengers jumped out of the plane in excitement. Chuck fell to the ground in an attempt to hug it like a long lost love.

"I am so glad to see you," he said looking down at it with adoration.

Both Tommy and Laurie fell to the ground mentally exhausted from the experience.

"I feel like I just ran a marathon."

"Sorry I let you two down."

"Are you kidding, honey bunny? You did great! You stayed cool under fire, not freezing up or anything. I am really proud of you," he said reassuring her.

She smiled slightly from the complement and rolled over to kiss him. He held her tightly kissing her back with the passion of life that filled every cell in his body.

"Isn't being alive great!" said Chuck's voice from underneath the tall grass. "Go ahead and have sex with each other, I won't listen. I'm fucking the earth right now!"

Chapter 29
A Rendezvous with the Government

With weapons holstered and packs hoisted onto their backs, the three travelers took to their feet and began the final part of their journey to the coast. They marched single file through brush and sand dragging along toward the coast relentlessly to meet their deadline with the government. Although the trip ahead would be a monumental one on foot, traveling most of the way through the air had left them plenty of time to reach the coast in time. Just having their feet planted firmly on the ground after a near crash was more than enough motivation to carry them through to the end of their trip with wide smiles. They spent the next week hiking across California's sparsely populated terrain skimping along on scanty rations from their nearly exhausted supplies. Under the cover of stars, they shivered through the nights on empty stomachs only to sweat under the relentless sun during the day. Nine days with each appearing no different than the other passed as they wandered on toward a seamlessly endless horizon desperately seeking the image of their destination.

The hazy image of an infected dotted the horizon through the blazing sun. It stumbled clumsily, dehydrated by the effects of the scorching sun walking aimlessly through the desert. It didn't make sense to any of the group why some infected when without stimuli seemed to go into a type of hibernation mode, while others seemed to roam randomly as if in search of it. Chuck dropped the decomposing creature at a distance of over two hundred yards.

"He never even saw us," bragged the sniper.

"Hopefully finding infected means we are close to a town," stated Tommy eyeing the horizon.

They hiked over to the man Chuck had just shot but found nothing of use on his badly decayed body. Flies buzzed in and out of open cavities in his body living off the nourishment of his flesh. Laurie turned around vomiting uncontrollably.

"You okay, pooh bear?"

"Yes," she replied wiping her mouth clean, "I've had an upset stomach over the past few days and the sight of that disgusting thing set it off."

"I'm sure it's all that water you drank on an empty stomach," said Tommy reassuring her as well as himself.

They traveled on for several more hours before coming up upon a road and a sign.

"Paso Robles," asked Chuck confused by the obviously Hispanic name, "where the hell are we, Mexico?"

Tommy scrambled through a pocket in his backpack and pulled out a dirty folded up map, unfolding it to full size. He ran his finger along the city names and then found its location on the grid.

"We're only about thirty miles from the coast!" he said in anticipation of ending a long journey.

"Really?" asked Chuck unbelievably.

"That's what it says," he answered back happily.

Laurie leaned over and sat down holding her abdominal area. Tommy noticed her lack of excitement and sat down beside her.

"You going to be okay?"

"Oh yeah, I just don't feel very well."

"Once we get you something solid to eat you will be right as rain."

"Come on, let's get moving! We can rest all you want once we reach the beach!"

Laurie stood up hiding how she really felt under the cover of a fake smile. Her stomach was churning like an active volcano ready to erupt and she felt light headed, but not wanting to make Tommy worry, she followed the two men as if she felt fine. Being in no particular rush, they walked out the rest of the day casually stopping to scavenge food or anything else of value when the opportunity presented itself, but they found little of value among the abandoned buildings they passed along the way. Chuck did find a can of beets in an old shed, but neither of the three's hunger had reached the point of canned beets as of yet. With the loss of light from the sun, they bedded down for the night taking turns pulling two-hour guard shifts. Laurie, glad for the opportunity to sleep off her nausea, volunteered for the third shift and fell asleep almost instantly under the watchful eye of Chuck who had taken the first shift. Tommy took the second shift, but never woke Laurie, letting her sleep through the night. When he awoke Chuck for his second shift, his friend rose up groggy looking at him like he was a fool for taking two shifts.

"Damn dude, you been up for four hours?" he asked.

"Yeah, Laurie has been feeling bad, so I decided not to bother her."

"Well, my back is sore. You want to cover mine too?"

"Wake me up in to two hours wise ass," he said ignoring his comment rolling over under his jacket.

Chuck made a whiplash sound to aggravate his friend by suggesting that he was whipped, but he really didn't believe it. It was fun to mess with him about it. In actuality, he was glad to see the two hit it off so well. Instead of waking up his friend, he sat up the remainder of the night and even took the blame for falling asleep on his shift so the other two wouldn't barrage him or each other with a throng of questions.

After eating a diminutive breakfast of Frito chips and beets, the three loaded up to finish their long hike. No one in the group enjoyed the peculiar taste of the odd breakfast, but the substance of it did add some weight to their stomachs, somewhat reducing their hunger pangs. They quickly took to the trail and by noon it appeared before their weary eyes. A vast sheet of still blue expanded out from the coast creating a resolution into the skyline almost inseparable to the naked eye.

The three felt a wave of accomplishment sweep over their souls upon the sight of such a wonderful spectacle sparkling in the distance. They had made it, a group of three against an entire nation of infected. There had been squabbles along the way, but each had grown closer for it, Tommy and Laurie together as a couple, while Laurie and Chuck had turned a competitive grudge into immeasurable respect for one another. No greater journey had been accomplished since that of Lewis and Clark. Laughter and cutting up followed the group to the coast as they joked about anything and everything, much like children would on a final field trip. They watched the swelling tide rush up and down the beach breathing in the fresh salty air.

"So what now?" asked Laurie after pulling her knees up against her chest to support her position in the beach's soft sand.

"I don't know really," admitted Chuck. "We are about a week ahead of schedule, are you sure this is the place?"

"I don't have an exact location, since the GPS went under with Doctor Ledbetter, but according to the map the coordinates we were given are between Harmony and Cambria, meaning we couldn't be off by more than a few miles," stated Tommy looking at his worn map.

"So then all there is left to do is wait, kind of like a weeklong vacation on the beach, except we don't have a room and not one of use brought sun block."

"I don't care," said Laurie. "I'm just happy that the infection is behind us forever and the only thing we have to worry about now is sun burns!"

"Wake me up when our ride arrives," said Chuck.

"Fine, you two can sleep in your own stink, but I am going to go take a bath!" said Laurie jumping up and pulling off her shirt.

Tommy jumped up and raced after her stripping off his own clothes on the way to the water's edge.

"I forgot to bring my bathing suit…" said Chuck raising up and pausing after seeing that neither of the other two had any clothes on as they jumped into the ocean playing like two naked children. "Hmm… guess I better stay out so things don't get all weird and stuff."

Being physically drained from the long trip and the consecutive guard shifts he pulled the prior night, he nodded off under the cool ocean breeze as soon as he closed his eyes leaving the world's last two lovers alone. They made the most of it acting like newlyweds on their honeymoon dancing after each other through the waves without a care. With the state of the world, it would be easy to say they were the happiest people on earth.

They spent three more days playing under the warmth of the sun, building sand castles and swimming in the surf, linking it all together through long catnaps and brilliant nights underneath the glistening stars. They discussed the remaining matters of the world that still held any importance under their mysterious glow debating the futures of both themselves and mankind. If it were not for their shortage of food, they would be living as man had been meant to do so in the Garden of Eden, but on the fourth day Satan arrived, this time in the form of a helicopter.

Three helicopters buzzed along the coastline coming from the north heading south skimming a few hundred feet out from the beach. The staggered chops of their blades cut through the air beating down upon the earth awakening three peaceful forms lying on the beach. Tommy, Laurie and Chuck jumped to their feet and began to wave at the helicopters in cheers as they hovered above the water. The crafts soared overhead slinging sand and dirt along the shore pelting their vulnerable eyes and mouths surrounding the group in an artificial whirlwind, before lifting up and disappearing over a small ledge overhanging the beach. They chased after the airborne objects in ridiculous full stride through the deep sand like children being left behind by their parents.

The helicopters sat down in a perfect line formation letting their blades come to a slow rotation before sliding open the side doors. Men or relative facsimiles filed out in unison fully clad in thick white glossy protective suits. The first men to rush out of the helicopters brandished long black assault rifles with scopes. The men stepped to the sides of the aircraft allowing two more forms in protective suits carrying shiny metal briefcases to step out. The last two men to exit the craft began to make hand gestures toward the three pointing in their direction. Immediately the men carrying rifles lowered their barrels at the haggard trio and spread out, completely encircling them. An uneasy feeling overwhelmed the three who had just rushed up the hill in enthusiasm as if the group of clad men radiated fear. Their smiles of relief transformed into looks of concern as they found themselves surrounded by a group of silent white suits with gleaming face panels. A long white rubber glove seized Laurie's arm from behind and she jumped forward with a scream. Spooked, both Tommy and Chuck drew their pistols pointing them at the smoky mirrors that continued to close in. Tommy swung his around wildly trying to stop their advances.

"Get the fuck back!" he screamed.

Chuck fixed his barrel on one target and pressed it up against the glass where a man's head would rest on top of his body. He concentrated his eyes upon it until he could see its eyes through the cloudy glass; they were radiating their own fear. Rifles clicked around the three fixed upon them ready to turn a rescue attempt into a bloody massacre.

"*Stand down*," said a scratchy voice from a small screened hole below his pistol.

"You drew first," Chuck replied pushing back the thing's head with the tip of his pistol.

"*This is your last chance!*" filtered the small abrasive voice. "*Stand down!*"

"I'm ready to answer to God for my sins. How about you?" Chuck said looking through the glass in the suit's facemask directly into the white beast's eyes. "Pull that trigger and we can skip into heaven together… hand in hand."

One of the suits carrying a silver case stepped up toward the encircled standoff.

"*Please lower your weapons. This is a mere formality,*" said the filtered voice.

"There was nothing formal on how you just greeted us," said Tommy nervously.

"*These men have orders to disarm everyone for the safety of the mission.*"

"Then disarm yourselves," replied Chuck stubbornly. "I make it a rule not to lower my gun when one is pointing at me."

"*They're orders are to disarm anyone we encounter and they will not leave until that has been accomplished.*"

"Lower your guns," said Laurie's voice. "If they wanted us dead they would have blown us away on the beach."

A tense moment passed, as stern guns with tight fingers on both sides failed to waver under the cool morning air. Tommy was the first to lower his pistol, followed by Chuck who swung his backwards in his hand holding the butt of his pistol grip out toward the very man he had so tightly held it against.

"I'll get you next time," he commented with a wink.

A cautious hand rose up and took the gun from him leaving the three unarmed. The man with the case then pointed at the three again and suddenly white hands engulfed the helpless group mauling them to the ground forcefully binding their hands with thick plastic ties. All three of the fatigued travelers struggled against their aggressors but were utterly outnumbered and were quickly subdued. The suits held them down with their knees like wild game trophies. Chuck managed to slip one of his hands free and pull out a small knife he had hidden within his waistline. He swung it up beside him connecting with a pant leg that was holding his face in the dirt. It ripped the suit in a long gash, not drawing blood, but separating the thick rubber material. The figure on top fell over backwards holding the rip with its hands screaming.

"Oh my god, I have been exposed!"

One of the men holding a briefcase dropped it and alertly ran over to the man patching the hole with a roll of red tape. Fist, knees and feet began to crash down upon Chuck breaking his grip upon his small knife vehemently bending his arm behind his back. When he tried to resist, blows began to rain down upon his head until flashing lights began to flicker before his eyes and he lost consciousness.

"Hold out his arm," said a suit holding up a syringe.

Tommy's eyes cracked open slightly revealing a room that would better be described a small metal box. He peered around the room disoriented from the anesthesia and shakily stumbled over to the only other object in the room, a door. He fumbled with its handle in a daze but slid back against the wall after finding it locked. His head throbbed mercilessly as he held down upon it with his palms feeling the lumps upon it. Made curious by the pain in his right antecubital area, he pulled up his sleeve to find it severely bruised, similar to that of a common drug addict. Someone had taken a lot of his blood or far worse, injected him with something. The homecoming that they had daydreamed about their entire trip out west had been shattered by a welcoming nightmare. Angered by his treatment, he began to pound against the thick metal door with the flat of his fist, but it stood solid hardly vibrating a sound. His head began to swim from the exertion and he fell backwards collapsing against the wall. He hunched over on the floor recomposing his equilibrium. The handle to the door lifted in a jerking motion discharging a flood of light into the small room. Two dark forms stepped into the room eclipsing the bright light. Tommy looked up to see two elderly men in glasses and white smocks peering down at him.

"I am surprised to find you awake so soon," said one of the men.

"Who the fuck are you?" asked Tommy unimpressed with his host.

"Oh, I am sorry, how rude of me," he said cordially. "This is Doctor Leben and I am Doctor McGee."

"Doctor Leben… Doctor McGee," he said with a polite nod to each of the men, "go fuck yourselves!"

"I understand your frustration, but we had to be absolutely sure no one in your group was infected."

"Does being absolutely sure mean you have to beat those in question into submission?" he asked irritated. "I feel like I just got gang banged."

"You have to understand the risk the men of this ship undertook coming back to the mainland to rescue you."

"I just crossed an entire continent infested with zombies without shit, except for what we could salvage from the dead and you want to talk about risk?"

"Neither one of us is attempting to diminish such an accomplishment, but besides the two of us, not a single man on this ship volunteered for this rescue mission and not one was happy with being pressed into service for it. There were times when I was sure that the men of this ship were going to turn to mutiny and abort the entire mission. If one of you had been infected, the men on this ship might have become exposed, turning this modern ship into a floating fortress for the dead."

"Where are Laurie and Chuck?"

"Resting…" he said turning the conversation to his own request. "Will you come with us? We would like to ask you a few questions.

"Go ahead and ask them now."

"Please, let us go somewhere more comfortable. Are you hungry?"

Tommy's head stung and his stomach grumbled, "You got any coffee?"

"Why yes, I think we can accommodate that with little difficulty."

The two men helped him to his feet and out into the hallway before telling a man in a sailor's uniform to bring some coffee and breakfast to his quarters. The sailor looked at Tommy apprehensively, then double timed down the long hallway. They walked along slowly as Tommy regained his bearings and turned around the corner startling three sailors who immediately scattered upon their appearance. They came to another small door and stepped inside leading Tommy to a stiffly padded chair. The room was larger than the one he had awoken in, but considering it had been about the size of a walk-in closet, didn't say much for the new room.

"I want to be told the minute either of the other two wake," said one of the doctors to the sailor before shutting the door.

A dim light on the wall illuminated the three slightly giving the tiny room a dingy yellow hue. They sat down and began to barrage him with questions.

"What happened to Doctor Ledbetter? If I am not mistaken, he is the one that arranged the pick up."

Tommy knew what the conversation was going to come down to, the cure.

"We lost him in Atlanta."

"Hmm… that is terrible," said Doctor Leben the shorter of the two men. "It is a shame to lose such a brilliant man."

"What about his inoculation? We did not find any trace of it."

"Gone."

The two men sat back in thought silently contemplating their dwindling options.

"Have you been immunized against the infection?"

"Yes, all three of us have."

"How do you know you are immune to the infection?" asked Doctor McGee holding his chin.

"All three of us were infected and brought back from near death by Doctor Ledbetter's cure."

"You mean to tell me it not only immunizes, but cures the infection?" he asked astonished by the statement

"Yes."

"Incredible!" declared Doctor Leben.

"Did Doctor Ledbetter keep any records of his research?" asked the other doctor.

"Yes, but we lost them somewhere in the Chattahoochee river the night we left Atlanta."

"What do you mean you lost them in the river?"

"I mean when we jumped off the bridge to avoid a bloodthirsty mob of infected we lost them along with Doctor Ledbetter."

"Did you get a chance to look at them?" asked the other Doctor.

"No."

"Why not?" asked the other.

"Because Doctor Ledbetter wouldn't let me."

"Wouldn't let you?" said the other strangely.

"You guys are bouncing me back and forth like I am at Wimbledon with these questions."

There was a knock at the door and Doctor Leben got up to answer it.

"I'm sorry, we are just curious, it's all we have spoken of since we first got the report. This cure may be man's last chance to survive this outbreak."

"Let's let him eat before we continue," said Doctor Leben holding a tray of eggs, bacon, toast, coffee and tea.

Tommy's eyes swelled open at the sight of a hot meal that didn't come out of a plastic bag. He quickly chopped up the eggs with his fork and soaked up the yoke in his toast consuming it like a savage.

"Surely he told you something or maybe you saw something that might give us a clue."

Tommy looked up from his breakfast at the two men. He could see the desperation in their eyes, they were grasping for any shred of hope he might be able to divulge. Had it been his friend who had awoken first and not he, Chuck would have given an elaborate impromptu speech carrying on with their ruse fabricating whatever falsehoods best fit the current line of questioning. He had always had an aptitude for tall tales, a talent that Tommy never excelled in primarily because he didn't have the stomach for lies. He never looked down on his friend for having done so ever since they were boys when it might benefit them in one way or another. It just left him with an empty feeling whenever he personally lied.

"I am going to be straight with you," he said coming clean. "The three of us heard about Doctor Ledbetter's cure and along the way to meet up with him, we were exposed to the infection. He saved us with his cure."

"You mean he reversed the infection?" asked Doctor McGee.

"Yes, we were bad off."

"Fantastic!" he replied.

"Do you know if you three are immune to the infection?" asked Doctor Leben.

"Chuck was bitten several days ago.

"And not one of you showed any signs of infection, everyone one of you had normal RBC and WBC counts, absolutely amazing!" said Doctor Leben standing up in excitement.

"Doctor Ledbetter wouldn't tell anybody anything about his cure, in fear of being abandoned at the CDC in Atlanta," said Tommy concluding his regretful news. "We lost both him and the hard copies of his cure in the Chattahoochee River on the way here."

"Hmm… maybe we are not at a total loss, with the three of you, maybe we can discover how your body fights off the infection," the doctor said scheming.

"I can assure you, we will be glad to help out in any way we can."

"Yes, I'm sure you will," answered the doctor.

An abrupt pounding at the door broke his concentration bringing his statement to an end as he walked over to the door.

"Sir," said a sailor at the door, "the young lady we brought on board is awake and is asking for someone named Tommy."

Tommy jumped up from his clean plate nearly knocking the doctor onto the floor so to come face to face with the sailor at the door.

"Take me to her," he ordered.

Chapter 30
An Hawaiian Cruise

Having had to be detained a little more forcefully than the others, Chuck had received an extra sedative and did not wake until eight hours after Laurie. Once he came through, the memory of their apprehension awoke a rage causing him to rant and rave among the astonished crew.

"Settle down now," said one the three sailors trying to detain him.

"Which one of you mother fuckers kicked me in the gonads back on the beach?" he screamed in anger.

"No one kicked you in the gonads, so calm down," replied the sailor.

"I think I know when I've been kicked in the jewels!"

"Please calm down," said another sailor trying to control his flailing arms, "the doctors are on the way."

"Good because you are going to need them after I get done kicking all three of you fuckers in the nuts," he yelled in frustration of being detained.

"What is going on here?" asked Doctor Leben running toward the scuffle on deck, followed by his colleague, Tommy, Laurie and two marines.

"Sir this man is out of control!" reported one of the sailors holding him.

"Please… please," said Doctor Leben trying to diffuse the situation, "let go of this man."

"Not until he settles down!" responded one of the sailors.

"Let me go you bitch!"

"Please stop resisting!" implored Doctor Leben. "I will not let anyone here harm you."

"Oh really?" asked Chuck sardonically. "The last time I quit resisting I got the shit kicked out of me."

"I am as pissed as you about how we were treated back there, but he is here to help," stated Tommy to his lifelong friend.

As if listening to reason, Chuck finally calmed down and by a nod from Doctor Leben the three sailors released him. He turned around and apologized for his behavior to the three sailors just before kicking one squarely in his genital area. The sailor collapsed to the deck holding his groin in agonizing pain. The other two sailors pulled out their batons and began to advance on Chuck with the intentions of cracking open his head, only to be stopped by a frantic Doctor Leben.

"Gentlemen put those away!" he ordered loudly.

"Get out of my way!" said one of the determined sailors. "I'm going to bust his head open."

"You will do no such thing!" shouted Doctor Leben blocking the sailors with his body. "This man is under the protection of the President of the United States! If you lay one hand on him you will have to answer directly to him!"

The young sailor's eyes shifted from squinted anger to widened fear as he stepped back and lowered his nightstick.

"We'll get you," he said before helping his friend out of a fetal position.

"Yeah, well I'll be careful not to drop the soap!"

The two parties parted reluctantly as the two doctors led their subjects away from the rest of the crew toward their quarters where they had been given their own marine detachment and complete control by presidential orders.

"Many of the men on the ship are a bit skittish about your presence, so I believe it would be the best if the three of you stayed as far away from the general population as possible," commented Doctor Leben. "We have made accommodations for each of you for the trip back."

"Where are we?" asked Chuck curiously looking at unfamiliar surroundings.

"You are on board the mighty nuclear powered aircraft carrier the USS Ronald Reagan," replied Doctor McGee proudly.

"Great, even the ship is a republican," said Chuck under his breath so that only Tommy and Laurie could hear.

His companions smiled and followed the two doctors into their new sleeping quarters. Three new passengers roamed the giant ship's deck under the watchful eye of a marine guard. They were free to go wherever they wanted, as long as they were under escort. Laurie leaned up against one of the ship's rails staring down the side of the hull as it churned through the ocean toward its island destination. All that she could see was ocean and sky and suddenly she felt isolated, but not safe as she thought she would have felt once she left the mainland.

Later that night when everyone else was asleep, Laurie lay motionless next to Tommy staring at the ceiling while he snored. Something wasn't right she thought. They were obviously safe, safer than she had been since the infection began and yet she couldn't sleep. Somehow she knew that they were going to have more hardships to endure, maybe even more difficult than those they had already incurred. She stood up and tiptoed to their door, gently cracking it open. A full moon hung over the ocean gleaming down upon it portentously reflecting off its surface illuminating her face. An empty chair sat outside their door where a marine was supposed to be standing guard. She quickly ran back over to Tommy and began to shake him vigorously to wake him. Her efforts managed to break the rhythm of his snores, but not to awaken him from his deep slumber.

"Tommy get up, let's go for a walk."

"What?" he asked half asleep.

"Let's go outside and get some fresh air."

He rose up groggily looking at her like she was crazy, "What time is it?"

"I don't know. I just want to get out of here and walk around without someone looking over our shoulders."

He was absolutely worn out, but he could see in her eyes that this was somehow important to her, so he roused himself away from the desire to go back to sleep and followed her outside. They ran down the long walkway and took several turns, until they found a small terrace like area out of sight facing the moon. He pulled her up close to him and they snuggled under the cool ocean air.

"Tommy, I know I am usually the most optimistic of the three of us, but I have a bad feeling about this trip."

"Ah, you're just homesick. Everything is going to be fine. We're headed back to civilization, no more hiding in basements or scrounging for food…" he paused hoping what he was saying was true, "no more zombies."

"I know but I don't trust these doctors, why do they have to have us under watch night and day? Even if we could escape, why would we choose to do so?"

"I guess because we are the closest thing they have to a cure and they don't want anything to happen to us."

"I think those doctors are holding something back, it's like you are the only one I can trust."

Nausea took hold of his innards as guilt twisted them mercilessly from within tormenting him far worse than any physical pain could ever inflict. Sweat began to pour out of his pores drenching his skin in the cool wind raising chill bumps along his arms and legs. He couldn't hide it from her any longer no matter what the cost. If he couldn't have her honestly, then he didn't deserve her at all.

"Laurie there is something I need to tell you," opening the gates of truth he had kept locked for so long.

She had grown to know him well, even in the short time they had been together, and she could tell from his tone what he had to say was important.

"What is it sweetie?" she asked turning around facing him while sitting Indian style.

"There is something I haven't told you, that you have the right to know."

She looked at him strangely completely unaware of where the conversation was going.

"See, back at the nuclear plant we didn't happen to come along at the right time," he said sorrowfully.

"I don't understand," she said dumbfounded.

"We brought those infected with us," he said ashamed.

"You didn't mean to, it was an accident," she said making excuses for the man she loved.

He didn't say anything.

"But you two saved me."

"We didn't want to hurt you," he replied scrambling for an explanation, "we were after the soldiers… they shot our friend in cold blood."

Her eyes changed and she stood up slowly backing away.

"But Brian, Doctor Werner they were…"

She stopped for she could not bear to hear those words cross her lips.

"I'm sorry. I wish I could take it all back."

"You monster!" she screamed backing away. "You have been keeping this from me all this time! You are no better than Chuck or those soldiers back there you helped to murder! You took everything from me and made me a mockery! Look at me! I am married to the man that murdered my husband! No wait, I'm not really married to you… our marriage is just a lie like everything else!"

She took off the ring he gave her and slung it at him. It bounced off the deck of the ship and floated away into the wind to be lost forever beneath the sea. The ring of his father was now gone to him as well. He reached out toward her, but she jumped way from him like he had the infection.

"You stay away from me!" she ordered. "I don't know who you are anymore!"

She ran off into the darkness, disappearing from his sight. Her image faded into the haze of the night, and had he had conscious control over his heart, it would have stopped at that moment. He lay in that very spot through the night hardly having the energy to move, not caring at that moment if he lived or died. The sun rose up over the sea breaking the cold shroud that had engulfed the large ship throughout night slowing down the chatter of his teeth ever so slightly. A tall shadow cast upon onto his face blocking the warmth of the early morning sun.

"What the hell did you do rub salt in your eyes?"

"I told her," he said desolately.

"I kinda figured," said Chuck, "I ran into her about an hour ago and when I said hi, she spit in my face."

"Where is she?" he asked curiously.

"She asked the Doublemint twins for different quarters on the other side of the ship."

Tommy lowered his head without say a word.

"Come on man, we're back where we started… two bachelors," he looked over at his marine escort. "Come on…if you are going to be my shadow, then at least be of some use and help me get him back to the room."

The marine looked at him crossly before finally giving into his command and helping him bring his shattered friend to his limp feet. They drug him back to the small cabin selected to serve as their quarters, where Tommy slid into the bed crumbling into a motionless heap. Chuck left him in silence to sulk out the problem on his own, following an unwritten code the two had followed since they were children. When one had a personal problem the other one never asked anything about it. If he wanted to talk about it, he would bring up the issue on his own. So to avoid the awkwardness of the situation, he left him in the room alone and roamed along the deck with his personal bodyguard.

"So where are you from?" he asked the uniformed man shadowing his every move.

"What?" he asked surprised to hear the man he had been keeping an eye on for two days actually speak directly to him.

"Oh I'm sorry, do I need to rephrase the question so you can understand? Where are you from soldier?" he said screaming his last sentence as if he were a drill sergeant.

"Why are you always such an asshole?"

"Are you insulting me?" he asked bumping up against the marine in a challenging manner.

"That's what I mean, I haven't done a thing to you and here you are ready to throw down."

"Maybe I don't like being followed around like a criminal."

"I don't know exactly why I am supposed to keep such a close eye on you, I'm just following orders."

Chuck stepped back cooled off by the young marine's words and turned around almost ashamed of his actions unclenching his fist. He had been ready to deck the soldier had he answered his challenge.

"Give me some breathing room okay?"

The young soldier stepped back a few feet quickly respecting his request, bringing the two completely different men into a moment of laughter.

"Hey, I'm sorry, so where are you from?"

"Oklahoma, I was lucky to be stationed in Hawaii when the infection struck. How about you?"

"Back east… right in the heart of zombie country."

"Damn, last estimate I heard was that there were over one hundred million zombies in the continental US."

"So, what's it like in Hawaii? Still a postcard moment?"

"It's more like a refugee camp now, than a tropical paradise, crowded with everybody who's left from the United States."

"What's left of the world? Anywhere else escape the infection?"

"New Zealand is still there. France relocated to the Marquesas Islands, Fiji was still there last I heard and I think Chile actually set up on Easter Island."

"That's it?" asked Chuck stunned at the few locations where man still ruled the earth. "Australia?"

"Gone, besides a few tiny Pacific islands that about covers it."

"Well at least it'll be nice to be able to walk outside again without worry about being eaten," he paused going silent for a long moment. "Sorry about being an ass earlier. Think I will take a stroll, you coming? Oh that's right you don't have a choice."

The marine laughed slightly and followed him down the ramp, but this time, he gave him a little extra room.

The monstrous metal island cut through the deep protective walls of the Pacific Ocean nautically churning toward its destination of Hawaii, carrying its nation's three most precious assets. For within their veins flowed what every man, women and child desired, with only the slightest of problems. How would they retrieve the secret within? Day and night fell in quick succession as if the sun and moon were upon a wheel rotating around their ship. Besides eating, and doing regular checkups with Doctor Leben and Doctor McGee, Tommy rarely left his quarters and neither of the men saw or heard from Laurie the reminder of the trip. The day they were supposed to arrive, Chuck spent the entire day up on deck so as not to miss a moment of its image. He watched it with anticipating eyes as if he was watching the golden city of Atlantis rise from the depths. It came into to view slowly rising up from the waters anchored in the center of a gleaming sunset. Upon its appearance the sailors upon the deck of the ship cheered in excitement of surviving their mission to the mainland.

"Welcome to the United State of Hawaii," said the sailor assigned to Chuck.

They had become fast friends during the long trip, graduating from an early hostility to downright current camaraderie.

"It's beautiful!" said Chuck awestruck by its crystal waters and swaying palm trees.

"Give it some time," said the sailor.

"There you are," said Doctor McGee in an obvious hurry, "we are about to leave."

A helicopter lifted off the runway and soared overhead drowning the three men out in a whirlwind forcefully pressing their bodies down toward the steel grates below their feet. The doctor continued to scream but the artificial windstorm swallowed his words drafting them away with the soaring craft.

"This way," he said after the helicopter was out of range.

"Aren't we staying with the ship?"

"No, this ship is docking in the harbor… we are headed to the other side of the island."

"Who was that?"

"Doctor Leben and Doctor Connelly went on ahead of us," he said leading the way.

Chuck knew Laurie was mad, but deep down he had assumed she would at least eventually forgive Tommy, but after hearing that she had taken back her first married name, he wasn't so sure.

"Come on G.I. Joe, you can drag my shit onto the copter, I'll drag Tommy."

"Great now I am taking orders from a civilian."

"You know you love it."

Chapter 31
The United State of Hawaii

The blades began to slow down as soon as the tires of the HH-60H Seahawk touched the ground grinding down to a hypnotic chopping sound. Four forms hunched underneath its swirling blades running through a mixture of shifting air and sand toward a covered walkway. Doctor McGee led Chuck and Tommy up to a dual glass sliding door, quickly flashed an identification card to pass by two armed soldiers then stepped into a bright white waiting area that sat empty. At a desk on the far wall was an older woman, somewhere in her fifties wearing pokeadot scrubs.

"Welcome back, Doctor McGee," she said quickly.

"Thank you my dear. I am going to show these men to their room. Has Doctor Leben arrived yet?"

"Yes, he and a woman arrived a few minutes ago."

"Wonderful," he stated.

Both men knew who his guest was as they followed the rushing doctor through a set of swinging double doors out of the waiting area. He took them down several long halls with numerous twists, turns and elevator rides before stopping in front of a door with a frosted glass window. He opened the door with a jolt and motioned for them to enter. The two men stepped in eyeing their new surroundings. It was solid white with two bed and had a multitude of low cabinets, a cornered bathroom and barred windows.

"This is a hospital room," said Chuck surprised at their accommodations.

"It looks like the room of a mental patient," stated Tommy.

"Yes, I am sorry about that. Rooms are hard to come by at the moment, but I promise you will find it to be quite comfortable."

"What are the bars for?" asked Chuck sarcastically. "Expecting a zombie attack?"

"Those are there for the protection of this facility. Even a worldwide epidemic doesn't stop crime," laughed the doctor. "If either of you need anything, just push the nurse's button."

The pale doctor latched the door and left the two worn men behind in silence. Chuck promptly stepped up to the door and checked its handle. It clanked stubbornly against the deadbolt refusing to open. He frowned, aggravated at being treated like an overgrown hamster. He turned around and gave Tommy I told you so look, who in turn flopped backwards onto the bed not caring either way.

"Guess we spent the last year hiding behind locked doors and traveling half way around the world to end up behind locked doors again."

Tommy's body lay silent as if he hadn't heard a word spoken by his friend, motionless. Suddenly a tap at the door burst the tranquility of the small room bringing the earlier static Tommy to his feet at near attention. A young man stepped in dragging two green army duffle bags.

"Hi," he said nervously trying to drag in the two heavy bags through the door on his own.

Neither of the men in the room budged to help him, leaving him standing in an awkward silence.

"Doctor Leben said that everything you need should be in these bags, but if not, feel free to ask."

The two men stared at him without saying a word. They smelled fear in him the moment he stepped in the room and they were going in for the kill, the silent kill. It was something they had practiced together since childhood. It was a method they had used against teachers, their classmates and as they grew older, on the basketball court and in bars. Chuck walked up to the young man bumping him slightly away from the door before closing it shut. The startled man turned around to put some space between him and the imposing figure, only to bump into a stone-faced Tommy. Feeling the room closing in on him, the young man scrambled for the door only to find he had been locked in with the two men. He leaned up against the door spinning around with wild dilated eyes. His sympathetic nervous system took hold of his bodily functions and with the option of flight taken away, he stood ready to fight.

"I don't want any trouble," he shouted in a cold sweat.

The two men cornered him responding only with heartless eyes.

"How the fuck are we supposed to ask for anything if we are locked up in here by ourselves?" Chuck asked firmly.

"You are under surveillance twenty four seven," he sighed, appreciative of the conversion, "just wave at the cameras.

The two men's eyes roamed the four walls of the room, coming to rest on a small camera hanging in the back right corner. The blurry image of uniformed men appeared in the frosted screened glass behind the young man, as four armed guards burst into the room separating the three.

"I guess the cavalry arrived in time to save you this time, bitch," said Chuck frustrated at their treatment. "You're going to have to stroke some balls as payback tonight."

"Gentlemen please!" screamed Doctor Leben stumbling in through the door.

"When were you going to tell us we were being watched?" asked Tommy.

"A simple misunderstanding I assure you. You are in this room merely for your own protection," he pleaded. "Since the presidential decision to allow you three to come over from the mainland, the entire island's population has been in an uproar. Your well-being is directly linked to our own and we are just trying to be certain of your safety."

"Ah shucks, doctor, I bet you tell that to all your prisoners," replied Chuck.

"I sympathize with your situation, but you must understand that this is only a temporary situation until we get your residence finalized. Since the infection, the island's population has tripled and at the moment space is extremely limited. Take a few moments to get settled in and I will be back to see both of you in an hour or so. Also if you desire anything, please ask," he said leaving. "Oh one minute, I almost forgot. Dr. Connelly prescribed this for you."

Chuck took the white bag from him and dropped its contents into his hand as the doctor left closing the door tightly. Tommy eyed the bag from his wife curiously.

"It's Grifulvin," he said reading the label on the bottle slowly.

"What the fuck is that?"

"Antifungal pills for jock itch. Hmm…" he said staring at the small bottle in his palm, "thank God, my nuts have been driving me crazy."

"Your nuts have made you crazy since you hit puberty," said Tommy glumly.

"Well well," laughed Chuck, "nice burn there, about time you lightened up. I thought you had developed the personality of a zombie."

Chuck began to fumble through the bags left in their room tossing stuff sporadically.

"What the fuck? All this shit is military, hell the damn socks are wool!" he screamed up into the air talking to the cameras. "I want something all right. I want some real clothes and I didn't sign up for boot camp!"

He slid up onto the bed and said sarcastically, "And can you give me a wakeup call in two hours?"

Tommy fell backwards onto his own bed and slipped into unconsciousness before his friend finished ranting.

The two men spent the next ten days being poked and prodded in one of the world's most beautiful locations, seeing little more than their room, Doctor Leben and Mc Gee's laboratory and the hallways between the two as the government of the United States tried to unravel the secret of their immunity to the infection. It was an ordeal that wore heavy on the two young men.

"You know why they are feeding us so well?" asked Chuck while presenting a piece of steak on the end of his fork.

"No, but I am sure you know exactly why," said Tommy as dully as the room in which he had been imprisoned.

"So we can make more fucking blood for those God damn vampires to drain from us!" he screamed throwing his fork across the room in protest. "Well I am sick of it! You hear me you fuckers? I'm not going to do it anymore!"

"What are you not going to do?"

"Eat."

"They'll give you an IV."

Chuck stood up frustrated and walked over to the door pushing a nurse's button on the wall to signal that he needed to go to the bathroom. He didn't like for anyone to tell him what to do, even if it was something he had to do, like eat.

"Come on you fucks, I am about to piss my pants," he said stuttering as he shook his leg.

In a couple of minutes two armed guards and a male nurse came down the hall and led him to the bathroom facility down the hall. Chuck stood up next to the stall staring at his male nurse sentry.

"Don't get to see enough dicks in your line of work?" he asked unzipping his pants. "Of all the nurses in Hawaii I have to get one with a set of balls. Where are all the Hawaiian Tropic bitches when you need one?"

"What are you bitching about?"

"I'm under a fucking microscope twenty four hours a day. I can't even take a piss without someone else watching. Look at my arms," he said holding out his bruised arm, "I look like a fucking crack addict."

"You don't know how good you got it."

"What are you talking about?"

"I've seen them bringing your food to you, three square meals a day. You should be thankful for what you got. Hawaii isn't a vacation destination anymore smart ass. It's the last stop before Hell."

"I just got back from Hell. You don't know what you are talking about."

"The rest of us who aren't national treasures, are on rations. You know what that piece of steak cost that you threw across the room?"

Chuck stood quiet unaware of what he was talking about.

"Four hundred rations for a steak dinner."

"Is that a lot?"

"I get 780 a week and I am married with two children. Goes without saying the only steak I ever see is the ones they bring you.

Cattle are kind of rare out here and so are those baked potatoes you eat with extra butter and cheese."

"Damn that's fucked… is everyone on the island on rations?"

"Yes, but not everyone gets the same amount, the more valuable you are to the government the more you get. About the only thing your average citizen can afford to eat all week is seafood."

Chuck stood stumped. He had never been considered elite. He had always been on the outside criticizing those in power, his life had been built as an outsider. It had been the only way he could live with himself.

"How would you and your wife like a nice steak dinner tomorrow night?"

Chuck returned to lockup and flopped onto the bed next to Tommy. His friend looked over at him queerly as he lay uncomfortably close for no apparent reason. He instinctively scooted over, only to be held back by a covert grip.

"We are getting out of here tonight," he whispered quietly so to avoid the detection of any microphones.

"What," asked Tommy surprised at the suggestion, "where the hell to?"

"Tonight the guard is going to leave the door unlocked when he brings our dinner."

"I don't get it… what are we going to do?"

"If you want to stay here and mope around that's cool, but I'm gone," he said ending the conversation in a murmur.

Chuck got up and flopped down onto his own bed falling asleep in the lackluster room enclosing the trapped men. Tommy wasn't sure what his friend was up to. Where could they go? It wasn't like there was anywhere else left in the world. Their planet now belonged to the zombies; except for a few safe pockets like Hawaii, mankind could no longer claim its dominance.

Later that night a man came to their room to deliver their dinner as he did every night and as always he closed the door shut, but this time there was one difference, the door didn't latch shut. Both Chuck and Tommy leaped up from their beds as their ears caught the slight differentiation like a dog after newly discovered prey. Tommy lifted up the lid from his dinner to find it empty. His stomach growled ominously at the bare plate as he looked up at his friend not sure if he should punch him or thank him for getting him involved in another one of his half baked plans. Chuck leaned forward grasping the door handle hopeful that his deal and ears had not failed him. The door glided open without a hitch almost as quickly as did his smile.

"Wait, what about the camera?"

"The guy watching it gets our dinners tomorrow night," he said scratching the doorknob with a fork so if they got caught it would look like he had somehow picked the lock.

Tommy's stomach growled again at the notice of another lost dinner.

"Are we ever going to eat again?"

"I will on Thursday, but you are out there until Saturday," he said joking. "Let's go, we only have six hours until the next shift and if those guys find out we might not eat again."

They ran down the hall toward a pre-planned exit. Their steaks were of high value and Chuck had struck a good deal. Just around the corner they came to a row of windows shrouded by a line of tall bushes outside. He fumbled with the levers and as promised they were unlocked. He slid out through the cracked window slipping down onto the ground behind the cover of a long row of trimmed bushes. They low crawled under the darkness of night through damp sandy grass before climbing over a high fence and dropping outside the compound area. Tommy followed and the two men stole off into the warm tropical night disappearing from the safety of their medical complex.

"What now?" asked Tommy wondering why they had actually escaped.

"This is free America," he said holding out his arms in excitement, "and I want to see it!"

They roamed through dark alleys and trash-strewn streets until they wandered up to the docks were the poorest of the poor lived or struggled to do so. Cheap neon lights lit up the night unglamorously revealing the worst of human nature in the worst of times. An old man with a haggard beard stood at the corner begging for money from bystanders.

"Hey man where are all ladies around here if you know what I mean," asked Chuck.

"Ladies?" laughed the scraggly man. "Ladies? There aren't any ladies."

"Come on, where can we find a good time around here?"

"If you are talking about relations, you are too late. When the government and the army came in they brought in a heap of men, making the ratio of men to women something like six to one. Hell, every old bitch and hooker on the island had their choice of proposals. I sat right here and watch a twenty year old man marry some sixty plus wrinkled old bitch because she was the last cunt left," he said laughing.

"Is there anywhere we can get a drink?" asked Tommy trying to save what he could of the situation.

"Yeah there's liquor if you got the rations," he said looking at the two young men in drab green unmarked clothing. "Say where are you two from anyway, the army?"

"No," replied Chuck quickly.

He eyed them strangely as if something was up. They were too well fed to be civilians.

"If I had any rations, I would go to Blind Fish around the corner."

"Thanks."

The old man seized Chuck's sleeve, "If you are looking for a BJ I'll do it for two hundred. I'll do it nice and smooth too, because I ain't got any teeth."

"Get away from me, you homo," demanded Chuck pushing the old man away.

"I even got a beard so it will feel like a real pussy!" he yelled in a sinister laugh at the two men as they walked away.

"I hope there is more than that to free America," said Tommy.

They walked up onto the deck of a broken down old building with a crooked sign hanging above its entrance spelling The Blind Fish. On its door was a large circular wooden carving of a fish wearing black sunglasses. Inside it was somehow hotter and sticker than it was outside. Scattered around the room were thick wooden tables hovering in and out of the darkness under the light of worn shrinking candles. A thin elderly man who couldn't weigh much more than a hundred pounds nodded from behind the bar as they sat down. About half of the tables had occupants, all men.

"What can I get ya?" asked the scrawny malnutritioned man.

"Can we get a couple of beers?"

"Sure that'll be twenty each," he replied, "up front."

"Can you cut us a break? We've had a rough run at it."

"I'll cut you a break. Get out of here before I bust your free loading asses down the dock!"

"Hey calm big guy," said Chuck laughing at the little man. "We're not here for a fight."

"Sir, we just got into town, we didn't mean any disrespect."

He looked down at their unmarked uniforms, "Just got in, where from a ship or something?"

"Yeah."

"I know you government fuckers have rations, now pay up or get out before I throw you out," he said as though in loathing of their uniforms.

"Hey we're not with the government!" replied Chuck as if the suggestion had insulted him. "Listen, we will wash dishes, whatever it takes."

"I've got some old shit in the back that I wouldn't give to my dog. If you want a drink, it's your last call."

"Sounds good," said Tommy kindly.

The old man left, went into the back and returned carrying a dirty bottle and two shot glasses. He slammed the glasses onto the table without saying a word before leaving and taking his place back behind the bar. Chuck gave him a nod before filling their glasses.

"My God this stuff is strong," said Tommy choking back tears.

Chuck's eyes rolled back into his head as his chest gasped for air. Unable to speak, he held up his glass complimenting the bartender. Whether it was horrible whiskey or good horse piss neither of the men could tell the difference, but it warmed up their miseries as the slow poison of alcohol took hold. With a third of the bottle gone, Tommy leaned over drunk laughing along with his friend.

"This stuff doesn't taste so bad now."

"That's because it dissolved your taste buds!" replied Chuck laughing.

The door to the Blind Fish burst open behind Tommy's shoulder letting in five unruly sailors. As soon as Chuck saw the face of one of the men, he sobered up and turned his head.

"Ah shit," he said under his breath.

Tommy spun around to see what had changed the mood of his friend so quickly only to spin back around when he saw the face of the sailor his friend had kicked in the groin on the ship from the west coast.

"Does trouble follow you around or something?" he asked in a whisper across the table.

"I don't know, but once they pass us let's get out of here."

The sailors strolled in slowly joking and bumping into each other loudly coming in to finish up a night of drinking on the town. Chuck and Tommy overtly turned their heads as the group of men passed by catching the attention of one of its sailors. He quickly tapped another person in his group on the shoulder telling him of his suspicions. The man came around the table and looked them over aggressively.

"Having a good time on the Island?" he asked.

The rest of the sailors surrounded the table cutting off their escape. Chuck saw their intentions and watched them surround the table. Normally he would have been up swinging or out the door before they could have done so, but sharing a bottle of old hard whiskey had impaired both his reflexes and judgment. He was behind the eight ball and it was going to take one hell of a shot for him to get out of this one.

"It's not quite as I had anticipated it," he said.

"I know you recognize me," he stated angrily. "I pissed blood for two days you son of a bitch!"

"I'm sorry but I think you have me confused with someone else," replied Chuck looking at Tommy with an unflinching stare.

Tommy saw it and even under the influence of alcohol he knew what it had meant. They had practiced the stare since childhood and it had gotten them the upper hand in many a tight situation, but this wasn't neighborhood bullies they were up against. These guys had weapons and attacking them might end up in a game for keeps.

"Stand up you pussy, I want you to try to kick me in the nuts again."

Chuck sat motionless still engaged in stare.

"Stand up you fuck or I swear to God I will blow you away right now," he said lowering his hand toward a pistol on his hip.

Chuck got up slowly and blinked giving Tommy the signal. Before the man knew what hit him, Tommy ripped the bottle up from the table, spun around and brought it down across the bridge of the surprised sailor's nose shattering it on his face. Blood and glass splattered across the table escaping the nose of the hapless sailor that now lay against his face without shape. Chuck took to action at the same moment buckling the sailor closet to him at the knees under the force of a heavy swung chair. Another sailor drew his gun and turned it toward Chuck firing it as Tommy shoved him into the bar. A blast ripped from the tip of sailor's pistol missing its target disappearing into the splinters of the bar's back wall. The fourth and fifth sailor rushed at Chuck knocking him onto the floor. The three in an entangled scuffle slid across the bar's greasy unmopped floorboards crashing into another table. Tommy struggled for his life with the armed sailor stopping as the tip of a huge double barrel shotgun appeared inches from his face. His eyes bore down the long thick barrel of the shotgun into the eyes of the skinny bartender who from his current perspective looked barely half the size of the gun's barrel.

"No one shoots a gun in my joint but me," he declared. "Drop that pistol right now before I separate you from it."

The sailor complied quickly by dropping it with a thud to the dirty floor.

"Now everyone get up real slow, remembering I have enough buckshot in each of these barrels to cut a man in half."

Chuck broke loose from the grips of the two men that had him down in a bad position as they stood up slowly.

"I don't know what you guys got between yas, but you're not going to settle it here," he said taking back control of his business. "Every one of ya pick up your stuff and get out."

Chuck and Tommy's face changed to mortal shock upon the realization of the old man's intentions of sending them out into dark with a mob of armed and vengeful sailors.

"You can't send us out there with them. We are unarmed," pleaded Tommy.

"That's not my problem. My problem is the mess you all made in here."

"Go ahead and shoot me now, because I'm not going out there with them," said Chuck determined.

The old bartender swung the long barrel and pointed it straight at the young man, "You think I am kidding boy? You better start steppin because I'm about to put a hole in you."

"Do it, because I would rather die right here than give those government sons-a-bitches the satisfaction of getting to do it!" he yelled back.

The old man peered into the eyes of his defiant target and without flinching cocked the lever on his shotgun raising it to eye level. Chuck stared down death ready to die for his convictions. He wasn't bluffing, the manner in how he died was important to him and he was ready to go at the hands of an old broken down bartender in the slums of Hawaii. A vacuum of silence took hold of the small bar and its occupants as the standoff reached its peak. The cards were dealt and the bids placed as the old man pulled back on the trigger, letting it go at the last tenth of a second.

"Get out of here you government stooges," he said turning the gun toward the sailors.

"We come in here all the time and you are kicking us out?" asked one of the sailors stunned at the situation.

"And I never liked anyone of you, so get out of here with your blood rations!"

"We protect this country and you're going to let these fucks get away with this?" petitioned the sailor with blood streaming down his face.

"You guys don't fight shit. When is the last time you fought a zombie? Your commitment is to your president, I know because I've seen you guard his assets while the rest of us slowly starve to death from that damn ration program. Now get out, I won't ask you again."

The five sailors saw the conviction in his eye and in the interest of survival hobbled out the front door beaten and battered. As soon as they left, the bartender quickly swung a heavy bar down across the thick old door bolting it shut. The old man spun around and made an announcement to his patronage that had hardly twitched a muscle during the encounter.

"Closing up early tonight, everyone out the back."

The rugged men of the bar stood up, some finishing their drinks quickly, some collecting their belongings, but not one raised a query as they shuffled out the back door like driven cattle. The old man bolted the back door as the last customer left, closing the bar down tight almost as if preparing for an assault from the infection.

"So what's the story with you two? I ain't ever seen you around before and from the way those sailors were talking you two aren't military."

They sat down with the old man and over some good beers, told him how they happened to arrive in free America. He listened intently hanging on every word, for news from the mainland was rare since the scattered broadcasts from it had faded away nearly six months ago.

"You going back to the base?" he asked bluntly.

"I don't see where we have an alternative, we don't have jobs, a place to stay… rations," stated Chuck.

"You can't stay here, that's for sure. Once those drunkards sober up they are going to want some revenge and if they can't get it themselves, they will start talking so to get it through your capture. Once they find out you left, you may never get out again."

"Oh I assure you, they haven't made anything that can hold me."

"Or his ego," interrupted Tommy. "Come on, let's get out of here and head back before they realize we're gone."

With directions from the crafty bartender, the two men made it back to the hospital before light and crawled into their beds, minutes before a male nurse came into the room.

"Dr. Leben would like to see you two in the lab for a hematocrit and urinalysis."

"Tell the doctors we are taking the day off," yelled a lump under the covers.

"Come on guys, you know if I go tell them that, they're going to send me back down here with a guard to get you."

"Great, see you in a few minutes," said a voice.

The young nurse sighed in frustration and returned to the lab empty handed. Ten minutes later Doctor Mc Gee, the same nurse and two marines returned to the room.

"Gentlemen what is wrong?"

"Nothing at the moment so let's keep it that way," said the voice.

"Are you not feeling well?"

"We are feeling like prisoners, ever since we arrived all we have done outside this room is give tissue, urine and shit samples," said Chuck still hidden from view.

"That is absolutely absurd! You are here merely for your safety!"

"Do you feel safe?"

"I live in fear of an outbreak every day," he replied solemnly.

"No, I mean besides the fear of infection do you feel safe here?"

"Why yes of course!" he stated unsure of the direction of questioning.

"Yet you don't live in a locked room, with twenty four hour surveillance."

"Why yes," he responded scrambling for a response, "but I do not carry the secret to the infection within me as do you."

"Is this all we have to look forward to?" asked Tommy sitting up in his bed.

"No, as I explained earlier, this is only a temporary arrangement until your permanent residence is ready."

"How long is that going to be?" asked Tommy suspiciously.

"No longer than a week or two more!" he said reassuringly.

"Wow it must really be a dump to take that long to fix up," retorted Chuck.

"It is more of a relocation issue."

"What about until then?" questioned Tommy.

"What if we got a television in here with some movies or something?"

"Come on, doctor, our blood is worth more than that."

"I don't understand. Is this some sort of negotiation?" the doctor asked confused at the sudden dissension.

"We're going to stop cooperating with you if we don't start getting treated like regular citizens."

"That's impossible!" he said alarmed at the request. "We cannot allow you to simply walk out among the general population. If anything happened... the last hope for mankind... the chance to unravel your cure could be lost forever. We need to be able to study your immune system, your T-cells, your B-cells in action not theory."

"This isn't a request beaker," declared Chuck.

Doctor Mc Gee scrambled within himself to find a workable solution. They could easily force the two to comply with their wishes through detention as they did mental patients both physically and mentally through sedatives, but such measures could compromise their homeostasis and therefore their value.

"Leaving the base is out of the question, but I can offer you free run of the Green Zone. I myself never leave it."

"Starting now?" asked Tommy.

"In twenty minutes, I need to take the time to update your status in the computer and print out your ID cards."

"And we get weekends and holidays off… no lab appointments and go ahead and consider today a holiday," added Chuck.

"I will make Doctor Leben and security aware of the situation," he said turning around to leave."

"Later junior," said Chuck taunting the young male nurse.

The four men left the room shutting the door, but this time without latching it. Both men flopped back into the bed, threw the covers back over their heads and spent most of their first official day of freedom sleeping off a horrible hangover.

Doctor Mc Gee quickly dismissed the two guards and his nurse before walking back to his lab. He flung open the door, finding Doctor Leben working relentlessly to replicate Doctor Ledbetter's cure.

"Well, where are they?" he asked curiously.

"We have a problem," he stated with wrinkled eyes of concern. "They refused to come unless we gave them the day off and free reign of the Green Zone.

"You agreed I assume?"

"What other choice did I have?"

"It doesn't matter," he said returning back to his microscope. "We have learned about all we can from their living tissue."

Chapter 32
The Green Zone

Tommy and Chuck walked proudly around the Green Zone a heightened area of security that enclosed the President of the United States, his staff, Congress, the Judicial branch, the highest ranking of the military, those necessary to run the government, the essentials such as doctors, scientists and finally, but certainly not least, those immune to the infection: Tommy, Chuck and Laurie. Outside the Green Zone was an area called the Yellow Zone that encompassed the remainder of the island's general population. The final zone, the Red Zone, was defined as any area where infection was likely and basically started two miles from the coastline and engulfed the rest of the world. Only those with green passes were admitted to the Green Zone and no one without authorization was allowed to enter or leave any part of the red zone. Anyone found in the Red Zone without permission was classified as kill on sight by the military, no questions asked. In fact, the military did regular search and scout missions around the island, and any unauthorized sea vessel or aircraft found was destroyed to prevent possible transmission of the dreaded infection. Hence no one came to Hawaii for freedom for doing so meant death. That was why the leak of news that three people were being brought over from the mainland spurred both peaceful demonstrations and violent riots. To diffuse unrest, the Government officially declined to disclose if they had ever arrived.

Although they had come over a trio, neither Chuck nor Tommy had seen Laurie since their arrival to the island. Tommy had asked Doctor Leben about her during one of his physicals, but was only able to learn that she was doing well physically. He had held the slightest of hopes that he might catch a small glimpse of her around the compound, but after a week of roaming it from one end to the other, he never saw, heard or spoke to her or to anyone who had come in contact with her. There was little to do in an area of such high security except walk, soak in the tropical sun and inhale the salty sea air from the coast that was nowhere in sight from the fortified compound. It was like serving time in one of the most exotic locations in the world.

Two weeks passed before the two doctors made good on their promise of finding Chuck and Tommy somewhere to stay outside the hospital. It was a small building that had previously been used as an office. It had a main entryway, which had been the reception area, two small offices, which became their individual rooms and a bathroom without a shower. If they wanted a shower, they had to use those in the medical complex.

Although it wasn't much, both men were glad to finally be out of the sterile halls of the medical complex that had become more of a prison within a prison than a hospital. It was on a trip to the shower in flip-flops and a towel around his neck that Tommy caught a glimpse of a man motioning to him from around the side of a building. The man stepped around the corner and from behind a row of neatly trimmed bushes signaled for Tommy. Tommy stopped sliding his feet across the sand particles lying invisibly on top the sidewalk that led from his converted office building to the hospital and watched for the man who had disappeared around the corner. Within seconds the man's face reappeared around the corner and once again he made the same motion for Tommy to come before disappearing around the corner again. Curious, but cautious, Tommy slid his feet across the sidewalk again this time heading toward where the strange man had appeared the two previous times. His head appeared again as Tommy got closer and once again he motioned for him, but this time he expressed exasperation as if he was frustrated at his slow pace. Tommy walked up to the bushes.

"Hello?"

"Hurry up and get in here before someone spots us," said a voice from the bushes.

Tommy gripped his bar of soap as if he could use it as a weapon if needed and leaned toward the thick green bushes. A hand leaped out from the foliage seized his arm and pulled him into the bushes. Branches scratched against his face, neck and arms as he fell into the thick structure, vanishing from sight of the compound's courtyard.

"What the hell?"

A man with dirty red hair and bright green eyes peered through the brush nervously, obviously not a native of the island. He was skinny looking almost anorexic as his skin seemed to merely lie upon his bones, "Sorry about the secrecy, but this is the only place we can talk without being monitored."

"Monitored?"

"Yes, we have been trying to contact you and your friends since your arrival to the island, but due to the many surveillance devices within this area this has been the first chance we have gotten."

"Who is we?"

"The People's Movement for Democracy."

"Democracy?"

"Since the President, Congress and the Judicial Court arrived on this island we have been under martial law. Over twenty percent of the population is in the military or part of the government. No one has rights. Our once-elected President and Congress under the provisions of the Isolation Act have extended their terms indefinitely."

"What do you want with me?"

"Up till now, we have been powerless against the government, having to remain underground as anyone caught or even thought to be part of the PMD is immediately put to death, but you three are immensely important to the government and ultimately to our cause."

"I have been told that the government is using us to find a cure so no one has to worry about infection. Then the army can swoop back into the mainland and clear out the infected, so we can take the world back."

"Then why haven't they told the people about your arrival, the possibility of a cure? Why do we still not hold elections? This government is mad with power, lying and starving its own people all the while using a military funded by the people to suppress their rights. Did you know that when a refuge boat from either the mainland or an island approaches the coastline our military destroys it? Men, women, children, foreign or U.S. citizen, it doesn't matter. Everyone is slaughtered."

"What can the three of us do about that?"

"If the rest of the population knew that the government was hiding you and we had all three of you as leverage, then we believe through popular support we could force the government to hold elections. If they refused to do so, with the support of the people and those from the inside that stand with us, we could overthrow the government and start anew with a government by the people and for the people."

"Sounds kind of Latin revolutionary to me."

"It was a revolution that first formed this great country and if you refuse to help the people how long will you be able to live with yourself while living inside the security of the Green Zone eating the people's food and getting fat while others outside skimp and save just to starve? It is easy to sit back and watch others suffer as long as you do not share in their misery, but it takes a man with heart to risk all so others may share in his blessings. You have the chance to be part of something, to be a forefather and mold a government that will serve the people instead of enslave them."

"What do you want me to do?"

"Go back speak with your friends and tell them what I have told you, but don't discuss anything inside a building or structure as they will surely be bugged. Do it as we are now outside in an inconspicuous place. I will meet you here tomorrow at the same time… at that point I will help you and your friends escape."

"How do you know you can trust me?"

"Unfortunately I don't, but great men seize great opportunities and I believe this may be our last hope to save our people."

He scurried out of the bushes and stood up straightening his ID badge that had both green and yellow markings, unlike Tommy's which only had a green marking. Then he walked off casually down the sidewalk. Tommy waited a minute in the bushes, not quite sure what to do, before finally stepping out and composedly returning to his new residence without a shower. When he returned he oddly enough found Chuck on the couch in the reception area watching an old zombie movie, Day of the Dead.

Chuck noticed his entrance as light poured in from outside bleaching the screen on the television.

"These things move too slow to be real zombies," he said criticizing the old film from personal experience.

Mindful of the warnings from the man in the bushes about surveillance, Tommy didn't say a word.

"What happened to your shower?"

"Changed my mind," he said blankly.

Thinking little of it, Chuck leaned back on the couch and continued to watch the old prophetic movie. Not sure what to do, Tommy sat down in a folding chair by his friend in deep thought. He tapped his friend on the shoulder and motioned his head toward the door.

"What?" said Chuck looking at him like he was crazy.

Tommy put his finger up to his lips shushing him silently, directing his head once again toward the door. Chuck took the hint and paused his movie before following him outside. They walked along the compound, finally stopping out in its center under a tall flagpole that held the United States flag up proudly in the strong Pacific wind. Underneath this symbol of freedom, Tommy detailed his conversation with the mysterious man in the bushes along with his governmental allegations and revolutionary intentions.

"We've got it pretty good here, no zombies running around, good food, hell we got everything we need but pussy. I don't want to risk my life for such a minute chance of success. Do you think they can overthrow all this firepower? We rode in on a nuclear aircraft carrier with fighter jets. You can't fight that! All governments are crooked and even if this PMD did overthrow the government they would end up just as corrupt."

"I don't know… he made it sound like they had some people on the inside that could help them take it from within."

"If they got insiders, why haven't they done it yet? And we don't even have a way of contacting Laurie without raising suspicions. For all we know, these guys might be terrorists. The last thing I want is to have our heads cut off with a knife on video as a ransom note. I say we let it lie for now and see what happens."

His friend actually made some sense and for the moment Tommy let the situation die in action only, as it lived in his mind vibrantly. He wasn't completely sure if it appealed to him out of charity for the starving or if because it required him to contact Laurie. A wave of guilt rushed over his conscience for all the people he had a part in killing. While Chuck was content to accept the status quo in trade for his own luxury, Tommy could not.

The next morning Tommy got up early so as to leave without waking his roommate and went outside for a morning walk within the compound. He had hardly slept a wink tossing and turning the entire night while wrestling with the decision of whether he should speak with the man from PMD or not. Everything in his life, even the succulent meals he ate at night had lost their flavor since Laurie had left. Tired physically and mentally, the young man weighed the physical risk of joining a revolution to the mental price of doing nothing for those that suffered so greatly. He couldn't stand how he felt about himself for his part he played in the deaths of those at the nuclear plant and he wasn't sure if his conscience had any more room for guilt associated with the suffering of others.

He walked around the hospital and once he got halfway around, realized he had never been on the backside of the building as it was primarily used as a break area for the hospital staff. He circled the hospital finally stopping to rest at a small garden bench set on the backside of the large complex. Cigarette butts littered the sidewalk burned to the tips of their filters in a time where the stress of their users was at an all time high, as they feared an outbreak with every cognizant thought. Hanging over the shadowed backside of the hospital were numerous tall white and light pastel buildings blocking the rising of the sun. He scanned their rooftops awaiting the arrival of the warm morning sun, when his eyes met hers. They bore into each other for only the slightest of moments as she disappeared from the window almost as quickly as she appeared, but even from the great distance of his bench to the tall white buildings above, he had no doubt that it had been her. Her quick disappearance also left no doubt about her feelings toward him. He got up slowly eyeing the small empty window so not to lose it place, before finally continuing on around the compound. As he walked off, two deep brown eyes returned from around the corner intently following his shadowed form until it disappeared.

In passing along the fence line of the compound, Tommy noticed he also had the attention of a young boy leaning against the fence, just outside the Green Zone. His small hands grasped the tight fence supporting his small frame. From Tommy's best estimate the young boy couldn't be more than six or seven years old.

"Hello there," said Tommy kindly walking up toward the young boy.

"Are you in the army?" asked the little boy curiously.

"No," said Tommy smiling at the youth.

"Are you rich?" he asked with jet-black hair glistening under the rays of a tropical sun.

"Why no," he laughed.

"Then how did you get in there?" he asked looking through the thick chain link fence. "Mama says only those in the army and the rich are allowed in there."

"Well that's not completely true," he said defending himself.

"Are there any kids to play with in there?"

"I haven't seen any," he said studying the young boy closer, his eyes sat deep onto his face sunk tightly to his cranium as if he were much older. "Where are you going?"

"Down to the beach to hunt for clams."

"Sounds fun."

"Mom sent me to get them for dinner."

Tommy leaned down to the boy examining his exterior features. He was battling malnutrition and from the look of his flaccid muscles, he was slowly losing.

"Hey, got a moment?" asked Tommy.

"For what?"

"Stay right here, I am going to go get you something. Promise you won't leave?"

The young boy nodded quietly. He rushed across the compound bursting into the door of his residence startling Chuck who scrambled for a gun he didn't own.

"What the fuck man?"

"Nothing," he said rumbling through their small icebox. Since Chuck and Tommy were special cases, Doctor Leben and Mc Gee had three square meals a day delivered to their apartment every morning so to ensure their optimal health.

"Where are you going with all that food?"

"Don't worry, it's not yours," he said running outside.

He slid his dinner underneath the fence to a delighted boy who snatched it from him like a wild dog.

"What about my mother?" he asked. "She hardly eats at all anymore."

Tommy stood up with a frustrated look, "I'll be right back."

He returned to his apartment gathering up the rest of their food into his arms. Seeing all his food disappear, Chuck stood up to confront his friend.

"Where are you going with all our grub?"

"I made a deal," he said leaving the room.

Chuck racked his brain trying to figure out what his friend could have traded for that was worth two steak dinners, when suddenly it came to him.

"Hey try and get me a blond!" he screamed in excitement.

Chapter 33
Revolution

Seeing the young boy run away in jubilation holding two plates of food as if they were brand new toys was too much for Tommy to let slide any further. The man from the PMD was right, it was easy to sit back and let others suffer when you yourself had it made. He wouldn't get trapped in the ease of hypocrisy again. He returned to the bushes where he had met the man the day before and waited on a towel as if soaking in the sun. A few male nurses and guards looked at him queerly as they walked by, but they left him alone without being suspicious of his activities. He waited three hours past the rendezvous time given to him by the strange man before finally giving up and heading back to his quiet apartment.

Along the way, he noticed groups of hospital workers and guards converging together chattering with each other curiously as if something big was about to occur. He stopped one of the groups and to his dismay discovered that there was to be a public execution at noon near the east wall. Curious, he followed the clusters of people migrating toward the execution like mindless sheep. They ended up near the east side of the compound where a huge wall nearly forty feet high had been built to keep a hillside from collapsing into the military base. Standing alone in the middle of the huge wall was the red haired man he had spoken to the day before. Across from him was a platoon of soldiers holding rifles. The men stood casually smoking cigarettes with their rifles at their sides as they waited to perform their detail.

The poor man stood quietly in solitude, as no one spoke to him, awaiting his sentence of death.

"What did he do?" Tommy asked a male nurse.

"They caught him last night trying to get out of the compound with a false ID."

The color from Tommy's face drained into his stomach leaving him ghost white and nauseous.

"They convicted him this morning as a member of the PMD. The guard that caught him said he could tell he was one of them by how skinny he was," said the nurse sniggering.

Tommy almost belted the man's smile off his face, but wisely held up, choosing to watch what was about to transpire instead. A man wearing a dress green uniform covered in badges and medals stood before the large group of people and made an announcement.

"David Kern, you have been convicted in violation of the Constitution article three, section three, treason. For this crime in a time of war, you have been convicted to death by firing squad. Do you have any last words?"

The man stood proud and tall showing no signs of fear, "We stand in the last days of man and although we fight a global war against the infection of our people, we are starving and killing one another for the scraps of power left over man. I beg of all of you to think of your brothers and sisters on the other side of the fence and show compassion."

Silence overtook the small group of onlookers as only the wind spoke with a whistle through the tall fence that separated the privileged from the unprivileged. In his heart, Tommy pleaded for the poor soul standing defiantly against tyranny, but he dared not let his feelings be known to the mob in which he stood. Upon orders from the officer in charge, the five soldiers raised their preloaded rifles some filled with blanks, some with live rounds. None of the men knew which they held as they placed their sights upon his heart. The man's eyes focused on Tommy's own sending a chill to his heart, as the man he hardly knew stood ready to take his mission to the grave. The man fell to the ground before the sound of gunfire left Tommy's ears. The crowd around the scene slowly began to disperse, as if they were returning to work from a simple lunch break. One man died and was taken from the cause of freedom under the tropical sun, while another had been brought to it. Stunned and unsure of his next move, he returned to his apartment and went to bed, choosing not to tell his friend about what had transpired.

The next morning Chuck lay on the couch watching old zombie movies as in their situation, they were the closest things to current reality in movies. A knock at the door prompted him to press the pause button and get up from his easy chair. The daily meal deliveries must be early he thought while scratching his head and shuffling to the door in his slippers. He swung the door open expecting to see a man in military uniform, but instead standing in the frame of the door was the slender body of Laurie. She was wearing a lab coat dressed like the doctors from the hospital.

"Oh hello Laurie," said Chuck stunned at her presence after not having seen her for so long.

"How's the old groin?" she asked walking past him into the small office space.

"Oh great, that shit worked… thanks."

"Is Tommy here?"

"He's sleeping in late this morning."

"I've got to talk to you two, it's urgent."

Chuck knew Laurie wasn't one to joke around and after hearing the seriousness in her voice he yelled out to his friend drooling on his pillow in the next room.

"Hey Tommy, get your ass up, we've got company!"

"Fuck you!" said a tired voice from behind the thin door.

"It's Laurie!"

The sound of feet hitting the floor promptly followed his words. In a matter of seconds the knob on the door turned revealing Tommy with his hair standing straight up. He looked around the edge of the door to see if his friend was teasing him. To his delight stood Laurie in the reception area of their office converted home.

"Good morning," he said unsure what to say.

"Good morning," she replied in an uncomfortable tone.

"Well, I better go and let you two talk," said Chuck getting up to leave.

"No," she replied firmly, "this concerns both of you."

Tommy's mind quickly turned to the words of the man he saw executed the day before and his warning of the government's secret surveillances.

"Wait!" he said quickly stopping her in mid conversation. "I've grown some flowers outside I've been dying to show you."

Chuck looked at Tommy like he had lost his mind.

"Flowers...what the hell? You're not growing any flowers," he said not understanding Tommy's stalling tactic.

"Um... this is really important," stated Laurie confused to why Tommy so rudely interrupted her.

"Yes I am, you remember I showed them to you the other day out near the flag."

Suddenly his intentions sunk in and Chuck gasped in revelation ready to play along.

"You've got to see these flowers! Oh my god, they are gorgeous!" he said in a bad stereotyped homosexual voice.

Laurie looked at the two as if they had finally lost their minds as they led her outside away from any buildings.

"What has gotten in to you two? What I have to say is important! We don't have time for shenanigans!"

"I'm sorry about that, we have reason to believe our room is bugged," explained Tommy.

"Oh, well..." she said trying to return to her original thoughts. "I have been working close with Doctor Mc Gee and Doctor Leben trying to reproduce Doctor Ledbetter's inoculation, but without success. We have been working for weeks and none of our experiments have even come close and the whole department has been frustrated working around the clock. Last night I happened to overhear Doctor Leben and Mc Gee discussing their next plan of action."

She paused leaving the two men hanging in suspense as she fumbled for the right words to describe the dreadful plan she had heard between the two doctors.

"Chuck," she said nervously, "they plan on dissecting your brain next week to observe how your blood-brain barrier is protecting your central nervous system from the virus."

"What the fuck?" said Chuck shocked by her statement. "Why me?"

"I don't know, but Wednesday you have an appointment for some blood work and if you go, you will never awaken again."

"We've got to get out of here!" avowed Tommy remembering the PMD.

"But where?" asked Laurie unsure where there was left to run.

"There is a group here on the island we can go to for help. They have already contacted us."

"Who?"

"The PMD… they're like an underground movement against the government here on the island," he said trying to explain an organization he knew nothing about.

"I'm going to cut those fuckers nuts off and shoved them down their throats!" replied Chuck completely ignoring the conversation between Tommy and Laurie. His anger rose as he thought about what the two doctors had planned doing to him. "I'm going to go medieval on those shits!"

Laurie looked over at Chuck who was engulfed in a world of plotting retribution, before returning to Tommy.

"How will we get off the base?" she asked concerned.

"Chuck knows all the guards as well as the ones we can bribe to look the other way while we take a little tour of the island. Isn't that right Chuck?"

"An entire nation of zombies couldn't bring me down and those two little educated shits think they're going to cut me up alive?" he mumbled still fuming over the news broken to him by Laurie.

"Chuck," screamed Tommy to get his friend's attention, "can you get us out of here?"

"Uh?" he replied awoken from within deep thoughts of rage. "Oh yeah, I'll get us out of here, but I'm coming back!"

Having nothing of real value, Chuck and Tommy loaded up a few clothes and made ready to leave the compound to avoid the deadly intended experiments planned for only one, but each knew that they would eventually lead to all. Chuck walked to a small refrigerator they had in the break room of the office which served as their kitchen and pulled out the last of their pork chop reserves.

"Pig for pigs!" he said with an evil grin coming back into the living room.

Having nothing of value to retrieve, Laurie was ready to leave the nightmarish government in which she found herself trapped. Chuck wily bribed his favorite guard for a turned head while he and his friends went into town for a late night party. The three under great duress agreed that they would need help to avoid the long reach of the United States' government and that the PMD would be their best bet, but with their only contact dead, they were unsure where to make contact.

"Now what?" asked Chuck unsure where to go once they got out of sight of the compound.

"What about that old guy down at the Blind Fish?" asked Tommy. "He seemed shady and he didn't seem to like government types very much. He may not be a part of the PMD, but I bet he might know someone who is."

"You two have been off the base?" asked Laurie surprised.

"We jetted out for a little snatch," commented Chuck being mean.

Tommy got an agitated look afraid his friend might ruin what little progress he had made with Laurie.

"I'm just glad us ladies don't have to pay for it," she replied teasing him back.

Chuck started bursting out in laughter and in a few moments Tommy joined him once he felt she was joking.

The fugitives walked down to the wharf finding the shabby old bar closed, as it was still midday. Desperate, the three renegades went to the back door and began to bang on the old door. Surprisingly, it held firm rattling the echoes of their knocking into the interior of the old building. After about three minutes of constant thudding, the door swung open exposing a scrawny old man holding a giant shotgun in their direction. From such a close distance, the barrels looked like trashcans.

"Knock on that door one more time and I will blow you out into the street for the sea gulls to pick at your bones!"

"We need your help!" replied Tommy.

"I'm running a bar here, not a free clinic. Now get out of here, I work until three in the morning and I usually don't get up for another hour or so."

"Please," pleaded Laurie to the near skeleton of a man, "we've escaped from the compound and we don't have anywhere else to turn."

"Why the hell would you do that? Everyone around here is trying to get in that place. Hell, the three of you look like you haven't missed many meals."

"I think he called us fat," replied Chuck messing with the ill-tempered old man.

"I mean nourished, you little shit!" he screamed angrily. "It may be funny to you, but when you don't know when your next meal is, it a far sight from funny!"

"We're sorry, but a member of the PMD contacted us, but was executed before he could tell us where we should go."

The old man heard his words and after looking up and down the old alley behind his bar, he shrugged his head for the three to come into the shadows of his bar. He quickly shut the door bolting it shut with a long board, several locks and multitude of chains.

"Don't ever mention that name out in the open, just being suspected of knowing someone in that organization will put you in front of a firing squad," he said warning the three. "You don't have very long, once they discover you missing from the base, they're going to be crawling over this town and I don't have anywhere to hide you."

"What should we do?" asked Laurie in concern.

"What did the man look like?"

The three fugitives stood still without saying a word as if they didn't understand his question.

"Oh," said Tommy realizing he meant the man whom he had seen executed, "he had red hair and real pale skin."

"Damn," cursed the old man in disappointment, "they got Red."

He walked back and forth racking his brain on their best course of action.

"There is this guy that comes in here sometimes. I've seen him with Red before. He's a native… most of the guys in the PMD are natives. Maybe he will show up tonight, but if he doesn't, you have to be gone before light tomorrow morning," he said with a serious look. "Once they find out you are gone, they will be out hot and heavy tearing up the streets and with all that meat on your bones, you three are going to stick out like a sore thumb. I don't have to tell you, anyone caught harboring you is going to sitting next to Red in Hell, because after the way the world has turned, heaven is just a pipe dream."

Having nowhere else to turn, the three sat in the bar during the morning hours waiting the bar's opening later in the night. Tommy and Laurie used the time to reacquaint themselves while Chuck spent it getting drunk. He conned the old bartender into donating a bottle of the strong liquor he had given Tommy and him their first night in the Blind Fish. The old man slammed a half full bottle of the drink on his table affectionately calling it sewer water.

"Here you go you freeloader, if I had more customers like you, I'd be out of business."

It burned Chuck's throat and stank to high heaven and only God knows what it did to his liver, but in a matter of minutes, he felt better buzzing the day away.

Tommy and Laurie sat on the other side of the bar at a corner table in the dark talking to each other like long lost sweethearts.

"I have to admit," said Laurie looking over the old wooden table at Tommy through the shadowed bar, "I wanted to speak for other reasons besides the planned experiment on Chuck."

Tommy eyed her beauty through the darkness hardly believing he was sitting across from her. He had missed her dearly.

"I'd find a dictation of your laundry list enthralling," he commented.

"This is a slight big bigger than a laundry list," she said fumbling for how to break him the news. "Remember how I was sick a lot back on the mainland?"

Tommy's eyes swelled with hideous speculation, as its human nature to assume the worst of those you love in fear of losing someone you love.

"Are you okay?" he asked nervously taking her hands into his own stretching them across the table.

"I'm pregnant," she said simply.

Tommy leaned back unsure what her avowal meant for the two. Would it be wrong to bring a child into a world of such deprivation? Would the child have the inborn immunity of its mother or would they have to spend the rest of their lives worrying about their child being infected? What of their current dilemma? At the moment, they were fugitives from their own country. He didn't even know where he was going to sleep tomorrow night let alone know where they could find food.

"Well, don't sound too excited," replied Laurie breaking the silence that had seized the table after she mentioned her pregnancy.

"It's yours."

"I never doubted that," Tommy said assuring Laurie after coming out of deep thought. "I was just wondering about its well-being."

"I'm keeping it, if that's what you mean."

"No!" replied Tommy quickly. "I didn't mean that, I've never been a father before."

"It will be the first time for both of us."

Tommy got up from his seat squeezing in next to Laurie in the dark booth holding her in his arms. They would figure out something, he vowed. Failure was no longer an option. Chuck stumbled over to the two in the corner dragging his feet and bottle along with him.

"Kinda boring over there by myself, mind if I join ya?"

"Grab a seat," instructed Tommy.

Drunk and seeing double, Chuck fumbled with the bulky chair as if it were some ancient enigma before falling into it and almost turning over onto the floor. He caught himself laughing at his gaucheness before finally sitting across from the two struggling to focus as if he were swaying on a ship.

"We have some news," declared Tommy to his old friend.

"Let me guess," said Chuck playing fortuneteller, "you two are getting back together."

The two lovers smiled realizing that their friend though drunk, had brought out into the open what both so greatly desired. They were back together.

"Laurie is expecting."

"Expecting what?" asked Chuck too drunk to catch his meaning.

"A baby!" declared Tommy happily.

"Damn, I thought you two hadn't spoken to each other in a while."

"I'm several months along," stated Laurie.

"Well I'll be damned!" stated Chuck in excitement of the news. "Bartender, three glasses over here, we have something to drink to!"

The bartender grumbled at the trio not partial to being ordered around in his own establishment.

"Chuck, the baby?" said Tommy.

Chuck looked at him funny then turned his head as if understanding his comment.

"Make that four glasses, she's drinking for two!"

"I'm going to split your head in two if you don't stop shouting orders, you penniless bastard!" yelled the bartender.

Once the bottle was empty, Chuck passed out in his chair collapsing to the floor where Tommy, Laurie and the bartender left him to sleep it off. As the day rolled by unseen by the hidden patrons of the bar, night came in on the distant islands of Hawaii bringing in sailors, armed soldiers and various dregs from the streets of the city ready to drink away the misery of the world. Afraid of being seen, the three renegades stayed upstairs in a room hoping the native man mentioned by the bar's owner would show. If not, they would be out on their own by morning. As each hour passed, the three waited anxiously for the skinny bartender to come and announce that the man had arrived.

The night passed quickly with each hour on the clock bringing no news and before the three knew what hit them, it was nearing three am, the closing time of the bar.

The clock in their dirty room struck three am and the three sighed with lost hope. Now what? Thought the three looking at each other with confused eyes? Not one had a plan of action for the coming morning. Chuck leaned back onto the only bed in the room groaning from an awful hangover.

"One minute you're running from the dead wishing for people, the next you're running from people, wishing you were back with the dead."

Suddenly there was a knock at the old door. It rattled on its hinges as the force of the knocks threatened to burst the aged and warped door. Chuck and Tommy moved to the sides of the entrance ready to jump up the visitor if needed as Laurie opened it slowly. The cock-eyed face of the bartender peered in at her.

"He's downstairs," he said motioning for them to follow.

Relieved it wasn't the police or some other government official, the three escapees followed the skinny man downstairs into an empty bar. A man with dark tan skin and long black hair sat in the corner with his back turned. The bartender pointed at the man so to let them know he was the one they had been waiting for and then stepped back behind the bar leaving the group of three to introduce themselves. They walked over to the man standing by the table at which he sat. He was covered in dark tattoos that ran up his arms and all over his neck. He looked at the three people and noticed they had been fed well.

"So you are the three from the mainland who are immune to the infection?"

"Yes," said Tommy.

"All three of you lean up against that table so I can frisk you."

"What is this, the start of some porno?" asked Chuck.

"I have to be sure none of you are wearing a wire or GPS device," he replied coolly, "so if you want out of here, bend over."

Having few options, the three awkwardly bent over the table. The man began to frisk them leaving little to hide searching their groins and even the crack of their butt. When the three protested, the man drew a gun so to finish the search.

"Damn man, you got to second base, I don't usually go that far on a first date," said Chuck responding to how he had been handled.

"I'm sorry," he said feeling secure that they were not bugged after searching their bodies, "but lives are in the balance. The government has been trying to discover our hideout for a while now. I had to be sure the three of you were not in on it. Two of my associates are out searching the area now making sure no one is following you. Once they get back we can leave."

Although rattled by the search, in retrospect all three were glad he had showed up instead of being left alone. After a few minutes there was a knock at the back door. The owner peered through a crack in the door and then let in two more men who also had the dark skin of natives.

"It's clear," stated one of the men."

"Follow me," stated the tattooed man.

Slinking out the back of the bar they followed the men through dark alleys and down into a sewer drain. An offensive odor poured up from the hole seemingly unnoticed by the three men, while nearly knocking out the three fugitives. They dropped down into the shadows of the dark hole sloshing through dirty stale water which nearly caused Chuck to vomit out the alcohol he had consumed earlier.

"We throw our shit over here by the entrance to deter any would-be explorers. The smell gets a lot better," announced one of the men leading the group.

The tunnel was about eight feet high and after turning corners and walking through a maze of tunnels the men stopped at a hastily built door. It leaned over, crooked on its hinges and creaked as the men opened it. A barrage of voices arguing gushed out the door as it opened. Chuck, Tommy and Laurie followed the men into the large dark room lit by lanterns which gave the room the feeling of an older time. Men were arguing as if on the floor of the stock exchange shouting over each other all trying to get in their opinions over their peers. As they walked into the large cool concrete room, every one stopped upon recognizing their guest. They were all exceedingly skinny giving the appearance of a room of skeletons eyeing them hungrily.

"So there are the people of the moment," declared a stately looking man from the front of the room.

"They have started doing house to house searches!" broadcast another man.

"The word is if they do not find them, they will cut off all rations!" shouted an unseen man.

"That is good!" proclaimed a man from the corner. "This is what we needed to get the full support of the people!"

"Yes, but now that they are here, what will we do with them?" inquired a man curiously before the crowd.

"Listen," shouted the man who had announced them, "with all three, we will have enough leverage to force the government to recognize the rights of the people! If they want them back, they will have to hold elections and allow the people to select their leaders!"

"Wait!" screamed Tommy getting the attention of the entire room. "We're not going back, they want to dissect us!"

"What good are they to us if they're not willing to go back!" screamed a man raising the room into a commotion of shouting and arguing.

The men began to shout at each other like mad dogs pushing and shoving as they tried to get their proposals across the floor. A man stormed into the room behind Laurie screaming an announcement into the room.

"The revolution has begun! The people are fighting the government in the streets!"

Some of the men cheered while others moaned about the upcoming fight with an obviously superior force.

"Okay everybody, remember our plans. We must organize the people and instruct them on guerilla warfare. Use the weapons we have stockpiled to do quick hit and runs. No drawn out firefights, as they will call in air strikes. We tried to do this peacefully, but the people have spoken and the time for words is over!" pronounced the leader of the People's Movement for Democracy. "What they would not give us freely, we will take by force!"

Men proceeded to storm out of the hidden meeting place rushing up to the streets to take their place in the rebellion. They rushed by Chuck, Tommy and Laurie, ignoring them as if they suddenly meant nothing.

"What about us?" asked Chuck pulling the tattooed man around.

"You have served your purpose," he stated calmly. "The search for you and the threat of no more food has finally convinced the people that there are no more options besides violence to overthrow those that were meant to serve them. You are welcome to join us in the struggle. I expect it to be a long hard fight."

"What have we gotten ourselves into?" asked Chuck. "We've started a war with the most powerful military in the world! Those fuckers have fighter jets and bombs! What am I suppose to do, swim out into the bay and stab their aircraft carrier with a knife?"

"It's not like we had a real choice," said Tommy.

Within a matter of moments, the room that was filled to capacity with arguing men was empty, leaving Chuck, Tommy and Laurie its only occupants.

"I guess we should follow and see where they are going," suggested Tommy.

Chapter 34
The Second Revolutionary War

The war in the streets was a vicious one as the revolutionaries struck the soldiers with Molotov cocktails and small arms fire. The battle within the city lasted for days as tanks and aircraft were called in to try to quell the rebellion, but the people were fed up with oppression and starvation and had taken to revolution and now nothing but the government's overthrow would suffice. In an attempt to save themselves, the president and members of congress in the relative safety of the green zone, declared everyone outside the compound to be enemies of the state and therefore legitimate targets for its military personnel. Leaders of the PMD hid underground during the conflict moving daily so not to be easily targeted by the technology of smart bombs and the viciousness of organized swat teams, which regularly stormed into buildings wiping out their inhabitants in firefights and more than not, in cold blood.

The soldiers who were well fed in comparison to their revolutionary counterparts regularly joked among themselves that the rebels were harder to hit since they were merely skin and bones. With a rifle being the only thing he had ever really been good at, Chuck took up with the tattooed man Akamu and two other natives creating a vicious sniper team that regularly did hit and run missions against American soldiers, using the city to fade away after making their kills. Tommy, having Laurie to worry about and a child on the way, stayed out of the conflict, moving with the leaders of the PMD hiding underground so to avoid capture.

A drop of rain trickled from a rooftop landing on his cheek running down his face and onto his neck. Chuck ignored the cold bead as he stared down the barrel of his rifle placing the crosshairs of his scope on a group of soldiers moving quickly through the city. They were Special Forces moving like lightning between structures and rubble so to cover themselves, but they had no idea a sniper team in high-rise apartment was watching their every move. It was the eye of a hunter that watched the six men, but this time he was not hunting wild animals, this time he was hunting men. Chuck exhaled, releasing the air from his lungs holding it as he focused his shot. He slowly squeezed the trigger firing off a round that burst into his target's face crushing it as the soldier's body went limp collapsing backward onto the street. Akamu took the next shot hitting another one of the soldiers in the neck nearly decapitating him. The remaining soldiers scrambled behind cover unsure from where the fire had come.

The other two men in the sniper unit took their assault rifles and descended into the stairwell coming out onto the street below. They advanced on the position of the soldiers as the snipers above kept them pinned down. The helmet of one of the soldiers emerged from the wall as the man tried to get a better look at the assailants who had exited the building. It appeared only inches above its top, but it was enough for the deadly aim of Chuck's rifle. The heavy round bore through the Kevlar helmet punching through the thin bone of the man's skull sinking into the center of his brain. The other two rebels on the ground below moved in on the soldiers' position using alternating machine gun fire. They slowly walked in on the trapped men firing so as to keep them at bay. A soldier rose up to try and fire back, but fell to the ground as a round from Akamu's rifle hit him in the back spilling out his heart and lungs from his chest onto the wall between him and the firing rebels. Taking advantage of their firepower the two rebels fired over the wall killing the last two soldiers pinned down by sniper fire. Upon the death of the soldiers, the two rebels rummaged through their gear taking their weapons and ammunition, but as usual, the men had no food. The men of the armed forces were not allowed to carry any as the government planned on starving out the rebels if they could not beat them militarily, a decision that turned out to be a drastic mistake, as starving men make ferocious foes.

Chuck and the three native rebels in his team quickly vanished into the city slipping underground into the sewers before the army could counterstrike, something the army did regularly, as those that hung around after a fight usually didn't return. It was better not to be greedy, Chuck thought. Make a kill and get out before they could pinpoint your whereabouts. It was his method so to fight another day. Hundreds of men who had swelled into the ranks of PMD once the revolution began greeted the men as they were legends among the movement slipping in and out of the city striking the enemy and mercilessly racking up kills beyond any other group of rebels.

"How many tats today?" asked a man from the shadows.

"Tell Keahi to warm up the needle. We need six marks," replied Chuck bragging.

His sniper team had made a tradition of getting tattoo marks for every kill. He had sixteen; his team was up to thirty seven. The war was bogging down in the city with neither side making any progress with the force of weaponry; the real struggle was for food. The government cut off the bay by firing on anyone seen in the water or on the beach successfully sealing off the city from supplies. Its residents were ravenous, fighting tooth and nail against the military and for the moment held their own. Chuck fell into a corner hungry and tired and since there wasn't any food, he closed his eyes.

"Chuck," whispered a voice waking him from his slumber.

He opened his eyes to find Tommy.

"What's up man?"

"We need to talk."

"Shoot," said Chuck half asleep.

"We've got to get out of here."

"It was your idea to join the PMD." Chuck said reminding Tommy. "These guys need us and besides I've never been good at anything but hating and killing. This is my calling."

"You know as well as I do, these guys can't hold out much longer. They're starving before our eyes and it's only a matter of time before they find this place."

"You know I'm not one for bailing out because things look bad."

"I've got Laurie and a child to think about and she hasn't eaten in two days. I won't expose them to a losing cause."

"You know as well as I do, if you hadn't gotten back together with Laurie you'd be out there right along with me."

"But I am back with Laurie and I'm smart enough to know staying here is going to lead to nothing but death."

"Well, you're going to get your wish anyway. Sounds like we're going to move the whole outfit up into the mountains. Things are getting a little too hairy around here."

"Chuck, there is this man named Doctor Hansel with a group of sailors that has gone AWOL and they have a nuclear submarine!" declared Tommy. "And he has agreed to let the three of us go along."

"I'm going back to the compound tomorrow for some blood work!"

"Are you fucking crazy?" his friend asked. "This whole island has been converted into a police state that's on constant alert, crawling with Army, Navy, Air Force and Marines. If you go in there after those doctors, you won't make it back out."

"Ah… I'll be in and out so fast those stupid fucks won't know what hit them."

"But why risk it? Let's just jump this place and find somewhere where it's constantly cold," he said offering a safer alternative plan. "Doctor Hansel and his group are leaving for Northern Canada tomorrow. With the submarine, we will be able to get away without being seen. He says there are places up there… he called it permafrost. The soil never gets above thirty two degrees, so the infection never spread there."

"Because those two fucks planned on slicing up my brain and if I hadn't found out about it, they would have gotten away with it and you know I never let anybody screw me or even plot to screw me without getting even."

"So that's it, you would rather die and get even than live?"

"No, but I'd rather risk death than live knowing that someone tried to screw me and I didn't do a thing about it."

"Laurie and I don't want anything to happen to you, we want you to come with us."

"That's cool man, but I'm not the same person anymore… I don't have enough soul left to care if I live or die anymore."

"What is that supposed to mean?"

"I don't know it's hard to explain, but it's like everything I've killed over my life has finally caught up with me. Kind of like I traded a little piece of my soul for every life I took and I just don't have any left. I don't hardy have any feeling anymore. I'm empty inside Tommy…. just empty."

"That's called depression, a few pills, some time you'll get over it. How do you think I felt when Laurie dumped me?"

"No, it's more than that. I've felt it since my first kill. I'm not counting stepping on ants and shit like that, I mean really killing. I was ten and my dad bought me a new twenty gauge for the opening day of dove season. God, I was so excited. I couldn't wait to shoot something. I remember it like it was just yesterday. On my first shot I wounded a dove just enough to where it couldn't fly and I didn't know what to do with it. So, I carefully picked it up in my hands and took it over to my dad to show it to him. "Pull off its head," he said and I asked, "But isn't that cruel?" "What's cruel is to let it to continue to suffer," he said. I remember looking the bird in the eyes and then pulling its head off like it was nothing more than a cap on a bottle of coke. It came off so easy and I felt a little bit of my soul disappear as if I traded it for that bird's life. It was the same way over the years, as I became an avid hunter, with each life I took whether it was that of a squirrel or a deer, I felt the same phenomenon. Then once the infection hit…" he stopped in deep thought, "I've lost a lot since then."

"We've all lost a lot since the infection hit. You're not the only one."

"I never told you why I happened to drive by your house that day I found you up in a tree. I'd gone to my parents' house to see if I could find them, but the infection had found them first," he paused painfully with tears streaming out of his eyes. "I killed them, I killed them both and from the pain I felt, I know I lost at least half of my soul that day."

"I'm sorry… everyone alive has had to do something they aren't proud of to be where they are right now; the infection has changed us all and not for the better. I'm ashamed of what I did at that nuclear plant, but I'm not going off on some half baked suicide mission."

"How many people did you kill that day?"

"I'm as responsible for the death of those people as are you."

"No you're not. It was my idea, my plan."

"Our plan," interrupted Tommy. "I've been involved with a lot of your schemes over the years, but every time they were our plan, by the time we put them into action."

"You didn't kill a single person that day, you actually managed to save a person despite my rampage. I shot three men, three uninfected men and it didn't bother me a bit. They were the last of it. I don't have a soul left to trade."

Tommy sat silent unable to find the words to console his lifelong friend.

"I have an appointment tomorrow with the two good doctors that I wouldn't miss for the world or even for what is left of it."

"Laurie and I are going to be on that submarine in the morning with or without you," he said. "If you go into that compound we won't ever see you again."

"I got the name of the place, I'll meet you there later," stated Chuck carelessly. "Did you say it was called permafrost?"

Tommy looked at his friend walking away knowing from experience his mind could not be changed once it was set, the only difference being this time, he wasn't sure if he would ever see him again.

The next morning before the sun rose, Chuck put on an army uniform he had confiscated from a soldier and slipped out into the darkness. He moved through the city slinking between crumbling buildings avoiding army patrols, which roamed through the city in armored Humvees. If he could make the compound without running into a patrol or rebels and pass the heightened security around the perimeter of the base, he would be able to move around the lax security of the interior with ease. He ran down a dark alley near the edge of the city nearing the compound's fence when the thuds of helicopter blades swooped down the alleyway reverberating along its walls and beating them in a rumble. The air around him swirled in a whirlwind lifting up small particles of wood, brick and dust trapping him in a mini-storm. A black attack helicopter rose above the city's roofline hovering with an M230 30mm chain gun pointed at Chuck who stood in the street defenseless. In the sight of a great predator, his first reaction was to run, run as fast as he could for the safety of a building but his legs froze in place. He could never outrun such a weapon. It would mow him down with the slightest of movement. He raised his hand waving at the shadowed silhouette of the pilot through the helicopter's rectangular window, using his last hope, a simple bluff. Sweat rolled down his face under the heat of his Kevlar helmet as he waited helplessly at the mercy of the pilot. The large craft drifted back and forth hanging over the street for a long minute before lifting up into the air and passing over him going deeper into the city. Chuck reached up and supported his heart with the palm of his hand as it beat mercilessly against his chest. The twisted air spun away with the helicopter leaving Chuck in the calm tropical wind once again.

He ran to the edge of the city seeing the compound off into the distance. If he was spotted in the open space between the city and compound, it would be a shooting gallery and he would be the duck. His legs moved across the grass taking him behind palm trees and brush whenever it was available. He felt vulnerable, and to escape the queasy feeling he ran until he almost fell forward landing next to the fence encircling the Green Zone. He touched the fence and a shock ran down his finger jolting him as he jerked his hand back. It was true, he thought, they had electrified the fence. He had heard rumors from people within the resistance that as a security precaution they had done so to keep out scavengers and to hamper raids or assaults. Although electricity flowed through its links, Chuck had come prepared slipping thick black rubber gloves onto his hands before pulling out a pair of wire cutters. Sparks shot off the fence as he quickly cut a hole into the bottom of the fence which turned into flickering flame. He dove through it receiving a massive jolt as he flew through, using his momentum to escape its range. His body shook as he recovered rising to his knees and looking around. Having lived in the compound, he knew it inside out and used his knowledge to his advantage heading to the hospital where he knew the good doctors did their experiments. He walked up to the front of the hospital where two guards stood. One of the soldiers stepped up toward him casually unsuspecting his identity, as he was in the same uniform.

"I need to see your ID and pass," stated the man in uniform.

Chuck walked up to the men in a rapid pace as if speed walking and pulled out his pistol. He fired into the first soldier's chest dropping him to the ground before he had a chance to react. The second soldier scrambled for his rifle but collapsed against the wall dragging blood along it as he slid to his death. Chuck threw the hot bulky helmet that sat upon his head to the ground, revealing a waffle mark on his head from the inner straps of the heavy helmet. Knowing the sounds of gunfire within the green zone would bring a barrage of soldiers he rushed into the hospital ignoring nurses and doctors that ran by in a panic. Seeing him in uniform, they thought little of him as an attacker and ran around believing there was an assault on the compound. Alarms began to sound within the hospital as Chuck took the stairs instead of the elevator upstairs to the laboratory where the two doctors did their research. He walked up to the lab and stared through its frosted window seeing two shadowed forms within. He slowly opened the door finding both doctors working diligently ignoring the sirens which were a daily event.

"Doctor Leben, Doctor McGee."

The two men dressed in white lab coats spun around taking on a fearful look upon seeing Chuck.

"I'm here for my lobotomy," he said serenely.

The two men looked at each other as if their secret was exposed and then back at him strangely.

"I'm sorry, young man, what did you say?" asked Doctor Leben.

"I ready for the two of you to cut my head open."

"What does that mean?" asked the other doctor.

"It means I know what you planned on doing to me and now I'm here to give you that chance."

"I believe there has been a misunderstanding," said Doctor Leben, trying to diffuse the hot situation in which he suddenly found himself and his partner.

"No, there has been no misunderstanding. You're going to have to dissect me by force instead of trickery," he said boldly. "So how were you going to do it? Put me to sleep under false pretenses? That sounds about how a couple of cowards would do it."

"I'm not quite sure where you got this idea, but neither of us planned on doing any such thing," said Doctor Leben defensively.

"Have you ever wondered why this infection began?" asked Chuck out of the blue.

"Random chance, as was the Bubonic Plague and smallpox," answered Doctor Mc Gee.

"That's a pretty good scientific answer," said Chuck holding up his rifle letting the two doctors know who was in charge, "but I think it's wrong, dead wrong. I think mankind has become a pest upon the Earth. Stripping its resources so to pollute it, wasting our intelligence to make weapons of mass murder, starving each other out of greed, senseless power struggles… see, I think the earth has finally decided to cleanse itself of our presence using the infection, as would you or I might by spraying for roaches."

The two doctors looked at him queerly figuring him a rambling madman.

"Which leaves me with a tough decision, which side should I choose? The side that has done nothing to me or the one that planned on dissecting me for the slight hope of saving themselves?" he pondered out loud. "I think I choose the Earth!"

Upon his declaration the two doctors panicked and tried to escape by running for the door, but Chuck shot one in the head blowing his brains out splattering cranium tissue over the once sterile lab. He then tackled Doctor Leben who was running to the door knocking him out from behind with the butt of his rifle. He dragged the doctor by his collar through the blood of his dead partner strapping him down in the chair they used to draw blood from their patients for their research.

"You wanted to learn everything about this virus, didn't you Doctor Leben," said Chuck to the unconscious man as he tied him down. "I'm going to give you a firsthand look at how it works."

He stood up looking at the thick window of the room where the doctors kept live viruses of the infection for research. He raised his rifle and began firing into the thick window, shattering it into the room and throughout the laboratory. Another alarm sounded, screeching through the small lab causing Chuck to instinctively cover his ears. He kicked shards of broken glass from the window seal carefully placing his hand on it and leaping in. He began to slam Petri dishes and test tubes on the floor before seizing one marked as a biological hazard.

"There are those fucking viruses!" he declared.

He climbed back over into the lab holding it into his hands without concern being one of only three in the world immune to its infectious nature. He shook Doctor Leben smacking him gently until he regained consciousness. The man awoke in shock of being tied down in the very chair he conducted research on his patients.

"What are you doing?" he asked shaking his hands in an attempt to break free.

"I need someone to kick off the infection on the island," he said holding up the vial containing the contagious agent.

"Get that away from me!" he screamed, trying to scoot his chair away.

"I think you are the perfect specimen. Being a greedy son of a bitch, you will try and save yourself, therefore spreading it all over."

Chuck poured the contents of the tube in his hands holding it out toward the mortified scientist.

"So begins the final infection."

"No!" screamed the doctor terrified of the virus he had studied so intently.

He knew exactly what it would do to him and he could think of nothing worse. Chuck smeared his hand upon the face of the doctor rubbing it in eyes, mouth and nose so to ensure infection as the doctor screamed for mercy.

"Murder and greed is what ended the world," stated Chuck leaving the man helplessly tied to the chair, "the infection was just a means to an end."

Chuck walked out into the hall of the hospital which had been evacuated by warning sirens indicating the infection had spread.

Back at the state house of the president and congress, which was in the middle of the Green Zone, an officer of the army carried a message to the President of the United States.

"Mr. President, we just received a report that there has been an outbreak at the hospital."

The president stood up from his desk hearing the news he feared would come to pass every day since arriving on the island after the infection first struck. His worst nightmare had finally come to pass. He and what remained of his people would be forced to live on floating fortresses becoming a people without a land. Enacting the desperate contingency plan voted on by congress in case of infection on the island, the president dictated his orders.

"Major, I want everyone within the building evacuated immediately. No one who has been outside this building is to be allowed to leave with us," he said to the man strongly. "Contact Admiral Hargrove and tell him that once the last helicopter from the state building arrives on deck, that no one else is to be permitted to leave the island. Not a boat, not a plane, not a man on a log. Anyone or anything attempting to do so is to be destroyed. This is very important. We must contain the infection on the island."

"Yes Mr. President," replied the major.

The officer left the room to fulfill his orders leaving the president of the nearly defunct United States alone to gather his possessions and thoughts.

What would become of man? He thought to himself as he rummaged through his desk. What would come of the world?

He ran from the office, which had served as his oval office during his stay on the island. He would have to make a new one onboard the USS Ronald Reagan, but this time they couldn't fail, as there was nowhere else to run.

Chuck ran through the deserted hospital toward the exit holding up his rifle. He stepped outside the building into the bright sunlight unsure where to go next. Should he try to catch up to Tommy and Laurie or follow the PMD into the mountains? The whole island was about to be roaming with dead in a matter of days anyway, so nothing mattered. A volley of gunshots rang out bursting into the walls, stairs and sidewalk. Another struck his right hip sending an acute pain throughout his body as he collapsed to the ground. Bullets glanced off the sidewalk and stairs as he crawled back into the building shattering concrete upon him as it trickled from the air. Another bullet struck the back of his right leg splintering bone. He screamed out in pain as his leg throbbed from the wound, which entered the back of his leg and exited out the front. He quickly ripped part of his shirt creating a makeshift tourniquet restricting the hemorrhaging from his leg. He peered around the corner spotting a squad of Special Force soldiers guarding the exit. Upon looking out, the men fired bursting brick and mortar into the hallway.

"You fuckers!" screamed Chuck pressing down on his hip wound. "You think you are special? Come on in here you pussies and we'll see who comes out alive!"

The soldiers ignored his challenge, moving along the outside for better position upon the door so to complete their mission, unaware that their own government had abandoned them. Chuck pulled himself up to his feet sliding along the hallway smearing blood along the walls as he stumbled into the closet room. He crawled across the floor below the bottom of the window line peeking out its bottom. He could see two of the soldiers leaning up against a small wall watching the entrance. He set his sight upon one of the soldiers squeezing the trigger of his rifle ending the man's life. The soldiers returned fire shattering the windows above slinging glass shards into the room with a crashing boom. He spun around to guard the door to the room; he knew how the Special Forces worked, having fought them within the city on the side of the resistance. Now that they knew he was in the room they would rush the doorway and with his leg injury, he could not reach the doorway in time to stop their advance. A man came up from behind the advancing squad of Special Forces shooting the men in the back in cold blood. His rounds tore through the men ripping out their chests leaving them in a pool of blood. Tommy ran past the dead men and into the building to save his friend.

"Chuck!" he screamed before going in, so as not to be shot by the man he was there to save.

"In here," said a weak voice.

Tommy ran into the room finding his friend lying in a rubble of blood and glass. He lifted his friend up trying to help him to his feet. Blood gushed from the wound in his hip.

"Did you get the bastards?" asked Chuck in excitement.

"Every one."

"Just like the old days," he said smiling, "the best team ever!"

"Come on man, let's get you out of here."

"What about your submarine?"

"I missed it to save your sorry butt."

"I'm touched," he said laughing.

"Now come on let's get out here," he said lifting up his partner, "the island is falling apart, there has been an outbreak."

"I'm not going," he said pushing his friend away. "I'm done."

"What are you talking about?"

"I'm the one you who started the infection," he confessed. "I've started the end of the world and I'm ready to go along with it."

"Are you crazy?" asked his friend finding what he was hearing hard to believe. "You turned the infection on everybody here, the army... the resistance? Why?"

"I'm sick of man and all his bullshit. We've had our time and we blew it!"

"Well thanks for deciding my future for me!"

"You and Laurie are supposed to be on that damn submarine."

"We have a personal airplane. Come on, let's get out of here before the dead start rising."

"Oh no, I'm not getting on another airplane with your wife! I'll take my chances here."

"In matter of days, this place is going to be crawling with zombies. Do you want to end up supper?"

"Look at me Tommy," said Chuck looking down at the open wound in his hip. "I'm not going to be alive in a couple of days."

"Laurie is a doctor!"

"A doctor with no equipment, if you don't get out of here now, you're never going to make it off this island. Now go!"

"I didn't want it to end this way."

"Ha… that's funny, because I just want it to end."

Tears filled his eyes, while a muted lump lifted into his throat, as he could not form words to express how he felt about his friend.

"You are Noah now. The world will be cleansed and you will have to start it anew. You have to spread your seed. I know it will be hard work, all that fucking, but don't let us down."

"Yes oh great prophet," said Tommy standing up and leaving never to see his friend again.

"Hey!" screamed Chuck. "You remember that night back at the airport hangar where Laurie checked out my jock itch?"

"Yeah," said Tommy turning around.

"She tried to give me a hand job," he said laughing for the last time.

"Fuck you!" said Tommy breaking out an unwilling smile.

He had always been able to do that since they were kids, make him smile when things seemed the worst. He had first done it when they were in the seventh grade, making the two of them laugh like crazy while they waited in line at the assistant principal's office for a paddling. They got good ones too for laughing at the assistant principal while he paddled them, but it had been worth it.

"Thank you for the friendship," said Tommy seriously.

Chuck nodded to his friend as his left him alone.

"It's been the best," he said quietly to himself.

Tommy ran through the compound that had turned into the pits of hell as people struggled with what to do about the coming infection. He rushed to the airstrip where he had left Laurie. He found her waiting nervously as he ran up to the small personal aircraft.

"Where is Chuck?" she asked not wanting to hear his answer.

"He said he wasn't going to waste his time running, as he didn't want to die tired."

She saw how hard it had been for him to mention his friend, so she left it at that starting up the small single engine plane preparing for takeoff. Tommy crawled in with her slamming the door of the tiny aircraft compartment shut. The small craft ran down the runway lifting into the air and soaring over the island. Tommy looked below as they passed over the island bellowing smoke as its occupants continued to fight each other in madness as the end approached. Even as the end of the world came men could not unite as one, they still struggled among each other for the scraps that were left like squabbling dogs.

A small boat of men, women and children left the harbor churning out into the ocean so to escape the effects of the infection. A fighter jet soared from the sky, streaking over the boat as it left the shore heading out into the open sea.

"I have a small boat in sight," reported the pilot confirming his earlier instructions. "What are my orders?"

"Blue twelve, your orders are to destroy anything leaving the island," stated command.

"You heard him," said the navigator from the back, "take it out."

"This is bullshit," stated the pilot as he leaned the plane into a dive toward its target.

The small vessel had no chance of escape as a missile veered from the fighter jet's wing exploding into the small boat. Flames burst from the deck as the boat tore into tiny pieces incinerating its inhabitants. The pilot lowered his head ashamed of his actions.

"We have a bogey," stated the navigator looking at his radar screen.

"I have him," asserted the pilot changing his course.

Laurie piloted her plane high into the air passing along the beautiful beaches of the tropical island that would soon belong to the forces of the dead. A fighter jet streaked by the small plane shaking it in its jet wash, rattling its two occupants as Laurie held on to the plane's steering wheel trying to keep the small craft out of going into a flat spin. The turbulence passed quickly as Laurie kept the craft under control nervously picking up speed.

"Why did it pass by so close?" asked Tommy tensely looking out the window for the aircraft that seemed to disappear from sight after passing by.

"I don't know," said Laurie visibly shaken, "but I can't shake something like that."

The jet plane pulled up behind the slow target locking onto its target.

"I have a lock," reported the pilot.

"Take the shot," replied his navigator.

The pilot placed his finger on the button ready to fire a missile that would shred the small craft apart. Sweat rolled down his forehead as he wrestled with his conscience. What was he doing? The aircraft in his sights was not being flown by a zombie, but a human being. It was being flown by a pilot like him, who deserved to live as much as he. The pilot lifted his finger from the button refusing to fire on the tiny plane.

"I'm not doing it," replied the pilot to his navigator.

"We have orders," said the navigator through a line within the plane.

"I joined up to protect the people of America, not kill them."

"Target down!" reported the navigator back to the aircraft carrier.

The pilot pulled up, leaving the small craft to its own fate, vanishing into the sky like a rocket.

"Oh thank God," replied Laurie relieved. "It left."

Tommy sat silent thinking of their future.

"There are several islands we can land on where the infection hasn't struck yet," said Laurie offering a suggestion.

"Let's find someplace where the three of us can start over."

Laurie rubbed her stomach at the suggestion of their child.

"Someplace cold," said Tommy.

The small plane soared into the blue skyline disappearing into the horizon with two people willing to give the world another chance.

Satan's Side of the Story

An Interview

How art thou fallen from heaven, O **Lucifer,** son of
the morning! how art thou cut down to the ground,
which didst weaken the nations!
Isaiah 14:12

On Wednesday the 15th, 1992, I received an unannounced visit from an odd gentleman. He was a small man, about five foot six to be exact, neatly dressed in an out of date but finely pressed suit with a knit bowtie. His face had fine features with a small thin mustache attached to his upper lip. Standing behind the door at a late hour, he claimed to me that he had a story to tell. Being a journalist, his claim interested me, but it was late and something about him didn't seem right. So I politely refused his offer and attempted to end our conversation by closing the door. He quickly placed his foot in the doorway, blocking me from shutting it and then kindly assured me that I would want to hear this particular story. Fearing he might be a persistent salesman or even worse a burglar, I tried to close the door and force him back outside, but refrained upon looking into his eyes. They bore into mine with an air of dominating confidence pushing me backwards away from the door in an ice-cold grip. It was as if I felt death slide over my body in a shiver and I had no more will to resist him. Troubled by the encounter, I invited him inside and he cheerfully accepted. Wasting little time, he sat down as if he owned the place and explained to me that he was not what he appeared to be and that he had a story to tell beyond any story ever told. He explained it was the first story and had shaped the destiny of every being from its beginning and would eventually shape it to its end. He boldly claimed to me without flinching that he was Lucifer, God's greatest creation. The statement nearly bowled me over and I almost broke into laughter, but his stern face and cold eyes froze my chuckle in mid throat and I starting coughing profusely. He patiently waited as I regained my composure and then continued by telling me that he had chosen me over millions of prospects. I explained to him, with an underlining objective of possibly avoiding his intent with me, that I was hardly qualified for such a task and that he would fare better with a more experienced journalist. He claimed to appreciate both my reservations and suspicions and offered outright to prove to me that he was Lucifer. Such a boast intrigued my journalistic nature and when I asked him how he could prove such a thing to me, he replied that I should declare to him how he could do such a thing. This time I managed a small chuckle and a long grin spread across his face. Being in a biblical state of mind, I asked him to turn his hand into ball of flame. As soon as I asked him, he burst into laughter. A strange feeling overcame me and I began to laugh with him hysterically for no reason. The laughter continued for what seemed like minutes and then my laughter gelled into a cold fear and I stopped laughing. It was his laughter that struck fear into my heart. It had an essence to it, a magnitude of power that I can only explain as similar to the unstoppable force of a raging tornado. Suddenly the room fell silent when his laughter ceased and a strange calm engulfed me as if I were in the eye that powerful tornado. He enlightened me about his laughter thinking of all the things I could have asked, such as filling the room full of gold or making it rain fish in my living room, all I required was to see his hand in a small ball of flame. I nodded my head almost as a challenge and suddenly his hand engulfed itself in flame.

"So you want to see Hell?" he asked with an evil smile.

As soon as he spoke the world hell, the fire from his hand leaped into the air engulfing my entire body in searing pain. I screamed in agony as the flesh on my skin began to melt from my bones before my eyes. Then suddenly as I collapsed to the floor in torment, the flames feeding on my tissues disappeared along with the pain I had felt, leaving me completely unharmed. I vaulted backwards from him unnerved by the experience, fearful of the calm and collective beast I had unwittingly allowed into my apartment.

"Would you like to hear my story now?" he asked.

I hastily went to my desk and retrieved some paper, a pen and a tape recorder.

The interview I am about to transmit to you is true, at least in the regard that it did indeed happen. Everything in the following interview was written down word for word from the master recording by my own hand. If the interviewee's words have any falsities I cannot say. The story he told me couldn't be verified in any way, for it is the first story that can ever be told. It is your choice whether you choose to accept this parley as factual or fictional.

Interviewer: So, you claim to be Satan?

Interviewee: I prefer my God-given name, Lucifer.

Interviewer: Why would someone such as yourself want to be interviewed?

Interviewee: To enunciate the perfidy that has befallen upon my confreres and me.

Interviewer: Perfidy... do you mean like treachery?

Interviewee: I'm referring to my anathema from the grace of God.

Interviewer: If I not mistaken, isn't it written in the Bible that you were thrown out of heaven for betraying God?

Interviewee: I am aware of what is written in the Bible better than anyone besides God himself! What I claim is true and I shall substantiate it.

Interviewer: Do you have some kind of proof?

Interviewee: Not the type of evidence that man has come to expect, such as witnesses or pictures, but an axiom. What I am about to tell you will explicate my innocence. I do not expect you to postulate my claim as true because I say it is so, but because of what I tell you will make sense.

Interviewer: Are you trying to say that someone betrayed you?

Interviewee: (He chuckles). I knew I chose well. Yes, I was betrayed by the one who had the most to gain, Michael.

Interviewer: Michael? It seems to me that you would have been the one with the most to gain.

Interviewee: That is where you are mistaken. First, you must comprehend God to see why I had nothing to gain. God is not a single entity; he is the universe and I am a part of that as it is told in Colossians one seventeen. What would I gain from destroying the universe? God is my raison d'être, without God there would be nothing. God is beautiful. It is impossible to have ill will against him. All you want when you have known God is to be with him. I had nothing to gain from trying to subvert God. I was already the most beautiful and powerful creature created by God, closer to him than anyone. I was the envy of all his creations. Michael was jealous of my position, like a younger brother is of an older brother. Michael had the most to gain. With my downfall he became the closest to God.

Interviewer: But isn't God supposed to be perfect? How could he have been so easily fooled?

Interviewee: God is perfect, perfectly pure! To be pure is to be without evil and to have no knowledge of it in any way. Not only is God completely pure of evil, but he cannot see it or understand it! Why do you think God allows such appalling tragedies to occur? God would never allow the crimes that man commits if he could see them! Adam and Eve were created in his likeness and were also pure at one time as it says in Genesis one twenty seven. They did not even realize that being naked was a sin. Why do you think God asked Adam and Eve if they had eaten from the Tree of Knowledge in Genesis three eleven? Also, do you not think God would have seen that we were going to sin and stopped all of this before it happened or not even created such failures? He could not see such sins. Your connotation of perfect is different from that of the bible. Your contemplation of perfect is to see and know everything, but if you know everything you lose that innocence or purity. God is pure, not perfect. If he were, he could not have created imperfect creatures such as you or I.

Interviewer: So you're saying to be perfect is not to be without flaw, but to be pure?

Interviewee: Yes.

Interviewer: That still doesn't explain your reputation. Look at all the references in the bible to your character.

Interviewee: I chose to speak to you because of your impartiality, not for your vague biblical remarks. Being a journalist, you of all people should know that there are two sides to every story. That many authors slant their prejudices into their writings. These "references" that you spoke of, do you believe that they were written in an unbiased manner? Do you believe that every word in the Bible is the direct word of God? If that were so, do you truly believe that God would have dictated chapter twenty one of Exodus setting down laws governing the ownership of slaves? God would never justify slavery by setting down rules and regulations for it. Why would God create men to belong to other men?

Interviewer: Honestly, I don't know.

Interviewee: Nevertheless, you refer to the bible as the absolute word of God. Hence if you follow these words slavery is the will of God. I have never met most of these authors in person, nor were they there, yet they write these allegations as if from firsthand knowledge. Do you know anything about these men's credentials or if they were influenced by their beliefs? *

Interviewer: Well, no.

Author's note: (At this point after going back through my notes, I now realize that I was no longer in control of the interview. I was asking exactly what he wanted me to ask.)

Interviewee: None of these men who slandered my name or wrote about my betrayal of God were there as witnesses. All of these scribes have no basis to substantiate any of these calumnies. All of their lore about this situation and me comes from other men who were not witnesses and whom I also have never met.

Interviewer: Where did these stories originate then?

Interviewee: With Michael and the other Angels.

Interviewer: What would the rest of the Angels have to gain in helping Michael to slander you?

Interviewee: Once again you are jumping to conclusions. I never claimed that the other Angels had anything to do with it. I honestly do not know which ones, if any, have any knowledge of this fabrication. They may have accepted what Michael said as the truth and do not conceive the maliciousness of their acts.

Interviewer: Okay, the concept of Michael betraying both God and you for his own personal gain seems far-fetched.

Interviewee: First of all, I don't think Michael believes he betrayed anyone but me. No creature that has been in the presence of the Lord could do him any iniquity. Secondly, it was not too hard for you to accept my guilt, even given my angelic nature. Why is it so difficult to believe that Michael an Angel would betray the only Angel between him and God?

Interviewer: A this point, all you have established is a reasonable motive, but you can't convict someone on motive alone.

Interviewee: Was it not enough to convict me?

Interviewer: You have a point, but you're going to have to give me a little more than that. You could just be vengeful against Michael since he threw you out of heaven.

Interviewee: Michael did not throw me out of heaven! God himself expelled me! Read Second Peter two four and Ezekiel twenty eight sixteen, if you want some kind of reference! We did not resist the authority of God or fight back, for we loved and feared his wrath. Michael knows of my torment and intends to see it through. In Jude one nine he reminds me of my sentence, knowing that is the most painful thing he could say. He intends on seeing my judgment through in the final battle.

Interviewer: I know you said Michael betrayed you, but you never explained how he did it.

Interviewee: It all began with the creation of man. One day God spoke with us about what would be his greatest creation, man. God told us that he would be made in the perfect image of him. This new creation would not understand evil as we the angels did. We were to be second to man! This filled all the angels, not with hatred, but with jealousy. We were God's first creation! We loved God and did not want anything to get between God and us. So many of my fellow Angels feared that they would lose their closeness to God that a third of us met in secret, or so we thought. I was included, for I was the closest to God and had the most to lose. This gathering was meant to be a peaceful protest against the creation of man and his new position. Michael took advantage of this and contrived this mendacity of our intention to overthrow his kingdom.

Interviewer: But the bible says you're condemned to Hell. Why even try if you can't win?

Interviewee: For the opportunity to be heard. Hell is not fire and brimstone, but distance from God. Hell lacks the presence of God as it is told in Second Thessalonians one nine. There can be no greater punishment than to be locked away from the brilliance of God!

Interviewer: You mentioned earlier that Michael intended on seeing your judgment through. What did you mean by that?

Interviewee: He intends to make sure I do not get the opportunity to proclaim my innocence.

Interviewer: Doesn't the bible declare that Michael and his Angels will defeat you?

Interviewee: Yes, but those scriptures were written by the impressionable hands of men inspired directly by Michael and his Angels. It says in Revelation one one that all of these prophecies were given directly to John by an Angel. When the time comes, the other condemned Angels and I will fight like savage dogs, for we have so much to lose and so much more to gain. We will never give up. We must defeat Michael and expound our innocence.

Interviewer: It seems that your story is leaving out a lot.

Interviewee: Please, could you elaborate on your last statement?

Interviewer: Well, for example your influence on Adam and Eve in the Garden of Eden and the sins of man throughout history.

Interviewee: I have never claimed to be pure, but I assure you I am not responsible for most of the sins for which I am given credit. When men sin they don't want to accept the responsibility of their actions. It's easier to put the blame on someone else, a scapegoat if you will. The phrase, "The devil made me do it," is not sufficient evidence of my guilt.

Interviewer: You avoided part of my question. Adam and Eve, did you seduce them into eating the forbidden fruit?

Interviewee: Both ate from the tree of knowledge by their own free will. I did not force them to do anything. What I told Eve about the tree's fruit was the truth. They made their own decision.

Interviewer: I'm not a religious man, but I believe the Bible makes you look guiltier than you're letting on.

Interviewee: Remember that man, who is an imperfect creature subject to prejudices and hearsay, wrote every verse in the bible. The Bible has not always been equitable, especially on my behalf.

Interviewer: If the Bible is not a reliable source to prove your guilt or innocence, what is?

Interviewee: Nothing, there are no records or substantial evidence of any kind. It is the word of Michael against my own. For now all we can do is gather allies and prepare for the final battle.

Interviewer: You just mentioned something about allies. Who are these allies?

Interviewee: Men, when men sin they are condemned to Hell for their sins becoming powerful allies. Men will turn the tide against Michael and his Angels. Men will swell our ranks and give us a numerical advantage. With this and my tactical skills I assured you, we will emerge victorious.

There is a knock at the door.

Interviewer: I'm sorry, give me a second.

When I returned, he was gone.

The Other Side of the Blackened Mirror

Madness is only one look away.

Its slick glossy center glistened as it was rolled onto the auction floor.

"This piece of art called *The Blackened Mirror* is a Barlew original. The bidding starts at ten thousand dollars," announced the auctioneer.

Arthur Pensley gently raised his right index finger and the biding continued.

"I have ten thousand. Who will give me fifteen?" continued the auctioneer.

Another hand went up and the bidding price went to twenty. Arthur's finger lifted the price over and over again until it finally stopped and rested at twenty five thousand. A young man entered from the side of the auctioning floor and rolled away Arthur Pensley's newest piece of art. He had studied it for nearly an hour before the auction and had been so taken by its strange beauty that he would have raised his finger for twice the amount he had paid. Neither the piece nor its sculptor held the level of recognition or prestige the rest of his collection held, but it did have its own unexplainable allure. Its creator, Roland Barlew, had been a mysterious sculptor whose work consisted mainly of bizarre distorted figures of humanity. *The Blackened Mirror*, which was his only non-humanoid piece as well as his last, had been found three days after his untimely death. It was the circumstances of his death that had raised the value of his works and brought them to the limelight of the local art community. Arthur knew little about the details of his death, except that it had been a suicide. Caring little for what was left to be auctioned, he followed his mirror back behind stage to see it one last time before it would be packaged and sent to his estate.

Its highly polished center was made of black smooth marble casting the reflection of its gazer, but not anything beyond. Surrounding its shining center was its thick copper frame covered with distorted engravings of hideous faces and maddening figures. At the bottom and centered on its frame were three words, *Into the Darkness*. Arthur stared into its black center and gently touched its cold surface with the tips of his fingers. Looking into its polished core made the admirer seem alone in utter darkness. Nothing but his reflection could be seen and for a moment it seemed to almost move on its own.

"Sir, do you want me to have them wrap it up?" asked his chauffeur.

Arthur jumped backed startled in a chill.

"Yes!" he said clearing his throat, "that will be fine Jennings."

"Are you all right sir?" asked Jennings.

"Yes, I'm fine. I was just admiring its simple beauty," he answered.

"Yes it is quite unusual," said his chauffeur before walking off to set up the necessary arrangements.

Arthur, who had almost been in a daze a bit earlier, went and wrote a check to make the purchase official. This was how Arthur spent his days outside his mansion, traveling the world collecting rare pieces of art to hide away in its many nooks and crannies.

His estate, which consisted of one hundred and sixty eight acres as well as a mansion nearly forty seven thousand square feet, was centered between elegant gardens, elaborate fountains and riding stables. His home housed his mother, eight servants and himself. His father had died at an early age while he was attending college, and being an only child he stood to inherit the entire Pensley fortune with the passing of his poor dear mother. Its extent was such that even a well-bred young man such as himself would have a difficult time spending in a single lifetime. He had attended and graduated from the finest law school in the country and his mother, through monetary influence, had secured him a position at a prestigious law firm upon graduation. He practiced law for a while, but found it petty and too demanding. To the delight of his mother, he eventually quit work altogether and returned to live at his families' estate.

Jennings took every precaution possible to ensure that the young men of the auction didn't put a scratch on Mr. Pensley's newest piece of art. It was because of his prudence that Arthur always took him along on his "treasure" hunts.

Once it was safely tucked away in their limousine, he quickly pulled to the front and picked up Mr. Pensley. Author, a young man, only twenty eight, had taken after his mother in every aspect except in his demeanor. It was in his countenance that he had taken after his father. He was easily subject to folly as was his father, which carried the two all over Europe in search of such art. Jennings believed that it had been the stern influence of Mrs. Pensley that had enabled his father to acquire and keep such immense wealth. Now it appeared she had a far greater task in her own son.

When they arrived at the mansion Arthur hovered over Jennings dictating a barrage of instructions as he carefully labored to free their latest purchase. It was a ritual that Jennings had gotten used to over the years and it would have done him little good to complain about it. Margaret, their maid, came out the front door to see what all the fuss was about and greeted the two.

"Margaret, where is mother?" he asked eagerly.

"Why…she's on the veranda having breakfast," she replied.

Then without giving her a chance to continue their conversation, he ran past her into the house.

"Mother, you won't believe the exquisite piece I found today!" he said excited as Jennings rolled a bulky yet flat object by his mother's breakfast table.

"Good lord dear! This place already looks like a museum," she replied lacking the enthusiasm of her son, "What is it?"

"It's a sculpture!" he said proudly.

"Of what," she said looking curiously at the large flat wrapped object as it rolled by, "a painting?"

"No mother," he said chuckling, "of a mirror."

"Oh dear, you're not going to start bringing in all that crazy stuff they call modern art are you?" she asked inquisitively.

"You'll see soon enough," he mumbled while chewing on a biscuit that he had snatched from the table only a few moments earlier.

His mother opened her mouth to respond, but he had already run off in pursuit of Jennings. She sat back and smiled. It was his boyish enthusiasm that prevented her from really getting angry with him. Oh well, she thought, there always seemed to be enough room for one more piece of art in their mansion.

Not wanting the copper to turn, he chose a location indoors at the end of the west hallway. Once he had found its spot, he went upstairs and dressed to play tennis, leaving Jennings and Daniels, their butler, the task of hanging it.

The next morning Arthur woke with the sun and quietly dressed for an early morning ride. His mother would reprimand him for skipping breakfast again, but he wanted to see the lake before the fog rose.

Taking the left stairwell, to avoid the dining hall and the eyes of his mother, he began his descent down the west side stairwell when a blackened flash struck his eye. Thinking little of it, he pulled on a pair black riding gloves and walked to the end of the stairwell. Once again a blackened flash greeted him, but this time it got his full attention. He stopped for a second and turned to look down the long west hallway from which it had come. At its end hung his Barlew original, the *Blackened Mirror*. A small beam of sunlight slid through a break in the curtains and glistened onto its slick black surface. Strangely, instead of bouncing off a reflection as a person might expect it to, it seemed to swallow it up. Arthur moved his head back and forth to see where the reflection went, but it wasn't there. It was as if it were shining into a black hole. If that were so, where had the flash that had struck his eye come from? Staring into its dark glossy surface, Arthur was met by a singular blackened image of himself. It seemed to smile at him in an unusual manner, as if it were someone else's image staring back at him. Nothing could be seen behind the image of that smiling face nor could any reflection of himself but his young delicate face. A compelling urge came over him to reach out and touch its smooth cold surface. A black likeness of his palm came closer and closer to the surface of the black mirror as his hand neared it until it seemed to actually come out. It touched his and long chill ran up his arm and down his spine. Startled, Arthur jerked his hand back and lost his balance nearly knocking over the table behind him. It slid across the slick marble floor in the hallway and banged against the wall. He shivered. A loud thud rang through the house and brought a distant response from his mother.

"Arthur," she screamed, "is that you?"

"Yes mother!" he screamed back toward her voice, while quickly replacing the table he had fell against back to its rightful spot.

"Are you all right?"

"Yes mother!" he yelled backed as if frustrated by her concern.

"Come and have some breakfast," said the distant voice.

Ignoring his mother's last request, Arthur tiptoed gently down the hall away from her voice and slipped out a side door which led out into the garden. The trickling sound of numerous fountains sprayed jets of water into the cool morning air, catching the swift breeze that blew through the open garden covering its many statues and hedges with a coat of beaded moisture. He let his finger cut through the long hedge pool that stretched the entire length of the garden as he walked through it toward the stables. The mornings were his favorite time. Every breath he took of the cool air seemed to invigorate his soul.

"Good morning master Pensley," said the stable hand. "Taking ole Mr. Saley out this morning?"

"You know I won't ride another horse as long as Saley is available."

The old stable hand smiled at Arthur's response and pulled off his dirty brown leather gloves setting them down on top of the fence before going inside the barn to saddle Mr. Saley. Mr. Saley was the last of a thoroughbred bloodline that had been bred by his father. He was a sleek black horse and although he was not a fast horse for his breed, he was as graceful as any creature created by God. Arthur could ride him across a damp morning field like sharp scissors through silk and never feel a jolt from a single hoof striking the damp ground. He was known in the game of horse racing as a mudder. Unfortunately Mr. Saley had been born sterile and there would not be another, hence Arthur enjoyed every moment with him all the more.

The stable hand returned leading a tall slender horse completely black from head to hoof. His well-groomed mane and short hair shimmered in the morning sun.

"Hey boy," said Arthur gently rubbing Mr. Saley's chin. "Good to see you looking so well."

He leaped on top of the waiting stallion and gently turned him around toward a long slender field with a line of deep trees down both of its sides. Mr. Saley knew what they were going to do and although he wanted to burst into a full dash, he waited patiently until his master gave him the command. It came quickly and the two took off as they had dozens of mornings before as two beings became one in a single gallop.

The wind tore through their hair and chilled their faces. Steam bellowed from the nostrils of Mr. Saley in perfect rhythm with his long graceful strides mimicking a runaway steam locomotive free from the restraint of rail. In a matter of moments they came near their destination and Arthur pulled upon the reins bringing the two to rest near the edge of a long and surreal lake. A deep fog lay upon it masking its true size making it appear as if it went off into the distance for an eternity. He climbed from his saddle and let Mr. Saley graze near its edge. He leaned down near its surface and stared into its glossy exterior. A clear bright image of himself appeared and sparkled with the early rays of the sun. It was an ebullient image full of life, unlike the gloomy lifeless image he had seen cast of himself in the sculpture he had gazed into earlier that morning. He instinctively reached out with the palm of his hand toward the pool and slowly brought it down until it touched the surface. Its calm exterior rippled as his hand made contact with it and plunged beneath its surface. It was like another world he thought, a world where the laws of physics were different than that of his own. A world where heavy objects could float or even sink depending upon their shape, a world where its inhabitants can roam freely in any direction up or down without the aid of machines. The only thing that separated the two worlds was a single barrier of where one rested upon another.

Arthur stepped down from Mr. Saley and gave him a long hug before he handed his rein to his stable hand and returned back through the garden toward his home. It was nearing noon now and the bright sun had nearly dried the dew and moisture from the surrounding bushes, statues and sidewalks. He began to sweat, not from his long ride, but from the change in the day. He found his mother sitting on the veranda.

"You really push that horse too hard dear," she said to him.

"Nah," he replied in bad slang flopping down in a chair near his mother, "he lives for the run. It is in his blood."

His mother let it go at that, for she had learned long ago that once her son got something into his head as had his father, there was no changing it. Besides her true concern was really for him and he knew it, that was why he gave her such a hard time about it and ran Mr. Saley extra hard when he knew she was watching. After the death of his father, she had coddled him so closely that he had grown to despise it throughout his childhood and even into adulthood she treated him as a child and he hated it. Upon entering the private garden, Margaret found him to announce a guest.

"Mr. Pensley, Miss Cartwright is awaiting you in the music room."

The young man's eyes lit up upon hearing the name of the beautiful young Constance. He ran into the manor without constraint sliding across the home's smooth polished wooden floors creating work for their servants. A soft melody poured from the piano in the music room washing down the long hallway like a tidal wave caressing his senses. She played most wonderfully on the ivory he thought walking into the large room used for entertaining large parties and small groups. Her naturally gifted fingers embraced each key controlling its output, as would a master, enabling musical notes of perfect harmony. The young woman at the grand piano sat proper at its seat as elegant as the music she created with her thin curly hair shifting with the strokes of her fingers. She stopped upon seeing him enter slightly embarrassed with red cheeks.

"My dear do not stop," he pleaded. "There are angels in heaven that sin at this moment with envy."

"Oh stop it!" she pleaded with her lover.

"I mean it," he said holding her in his arms, "you are a piece of heaven in my eyes."

"How was your trip?" she asked changing the subject.

"Good," he said looking into her beautifully clear blue eyes, "I found quite a nice piece. Would you like to see it?"

"If only I had the time. I must return right away to make sure everything is absolutely perfect for tonight."

"Okay," he said disappointed.

She wrapped her arms around his waist hugging him playfully.

"I'll have plenty of time to see it for the rest of my life. I'm sure you will have to display it at our place!" she declared happily speaking of their wedding plans.

Constance had talked her father into holding a huge dinner party, inviting everyone he knew of any importance to their family. What he didn't know was that Arthur was planning on asking him for his daughter's hand in marriage. She kissed him quickly like an excited little girl pulling away from him to complete the rest of her errands for the ever-important dinner party.

"Don't you be late, Arthur Pensley!" she declared running out the front door.

"I won't," he said softly "I wouldn't miss it for the world."

He watched her car disappear off the grounds before returning to his room to clean up. Along his way, he unconsciously chose the stairwell he had came down earlier in the morning, catching a glossy flash in the corner of his eye. Curious about his new piece, he walked slowly down the long hall coming face to face with the blackened mirror. It glistened unnaturally in the darkness of the hallway as if the flash he had seen had somehow came from within instead of from the reflection of light. His mysteriously floating profile shimmered in the frame as it had earlier in the morning at the lake. He instinctively lifted the palm of his hand placing it near the black surface, stopping as a chill ran up his arm.

"Touch my hand," said his blackened image, "and I will show you how things are on the other side."

His hand trembled at his own madness. His lips had not moved. The blackened replica of himself smiled with a long evil grin.

"Come over," it said in a whisper.

He pushed his hand against the cold surface touching the blackened palm firmly. The black creature grinned as its dark hand began to pour out of the picture engulfing his arm and crawling over his body. The black ice ran up his arm creeping up his neck as he vainly tried to pull away from the frozen tar. He began to scream as it swallowed him, pulling him into the blackened pool upon the wall. He fell into the black void shivering on the ground as the black skin molted itself from him leaving him the only unblackened object in the glossy shadowed world. The room he found himself in was an exact replica of the hallway he had been standing, only an opposite reflection. Black souls hovered above him with malicious faces viciously smiling at him with evil intent.

"What is this place?" he asked trembling from the bitter cold.

"Purgatory… purgatory… purgatory," whispered soft voices echoing in repetition.

"But I am not dead!" screamed Arthur straining to hold his sanity.

"Not yet… not yet… not yet," repeated the voices again in a hiss.

He stood up in the granite hallway backing away from the shadowed forms that swarmed around him violently.

"What do you want from me?" he screamed into the void.

"For you to die!" said a blackened image that appeared.

It was a glistening black form of himself.

"Then kill me and end this madness!" he shrieked.

"You must do it for us!" it replied coaxing him.

"Who are you?" he asked fearful of the horrid floating shade.

"Shadow, blackened, two sides, one light one dark," it murmured in cold riddle like the winter wind. "When light cast and illuminates one side it casts a shadow and blackens the other. When the sun shines upon the earth one side is bright and illuminated while the other is blackened. Everything has a dark side, day has night, the sun has the moon, light has shadow and you have me!"

A faint light leaked through the blackened mirror into the dark domain offering hope to the young man. He began to back away from the creature as it spoke in a ghastly tone.

"To murder oneself is to steal yourself from your destiny, leaving you without right to enter Heaven or Hell, leaving one in utter eternal darkness. Barlew built this portal to purgatory driving himself mad and becoming one of us! The more souls we collect, the less we suffer. Share our burden!"

"I'll never do it!" he declared in the horrid black cold. He could hardly tolerate it for the few moments he had been within it. He would never be able to handle eternity in such an utter cold darkness.

"To have you we cannot harm you, but by coming here you have given us the power to drive you mad!" announced the shadow disappearing into the streaking light.

Arthur leaped through the small portal bursting into the light falling to the floor shivering in the warm sunlight. He rose to his feet and spun around to the blackened mirror on the wall gasping at its sight. Had any of it been true or had he slipped into a temporary madness? He streaked his hair wildly trying to erase the chill upon him. A scream burst out from behind him. He spun around with wild eyes toward the sound. He ran down the long hallway and into the kitchen finding Margaret his maid lying onto the floor with hands gripped out as if trying to grasp something to stop a long fall. Her body was drained to a dull gray. He slowly reached over touching her shoulder. As he did so, it crumbled in his hands. He looked at his hands strangely as they were covered in a fine black powder. Margaret's mouth was frozen open as if in mid scream and her face was sunken in pulling her skin tightly against her skull. Her ghastly gray body fell to the floor where she clanked as if only skin and bones bursting into dust.

He pulled his hands back as if contaminated before remembering his mother! No, screamed within his mind. His feet leaped up the stairs to his mother's bedroom scaling the structures three at a time skidding to a stop as the grayed body of his family's butler Daniels. His face was stricken in horror as if frozen in ice. Arthur leaped over the body tearing through the door of his mother's room tumbling against the wall. Hovering over his mother's bed was the shadowed form holding her face between its hands. She began to scream in pain as the light within her soul drained through the pores in her skin shriveling up her body in the process. Arthur dove at the creature falling through its icy shadow landing on top of his mother as her face shrunk before his eyes freezing in pain forever.

"Stop it!" he pleaded with the shade shrieking in madness.

"Come to us!" it whispered in a long tone. "End this misery and take your life."

The reality of the creature's demand came to his eyes and he was not mad enough yet. It saw he was not ready to concede. He had too much to live for.

"There are others you love!" it stated fading into the shadows and out of sight.

He gripped his mother's hideous face and pressed it against his own. Her body began to crumble to black ash burnt by the darkness of purgatory.

"No mother, don't leave me!" he cried in grief.

He would destroy the mirror. He would shut the vile shadow off from his world. It would die in the light! He ran down the stairs toward the art piece he had so foolishly brought into his home ready to grab it and shatter it against the floor. It glistened appealingly down the hall as he ripped it from its perch and slung it against the ground. The metal frame clanked against the floor skidding against a wall without the slightest sign of damage. Seeing it still in perfect condition, he leaped onto its back with the base of his two feet trying to destroy it, but it only slid from underneath him ricocheting away harmlessly. He seized the structure again in a deafening madness beating it against anything within his reach collapsing in tears upon finding its seeming invulnerable.

"What must I do to expel that which I have called in lunacy?" he screamed with his hands in the air.

The creature's last comment rang in his head, "There are others you love!"

"Constance!" he whispered in realization of the monster's intentions.

He ran from the hall sprinting through his front yard slinging open the door to the family's limo. The gray ash body of Jennings fell to the driveway in a clump blowing away slowly with the wind. He crawled into the car stepping on the gas pedal bursting through the property's gate. He drove to the Cartwright home running cars off the road in a mad dash to save the last person in the world he loved. The front of his car shattered the thin gate blocking the entrance to the home of his fiancé as his tires spun along the pavement trying to gain traction. The car skidded to a stop in the middle of a flower bed as Arthur leaped from the vehicle trying to reach his love before the shadow from beyond the blackened mirror. He beat at the front door knocking down the butler who answered as he rushed past the stunned man screaming her name as if he were mad.

"Where is Constance?" he cried running around unsure where to start looking.

"Please sir calm down," replied the butler straightening up his clothes from the fall.

Arthur seized the man's collar and looked into his eyes with wild eyes, "Where is she? I must find her she is in danger!"

The man fearful to tell the madman where she was said nothing afraid of what he was going to do to the young lady of the house.

"Tell me!" he ordered throttling the man with his bare hands.

"Arthur is that you?" asked a voice from upstairs.

"My darling, where are you?" he said overjoyed to hear her voice.

"Upstairs," she responded. "What is wrong?"

The young man, glad to hear his love was still alive ran up the stairs leaping them three and four at a time rushing into her room frantically seizing her. He gripped her as tight as he could afraid she might turn to ashes at any moment.

"We have to get out of here before it comes!" he petitioned her with wide eyes of fear.

"What is wrong my dear?" she asked terrified from his actions.

"It has gotten everyone I love but you!" he said speaking of the hideous shadow from beyond the mirror. "Mother, Jennings, Margaret... they are all dead and I know you are next!"

A cold chill ran down his back and he turned his head nervously as if the creature was breathing down his neck. Its shadowed form was floating outside the window with a long grin.

"No" he screamed at it spinning around shielding his fiancé, "you cannot have her! I will not let you!"

He looked around the room eyeing a letter opener lying flat on her cosmetic table. He seized it within his hand jabbing it into his neck. Constance ran to her lover trying to stop the flow of blood pouring from his neck pressing against it with all her might. He began to gasp as air whistled through his neck taking his last breaths. His lover held him covered in blood crying as his body went lifeless in her lap.

"Someone help us!" she screamed in vain. "Oh my god someone help us!"

The next week Arthur's mother and Constance stood at the side of his coffin crying for the death of the young man they both loved. He had been everything to both of the women, an only child to one and a lifelong partner to the other. All of the families' servants were there to pay their respects, Margaret, Daniels and Jennings.

"It is a shame to see such a young man with so much promise take his life in his prime," whispered a distant relative.

"Mental illness no doubt," whispered another, "they say he was ranting about his mother being dead before he killed himself."

"I feel sorry for his poor mother," replied a woman, "she absolutely adored him."

"What of the pitiful young girl? He died in her arms the night of their engagement."

A month had past after Arthur Pensley's funeral and his mother sat on the veranda without a smile. She had not smiled since the day her son had died.

"Jennings!" she screamed in foul humor.

"Yes," he answered coming in from the kitchen.

"I want you to have all of Arthur's artwork boxed up and taken away," she suddenly ordered. "I can't stand to look at them. They remind me of him."

"What do you want me to do?" he asked curiously.

"Auction them off."

"Right away."

Primordial Beast

Ancient Memories

Part I

John Hark had walked the central beat for twelve hard years and in that time he had seen firsthand the many sinister depravities man inflicted upon his own species through prostitution, drugs, murder, rape, abuse and robbery. In that time he had been knifed, personally shot three men and lost a partner. It had changed him as if every crime he had witnessed had slowly hardened his once youthful compassion toward men making him cold inside. His family had been the first to notice the transformation, followed by his ex-wife. All of his friendships outside those of the force had faded long ago and he had become what those at the department referred to affectionately as a "lifer".

"Hey let's head up twenty-third and get a hot one to cut the chill."

Officer Hark nodded to his partner and they took a left from Ninth Street stopping to look into the dark window of a local business. The cold night air punished the exposed skin on their faces, nearly freezing the cartilage in their noses solid leaving them as red as a hobo's. John reached up with his cuff and wiped his nose, as he did constantly to keep it dry, nearly rubbing it raw. His partner reached up and lifted the heavy collar on his overcoat around his ears.

"Son-a-bitch, it's cold tonight."

"You say that every night," replied John.

"Well, when your nuts shrink up inside of you...it's cold."

They walked between the buildings on ninth and stepped out into the sharp wind on the corner of ninth and twenty third. Both officers instinctively tilted the top of their heads toward the biting air.

"Why the hell do they send us out when it's this cold anyway?" asked his partner.

"You know the Chief. He likes to do things by the book."

"We should be back at the station hanging by the radio and sucking down some java," said his partner bitterly. "No one is going to get out to do anything in this shit!"

A distant scream echoed from the alley behind, piercing the cold air and jumpstarting their hearts. Grasping their heavy belts, they ran into the dark alleyway facing into a long dead end. Their eyes searched slowly scanning the dark shadows, but nothing moved. A long moan came from a dark hump in the middle of the street. John's partner's hand relaxed from his belt and he stood up straight relieved in his finding.

"It's some wino with a hangover," he replied walking up toward the moaning man.

John had been a cop on the force three times as long as his partner and he had learned that sometimes things were not always as they appear. He kept his cautious stance, continuing to look around while holding the hilt of his gun.

"Hey buddy," said the officer, "you better get inside before you turn into a block of ice."

The body rolled over toward him and emitted a sad wheeze. The old man's bloody and tattered face rolled into the light startling the eyes of the looming officer.

"Oh crap!" he said shocked. "Call for an ambulance!"

John pulled his radio free from its holster on his belt and called into its cold microphone. "We need back up and an ambulance in the alley behind the corner of ninth and twenty third."

His partner leaned down toward the injured man and inspected him closer by using his hand to roll him over.

"Who did this to you?" asked the concerned officer with his hand on the old man's side.

The man answered in a low mumbling tone beneath a scarf that covered his face, but didn't make any sense. Carefully, the officer pulled the scarf aside and revealed his face. The skin on the man's face had been nearly been torn off the front of his skull sending cold oozing blood down onto the man's worn and tattered clothing.

"Oh god!" gasped the officer.

A screech echoed from within the darkness catching both of the uniformed officers by surprise. A dark hulking figure leaped from a dumpster and landed on top of the kneeling police officer. It began to rip and tear into the officer's thick clothing, shredding the cloth into pieces along with his soft flesh. The officer began to scream loudly as the creature hopped onto him like an ape and beat him mercilessly with his long wide-open hands. It all happened so quickly that John barely had enough time to reach for his gun before the beast had murdered his partner and sprung at him. It tumbled into him like a sack of bricks sending him onto his back and knocking his breath out. He quickly pulled his gun free and brought it toward his attacker. His eyes met its raging glare of hunger. There was something inhuman in its pupils, something animalistic. Its pointed teeth gnashed at his throat but caught his arm as he alertly shielded his face. His arm separated its jaws and game to rest at the back of its throat. Long teeth sunk down into his arm raining blood down onto his face. Its two hands began to beat down onto him making crunching sounds with the breaking of his bones. He fired his gun rapidly into its body. Fire jumped from the tip of his pistol, but the beast showed no signs of slowing its attack. Warm blood began to run through his clothes as John's eyes sunk into a black shadow leaving him unconscious while still firing his gun.

Part II

John awoke to a blurry world of bright light and distant beeps. Tubes and needles riddled his body and once he started to move, hands took a hold of him and held him still.

"Calm down big guy," said the voice soothingly.

John recognized the voice, but for some reason his mind felt numb and he couldn't connect the voice with the name from hence it came.

"The boys down at the precinct are going to be glad to hear you have come around. You are all anyone talks about down there anymore."

John looked up into the lights and saw the dark image of his captain's face looking down.

"Chief," said the weak voice.

"Don't waste your strength," said the fuzzy face. "You just do us all a favor and get better."

The exertion of his consciousness was too much for him to bear and he fell once again into unconsciousness. When he woke again he was still surrounded by bright lights and beeping noises, but one thing was different, everything was clear. His eyes no longer struggled to focus and now he could see the face of his old friend the "Chief".

"Damn boy you are one tough son of a bitch!" said the Chief fondly. "I have seen guys not even in half as bad as shape as you were not pull through and here you are almost fully recovered in less than a month!"

"I've been out for a month?"

"Yeah, someone with some pull with the big guy must have put in a good word for you, when you were first brought in. The doctors gave you a snowballs chance in Hell to pull through. I hadn't seen anything like it in my twenty four years on the force, but every day you got stronger and stronger."

"What happened to…" he paused not knowing what to call the thing that had attacked him.

"Oh you capped that fucker. He was dead when the other units arrived at the scene."

Suddenly he remembered his partner and the hope in his eyes faded when he saw the grave look in the Chief's eyes.

"I'm sorry about Breman," he said sadly. "They said he died instantly."

"What was it?'

"What was what?" asked the captain.

"That thing that attacked us, what the hell was it?"

"His name was Eugene Wallard, some attorney from uptown that flipped out or something."

"Chief I saw that thing up close!" he said excitedly. "That was not some blood sucking attorney from uptown! It had pointed teeth, claws…eyes, eyes that were not human."

"Son," said the captain reassuringly, "It was dark and you've been through a lot."

"I'm telling you it was some kind of monster!" he said in terror.

"Listen to me," he said calmly. "We found Eugene Wallard two blocks from the crime scene naked filled full of lead from your gun. He had blood and tissue from you, Breman and that homeless guy all over him."

"But what about what I saw?"

"Shadows play tricks on you," he said. "I have seen good cops swear up and down that a guy they shot had a gun in their hand, when it turned out to be nothing more than a pen or a cell phone."

"That thing had more than a pen or a cell phone to do this to me!" he screamed while showing the huge long scars along his chest.

"The weapon is the only thing we didn't find. We're assuming he ditched it somewhere between the crime scene and where he died."

"He ditched it with eight rounds in him?" asked John.

"He got two blocks with those rounds in him. I guess he could have had the strength to hide the murder weapon."

"Chief!"

"I don't want to hear it," he ordered. "The case is closed. All I want you to worry about is getting better."

John knew there was no arguing with the captain, he always won the argument, every argument because he always ended it.

"So I guess I can get back to work in a week or so, not on the street or anything yet, but maybe I can peck a few keys at a desk for a week or so…"

The captain interrupted him. "You are on medical leave for the next thirty days. The papers have already been filed. I don't want to see you till late next month."

John began to open his mouth but was interrupted once again by his forceful captain.

"That is an order!"

Part III

Another week past as John's wounds healed at a miraculous rate, confounding everybody, especially his doctor. On the day of his release he had healed completely having nothing more than large scars to show from the brutal attack. His parents as well as his older sister came to the hospital to pick him up and insisted he stay with them. Glad to have some company, he accepted their offer and spent the next week being waited on hand and foot by his loving mother. She relished the opportunity to baby her son once again, especially because since he had been on the force, she had rarely seen him more than three or four times a year.

"You know the Harsons are coming over for dinner tonight," said his mother in light conversation.

"How could I forget? It's all you have talked about for the past three days."

"I'm trying to give you a hint to go start cleaning up."

John looked at himself and brushed a potato chip off his shirt.

"That's not for another three hours," he complained.

"I know, but look at you. You need to take a shower and shave," she argued. "And please change into something nice. Angel is coming too."

"I know. You've told me that a thousand times too."

He went upstairs and stripped his dirty clothes off to take a shower. Warm water rushed out of the shower's nozzle and over his deeply scarred skin. The scars had swelled out upon his skin like welts and near the scars he had lost the feeling in his skin. His thoughts drifted from his injuries to Angel and he remembered how pretty she had been as a teenager. They had gone to the senior prom nearly fifteen years ago, but never got serious, going no further than a few innocent make out sessions. He hadn't seen her since high school and the last he had heard she had left for college nearly fourteen years ago. Although he had not obsessed about her over the years, he had never forgotten her. He turned the shower off and got ready to meet her once again.

When Angel and her parents arrived, his mother who played it well, turned into the perfect hostess. The home's interior was fumed with dried incense and decorated with set tables and strategically placed furniture. His mother beamed an approving smile at his clean-cut appearance and the civilized tie around his neck. She quickly hugged Angel's mother as they were old friends and kissed her father on the cheek. Angel stood behind them quietly, giving him only a slight glance before embracing his mother. It was a quiet night, as he and she had little to say in front of their two families and with each bite that slipped off of his fork into his mouth, he wished for it to end.

Apparently from the best he could make out from all the small talk around the dinner table, Angel had gotten married just after earning her degree in psychology and it had not gone well ending a year ago in a divorce much like his own, except on his own he knew why it had ended, exactly why. It had been his career or his devotion to it. His wife had always complained how he spent more time with his friends at work, both on and off duty, than with her. When she finally left him, it was of no surprise apart from how long it had taken her to finally do so. It went as most of his mother's entertaining went, with everybody attempting to impress one another and with nothing truly monumental occurring, until his mother decided to stir the evening pot with a slightly different ingredient.

"John," said his mother in a slight but forceful suggestion, "Angel lives uptown a few blocks away. Why don't you drop her off, to save Mark and Janet a trip?"

"Oh no," said Angel politely, "I don't want to burden him."

"Sure," replied John dryly shuffling through the pockets on his slacks, "I don't mind… let me get the keys to my car."

"Are you sure you don't mind?" asked Angel's mother.

"Of course he doesn't," responded his mother for him pushing him ever so gently toward the key rack on their wall near the kitchen. "Besides, how could she be any safer than with a police escort?"

They all chuckled graciously and the four left his mother's home in two separate cars.

Angel sat next to him in a quietly uncomfortably state that he could sense as soon as he sat down next to her and latched his seat belt. She followed his lead and did the same as his long dark unmarked car pulled out of the driveway.

"Seeing you tonight brought back some memories... back from the old days when we were young," he said.

"I don't know about you," she said laughing, "but I haven't gotten old since high school."

He smiled with her and over their ensuing conversation the cold barrier of their introverted relationship melted away and they were as they were fifteen years ago without failed relationships. His car came to a rolling stop in front of her home and like kids they walked together to the front door.

"Want to come in for a minute?"

"Maybe for a moment to make sure everything is clear," he said.

"Your mom was right about you," she said coyly. "You are a cop."

"Please don't let my mom know you think anything she ever said about me was right. She will never stop."

"I don't think there is anything that will stop that."

He laughed at the joke taken at the expense of his mother's meddling personality and stepped inside taking off his coat.

"Here, let me take that," she said pulling it free from his arm.

He instinctively walked over to her couch and sat down as she went to fix a drink.

"Wine okay?" she asked from around the corner of her dining room.

"Anything wet will do," he replied, "just no donuts."

She came back holding two glasses and sat them on the table gently before sliding down next to him. Something took hold of him, something that had always eluded his youth. He wasn't sure if it was that the taboo of sex between two teen-agers had long faded or if it was simply that they were older and now more mature, but he had an irresistible urge to embrace her. He reached over behind her neck and pulled her to him. Her body leaned up against his and he began to gently kiss her on the neck. She kissed him back along his cheek and ear. Passion filled his every thought and motion and he began to undress her. His lips crashed against hers roughly giving her every indication of what he intended to do as he began to tear off her clothes. She leaned back and looked up at him as he crawled up on top of her slim near naked body.

"What about protection?" she whispered gently into his ear.

He ignored her request and continued to kiss her as he reached behind her and pulled her panties down. He had an overwhelming desire to fill her, to make her his, to guarantee his survival.

"John!" she whispered loudly. "It's too fast, stop!"

He ignored her pleas and continued to stroke his body against hers. The warmth of their naked bodies blended together as they merged into one being. He pulled her closer to him with all his strength as she screamed for him to stop, but he didn't until he had finished the first step of survival. The lust in his eyes faded away, replaced by the horrid stare of two betrayed eyes. They bore into him viciously revealing what he had done.

"Angel," he pleaded. "I'm sorry.

Her leg jerked away from his touch and he left her jumbled on her sofa weeping. He drove home in shame and tried to figure out where things had gone wrong. They had gotten along so well and she wanted to be with him, but he had gone too far... pushed her too hard. Here he was, a good cop raping people. What had gotten into him, why hadn't he stopped he thought? He punched a hole into the plaster of his wall and fell down into the center of his bed, falling asleep as he gazed at the black ceiling of his room.

Part IV

He awoke the next morning to bright light of day and the cries of his mother from downstairs.

"You going to sleep all day?"

He rubbed his eyes with the palms of his hands and saw that he had slept the entire night in his clothes. His body was exhausted as if he had awoken in the middle of a deep rest. He stumbled down the stairs and collapsed into a chair at the breakfast table, consuming a hot cup of coffee his mother had left out for him.

"Did you drop Angel off at her house last night?"

"Why?"

"Because her mother called me this morning and said that she couldn't get hold of her."

He nodded his head to give both the impression that he didn't have a clue and to end her current line of questioning. Ignoring the rest of her endless conversation, he reached over and took hold of the morning paper and read the bold headline, **Midnight Mauler Murders Again**. John's eyes swelled open widely as they took in the entire story. He slammed the paper down onto the table startling his mother before knocking his chair back against the floor and stomping angrily to the phone.

"Let me speak to the Chief!" he screamed in the receiver.

"Oh hey John," said the voice over the phone, "How are you doing?"

"Fine Marge, can you get me the Chief?"

"Sure one sec, Hon."

The phone clicked as the Chief answered.

"Captain Linard."

"Have you read the paper?" asked John lividly.

"I saw more of it than I wanted to in person last night."

"I thought you said the case was closed?"

"John calm down. You stay where you are, we are on it."

"Some guy who gutted my partner is running around town and you tell me to calm down?"

"John, I know how much you want this guy. Hell, all of us want this fucker, but I swear to you if you come anywhere near this station before your medical leave is up, I will nail you to the wall!"

The line went dead and John slammed the phone against the wall ripping it off and shattering it across the hardwood floor. His mother stood quietly stunned as he walked by her going upstairs to his room. When he came back downstairs he was carrying his old duffle bag and he left quietly after a small hug from his mother. He returned back to his dirty apartment, which he had lived in since his divorce. Studying it carefully, he saw for the first time how dull and worn down it appeared from first appearance. No wonder his mother worried about him all this time. It had few luxuries, an old icebox that did little more than refrigerate air, a couch that complemented the lawn furniture in his den and a weight set in the living room. He flicked the light switch, but nothing happened and he cursed another blown bulb as he walked to his bedroom closet in the dark and found his gun through feel, instead of sight. His fingers slid down its smooth surface until they stopped at its polished handle. He tucked it in his pants and threw his badge onto his unmade bed, before leaving.

The cold wind found his dark silhouette in the shadows of 14th and 65th street, one block from where the last attack occurred the night before. Two men in dark uniforms stepped around the corner. The dull moonlight glistened off their badges. John quickly slid down behind a dumpster and waited quietly until they passed. He knew both of them well, Ed and Jay, good cops, he thought. He hated to hide, but if the Chief found out what he was doing, he would be in for it. One thing about the Chief, not only did he run things, but he always kept his word. If he said he was going to do something for you, or to you, he did it and although John wasn't sure what being nailed to the wall meant, it sounded like something he should avoid.

"They're gone, Sugar."

A worn, middle-aged woman in tightly revealing clothes stood with designing eyes staring directly at him. Although she was not particularly beautiful, her mannerisms were sexy and her eyes standing tall above deep crow's feet showed a sly experience. Not offering an excuse, John stood up tall and walked past her without responding.

"Hey Honey what are you looking for?" she said trying to get his attention. "I bet I can help you find it or do it to you."

John stopped, turned around and looked at the woman. He had taken a few prostitutes down to the station in his time.

"You're barking up the wrong tree," he said dryly. "I'm a cop."

"Oh please baby!" she said shaking her head. "I saw you take a dive when those pigs strolled by. You ain't no cop... hey listen, they ain't nothing wrong with two people havin a good time together!"

John walked on ignoring her without even giving a response.

"If you aren't looking for a good time... what are you looking for?" asked the lady while trying to keep up with his long strides. "I mean no one comes down to this part of town at this time of the night unless they are looking for something."

John walked on continuing his cold silence.

"So what are you looking for?"

"I am looking for a man."

"Oh you swing that way."

"No, I don't swing that way," he replied defensively. "I'm not interested."

"Is it a bag of something you want? Cause I know a guy that's got some good stuff."

"Are you trying to get landed into jail?"

"No, I'm just trying to make a buck. Since that serial killer has been running around downtown business has been kind of slow. Most of the girls have moved uptown, but I'm not afraid. I can handle myself."

John turned around with a new interest in their conversation.

"You know anything about this guy?"

"Yeah, my girlfriend Kitty saw him."

John's eyes dilated immensely as if attempting to swallow her image.

"Did she go to the police?"

"Yeah," she said giggling sarcastically, "girls in our line of work always run to the cops when we see something illegal going on."

"I need to talk to her."

"See, I told you if you wanted something I could get it for you."

"Fine, let's go."

She stood motionless with an open hand.

"All of my services cost money," she said defiantly. "And I mean all of my services."

John took hold of her shoulder and pulled her into the darkness of a near alley. Even his reputation couldn't survive being seen giving money to a prostitute.

"How much do you want?" he whispered.

"Make it forty and I'll take you to her."

He pulled out a single bill and handed it to her quickly.

"Well hello Mister Franklin!" she said with wide eyes. "Easiest fifty I've made in a while. If there were more suckers like you around a girl wouldn't have to work so hard."

John turned the collars up on his jacket, so as not to be easily noticed and followed her through town. They walked quietly for nearly thirty minutes under soft flakes of snow before she stopped in front of a shabby apartment complex.

"We got an apartment together upstairs," she said exhaling a puff of smoke.

She stopped and nodded to a man in a car across the street, flashing him a sign with two fingers.

"Ricky thinks I'm taking you upstairs for a deluxe trick. Come on."

He stumbled up the dreary hallway following her lead up a twisted dirty stairwell. They came upon an elderly man lying in the corner covered in a filthy jacket. John recognized him from the beat. The guys called him Charlie, but no one really knew his name. He was one of those anonymous citizens passed by and forgotten by society long ago. He had always wondered what had broken him. He had learned on the force that the homeless were made not born. Something had always driven them to it whether it had been a failed relationship or a bad business decision.

"Get out of my way you old fart," she screamed at the prone man. "It's trash like you that drop the property value around here!"

She pulled her leg back and stomped on the man, who groaned and rolled over. John quickly reached out and pulled her away from the helpless man.

"You better be gone before I come back down," she screamed at the unconscious man as John hurried her on.

Her key clicked into the door and she motioned him in. The room was drab, but well maintained. He looked around but didn't see anyone else.

"Where's she at?"

"Oh Kitty?" she asked while stripping from her winter clothes to expose a black lacy bra. "She's been working uptown since that murder. She should be in any minute."

She came back into the living room wearing just her bra and a short skirt.

"Grab a seat Honey."

She sat down next to him and touched his ear slightly with her finger.

"You sure you don't want to play around a little?" she asked. "Since you're already up here I'll cut you a deal."

He leaned away from her and tried to keep his mind on the matters at hand. Her leg came to rest on the top of his and he instinctively touched it with his hand. It was tight and smooth. His eyes caught on fire and something ancient in him awoke, a primal lust to procreate. He leaned over took her into his arms and began to kiss her.

"Whoa!" she said quickly as if correcting a school child. "Not on the lips."

He quickly stripped her skirt off tearing it as he pulled it free from her waist.

"Hey Tiger, if you like it rough it's going to cost you double," she declared from underneath him.

He ripped his pants down and pulled her over to him.

"One sec Hon, I've got a skin in my purse."

He didn't hear her comments, he couldn't hear anything, his urges had taken over his bodily functions. He threw her back onto the couch and penetrated her forcefully.

"What the hell?" she screamed in protest. "Get off of me you sick fucker!"

The more she struggled, the tighter he held her and the harder he banged his body against hers as if to finish before she could get away. The couch began to bang up against the wall, knocking old dry plaster from the ceiling on top of the two in a cheap artificial snow.

"Stop it!" she begged. "You are hurting me."

Being a prostitute, she had done it all, but the man on top of her ravished her like an animal forcing his sexual fever on her until he was satisfied. He had ensured his survival, he thought instinctively.

Part V

The next morning he awoke in his bed without any idea of how he had gotten home. The back of his head throbbed painfully as he rubbed it gently with the palm of his hand. Two large bumps close in size to walnuts rose up from underneath his hair like small peaks. He slowly crawled out from under his covers, flopping his bare feet onto the floor finding himself to be completely naked. He faintly remembered what had happened the night before up to having sex with a prostitute, but nothing after. He wondered what could have come over him to sleep with a prostitute, unprotected. He looked down between his legs and hoped he had not gotten something fatal. Hell, he thought, something that wouldn't kill him would be far worse, because once the guys down at the station found out he would never live it down. He pulled a pair of boxer shorts out of his drawer, slipped them on and dragged himself into the kitchen.

Damn, he thought, he hadn't set the coffee pot and now he would have to wait for it to brew. He dumped the wet coffee grounds out of the old filter, refilled it with two scoops of dry ground coffee and flipped the switch to red. It began to percolate as he walked over to his door to get the paper. It was bundled outside his door and he flipped it open as he waited for his morning coffee. The headline struck an unnerving terror into his heart and a bead of sweat broke onto his brow. It read, "**Midnight Mauler Murders and Mauls Another**." He fell back into his kitchen chair rocking it back against the wall and read the storyline. He dropped the paper onto the floor and looked at his hands as if trying to see to whom they belonged. He grabbed the phone with them as if fearful to trust them and dialed with shaking hands.

"The Chief please."

"Captain Linard here."

"Chief," said the voice over the phone lightly.

"John is that you?"

"Yeah."

"I already know what you are going to say," he said quickly, "but we got the fucker this time."

"What happened?" he asked with a sick feeling in his stomach.

"Well he stuck to his regular killing pattern and gutted some local pimp named Ricardo something, but this time he left us a witness. Seems he decided to rape one of his girls. She's a little distraught, but we've got her down here doing a sketch at the moment. We should have a good composite of him on the street before the beginning of the late shift."

John didn't say a word.

"Hey… John we lifted this guys prints from her apartment. We're going to get this fucker for you. It's all anybody is thinking about. You stay where you are and rest up so you can get back down here."

The doorbell rang.

"Thanks Chief."

He hung up the phone, went over to the door and peeked through the peephole. A thin short man with thick black rim glasses stared back at the hole. He lowered the handle and opened the door.

"I don't have time for anything today," he said slamming the door.

The bell rang again and he slung the door open with a rage.

"Listen, I am not going to tell you again."

"Your eyes…" he said strangely, "I hope it's not too late."

John stepped aside and the man walked past him cautiously.

"Who are you?"

"The question is who are you at the moment?" asked the man while setting up his briefcase.

"I don't know," he said with his head in his hands.

"I do," he said quickly. "I followed you from her place last night. I just had to wait until I knew it was safe to come up here."

"What do you mean safe?"

"Come on, you have to know by now you are the mauler, or at least one of them."

"I don't know what the fuck I am," he said frustrated, "or what the fuck I've done."

"I've been following you since your attack by Mr. Wallard."

"You knew him…what he was," he asked unbelievably, "and you didn't report him to the police?"

"Mr. Wallard had gone too far…had altered too much. He was too difficult. I couldn't work with him as I will be able to with you."

"It's too late for me too," he replied. "Within a few hours my prints are going to come up as a match and a lot of people are going to want to talk to me. What has happened to me? Why am I doing these things?"

"You have come down with an affliction, something like a virus, but unlike a virus which is detrimental to the body, this infection, changes you, awakens memories… ancient memories of lust, hunger and murder. I have been following your strain of the infection through three hosts, but I keep arriving too late to do any real research. They were too far gone…too unmanageable."

"I'm about to be gone. Do you know what they do to bad cops? They just put you away, it's those on the inside that finish the job."

"Technically you haven't done anything wrong," he replied coolly.

John's eyes nearly popped outside his head upon hearing his comment.

"Are you kidding? Rape! Murder! I can't think of much worse!"

"Men are nothing more than animals. When animals kill each other, it's not murder it's instinct… something natural. When an animal mates with a member of its species, it doesn't matter if it was consensual or not, the species survives. Under the laws of nature nothing immoral occurred. When you committed these crimes against humanity you were in a different state of mind, the mind of your forefathers, the mind of our forefathers."

"Are you fucking crazy? That kind of talk will have me put away into some mental institution!"

"I can defend you. All we have to do is identify whatever it is that has infected you," he said pausing as he ruffled through a jumble of papers. "I believe your particular infection as been around for several centuries, but never properly identified. Usually associated with mass murderers or serial killers, it has most commonly been held liable to mental health, but I have been studying several other references to another infection with similar symptoms… lycanthropy."

John sat still and wondered which one of the two were the craziest.

"I don't by any stretch of the imagination mean to try and prove you are a werewolf, but I think that whatever has infected you actually alters your genetic code, degenerating it, breaking it down to its most primitive state."

"I don't understand. What is happening to me?"

"I believe you are slowly un-evolving, almost reversing evolution. With every outbreak you suffer, the quicker it will occur."

"What will occur?"

"Your final transformation."

John stood up and began to walk around nervously.

"What the fuck am I going to turn into?"

"I'm not completely sure, but if your progression goes unchecked and you live long enough…" he paused nervously, "I can only assume you will revert to the most primitive form of man."

"Some fucking monkey?"

"Not a monkey, but whatever first form that man derived from."

He saw the look in the sick man's eyes and tried to ease him.

"This doesn't necessary have to happen," he said pulling out a needle from his briefcase. "I just need to run a few tests."

"What's that?" asked John nervously.

"I am going to need a few blood samples."

John jumped back and bulked over in pain, "What's going on?"

"You are having an outbreak brought on by stress!" screamed the man holding out his hands defensively. "You have got to calm down and reverse your transformation before it's too late!"

John began to stumble around the room banging into its walls and furniture knocking anything not nailed down crashing onto the floor. He began to scream and tear at his restrictive clothing.

"Please, you must calm down!" cried the man holding out his needle. "You are only speeding up your progression!"

John's eyes narrowed in on the vision of the man before him and he felt threatened. He could feel his fear.

"Here," he said soothingly, "let me give you something to help you relax."

The wild man began to jerk as his misshapen arms tightened into muscles and his fingers stretched out with long claws.

"Oh my god," whispered the small man holding out a needle.

The beast leaped at him, slamming him against the wall knocking him across the kitchen unconscious. The primal beast leaned up toward the still man and sniffed, the danger had passed. A beam of light and suggestion of freedom leaked into the dark room and the creature examined its strange transparency. Powerful fists came down upon the strange clear object shattering it onto the fire escape in long broken shards. The ancient creature sprung out the broken window effortlessly and climbed down the apartments high walls acrobatically landing on the street's hard surface. Its keen senses examined its new and strange surroundings looking for something that made sense. The sound of a car's horn disturbed it and it scaled the wall of the next building like a nimble spider landing upon its cold roof with its bare hairy feet. Its red eyes bore down the other side of the building and curiously watched the peculiar hustle of the cities' people before descending down the back of the building into a quiet alley. Its sharp eyes quickly caught the movement of a man and a women walking below. He had her it thought angrily, it had a woman in his territory. Rage burst through its arteries and a primeval strength came into its limbs as it landed upon the unsuspecting man, tearing him apart in a fury unknown to civilized man. Blood sprayed from the man's wounds as the beast's claws dismembered the poor man's body leaving him dead before his corpse hit the ground. The woman froze in terror as the brute beat her boyfriend to a pulp in front of her eyes. His eyes turned to hers and an ancient memory of her own crept from deep within her mind and she took flight. The beast, much physically closer to his own ancient desires of survival, ran her down and ripped her clothes from her body. She screamed and fought him the best she could, but he seized her ensuring survival.

Part VI

The frigid air aroused him from his slumber in a heap of trash. Unaware of his surroundings he found himself naked and covered in blood from his elbows to the tips of his fingers. The terror of unknown crimes filled his eyes and he couldn't bear the thought of ever discovering what he had done.

"You feel alive now?"

John jumped to his feet startled by the unsuspected voice.

"I feel like dying," he said looking at his savage appearance.

"We've got to get you out of here," he said warily. "The cops are out looking all over for you."

"The cops," he said in exasperation, "this damn thing had stolen everything from me. Being a cop is all I know and now because of this I don't know shit!"

"Come on," said the man holding out a long jacket, "I can stop this. All we need to do is get you to my lab where I can study you and keep you restrained."

"There's no cure for this!" yelled John shivering with his arms wide open.

"There is a cure for everything," he argued. "You think people didn't say that about small pox, the plague?"

"You can't cure what I've done. There is no way to justify or rectify the wrong I've done. It can't be changed."

"Calm down, it doesn't take much to bring on an outbreak. Any kind of primal emotion such as fear or stress could bring on another one."

"What about sex and murder?" he asked. "Think that sex and murder can bring on an outbreak or does an outbreak bring on sex and murder?"

"I don't know what you mean."

"I do and you don't have to worry about another outbreak, because I know the cure," he said calmly.

The man stood confused as John walked past him and out to the street full of people who stopped in awe of a naked man in the freezing snow covered in dried blood. John stood calmly by the side of the road watching the traffic go by as if there was nothing unusual about his appearance. He watched patiently until a bus came around the corner running full speed. The man, who wanted to help him, saw his intentions and ran toward the naked man.

"No you fool!" he screamed in vain as John dove directly under the buses' tires.

The bus slammed on its breaks acting like a thick blade smearing his body across the road like jam on wheat bread.

"You can't stop it," he said. "You've already set it into motion."

A crowd began to form around the scene of the accident and the disappointed man stepped back to get away from all the commotion.

"You've already passed on your genetic memories to your offspring," he said in curiosity. "The question is to how many?"

And Other Exquisite Delights:

Ocean of Mind

Staring out at the ocean
With its dark color
And its continuous rocking motion
Sways and moves my mind.

A lucid glance at the moonlight
With its power of brilliance
Brings me great delight.
As her ageless silence beckons.

Standing across the sky
The clouds beneath my feet
I am coming down
I'm tumbling to my defeat.

My form plunges into the cold darkness
Sinking deeper and deeper with every wave.
No thought of remorse enter my head
As I rest in a deep Cimmerian grave.

One Time for a Killer

Stalking, hunting, for the weak.
Searching, tracking, finding easy meat
Uncontained thoughts search the mind
Hatred rises against the ways of humankind
Stomping, running on concrete in utter fear
The predator chases down a dear
Screams cry out in total vain
Darkness gives way to the cleansing rain
Rain drops hit the ground pitter, patter in a flood
Dripping, dropping, filling and erasing pools of blood
Together joined by the weight of dark bleeding
The killer screams and marks his final greeting
A life is ended amid the trash of the street
Leaving the sound of only a solitary heartbeat

Dark seed

Quick thoughts of primordial insight.
Unlawful, wrong and not right.
Tearing at them like a gardener at a weed,
but they continue to grow in the mind and feed.
Traveling through dark tunnels like train.
Through the eyes of the freshly insane.
Laughing quietly in never-ending corners.
Hiding from a procession of black mourners.
Too Late! The dead are whispering in my ears
Of the song of life and tears.

Out Of Reach

Green Grass Rolling,
Souls Released Into The Earth.
White Stones Standing.
Finding A New Rebirth.

Seasons, Forms And Functions Change,
Only Our Lies Remain.
Unnatural Laws Have Found Their Range.
The Reign of the Worm Has Begun.

Condemned Convicts Stand Above The Ground,
Mumbling, Draining Like A Leech.
But They Are Gone, Control Is Lost
Finally They Are Out Of Reach.

The Creations of God

God created the lovely rose then he created the sharp thorn.

God created the luscious apple then he created the poisonous mushroom.

God created the warmth of the sun then he created the destruction of tornados.

God created the gluttony of the rich then he created the famine of the poor.

God created the pleasure of sex then he created the disease of AIDS.

God created the harmony of peace then he created the turmoil of war.

God created the sanctity of marriage then he created the routine of divorce.

God created the miracle of life then he created its end in death.

God created the bliss of Heaven then he created the torture of Hell.

God created all these things then he created something to enjoy and endure it all.

God created man then he created woman.

Miracle

A married couple had sex and both enjoyed it.
A pastor completed a sermon without judging his congregation.
A miracle occurred!

A doctor saved a life for free.
A senator voted with a clear conscience.
Another miracle transpired!

An honest man got the promotion.
A lawyer turned down a case because his client was guilty.
Miracles abound!

The war on drugs was finally won.
A farmer just repaid his loan.
I have seen miracles!

A war was fought and someone won.
A rich man made a taxable contribution.
The work of God is at hand!

A judge ignored a loophole and upheld justice.
A government served the best interest of its people.
I have seen the sign!

A life was lived without molestation.
A death occurred and it was the end.
I saw the truth!

<u>Catalog</u>

<u>Cosmic Contemplations</u>- Limited edition hardback (100 copies) signed by the author with black and white artwork and full color dust jacket. The collected science fiction of Charles Clemons containing the novel Intergalactic Eden, the short stories Suspended Hell, The Genetic Game and Death to the Queen as well as the poem Intergalactic Dimensions. 200 pages, $23.00. - **Sorry Sold Out!**

<u>Cosmic Contemplations</u>- Oversized paperback with black and white artwork and full color cover. The collected science fiction of Charles Clemons containing the novel Intergalactic Eden, the short stories Suspended Hell, The Genetic Game and Death to the Queen as well as the poem Intergalactic Dimensions. ISBN-13-: 9780615142876, ISBN-10: 0615142877, 200 pages, $12.00. - **In Stock!**

<u>Funky Shrooms and Other Exquisite Delights</u>- Limited edition hardback (100 copies) signed by the author with black and white artwork and full color dust jacket. Includes the introduction Strange has a New Name, the full length novel The Final Infection, the short stories Autobiography of a Necromancer, The Other Side of the Blackened Mirror, Primordial Beast, the interview Satan's Side of the Story and six poems. 436 pages, $28.00. - **In Stock!**

<u>Funky Shrooms and Other Exquisite Delights</u>-
Oversized paperback with black and white artwork and full color cover. Includes the introduction Strange has a New Name, the full length novel The Final Infection, the short stories Autobiography of a Necromancer, The Other Side of the Blackened Mirror, Primordial Beast, the interview Satan's Side of the Story and six poems. ISBN-13-: 9780615174679, 436 pages, $16.00. - **In Stock!**

Coming Soon From Portal Press!

<u>The Lands of Dream</u>, a realm where a multitude of Gods still compete for the worship of man and man is content with the luxuries of his natural surroundings, therefore he does not strive to invent or discover new technologies to better life, because it is as it already should be. This third collection of the exciting author Charles Clemons contains all his fantasy tales including the Mhorhaen trilogy, the Dreamer trilogy, a short story and four poems establishing the connection between the land of the waking and that of dream. Available summer 2008 in limited edition hardback and mass paperback.

Portal Press Books
Where Strange Fiction Lives!
Order online at:

www.portalpressbooks.com

Portal Press

Soddy Daisy
Tennessee

About the author:

Charles Clemons lives in Chattanooga Tennessee with his wife Joy and his son Alex writing short stories, poems, novels, essays and screenplays. A Desert Shield/Storm veteran and constant student, Charles spends his days in the beautiful mountains of Tennessee and nights "pecking" at a keyboard.